KAREN HARPER

HURRICANE

MIRA

ISBN 0-7783-2307-2

HURRICANE

Copyright © 2006 by Karen Harper.

www.MIRABooks.com

Printed in U.S.A.

To all our friends in south Florida, especially Barbara Nelson, Barbara Deyoung and other loyal readers. Special thanks to our friends Sue, Leo, Bill, Hank and Tom for assessing our damage when the real hurricane hit. And, as ever, to Don for past beach walks and those to come.

1

All right, heads up everybody out there on this lovely morning. Tim Ralston here from storm watch WSEA-AM radio in Naples for your 10:00 a.m. weather report, August 16, 2003. I know it's a beautiful Sunshine State Saturday, but air reconnaissance has just confirmed that the tropical storm we've been watching in the Atlantic has officially become a hurricane. Dana is only a Category One at this point, on a zigzag course 400 miles southeast of Havana and 88 miles southwest of Jamaica. But as she comes over warmer water, she will strengthen—how much, we're not certain yet. Be assured we'll be keeping an eye on her and let you know if her path threatens our own little piece of paradise.

Standing on the dock of the Gladesport Marina, Julie Minton saw Kaylin was keeping an eye on the girls. Julie counted them herself anyway as their Jet Skis cut sharp silver patterns on the windy, sun-swept bay. Were two of them missing?

"I only see ten girls," she called to her friend and coworker. Her stomach knotted instantly, for the young women they'd taken into their lives these last two weeks were more counselees than campers, and she was ultimately responsible for their safety. "Where are the other two?"

"At the last minute, Bree and Jen weren't ready to get on one of those things. I meant to tell you they're swimming at the beach just beyond the marina—still a buddy system," Kaylin assured Julie.

Yet Kaylin's voice sounded terse. She didn't turn toward Julie, but, with both hands shading her eyes, kept looking out into the bay. She had walked toward the far end of the dock, while Julie stood only partway out on the long, double-E-shaped structure to which fishing boats, sailboats, speed-boats and four visiting yachts were tethered, along with the old ferry that belonged to Julie. The dock was deserted for once; both locals and guests were at the Fish Fest up on the shore.

With Kaylin watching the girls so intently, Julie thought, she could take a quick break from two weeks of hard but re-warding work. Their charges were cutters, teens caught up in aberrant behavior in which they abused themselves with knives or razors in a warped attempt to gain control of their bodies and lives. It was a practice psychiatrists were calling "the new age anorexia." Julie owned the tropical island re-sort where she and Kaylin worked and lived alongside the girls and Julie's fourteen-year-old daughter Randi.

Just to be sure all was well before she got out of the sun for a minute, Julie counted the number of Jet Skis again. That simple task seemed almost impossible as they circled and crisscrossed in the sun and their own foaming wakes.

"I guess Randi's at the Fish Fest," she called to Kaylin.

But Kaylin evidently didn't hear her. She stood at the end of the dock, not shading her eyes now, but with both arms wrapped around the top of her head as if the sky were falling.

Randi Minton thought she would totally die of excitement. And not just because this part of southwest Florida was so awesome, even if she still did miss Michigan despite the three months they'd been here. It wasn't even because she'd gotten loose from her mom and their guests, for once. It was because, bouncing over the waves of Mangrove Bay on Thad Brockman's Jet Ski, she had the perfect excuse to be close to a guy who had no clue how much she liked him.

At least Thad hadn't freaked when Kaylin McKenzie, Osprey Resort's other guidance counselor besides Mom, had seen he was going out on a Jet Ski alone and had yelled at him, "Hey, got room for one more?" She'd practically pushed Randi on behind him. Randi hoped he didn't think she was one of the cutters who came to the resort for counseling. Thank heavens, sitting ahead of her in the long saddle seat, Thad couldn't see her red cheeks. She could hardly blame that on sunburn since she'd been fine when she got on the Jet Ski.

Wearing only baggy swim trunks, Thad looked totally phat, with his buff, bronze body, black hair and blue eyes he hid behind wrap-around shades. He was seventeen and really cute. She knew she had no chance with him, ever, even though they'd be in the same high school this winter. She barely knew him, though they'd talked briefly once or twice. But she'd thought about him so much, she felt she knew him really well.

As they whipped along with sun and wind in their faces,

Randi pretended he was her guy and that the rooster-tail spray behind them spit at everyone to just leave them alone. She hoped Thad didn't totally hate her for being dumped on him like this. He probably thought she was some stupid Northern snowbird with her cutoffs and Johnny Depp pirate T-shirt with red sequin flowers, especially when the other girls were in swimsuits today. Randi had her new two-piece on under her clothes, but she thought she looked too skinny in it, with hardly any boobs—so far, at least. Her mom was really built and promised Randi she'd get shapelier too, but when? She was already almost fourteen and three months old.

She pretty much kept her mouth shut because it seemed as if Thad was in a bad mood. That was probably because he'd just had an argument with his girlfriend at the Glades-port Marina, where he worked part-time. Their voices had been raised pretty loud. The girl's name was Grace Towers— gorgeous, slender, not skinny—who went to boarding school in Connecticut, but had spent the summer with her father over on Marco Island. Grace's father didn't like her hooking up with Thad, either. And Grace was leaving soon; Randi had overheard that, too.

Kaylin, who'd put her on the Jet Ski, and Bree Nichols, one of the girls being counseled, were the only ones who knew about her feelings for Thad. Randi had been watching him all summer, not like some sick stalker but like an admirer from afar, just like she might keep an eye on Hugh Jackman if she ever spotted him somewhere. No way she'd ask for an autograph—she'd just kind of memorize him and make up stories in her head about him, how he'd noticed her and started talking to her, how he was looking for someone real, not plastic like Thad's Grace, or Grace's sister Tanya Towers, who played sexy Ginger on the soap *Dangerous Women*. Thad and his dad were obviously working guys with a fishing boat, while Grace and Tanya's dad had a big yacht and sold luxury real estate worth gazillions around here.

After the girls' half hour rental time, two to a Jet Ski, Thad began to herd them in toward shore. Randi sat up straighter and waved to the girls, ten of the twelve, who would be going home tomorrow. A couple of them gaped to see her riding with Thad.

Randi looked back across the bay at the distant silhouette of the kiddie rides, game booths, and eating places for the annual Gladesport Fish Fest going on in the park behind the marina this weekend. She wondered if she'd see Thad there tonight and if he'd talk to her after this ride, even if he was with Grace.

"They're all heading in," he shouted to her, turning his head slightly so she could hear over the noise of the motor. His chin was so close she could see beard stubble on it. "Want to take a spin? I've been cooped up in the marina rental shop and pretty soon I'll be swabbing my dad's boat."

"Sure—great!"

Little did he know that she would have agreed to ride clear across the Gulf of Mexico with him.

Julie scolded herself for being paranoid and acting as if Kaylin were a babysitter and not a certified counselor. Everyone was heading back in and Randi was evidently off on her own at the Fish Fest. Julie understood that. She had no right to expect her daughter to hang out with the groups of girls who came and went from the Osprey Resort every two weeks.

The last she'd seen Randi, she'd been with Kaylin but had said she might head for the Fest in the park behind the marina. She'd joked about not getting hit by a flying mullet from a fish-throwing contest. Kaylin, who must have been reacting dramatically earlier to the sharp, show-off turns some of the girls were making, now waved to them as they headed, full throttle, along the dock toward the shore.

Julie was proud of this group of girls. Most of them had made progress in their two weeks of counseling and support activities at her Osprey Resort. It was only the fourth set of guests in this new endeavor, but it was great to see the old family lodge come alive again with chatter and laughter, even mingled with tears and troubles.

Osprey lay in a dazzling stretch of water called the 10,000 Islands, studded by tropical isles between glitzy Marco Island and the raw beauty of the Everglades National Park. On its long, narrow barrier island of the same name, the resort was a half mile off the coast, where tiny Gladesport still exuded its old fish-camp charm. The Osprey Lodge and outbuildings dated from the 1930s and had been her beloved great-uncle's passion. She'd been thrilled to inherit the island and resort last year, even if the place had become dated and overgrown while Uncle Phil languished for years in a convalescent center and then while his will was probated after he died.

The staff was still just the two of them: Julie was thirty-four and Kaylin twenty-six, but they had the same academic credentials in counseling. Eight years ago, Kaylin McKenzie had been the first cutter Julie had ever known and helped. The upbeat, bubbly woman had blossomed over the years. The big joke between them was that Kaylin had once sent her photo to the *Today Show* for a Katie Couric look-alike contest. Lately, the petite, once withdrawn woman had a man in her life. Nate Tomzak was the hunky assistant to the area's ecology and wildlife maven, Liz Lawson.

Her sarong skirt over her bathing suit fluttered around her legs in the hot blast of humid breeze as Julie shouted to Kaylin over the noise of the Jet Skis. "I'm going to pop inside the marina store and grab a soft drink before we head back. Want anything?"

"I'm fine right now," Kaylin said, though she still sounded on edge. Surely, she didn't think Julie was upset because she didn't mention two girls opted to go swimming. It was just that she'd paid the Brockman boy in the marina for six Jet Skis, and she'd have to correct that when she saw him.

Julie went into the old store; it was not air-conditioned, but open to the breezes. Distant country music—"Achy, Breaky Heart"—drifted in from the Fish Fest.

She greeted Loreen Blackwell, whose family had run the place for years. Julie remembered Loreen's parents and grandparents from the weeks she and her own parents had spent on Osprey Island years ago. Loreen might be near her age, but her eternally bronzed skin and sun-bleached hair made her look older. Still she wasn't nearly as ancient as the dusty black-and-white photos of long-dead anglers and their prize catches tacked to the wall behind the checkout counter.

"I need something cold to drink," she told Loreen who wore her usual ball cap, which read Swamp Buggy Races, 2000. Though Julie had the impression that the Blackwells were barely making ends meet, Loreen, husband Clint and their two kids were into all kinds of racing. The friendly woman was also into talking, so if anyone needed local news, this was the place.

"You could get you some *real* drinks up at the Fest," Loreen said, her voice its usual calm drawl as a radio droned away in the background. "The Seaside Restaurant booth makes great mai tais, better'n the Bloody Marys at the Flamingo booth. Skip the beer and head straight for those babies. We're closing early today, 'cause everyone's gonna be there by noon, including all the folks that came in by boat or plane. Our boy's parking cars for a buck in our side lot, some clear from Miami. Clint's charter's s'posed to be back in by noon. He couldn't pass up the extra money, even if he does hope to win the hundred dollars for the fish-cleaning contest later."

Though this was a small marina in a small town, two charter sportfishing boats docked here on a permanent basis. With so many extra people around today, no wonder both were out. Loreen's husband Clint had *The Happy Hooker*, and Zach Brockman captained *The Hooyah!*

Julie had also known Clint and Zach from her visits as a child. Local kids used to wait tables, clean or hold other odd jobs at the lodge in its heyday. Clint had carried guests' luggage on and off *The Manatee*, the same small wooden ferry which still linked Osprey Island to Gladesport. And Zach had helped on the resort's fishing boat and been the lifeguard—

until he screwed up big-time and was told to keep clear of the place and its people.

Since returning, Julie had no relationship with either of the men. She figured that memories of their very different, sometimes difficult pasts might make them as uneasy as she felt when she saw them. She tried to tell herself it wasn't her fault, but the result of the way her uncle and parents had treated the local "help." Sometimes she yearned to make it up to them—to apologize somehow—but so far they had just nodded, sometimes said a few words, then walked around each other. With Loreen, though, it was always old home week, for if Loreen met a stranger, he or she didn't stay that way long.

It felt great here in the back of the store: a pop and beer cooler, as well as one full of ice cream treats, wafted out chilled air. Between those coolers were two larger ones full of fish, shrimp and crab for those who weren't around when the fishing boats brought them in fresh. Evita, the local cook and housekeeper at the lodge, sometimes bought fish here. Julie decided she'd grab a cold drink, send two of the girls to find Randi at the Fest, then get everyone to Osprey on the old island ferry.

"I thought that was you, Julie," a man said, coming around from the ship supply aisle as she reached into the cooler for a can of soda. Grant Towers, suave, silver-haired and silver-tongued, extended his hand. A developer of local luxury real estate, he'd been out to Osprey more than once, offering her a fortune to let him turn the land into high-end homesites with private boat docks. At least for her little, low-lying barrier island, he hadn't envisioned the high-rise condos he had developed all over nearby, larger Marco Island where he lived.

"Grant, hi. Slumming today?"

He was immaculately dressed as ever, this time in a Ralph Lauren pink polo shirt and pressed khakis. She shook his hand as she let the cooler door bang shut. He held hers a bit too long and made the slightest bow over it before he released her. Even when Grant tried to blend in to the Gladesport world, where T-shirts or Banana Republic cutoffs were *de rigueur*, he stuck out like a manicured thumb on a calloused hand.

. "I figured you and your little brood would be off-island at the Fest today," he said. "Listen, I'm not kidding about making you a fabulous offer for Osprey—fabulous. I could cut you that deal we discussed right now. With that, you could move your counseling camp inland, where it's safer. After all, if the hurricane comes, wouldn't you rather have me worry about repairs instead of you?"

"Hurricane?" Her heartbeat instantly accelerated. "That storm way out they've been watching is now a hurricane?"

"True!" Loreen called from her perch by the cash register. "But those things are unpredictable. Odds are it'll zing right by. The last couple we got all het up over did."

"Dana," Grant was saying as he followed Julie back to the counter. "I think they've named it Dana. Is that a man or a woman's name? I had a male client, bought a penthouse on a condo overlooking the beach, name of Dana."

"Excuse me, but I'd better get the girls out to the island," Julie told them. And she'd find Randi herself, to be sure she went with them, even though they were coming back in for the dinner at the Fest tonight. "It—it can't hit soon, can it?" she asked Loreen as she laid a few quarters on the counter.

"This group of girls, except for two staying over, is leaving tomorrow, and the next doesn't come until Wednesday."

"Don't fret now," Loreen assured her. "The weather guys cry wolf all the time."

That made Julie feel a little better. The doughnut-shaped *Gladesport* life preserver hanging on the wall looked like a halo behind Loreen's head, and Julie decided to take that as a sign to believe her on this. The old preserver had Trust Me stenciled on it. Though Loreen had turned her down, Julie had offered to buy the antique for the large wall in the Florida room of the lodge where she had a collection of them, one for each girl. Kaylin had said Randi'd been upset there wasn't one that represented her too, but it wasn't as if Randi needed counseling and confidence-building like their guests.

"Don't panic," Grant added, patting her shoulder. "I'm not, and I'm selling luxury condos for a half-built megatower on Marco. It sure doesn't need any more rain than we've already had this month."

Julie hurried out to where the girls stood on the dock near the Osprey ferry, giggling about their rides. She hoped they'd taken turns steering as she'd urged, because feeling in control of something was key to almost every activity they did. The two who had gone swimming had joined them, so they made a dozen again. They'd be a baker's dozen with Randi, but she was still nowhere in sight.

"Get on the boat, and I'll be right with you," Julie called to them. "Kaylin, I've got to make a quick run through the Fest to get Randi."

Kaylin turned to her as the first girls jumped into the trusty old *Manatee*, while Captain Mike, another part-time employee, greeted them. Mike was in his upper seventies, almost the same vintage as the boat. But Julie wasn't looking at Captain Mike. The stricken expression on Kaylin's face made her stomach churn.

"She's not there," Kaylin said so quietly that Julie had to read her lips.

"What? Then where is she?"

"She went out on a Jet Ski, too," Kaylin admitted, looking as if she might burst into tears.

"But everyone's back in!" Julie cried, her voice suddenly shrill.

"I'm sure it's fine. She's with Thad Brockman, so she's not alone or anything. He knows what he's doing."

"That hottie?" she heard Cindy Markland say to another girl as the two of them high-fived each other. "Bet he knows what he's doing, all right. Way to go, Randi!"

Julie frowned in Cindy's direction. "Then where are they?" she asked, scanning the blue bay with its green confetti of mangrove islands.

"They probably just went for a little longer ride," Kaylin plunged on. "He's the one who services and rents out the Jet Skis, and he's lived here all his life."

"Believe me, I know who he is."

Julie gripped her unopened soda can so hard, it dented and hissed through the tab. She closed her eyes to steady herself, then opened them to take in all the watchful faces. "Okay, listen, everyone! All of you head back for Osprey with Kaylin. Mike, please bring the boat right back for Randi and me. I'll wait for her here. I'm sure she'll be right back."

* * *

Randi squealed in delight as their Jet Ski crested one wave and sliced through another before smacking down into the third. To her amazement, Thad cranked the big blue metal machine between their legs even faster. The sea breeze felt great on this humid day.

She understood how Thad felt about being cooped up. This summer she'd had some good moments, like when she and Mom were refurbishing the old resort. But when the guests started coming, Randi'd felt shuffled off to the side again, like all those years Mom had college classes or worked long hours after Dad left them. Randi still phoned or instant messaged her friends up north, but she could tell they were slipping away.

Mom's counselees, mostly girls from the midwest, rotated through the program every two weeks, though a couple of them were staying for two sessions this time. But they weren't exactly focused on making friends, since they were pretty intense about their personal problems. Not only were they gone in two weeks, but Randi couldn't see unloading on someone wacked or depressed enough to cut her own body again and again.

"There are a lot of shallow areas and sandbars out here, but I mostly stay in the deep water channels," Thad told her. "My dad has taken fishermen out here for years, and I've had my share of helping him, even steering his big boat, *The Hooyah!*"

He shouted that last word so loud it hurt her ears, but she didn't care. His voice vibrated right through her, despite the continued hum and delicious shiver of their Jet Ski. The bare skin on Thad's strong shoulders was warm where she held onto him in the mist of cool spray. She didn't care about anything but flying along with him, even if she got a lecture about going off without asking Mom. After all, Kaylin thought it was okay. She'd been pretty different since Nate Tomzak had started coming around.

Thad whipped their Jet Ski left between two narrow, leafy islands, then down another green alley of mangroves. This place was like a pinball maze, she thought, but she felt absolutely no worry that he didn't know where he was going. Mom said most of the locals knew every inch of this area, where outsiders could so easily be lost before the Gulf of Mexico began.

Thad called out the names of some of the small, long islands, called keys, and she was soon laughing at them: Needhelp, Cutshin, Halfway, Red Man, No Name, Squatters and Palm Shack.

"Oh, there's a little beach on that one," she cried, then hoped he didn't think she meant to stop there.

"Yeah," he called back as they took another twisting water road where the waves didn't wash through so big. "Quite a few have beaches or dry ground. Some still have overgrown derelict houses that were hunting camps or homes before the Everglades National Park started moving people out years ago—we're almost to their boundary. Before that, rum runners, Civil War deserters, even outlaws and pirates used to hide out here. There's still some weirdos who hang around."

"Like Leon and Jake Malvers down at the southern end of Osprey?"

"No—not them." She felt his shoulders tense. "I know them, and they been real good to me."

"Oh, I didn't mean—"

"People just don't understand them."

He took the next turn, plowing through the green water at such a slant that she feared they'd flip. Behind them, they left a broad, white wake, a jet trail like in the blue skies overhead.

Thad slowed to make another sharp right turn into a wider passage. This natural waterway looked the same as the rest with its walking-root mangroves and green puzzle pieces of irregular, small islands. He cut the motor to an idle.

"I should have been watching the gas," he said with a shake of his dark head. "I forgot to fill this one after some-one else had it for a while. We'd better head back, Randi."

He'd used her name. He'd remembered it. But their ride had almost run out of gas.

"Hot damn, a shark? Is it, Captain? A shark?"

"We're about to find out," Zach Brockman told his charter, a cosmetic surgeon from Clearwater who had flown his small plane in for some Saturday morning fishing and the "best Florida Cracker festival in the state." Zach hoped Dr. Ray Paul didn't decide to fly home tonight, if he was still drinking straight Scotch. Zach tried to get along with all his charters, but he hadn't liked this guy from the first, when he'd heard him telling Loreen Blackwell she needed skin abrasion to prevent that leathery look.

"Like I said, sharks have a real attitude about being caught," Zach told him. "Hang on to your gear, because he's really gonna go!"

The guy hooted with delight as the fish—maybe a four-footer, from the rising ripples—took them on a scorching run out of the mangrove islands towards the gulf. Zach had to haul anchor and move the boat to go with it so the line wouldn't break. Since it was so windy and they were only going out for half a day, he'd talked the guy out of deep-sea fishing in lieu of inshore casting. He hoped this hit didn't drag them out too far, but they were really moving.

The fish broke water in a sizzling, corkscrew leap. It was a four-and-a-half-foot shark with a distinctive, shovel-shaped head. "A bonnethead!" Zach yelled from the open, elevated bridge of his thirty-five-foot boat. He half hoped the shark would get loose by sawing through the line. Years ago the locals made big bucks taking charters shark fishing, but the *Jaws* ethic of monster-slaying had put most breeds on the endangered list. Today, given the severe limits set on shark catches, he always made it clear that shark fishing on his boat was strictly catch, tag and release.

"Yahoo!" the doctor, a short, stocky fifty-something shouted as the fish turned toward them to give some slack in the line, then took off again. "Or in your case," the excited man yelled up to Zach with a laugh, "Hooyah!"

Zach was a former navy SEAL. He'd left the service early to come back to raise his only son after his wife had accidentally drowned. Often, his thoughts were still with his SEAL team in other gulfs of water, chasing human sharks who, unfortunately, were not endangered yet.

In its fury, the shark shook its head and slapped its tail, dousing *The Hooyah!*'s deck and Dr. Paul. As an hour passed, both fish and fisherman began to wear down, so Zach killed the motor and came back down the ladder onto the stern deck. But when they got the bonnet close to the starboard side, Dr. Paul whooped again.

"Look at that ugly son-of-a-gun," he crowed. "Wait 'til everyone sees that! I'm gonna put that sucker on my wall."

"In a photo, you mean. We agreed on catch and release if you hooked a shark."

"But that was on the dock, with others in earshot. Listen," the guy said, as the thrashing fish thumped the side of the boat with his head and tail, "I heard with a nice extra donation— you know, toward saving sharks—you'd let me catch and keep."

"Look, Dr. Paul, you don't save sharks by killing them. It's strictly tag and release on my watch."

As the man continued to battle the struggling fish, he went on, "My lawyer said the sportfishing boat closest in on the Gladesport dock would let you catch and keep!"

"Right, other fish—snook, redfish, pompano, trout, tarpon—by quota, in season."

"You just trying to jack me for more dough? You *are* the one they call Sharkman, aren't you?"

"Because I tag them for the university. I don't kill them anymore. And it hasn't made me popular with other fishermen, including my best friend, so don't try to pressure me."

Damn, Zach fumed, this guy's lawyer friend must have been referring to Clint Blackwell's boat in the next slip. They'd changed positions lately. Clint said Loreen was always keeping an eye on his beer intake by just looking down the dock, so now Zach kept *The Hooyah!* closest in. And that meant he'd have to tangle with Clint again.

"When was this?" Zach demanded as he yanked on his leather gloves. "When the lawyer told you?"

"Last month, but—"

Just off the boat, the bonnet looked frenzied, as if he knew what they were discussing. The shark had a strange J-shaped scar just above his left eye; Zach wondered if it had been hooked before.

"Hey," Zach said, still trying to mollify the man, "it's a whole new sport to tag one of these. No fish has a worse attitude about being caught than a shark, so you want to help me dehook and tag him or not?"

When the guy pouted like a kid, Zach got his three-foot gaff hook to cut the fish free after he tagged him. He affixed the yellow tag on the end of a pole to the base of the first dorsal fin.

"You're not letting my prize catch go!" the man insisted again and tried to shove Zach as he reached over to cut the hook free. "You know damn well Florida rules are you can keep two sharks per boat or one per angler, whichever is less."

"And you know damn well what I told you when you boarded."

When the man yanked at his arm, Zach elbowed him back hard; the man bounced against the fighting chair and grabbed it to keep from falling. Zach wished he'd insisted the guy lay off the Scotch, but he hadn't known what was in his canteen at first.

Zach stabilized the bonnet and dehooked it. It was strictly his imagination, but the shark seemed to nod in thanks before it thrashed away and raced off with a final smack of his tail.

"I been lied to, or you're screwing me!" Dr. Paul accused, keeping the fighting chair between them.

"So get your lawyer pal and sue me," Zach muttered as he headed to the wheelhouse. "Just stay put until we're back at the marina."

"I've got time left on this trip!"

"I'll give you a partial refund, but we're heading in. Sit the hell down before you fall overboard and have to argue with the sharks themselves."

"You threatening me? I'll see that your license is revoked, that…"

Zach climbed the ladder to the wheelhouse and headed the boat back toward the marina. At first, when the livid fisherman grabbed Zach's digital camera from the second fighting seat where he'd dropped it, he thought he'd throw it overboard. But instead, the guy snapped photos of every boat they passed on the way in, as if he needed something to show his wife waiting for him at the Fish Fest. After all that drama, they hadn't gotten a shot of the shark at all.

Randi glanced around the area Thad was taking them slowly through as they headed back home. He said they'd have enough fuel to get back out into the bay, where someone would spot them.

He'd called the mangrove island on their right Fishbait Key, a fish hatchery spot. It was one of the few deep ones because, he'd said, it was directly out from the mouth of a river. She didn't see any fish, but she just tried to memorize how awesome everything looked, how free and safe she felt out here with Thad, low fuel or not. The sun was at such a slant that diamonds seemed to dance all around them on the water. Then, off to the side, she saw two shrink-wrapped packages bobbing, snagged in a mangrove root.

Evidently seeing them too, Thad swore under his breath. He stood on the footrests and looked around, though he probably couldn't see much over the height of the mangroves.

"What's that?" she asked, as her heartbeat kicked up even more.

"Drugs that someone's supposed to find but didn't—yet."

"Drugs? Shut up!"

"Probably coke coming in from South America. Big bucks."

"Should we take them and turn them in to the sheriff or park rangers?"

"Are you nuts? We've got to put as much space between that and us as we can. I'll tell my dad about where they are, and he'll report them."

"But how did they get lost here?"

"Planes drop them in a target area at night, and they're usually picked up by boats early morning."

"Local boats?"

He nodded and headed out faster the way—she thought— that they'd come in. But a sleek silver boat coasting quietly in from the gulf cut them off ahead, then turned toward them.

Thad slowed and made a tight U-turn, then kicked up their speed. She dropped her hands from his shoulders to clamp them around his waist. The boat roared to life behind them. It was going to chase them!

She glanced back. The big craft shoved waves into the

sides of the waterway, rocking the trees, picking up white foam under its sharp prow. Dark-tinted windows reflected the sun like wide-set, narrowed eyes with flaming pupils.

"Hold on!" Thad shouted.

Their Jet Ski jerked to a faster speed. Randi couldn't believe her dream could turn to nightmare so fast. Wind ripped her hair; salt spray blinded her. If only they had enough gas, they could outrun that boat. Or, if they could turn down some narrow, small alley where they couldn't be followed… Maybe that boat just wanted to scare them. It had gone way past where the drugs were floating, so maybe it hadn't come to pick them up.

"Hold on!" Thad shouted again as they took the next turn. She closed her eyes and hunched closer to him, certain they would fly into the web of branches and leaves.

But they hit something under the water, jolted, then turned. The Jet Ski soared sideways. Ripped from her grasp, Thad flew over the handlebars, head down, heels up. She too went airborne. She screamed as the little island came at her, tree limbs and leaves hitting, scratching…

But they cushioned her fall, clear to the clawlike roots pointing down into the lapping water.

Dizzy. Hurting. Thad—where was he?

She saw him in the water, close, bobbing facedown as the Jet Ski slowly sank behind him. Dragging herself across the web of roots, she reached for his floating arm just as the prow of the silver boat edged around the corner as if peeking at its prey. If they hadn't ditched, they would have escaped, because the boat evidently couldn't fit this far down the narrow path. It seemed stuck right where it was.

"Help me!" she half screamed, half sobbed as she tried to pull Thad toward her to get his face out of the water.

In answer to her plea, a man in a black baseball cap with a white handkerchief tied over his nose and mouth came out on the pointed peak of the long prow and heaved a huge, heavy net over both of them.

2

Tim Ralston, manning the storm center here at WSEA-AM, with an 11:00 a.m. update on Hurricane Dana. Our latest readings indicate that, in her current trajectory, Dana will not threaten the Dominican Republic, Haiti or Jamaica, but it looks as if she could impact western Cuba. That's not especially good news for the southwest coast of Florida. So keep it tuned right here, because we will have continual updates on Dana's speed and track from the National Hurricane Center in Miami.

Julie paced the dock, walking around two pelicans that were likely waiting for the charter fishing boats to come back and clean their catches. Laughter, music and the screeches of little kids on the rides floated clear down here. The local band and singer brought in for the Fish Fest were belting out an old Kenny Rogers song about knowing when to walk away and knowing when to run.

She squinted at the horizon, willing Randi's Jet Ski to materialize, then glared at the space where Thad Brockman's father docked his charter fishing boat. Next to it, affixed to a mooring post, a plastic box offered a neat stack of one-page ads for off-shore or backcountry fishing. She took one out and skimmed it.

The fees surprised her until she realized they were for up to four people: full day, $600 or half day, $300. One to six passengers could catch giant tarpon only from May 1 through July 1, but grouper, snapper, snook, king mackerel—and shark, no less—were evidently year-round. Bait, tackle and licenses were included.

The boat was described as a custom-built thirty-one footer with a restroom, or head, galley, dinette and a shaded, elevated bridge for the captain's cockpit. Sightseeing trips of Naples, Marco, or the 10,000 Islands were included, featuring sunset cruises with or without narrative.

Captain Zach Brockman. She frowned at his name. If she dialed his phone number listed here, could she reach him to demand he take her out looking for his son and her daughter—for free? But then, if he was already on a fishing trip, maybe he'd spot the kids on his own.

Julie pulled her cell phone out of her macrame handbag and only then realized she was carrying around her unopened can of pop. She set it on the wooden railing and punched in the local number. It rang, again, again, then a recording clicked on. The deep, rough voice startled her. "Hi, Captain Zach here. If you'd like to go either inshore or deep-sea fishing, just leave your name and number, and I'll get back to you about open dates...."

No, she wasn't leaving a message, she thought, as she hit the end button. But Zach Brockman and his son were going to get a piece of her mind. And Randi, too. If that girl thought she'd be welcomed with a calm, counseling chat after this stunt, she was dead wrong.

Loreen had walked almost all the way down the dock before Julie saw her. "Hey," the woman called to her, coming closer, "you worried 'bout your girl?"

"Yes. How did you know? She's out on a Jet Ski with Thad Brockman."

"Saw 'em go. That cute-as-a-button friend of yours put her on with him. They'll be back in. There's lots of nice beaches out on the islands and places to explore. I guess you didn't say she could go, huh?"

"Exactly, and Kaylin shouldn't have set that up. I just want Randi back right now!"

"You know, that storm's a couple of days away if it does hit, which it prob'ly won't. I got two of my own—kids, not storms, though sometimes it's the same thing."

Biting her lower lip, Julie nodded. Damn, but she was going to break into tears.

"I know it's tough," Loreen went on, leaning back against the wooden railing, "'specially for a single mom like you. But what I came out to say before I go meet Clint at the Fest is a warning about Grant Towers."

The last person in the world Julie was worried about was Grant Towers. "What about him?"

"I know he's been after you to sell Osprey to him for luxury homesites."

"He claims they would be what he calls 'cottages for boating, fishing and hunting enthusiasts, arranged in a small community.' But, with the lots, they'd start at over four hundred and fifty thousand dollars, so that sounds pretty luxe to me. Anyway, I'd never sell. End of conversation on that."

"Well, folks heard—I mean, you know how things get around in a little place like this—that he offered you twelve mill and is willing to go up."

"Loreen," Julie said, shoving her hair out of her eyes, but still staring out into the bright bay, "Osprey Island and Resort are a big part of my past and my future—the future for the girls who visit here, too. My daughter and I, when she gets her little booty back in here, have our own plans for it over the years. The last thing in the world I'd want there are thirty so-called cottages, a clubhouse and five hundred feet of dock space."

"Spoken like a deep south Florida Cracker after my own heart!" Loreen said with a broad grin. "Thank the Lord you're not like the old uppity-up guests your great-uncle used to entertain. Seemed that way to all of us who worked there, anyway."

Yes, Julie could see that now. It had been a real upstairs/ downstairs world. At the time, she'd thought nothing of it because she'd been too obsessed with her own loneliness and feelings of rejection. Sometimes she wondered if she hadn't majored in psych and counseling to learn to advise and comfort herself. The way her parents had treated her still hurt and rankled. As a young child, she'd tried to earn their approval and then had turned into a brat, desperately trying to get at least their attention.

"Thanks for the warning about Grant Towers," she told Loreen, "though I guess someone arriving in his yacht or his sleek white speedboat and offering to buy you out for a fortune is a nice problem to have."

"Us locals don't want fancy places and steep prices here, like on Marco Island or in Naples. No snooty outsiders who want to buy our places, build big, and jack up taxes! We're willing to do anything to keep that from happening, and I mean *anything*."

Julie turned to face her. Looking through both of their sunglasses, she could tell Loreen's eyes were mere slits; her lips were pressed so tightly together they trembled. Julie bet it wasn't only Loreen's husband Clint who could hold his own in a fight.

"I understand," Julie told her, looking out at the bay again. "But right now I just want my daughter to get back so I can take care of my guests, keep them calm when they hear about the storm, and chaperone them here at the Fest tonight."

"Speaking of Grant Towers, Thad's taken his daughter out on the WaveRunner or in a Hobie Cat sailer and then they've gone back to his place down a ways. You know, when his dad's been fishing and since his mother's dead. You could go check his house—but don't say I said so, about him taking a girl there."

Julie felt her tension unwind a bit. Despite her annoyance—and disbelief—that her fourteen-year-old daughter would have gone to a boy's house when she didn't even know him, at least that would mean she wasn't lost out in that labyrinth of islands. Man, that girl was going to lose computer time or her cell phone if she'd been foolish enough to do that, and with Zach Brockman's son!

"Do the Brockmans still live where they used to?" Julie asked. "Out on the edge of the Glades?"

"Not for years," Loreen said, shaking her flyaway hair

even harder than the wind was scrambling it. "That ram-shackle place got torn down, and the land bought up by a British guy, Ken Leigh—talk about moneybags—for a hunting camp in the Glades. Zach and Thad live in the guesthouse and rent their main place down off that second beach, right there," she said and pointed a brown arm so fast her bangle bracelets clinked. "Both of them can walk to work. It's a small place, painted dark blue, just behind a white tabby."

Tabby was an old but sturdy mortar, a homemade form of concrete, made from burned sea shells combined with sand, lime and water. Old places like the Osprey Resort had walls of tabby nearly a foot thick, so Julie knew what to look for. But she was torn between hoping or fearing she'd find her daughter with Zach Brockman's boy there.

As she quickly changed clothes in her room, Kaylin McKenzie prayed Randi had come back in by now. She felt terrible she'd more or less caused the problem by putting her on the Jet Ski with Thad Brockman, but Randi secretly had been so totally into him. Kaylin rushed out into the high-ceilinged Florida room of the lodge to wait for the girls to assemble for a talk about which activities had helped them the most while they were here. It was a debriefing session Kaylin knew Julie would not want to miss. Then, this afternoon, instead of the farewell beach cookout, they were going to the Fish Fest in town. On Sunday, most of the girls would begin to head home.

Through the large windows overlooking the bay, Kaylin could see Mike taking *The Manatee*, slow and awkward as its namesake, back in to pick up the Mintons. The 180-

degree view out the windows of this large room was only one of the things Kaylin loved about the old lodge, however much she sometimes felt stuck on a tropical isle, like Tom Hanks in that movie *Castaway*.

She'd agreed to only two days off every two weeks, but now that she'd found Nate Tomzak, she was starting to long for even more of a social life. With him, it would be an active, exciting one, too. He loved snorkeling and scuba diving, hiking, climbing and rapelling. The one thing he didn't like about Florida, he'd said, was that there were no mountains and the only climbing walls were on cruise ships, which polluted the oceans. No, life with Nate would not be luxurious, but it would be adventurous.

Kaylin sighed as she quickly straightened the sofa's throw pillows in the lofty-ceilinged room. Under the original tin roof of the resort, with its two wings, was an attic, top floor and main floor, since no Florida homes had basements. The sturdy white tabby walls, heart of pine ceilings and cedar floors anchored the light-looking rattan chairs and sofas, with their orange and fuschia cushions.

Through a sprawling screened-in porch just outside these windows, the interior seemed to flow into the lush outdoors. The big old kitchen was still in the nearest outbuilding, though Julie had installed a breakfast and snack bar when she updated the bathrooms. Still, the resort had that primitive, escapist feel, which was psychologically good for these troubled teens. It got them away from their environs to believe they could become someone new, someone who could cope with loneliness, longing and life.

Outside, a lawn dotted with wooden deck chairs and metal

tables with pastel umbrellas wrapped around three sides of the sprawling resort. Orchids swayed in the big gumbo-limbo tree while blue plumbago and pink hibiscus bushes under arching royal palms edged the flagstone walkway to the beach, where the sand was as soft as sugar. The island was about two hundred yards wide but a half a mile long. Its only other permanent inhabitants were Leon and Jake Malvers, father and son, who rented an old house from Julie at the southern end.

Kaylin ran upstairs to get her notebook from the office. Julie and Randi used this area for their living quarters; it included two bedrooms, a bath, and a large combined family room and office. Looking every bit like the big tropical flowers they resembled, area rugs dotted the polished dark wood floors. Julie had left her desktop PC running, and neon fish swam across the screen. Kaylin grabbed her notebook and headed back down.

Her spacious ground-floor room was in the north wing, which had three bathrooms, one of which was her private one, and four bedrooms; the south wing was a mirror image. In the good old days, wealthy people from the Detroit area had come down every winter, including, of course, Julie's parents, who'd had their only child, evidently a change-of-life baby, when they were in their late forties. Julie had always said her parents were terribly in love. Those were always her exact words: *Terribly* in love.

Kaylin sighed. How she longed for that herself. She'd often cried herself to sleep when she was a kid because her own parents fought and screamed all night. And here, Julie had said her folks loved each other so much that they hardly knew that she was around and just shuffled her off while they did their thing.

Kaylin could hear the girls' voices as they chatted from room to room or went down the hall to use the bathrooms. This group had bonded beautifully into a little family, one with a mother figure in Julie, a big sis in Kaylin and a kid sister in Randi, though it wasn't fair for Randi not to have her own life to live. Leaving her friends and coming to Po-dunk was the price Miranda Minton, like Kaylin herself, had paid for paradise.

"Kaylin, can I talk to you a sec?" A strident voice broke into her thoughts. Cindy Markland, a Grosse Pointe girl, bounded into the room from the south wing. Cindy had burned as well as cut herself to try to cope with her mother's expectations for a graceful, slender daughter. Kaylin and Julie were pretty sure she could cope with her problems and pressures better now, though she was one of the two girls staying for an extra session. Cindy came closer and leaned against the back of a rattan couch. She was plump and plain but her outgoing personality could take her far—if she could become her own person and not punish the one she would never be.

"Man," Cindy said, gesturing extravagantly, "I didn't mean to upset Julie. You know, blurting that out about the guy Randi went out with. He's way cool, and I was just happy for her."

"Tell me about it. I'm the one who finagled Randi a spot on his Jet Ski. I had no idea they'd just…disappear."

"Captain Mike heard on the ferry radio there's a bad storm coming," Cindy rushed on. "Can we still go in to the Fest tonight?"

"It looks like clear sky," Kaylin said, stooping a bit to glance out over the bright, azure water. A sleek silver cigarette boat with dark-tinted windows raced along the horizon, nearly blending in with it. "A storm coming? When?" she asked. "If it clouds up, we can always take umbrellas."

Loreen's directions had been good; Julie easily spotted the beach house that must belong to Zach and Thad Brockman. The small bungalow was painted a navy blue with white trim and, like the larger, white-with-blue-trim two-story house they rented out, it had a traditional Florida tin roof. A new-looking black pickup truck sat in the driveway, but the place looked deserted.

Her heart thumping, Julie strode up the flagstone path through the sprawling hibiscus hedge, knocked on the screen door, then opened that to rap on the wooden door. She thought she heard music from somewhere nearby. Surely, it didn't carry all the way from the Fish Fest. It didn't sound like the same down-home country twang; it was more like a salsa beat.

She gave up on knocking and circled the house. It was neatly kept outside. Opened vertical blinds hung in the windows. A small air conditioner jutted out from the house, but it wasn't running, and the window sashes were all up to let in the warm breeze. On the back side, hidden from the road by a stand of palmetto, she shaded her eyes and peeked in through a screen.

The small bedroom was evidently Thad's, with its movie posters, desktop computer, messy bed and general chaos. The next small bedroom looked shipshape, spartan and immaculate. She'd heard Zach Brockman had been a navy SEAL. A long dark wood dresser with no mirror above it looked bare, but for a phone and a framed photo of what looked like a man, woman and a child.

She jumped as the phone rang and darted away from the window so fast she almost tripped. It rang twice more and then the deep, recorded voice she'd heard before came on: "Hi, Captain Zach here. If you'd like to go either inshore or deep-sea fishing, just leave your name and number, and I'll get back to you...."

He'd better get back in person and soon, Julie fumed. He had to help her search inshore or out in the gulf or wherever those kids could have gone.

As she continued around the other side of the house, the caller's words pursued her through the open windows. "Good day, Sharkman, Victoria Leigh ringing you up. I'd really like to get another deep-sea lesson straightaway. Or, both the sightseeing and the sunset cruise sound lovely, luv."

The accent was British, and the tone a strange mix of aloofness and warmth. Julie knew Victoria Leigh and her husband only by name. Ken Leigh was a local entrepreneur who owned several import businesses in Miami but commuted to the city in his helicopter from here. They had a large home on the beach a ways outside of Gladesport, and Loreen had said today they'd bought the land Zach's family had owned on the edge of the Glades not far from here for a hunting camp.

Was the message a sexual come-on, a subtle allusion to more than a simple fishing lesson? Maybe she was being overly suspicious, but she'd been such an idiot to overlook signs her husband had been "cruising" with someone else.

And then she heard a girl scream.

She gasped and turned. She *had* actually heard that, hadn't she? It hadn't been her own inner scream at the memory of Steve's betrayal and desertion? Where had the noise come from? Not inside. No, it must have come from the large house. What if the boy had taken Randi there? What if…

Julie tore around the bungalow toward the house. She'd break a window if she had to…Loreen said they rented this place, so the boy would have access to it if no one were there right now….

Could that have been Randi?

She charged up the wooden steps, screaming, "Randi! Randi?"

The screen door banged open into her and sent her stumbling back. She barely managed to keep her feet.

"No, *señora*," the dark-haired young woman who came charging out cried. "My name is Rosa. Sorry if I hit you."

"Wait, wait," Julie cried, getting her balance and grabbing the girl's wrist as she tried to flee past. "Is Thad Brockman here? What are you running from?"

"Hurricane coming!" she cried, tugging free. "I cleaning the house like always, listening to my music and I hear it coming!"

"But it's days away and might not come here at all. They'll tell us if it's heading this way."

"They say on my radio station, in *español*," she added, "it coming over western Cuba." She pronounced it *Cuva*. "The mountains there, they slow it some, but it coming! I been through it when I grew up in western Cuva. But Thad—" she said the boy's name as if it were Tad "—he not here, his papa neither."

"Rosa, I'm looking for my daughter, who was Jet Ski riding with Tad—Thad. I just wondered if you had seen either of them around here."

"What she wearing?" Rosa asked, still poised for flight as she scanned the sky through the trees.

What *had* she worn today? Julie thought. Not a swimsuit like the others, but exactly what? What if she had to describe her to the police—or even to Zach Brockman, because she was going to demand he go out looking for them the minute his fishing boat came in.

"She's about five feet six inches—my height, with my color of hair, only a lot of it, straight and long," Julie told her, hitting her own shoulders to indicate its length. "She has blue eyes, a heart-shaped face, kind of thin and lanky body."

"Oh, *señora*, that sounds like a few others I seen, but I look. I keep looking." She started toward the beach, leaving Julie feeling desperate and alone. The woman had left the front door of the house open with the radio still blaring its Spanish station. Granted, few folks locked their doors around Gladesport, but was she planning to just walk off like this, all because a hurricane might be coming in a few days?

"Rosa, wait!" Julie cried and rushed to catch up with her. "Do you know Thad Brockman? What's he like?"

Rosa rolled her eyes. "Depend on who you ask, *señora*."

"Please, I'm asking you."

"I not know him much. His papa keep him in straight line, *sí*, make him do push-ups, yell at him if he not good."

"Not good? What do you mean?"

"Got hisself spelled from school last year. My brother is the janitor there, working, you know."

"But why did Thad get expelled from school?"

"For selling that sex stuff, you know, like drugs."

"What?" She had no idea what the woman could be talking about. Pornography? Marijuana, or worse? She actually thought she was going to be ill.

"I just wait for my husband come get me when he come back from fishing for crabs," she said and plopped herself down on a short stretch of low sea wall along the beach. "See," she said, pointing, "there Captain Zach's boat just come in, closest one to shore and that other one Captain Clint's. You can ask Tad's papa yourself, so—"

Julie was already sprinting back toward the marina.

The minute Ray Paul stomped off down the dock, Zach jumped on Clint's boat, despite the fact his friend was squirting the deck and scuppers down with a hose.

"Hey, my man!" Clint greeted him with a grin. "Ready for some suds up at the Fest, or you want some here? I've got a few extra brewskis stashed aboard."

"Not right now. My charter, the doc from Sarasota, had the definite idea I'd let him catch and keep shark," Zach said, folding his arms over his chest.

He and Clint had known each other all their lives. Even if they'd been apart for months, they had always picked up as if it had been minutes. The fact Zach had spent years as a marine and then an elite SEAL and Clint had spent three years as regular army had hardly fazed their friendship. SEALs lived in cycles of eighteen months of training or workup, six months of overseas deployment, then stand-down for six months, and each half year home, Zach had happily crewed on Clint's boat. Nothing had come between them until these last few years, when Zach had championed sharks and Clint had headed up the opposition of local fishermen who felt their livelihood was more endangered than the sharks.

The two of them looked somewhat alike, too, and had once passed for brothers. But Zach had stayed lean and his short black hair had begun to silver while Clint had developed a beer belly and wore his dark hair collar-length—or it would be, if he ever wore a collar, with his swamp buggy and speedboat racing T-shirt wardrobe. And, of course, Clint had been married to Loreen forever and had two sons, while Zach was widowed and just had Thad.

"Hell, nice to see you, too!" Clint muttered and turned the hose so it bounced off the wheelhouse to douse Zach with spray.

"So what about it?" Zach demanded, seizing the end of the hose and spraying Clint back with it. Ordinarily, such horseplay would have had both of them hooting with laughter or collapsing into a mock wrestling match.

"So what?" Clint countered.

"You evidently took the doc's Sarasota lawyer friend out a month or so ago and either let him catch and keep shark for a bribe or told him you would—and this guy today mixed you up with me. What's the story?"

"Gonna turn me in? You can't prove a damn thing. Would you get off this crusade, Sharkman? It's turning everybody against you—me included."

"It's the law, Clint. A moral one as well as a legal one."

"Oh, here we go with the college prof bit, huh? Or you gonna turn preacher on me now?"

"I've only guest lectured at the university a few times, so don't throw that at m—"

"Why don't you just give me your scare tactics talk about shark species becoming extinct. What's that you call it—'Man Bites Shark'?" he taunted, his voice rising, his face reddening through his deep tan. "Bet that gets the coeds all excited, huh, former stud SEAL, macho Sharkman and all that."

Zach felt like he'd been sucker-punched. He'd actually thought all that didn't make one damn bit of difference to Clint. "Look," Zach told him, "you're getting really good at an offense becoming your best defense. Or is it that you've been drinking, getting a real early start on the Fest? I had to practically detox my charter today."

"Hey, you want to clear the air with a good fistfight like we used to?" Clint demanded and heaved the still spewing hose up on the dock before advancing on Zach with his fists balled. "Or you want to go back to a drag race to settle things like the old days," he shouted, stopping about three feet from Zach. "You've never beat me yet with a swamp buggy or a speedboat!"

"You sound like some high school kid, and we're both way beyond that," Zach said, not giving ground. "Let's leave that stuff to our boys, okay?"

"The fun things of life may have passed you by, buddy boy, but not me. Maybe you just better get the hell off my boat and start hanging with Grant Towers's Marco crowd or Liz Lawson's eco freaks."

In truth, Zach knew Clint got only happier, not meaner when he drank. So what really had triggered this cesspool of hatred? Could he have a side business going from grabbing sharks illegally, then taking bribes?

"Maybe you're real different now," Clint raved on, "but I'm just the same old Gladesport townie I always was. I'm just trying to get by and seeing mor'n half my trade disappear, partly thanks to you and politicians. Everything's going down the drain with our friendship, just like this fish-bloodied water."

Clint reached over the side of the boat and grabbed the hose back. That sent an arc of water down the dock, followed by a squeal. Then someone shouted, "Hey, watch it! Captain Clint, I'm looking for Zach Brockman. Have you seen him?"

"'Fraid I have," Clint bellowed. Then he added under his breath with a wink at Zach, as if they'd never argued at all, "Now don't you have all the luck."

Up on the dock, a wet, distraught-looking blonde glared around the wheelhouse, frowning, especially when she saw Zach. The woman wasn't that tall, but from his angle under her it seemed that her bare legs, teasingly displayed by her red wraparound skirt, would never quit. Despite the fact she'd changed so over the years, Zach knew who she was. The few times he'd been near her this summer, she'd looked totally cool and put together. Now her hair was wild, her pretty face flushed, and her soaked blouse stuck to her full breasts. A raving fury, she was sweating, dishevelled, out of breath—and yet she took his breath away.

"What can I do for you, Ms. Minton?" Zach asked as he stepped off Clint's boat onto the dock and crossed his arms over his chest. His stomach muscles clenched. Long-buried memories of how her people had treated him and his friends assaulted him. Either she was furious about something he'd done—and he had no clue what—or, if she'd come to him, it was obvious she *really* needed help.

3

Tim Ralston here, southwest Florida. Time's 11:45. From now on I'll be giving you hurricane reports on the quarter hours and breaking in if there's any need. Nothing official yet about Hurricane Dana's exact path once she leaves Cuba or any possible evacuations, but she's picking up speed over warm water and is moving toward becoming a Category Two. She could be on a trajectory that would bring her to our coast. Those of you who have been here in the storm season know the drill. Beachfront property folks especially should dig out your board-ups, or buy plywood and nails before they're all gone. Batteries, canned food, and water will be disappearing from store shelves. Let's not panic, but plan ahead. This one could be a real unwelcome guest.

Julie noted Zach Brockman was about a head taller than her; his muscular body looked carved from stone, as did his expression. She tried to sound calm. "My daughter's missing—with your son. They didn't come in from a Jet Ski ride over an hour ago, and he should have brought her back when the other Jet Skis he rented to us were returned."

He frowned. His face was craggy with chiseled cheek-bones and thin lips, and his aquiline nose looked as if it had been broken. Even with his close-cropped hair, his ears were tight to his head. Because his hair was so dark, a slight shadow of beard stubble showed on his bronze cheeks and skin. It bothered her that she couldn't see his eyes behind the mirrored aviator sunglasses he wore.

"Thad's good on the water and knows the area," he said. "They probably just stopped to walk on a beach or explore out there."

"That's what Loreen said, but it's not like Randi. She's only fourteen."

He raised thick, dark eyebrows from behind his sunglasses. A small muscle at the base of his throat seemed to throb.

"Can't you do something to get them back?" she cried, her voice suddenly strident. The knot in her stomach tightened.

"Hang on a sec. It always pays to think, not just react." He wiped his wet hands on his water-blotched khaki shorts. He wore a black T-shirt and beat-up running shoes with no socks.

"I checked at your house," she told him, "and they're not there. Rosa said something about him getting expelled from school for porn or drugs, so you can't blame me for worr—"

Thrusting both palms out as if to shut her up, he interrupted, "I don't know what she told you, but it was just a toad."

"A what? Look, Captain Zach, I want my daughter back,

and I want her now. If you won't take me out, I'll hire that other boat right there, Captain Clint, I don't care what it costs—"

"I should have known you'd throw money around. I'll need to fuel my motorboat so we can take that. It'll get us down the mangrove alleys between the smaller keys where my big boat won't go. You may be going with me, but you're *not* hiring me," he went on, punching an index finger in her direction. "Zach Brockman doesn't work for your family anymore."

He turned and walked out on the dock to the fuel pump. He'd said that last comment with such contempt that, for a moment, she hesitated to trust him. But this man, who surely had a stake in the search too, was the best one to help her right now. However tempted she was to run to the police, she knew it was too early for that. *Dear God, please don't let it come to that.*

"If it's going to take you a few minutes to get ready," she called to him, "I'll tell my ferryboat captain I'm going out, so he can tell the others."

"Five minutes."

"I'll be here."

Julie told Captain Mike about the situation and sent him back to Osprey again, asking him to circle the island to be sure Thad hadn't taken Randi home or put the Jet Ski in on a beach there. That possibility made her feel better, but she still had to go out with Zach. She couldn't afford to leave one hidden inlet unsearched.

As she glanced at the old *Manatee*, lumbering out toward

Osprey, she recalled the times she'd ridden it years ago with the kids from Gladesport who'd held jobs at the resort. Ferry rides were the only times she could closely observe and overhear the local teens, since their orders were to be seldom seen and not heard as they did their tasks to serve the resort guests. They were supposed to ride the ferry only, since her great-uncle didn't want their boats taking up dock space or beach. Julie had managed to ride the ferry with them whenever she could get away with it.

Zach had been the exception to the seen-but-not-heard rule. Since he'd swum like a fish, her uncle had hired him as a lifeguard, so he was often on the beach, which ran in front of the lodge. She'd had a secret crush on him and had cried when he'd been fired. Her great-uncle had ordered him to stay away after he'd pulled that trick with the fake shark he'd made. It had caused not only temporary panic but cancelled reservations and made the lodge a target of ridicule when the story was picked up in the media. What Zach claimed was meant as a joke had infuriated her great-uncle and her father.

Even now, she could see in her mind's eye the coast kids, as her father disdainfully referred to them, whispering and laughing on the back bench of the ferry. Skinny Loreen, crazy Clint. Cocky Zach and pretty, sun-browned Becky. Becky, who cleaned the rooms, was the girl she'd heard Zach had married. Had to marry, Captain Mike said, so Thad was probably the result of that.

Each winter her parents had pulled her out of her suburban Michigan school, hired a tutor, and brought her here. How she had longed to be one of the coast kids' clique with their insider jokes, their local knowledge, their bonfires on the beach at night. She'd even asked to attend the local school during the season, but her parents would have none of that.

Growing up, she'd felt so alone in the midst of adults, especially since her parents always had each other. A great love story, but one that broke their daughter's heart. She'd always figured that's why President and Nancy Reagan's kids had each rebelled in their own ways. Perhaps Pattie and Ron Reagan's parents were so busy, so complete without them, that they felt like intruders.

After Zach's shark trick, Julie had pulled reckless stunts to—unsuccessfully—get her mother and father's attention. She'd ridden a horse through the house during one of their dinner parties, she'd brought friends they couldn't abide home from college, she'd even dressed punk for a while, though she hated the look.

Since her years of studying aberrant behavior in others, she realized now that she'd pulled her most destructive stunt in her headlong marriage to bright but belligerent Steve Minton. That, at least and at last, had made her grow up. It was the old story she should have been able to read before its sad ending: she'd worked hard for years mothering Randi and drawing a salary to put Steve through med school and set up his practice, only to have him desert her for another woman, a colleague at his new clinic.

Maybe it was the shock of a divorce in the family that finally impacted her parents, for her father had died of cardiac arrest and her mother of hypertension shortly after, leaving the bulk of their estate to the charities they'd founded. Julie had gone to grad school to get a masters in counseling, and—she hoped—had finally learned to counsel herself.

"You set to go?" Zach's deep voice broke into her reverie.

She was startled to see she'd walked the length of the dock. Since his motorboat sat below its level, she hadn't seen him at first. Walking to the edge, she looked down. As the waves moved under and around his dark blue boat toward shore, she felt a moment of vertigo. Pulled toward him, she almost toppled off the dock.

He extended a hand up to her, and she took it for the big step down. His touch was strong and warm. She was going to have to trust this man to find Randi. She had to work hard to be calm, to get along when she was so furious at his son.

"Thanks," she said as she settled herself on the first of two seats, facing the front, while he sat in the stern seat so he could steer the outboard motor. The boat, ironically, she thought, was called *Tracker*. Backing them out, he maneuvered it adeptly, then turned the prow toward the bay.

"I was especially panicked," she went on, gripping her hands in her lap and turning halfway toward him, "when I heard about the hurricane. But the sky's so clear, and they say it's at least two days out, if it comes our way at all. Did you…have you heard about that? Hurricane Dana?"

"On my radio coming back from fishing. There's a lot to do in case it hits, but nothing more important than finding our kids. I know one place to look."

She felt instantly grateful. Nodding, she held her visored sun hat on harder as he accelerated their speed. *Our kids* sounded strange, but good. At least he had agreed to help and had an idea of where to look. She felt a bit better already, but then maybe that was just because he'd been a navy SEAL. Surely they knew everything about water rescue.

He seemed to be staring at her from behind his sunglasses, or was he just looking out at the bay? She told herself she was going to have to play peacemaker during this enforced period with Zach, because it was pretty obvious he didn't like her. But she needed information above all.

"Now, what's this about Thad getting expelled over a toad?" she asked in a voice loud enough to be heard over the muted roar of the motor.

"Later," he yelled at her. "Take these binocs and scan the shoreline to both sides. Unfortunately, those WaveRunners are dark blue."

She took the heavy binoculars from him, removed her sunglasses, and adjusted them for her eyes. She soon recognized the south end of her own Osprey Island, where she'd allowed two eccentric old clam and gator hunters, Leon and Jake Malvers, to continue to rent a run-down house they'd lived in for years.

When the resort was in its heyday, Leon, Jake's father, had taken Osprey Resort guests on fishing trips in the 10,000 Islands. But now Leon was a paraplegic and the area's folklorist—or biggest liar, depending on whom you talked to. She'd considered having him tell the girls tall tales of Ponce de Leon and the Seminole Indian days, but big, hulking Jake, who was about forty, went everywhere with his father, and she was uncomfortable around the man. More than once she'd seen him watching her and her girls, though she'd told herself that wasn't so weird on such a small island. It wasn't like he'd been peeking in windows. Besides, she was sure the

Malvers wouldn't step out of line, not when she could terminate their lease. They knew it, too, for Jake had warned her about Grant Towers wanting to buy Osprey, just as Loreen had.

"I was hoping Thad might have brought Randi home," she told Zach as they skimmed the length of the island past the lodge. "Captain Mike checked, but I guess they might have hit one of the nice beaches on the island. I already sent Mike back in *The Manatee* to look all around here."

"Good, let him look. We're not going to search the island. We're going to see if Thad dropped in at his grandfather's."

"His grandfather's?"

"Yeah. Leon Malvers is—was—Thad's mother's dad."

Julie felt like an idiot that she hadn't known. "Then Jake was Becky's brother?"

"Yeah. So you remember her. She drowned right about here, swimming at night. They didn't find her for a while. If I hesitated back on the dock, it's just…as many times as I've helped save lives, one way or the other…I was thousands of miles away that time…" His voice broke. "It threw me for a minute, hearing Thad was missing where he knows every twist and turn here, that's all."

"I'm sorry Julie isn't back for our final group chat," Kaylin told the assembled girls as they sat around her in the Florida room. The guilt of having put Randi on Thad's Jet Ski was starting to really eat at her, but she tried to carry on for Julie, wanting to make it up to her. "But I know she'd like us to keep on schedule. Have each of you signed your life preserver?"

The girls began each meeting or group activity with a

touch of their particular preserver on the wall, which was the symbol of their decision to keep themselves afloat when they went back to their normal lives. Most of them had photographed or sketched their preserver; all of them signed theirs before they completed the program.

"Okay, then, I'm sure Randi and Julie will be back soon, or maybe they'll meet us on shore when we go in for the Fish Fest. Let's just concentrate on the things you've done or learned these two weeks that you think will help you the most. Your advice will help us, too, since we can use it for future guests."

Bree Nichols, a redheaded, freckled Detroit girl whose arms were crisscrossed with white razor scars, spoke up first. Kaylin was thrilled by that, for Bree had been painfully quiet, a mere mousy observer of others. Along with the outgoing Cindy Markland, Bree still had serious problems and was staying for two more weeks, but she'd made amazing strides.

"For just basic things," Bree said, her voice so quiet that everyone leaned forward to hear, "using red Magic Markers or paint on my arms and legs. You know, when I had the urge to hurt myself, just draw the pain instead. And that made me see how bad it looked. But my way best thing to handle the black feelings is to stab a piece of wood with a screwdriver and scream. You know, like Julie said it's okay to do. Just letting myself cry, shout and scream. That's the best."

Kaylin could tell some of the others were also surprised the introverted girl had said that. Bree Nichols, daring to scream? Others contributed their favorite ways to release the tension and inward hatred which so often triggered the self-torture they had hidden for so long. Doing a specific task, both mundane or unusual, exercising, just talking it out, even in front of a mirror—their list of coping skills they'd learned went on and on.

"When we first came here," Tiffany Troutman said, "we jokingly called this place the Osprey Last Resort, but our time here really helped."

Kaylin took notes so she could fill Julie in. Instead of jumping in first, Cindy Markland finally spoke. She'd spent the meeting glancing out the windows, as if she too were obsessed with finding Randi.

"I'm still way surprised at how the simple things work best for me," Cindy said. "I mean, even though my parents want me to stay another two weeks. My mom just doesn't get it that snapping an elastic band around your wrist or holding ice cubes in your hands can help something she thinks must be so…so mental-case stuff."

"None of you are mental cases!" Kaylin put in. Both she and Julie had stressed that repeatedly from the beginning, though some of the girls had gone through psychiatric counseling before coming here and would need more later. "You just have had difficulty learning how to express insecurity or emotional pain. But always remember that self-injury is not an answer. No one here is insane, crazy or evil, even though there is so much shame and guilt associated with what we all—me too, once, remember—used to do, before we found better ways to cope. Something else, Cindy?"

"I don't mean to get you off track, but a boat just put in at the side dock, and it's not the ferry. An old wooden boat— Ms. Lawson and that aide of hers, looks like to me."

Kaylin's pen went flying as if she'd actually flipped it on the floor, but she didn't take time to recover it. The girls knew Liz and Nate from their presentation about valuing and preserving wildlife last week. What would they be doing here today? Could they have found Randi?

"Stay here, and I'll see what they want," Kaylin cried and rushed out the side door toward the dock. She prayed they didn't have bad news.

As if to allay her fears, Nate grinned at her from behind Liz as the woman jumped lithely onto their dock and wrapped the rope around a post. Stenciled in green on the side of their vintage motorboat was the word *WorldWise* and the local phone number. Under that, smaller letters read, Don't let the Everglades become the Neverglades.

Liz and Nate worked and lived in a gated compound which included a renovated house, a guesthouse where Nate stayed, and some outbuildings in another fishing village called Goodland. Together they patrolled the entire Mangrove Bay area, gave talks promoting local ecology causes through the media or government. Liz always gave great sound bites to the local TV or radio stations. WorldWise was a privately funded, international activist organization, one that was becoming more high profile yearly, according to Nate.

"We were working on our manatee count and just stopped by to bid a hearty farewell to your girls!" the ever-exuberant Liz cried, giving Kaylin's shoulders a quick, one-armed hug.

Liz was in her midfifties, though she looked years younger, until you got close enough to see the wrinkles around her eyes and upper lip and the silver in her pale brown hair. It wasn't the sun which had aged her though, since she used massive amounts of SPF blockers, and wore big hats and long-sleeved light cotton shirts and slacks to stay amazingly pale for someone who was out so much. Kaylin had heard that some of the locals who didn't like Liz or her do-gooder causes called her "the glades ghost" behind her back.

Under her baggy garb, Liz was totally toned, not only from working out, but from her all-natural eating habits. Kaylin could tell that when she hugged her, and when she was inside, she often took off her blousy tops to reveal shapely arms. Since she never wore makeup to warm her complexion, darken her pale brows or outline her crisp blue eyes, she looked almost girlish—and she had been a real hit with the girls.

Liz had evidently been married several times, but was now only married to her job. She had told each group she'd spoken to here to find something passionate to do with their lives that was all-consuming. "Protecting nature brings rewards worth anything you might sacrifice for her," Liz had told them, as if nature were some sort of pagan goddess.

Square-jawed Nate was all dark eyes, blinding smile and quick movements. He, too, was passionate about protecting this mangrove wetland system. His mere presence always pulled at Kaylin like the underwater ebb tide when she'd gone snorkeling with him last week. Despite the fact he'd been furious when she'd touched a piece of living coral, she understood his protective nature. But now, as she looked at him and smiled, she also saw *The Manatee* going past the dock.

"Excuse me a minute," she told her guests, then cupped her hands to her mouth and shouted across the water to Mike. "Randi?"

"Nope!" he yelled over the chug of the motor. "Checking around the island!"

"What about Randi?" Liz asked.

"She went out with Thad Brockman on a Jet Ski, and they didn't get back yet, that's all."

"I'm sure Julie's upset. If they don't return soon, we can help look. Just let us know. Where might they have gone?"

"Liz," Nate put in, "if they knew where they'd gone, they wouldn't be looking. There may not really be ten thousand islands out there, but it's a bunch."

"Please, Kaylin," Liz said, taking her wrist in a firm grasp, "you tell Julie we want to help. If there's anything we can do...though we're going to have to board up the WorldWise Center in case this bitching storm comes in here... Sorry," she added. "Nature giveth and taketh away. We must remember that hurricanes are nature's way of change and renewal too, just like a forest fire, however brutal the process."

"Li-iz..." Nate sounded as though he was going to protest something she'd said, but she glanced at him and he shut up. Kaylin frowned at Liz, and not just because she kept Nate on too tight a leash. Sometimes the woman's grand pronouncements made no sense at all. The last thing anybody who lived on a barrier island or near the shore needed was the renewal caused by a brutal hurricane.

4

Tim Ralston with your WSEA-AM first alert forecast, so keep it tuned right here. It's 12:00 p.m. but not high noon for us yet. I want to warn you, though. Granted, Florida forecasters have predicted some storm landfalls which have been wrong, like Hurricane David, which veered offshore before hitting Miami in '79. But I'm going to ask you all to trust me and act on my information, if the word coming soon from the National Hurricane Center in Miami includes our coastline. For those of you who live in a high-hazard zone, voluntary or mandatory evacuations are a distinct possibility.

"Part of the reason I mentioned Becky's death," Zach told Julie as he put their small boat into the Malverses's dock and killed the motor, "is because we'll do better here if you check with Leon about whether he's seen the kids rather than me."

"Me? I mean, I know him, but why me? After all, if he was your father-in-l—"

"Just do it, okay? Leon, Jake and I haven't seen eye to eye for years. When I was in the Middle East and Becky died, he took Thad in, of course, but then he wanted to keep him."

"Not like—abduct him? I remember he told me a story about taking someone he loved captive on an island where a pirate once lived, or something like th—"

"I think he might have abducted his wife from her family years ago, but so much with him is tall tales. Miss Julie," he said, using her old, resort-era nickname, "are you going to ask him or not? I think we'll catch more flies with your honey than with my vinegar."

Doubly upset that she had to go back into that creepy place—why didn't someone see or hear them and come out to the dock?—Julie set her jaw and climbed out of the boat. A navy SEAL and he was acting scared to ask some old, crippled man if he'd seen Thad? But then again, if things were bad between them, she didn't need Zach shot at with one of those rifles they had hanging on their walls, amid the mounted skulls of alligators they'd killed over the years.

She strode briskly off the short dock where three boats were tethered. It seemed everyone in this area had two or more boats, just like most Americans had cars.

She'd make this visit quick. If only he or Jake knew where Thad was, or at least had seen him.

"Mr. Malvers? Jake?" she called and hesitated a moment where the sand became scrub grass. Their house was about thirty yards inland through the blowing screen of palmetto thickets. It was what she'd heard called a classic Cracker house, though nothing looked classic about it. The Crackers, as they were affectionately known to the locals, were evidently Florida's answer to hillbillies, people who were self-sufficient yet hospitable loners. That described these two all right.

The house was made of flaking white clapboard and shingled, built about four feet off the ground on thick stilts with a long front porch and a breezy central walkway which divided the place in two equal sections. Leon had pointed out in one of his rambling lessons about local history that it was built in a clearing to avoid lightning strikes from the nearby tall pines.

She walked up the long, rough board ramp Jake had cobbled together to allow his father's wheelchair to navigate the immediate area. Also supported by wooden stilts, it slanted up to the front porch and bounced a bit under her.

"Anybody here?"

She seldom visited, since Jake dropped off their monthly rental money, always in cash, at the lodge. But the last time she was here, she'd gotten a long harangue about not only Grant Towers but how they resented Liz Lawson's poking around. Julie hoped they didn't mistake her voice for Liz's. Liz thought Jake was a gator poacher and clam rustler and had said so.

"First," she remembered Leon complaining, "the gov'ment makes it illegal to shoot a gator after we been catching them for years. Then finally in '88 they allow two kills a year, then try to make us take gov'ment training programs to teach you how, no less. Got to rope a gator now like some damned cowboy, haul him too close for comfort to the boat and finish him off with a pistol or a bang stick. Then the 'glades ghost' Lawson shows up to lecture me 'bout even that. Now don't that beat all, and me in a fair fight with them gators these days, since I can't move nothing from the waist down?"

"But if there were no rules," Julie had said, "alligators would still be endangered."

"Listen, girl," he'd ranted, pointing a stub of index finger some trap or teeth had shortened long ago, "compared to folks like that British guy Ken Leigh, hunting with his fancy crossbows, it's real glades hunters like me and Jake's 'dangered 'round here!"

Please, dear God, Julie prayed, as she knocked on the screen door in the breezeway, *don't let Randi be endangered.*

Jake Malvers appeared inside, looking gray through the screen. His big, square head and broad shoulders blocked out the dim room beyond, though she could see the mounted rifles and silhouettes of alligator skulls along one wall. She took a step back.

"Sorry to bother you, but—"

"Who's that, Jake?" the old man called.

"Dad's just taking a lay-down," Jake told her and opened the door, though she didn't step in. "It's Julie Minton!" he shouted over his shoulder.

"Come to tell us to get out, with that storm a-coming?" Leon yelled from somewhere in the depths of the house.

"No, Mr. Malvers!" she called in the door. "I'm in a hurry, but I just wondered if you'd seen my daughter, Miranda—Randi." If there was bad blood between Zach and these men, should she even mention Thad? Yes, of course, she should, for they were related.

"We ain't seen hide nor hair of her," Jake answered for him, scratching his beard stubble. "She lost on this little island, you mean?"

"No, she went for a ride on a Jet Ski with Thad Brockman and they didn't come back," Julie blurted in one quick breath.

"So, who you with out there?" Jake said, frowning and squinting through the screen door he still held ajar. "That Zach's small boat out at the dock?"

"Yes, and—"

"Thad knows the area," Jake said. "Pa and me taught him, 'fore Zach come back from playing hero, chasing foreign terr'ists, 'stead of the kind we got 'round here. Then he gets in bed with one of them, that Lawson bi—lady."

Julie hoped "getting in bed with" Liz Lawson was a figure of speech. But then, there had been that provocative recorded phone message from Victoria Leigh which Julie had overheard at Zach's house. She realized how little she really knew Zach Brockman, despite how much she needed him.

"That's enough," came a gruff voice from behind Jake. "Mrs. Minton don't need to get in the middle of any of that…the things with Lawson or Zach. She got herself enough to fret about, keeping that snake in the grass Grant Towers away."

Leon reminded her of a gaunt, ill-dressed Santa Claus. The whites of his eyes and white beard seemed to glow in the shadows as he wheeled himself to the door, edging Jake aside. The younger man stepped onto the porch with her. His gray T-shirt read, I'd like to help you out. Which way did you come in?

"How long have Thad and your girl been gone?" Leon asked her.

"About two hours, when they should have come right back in. We just thought, with your ties to Thad, they might be here."

"He does come here at times. Least Zach's fine with that much. Two hours ain't long, Mrs. Minton. Why, Jake and me used to take the boy out all day when he was no more'n a tyke. He knows his way 'round here, from 'fore his daddy come home after his mamma died." With a sudden, hacking cough, he added, "That was 'fore Zach gave up saving the world to save his boy from being raised by the likes of Jake and me."

Now she wasn't quite so angry with Zach for sending her to do his dirty work. He might have wasted time here arguing with them. But she regretted Leon's hurt feelings. Ordinarily, she'd hope they could sit down and talk it out with a counselor, for she'd seen close up that festering family ties were the hardest to heal.

"I've got to be going," she told them and headed for the ramp again. "We're going to search the bay."

"I'll go out in my boat, too," Jake called after her. "There's a coupla haunts I'll check, places he might of gone."

"Thanks. I'd appreciate that—Zach, too."

"Don't count on that," she heard Leon mutter as she rushed back down the boardwalk toward the beach.

Around the first turn, Julie almost jumped out of her skin when Zach suddenly stepped from behind a palmetto clump beside her. She hadn't heard or seen him; for one instant, in the blur of motion, she thought Jake had followed her.

"What are you doing?" she cried. "I thought you were in the boat."

He took her arm and hustled her along. "Once I was sure they couldn't see whether the boat was empty from the house, I shadowed you to be sure you were safe. You handled that well."

"Talk about catching more flies with honey. You sent me into a hornets' nest. And then spied on me! Was that some sort of test or what?"

"It was necessary. Julie, I don't want to upset you more, but I don't think Thad would have stayed out this long of his own doing. He's hot for Grant Towers's youngest girl, and unless he's decided to try to make her jealous—and with a fourteen-year-old, I doubt it—it doesn't make sense that he didn't come back in."

"That's what I've been trying to tell you!" she cried and pulled free of his hand on her arm. At least, he was being honest and sounded fully committed to the search now.

In the dappled shade, he whipped off his sunglasses and turned her to face him. For the first time, they looked into each other's eyes without barriers. His were as dark as mahogany, and fringed with lashes quite thick for a man's. It was the Zach of her girlish memories and daydreams, and yet one so real, so close.

"Where do we start to find the kids?" she asked as she pulled quickly away again and rushed for the dock with him right behind her. She climbed in, sat down and retrieved the binoculars from her seat as if nothing had happened between them, for, really, nothing had.

"First," he went on, not missing a beat as he started the motor, "we stop at your place to see if any of your girls noticed which direction Thad's Jet Ski was heading." He raised his voice to be heard over the roar. "Then we find Loreen at the Fish Fest to see if she noticed anything, because she's better than any recon team I ever knew at gathering intel."

"But I thought we would go search the mangrove keys out

there," she said with a sweeping gesture. "That's why we took this boat." Her voice caught as her emotions plummeted again.

"I've replanned the plan. There are hundreds of keys and waterways out there, and if we can narrow the parameters of our search, that's just plain smart. To cut panic, time loss and mistakes, before you plan a dive, you dive the plan."

"What do you mean, dive the plan?"

He shook his head. "It means, stay calm, plan ahead. I'm going to call the local Civil Air Patrol, because I've seen them search the coastline daily."

"For lost people?"

"Or those in disabled boats, stranded by running out of gas. It's located on Marco Island, but they do daily sundown flights over the entire area."

"Oh, thank God! That's perfect! Let's call them now."

"As soon as we have a better fix on where they might be. These are volunteer pilots, but they've helped find and save people. They fly low. I've met a few of the guys."

"But they don't go up until sundown?"

"I'll see if they'll send someone up earlier." He leaned forward and took her free wrist in his big hand. Only then did she realize she was shaking. Zach still seemed rock-steady, despite how the motor vibrated the entire boat. "Are you with me on this?" he asked. "If we can't pinpoint the search area, we'll look everywhere by air, first with the air patrol, then with more than volunteer help. And we'll contact the police."

"The police? After only a couple of hours, I didn't think local law officials would respond yet."

"They won't, but we can at least report the kids missing.

The trouble is, if the hurricane targets this area, the police or even the park rangers might not be able to respond, as they'll have to oversee the evacuation of thousands. And pilots are going to have to get their planes out of here. But one step at a time. Let's do what I said, and if we turn up with no leads, even with the air patrol, I can try to get Ken Leigh to take me over the entire area. The Air Patrol flies about five hundred to a thousand feet up, but Ken could take me lower in his helo."

Ken Leigh, she thought. The rich guy Loreen had mentioned who had bought Zach's childhood home for a hunting lodge in the Glades. "A helicopter, right?"

"Right."

"But can't we do that right now? We have to do something now!"

"We are. You rush into things, you make big mistakes," he said and released her wrist.

She was surprised he still held it. Her skin tingled where he'd grasped it so hard. His plan sounded logical. She prayed she could only stay strong through this, for Randi. And she had to stay close to Zach to get all the help he'd promised her.

It had been years since Zach had set foot in the old lodge. Julie had done wonders with it. The place seemed airy and bright, not oppressive as he'd remembered it—not that he'd been allowed inside. By the time he resigned his commission and returned from duty, Philip White, Julie's great-uncle, had been in a Naples convalescent center and the place was slowly growing tattered in addition to being tacky.

At first he'd thought it was crazy that she'd renovated it for teenagers who were screwed up enough to cut themselves, but she'd obviously made a go of it. He couldn't imagine young American women, with all their blessings deliberately injuring themselves, when the downtrodden and deprived girls he'd seen during active duty fought to keep from being raped or blown to bits.

Julie's friend Kaylin had quickly gathered the girls in the Florida room for them. He heard Kaylin tell Julie, "I just want you to know that Liz Lawson and Nate Tomzak are willing to help search. They stopped by a while ago to say goodbye to the girls. I guess they had no idea we'd be in at the Fish Fest later. Are we still going?"

"You may have to oversee them alone—if the weather doesn't kick up," Julie told her. She had just run upstairs to change into cropped pants and a T-shirt. "Oh, Jake Malvers said he'd go out looking , too," she added, "but Zach is going to try to narrow the area we have to search."

"Okay, listen up please, ladies," Zach said. "For some reason, Randi Minton and my son, Thad Brockman, didn't come back in from a Jet Ski ride today. They may have gotten lost, run out of gas, had an accident—we don't know. But we're asking you to recall whether you saw them heading any particular direction as the rest of you came back to the marina on your Jet Skis."

"We were turned away from them then," one girl put in.

"Didn't anybody give a backward glance?" he asked. "At Randi, with a guy she evidently didn't know? An older guy? When you ladies have been marooned here all together, let's call it the look-at-the-lifeguard-on-the-beach reaction."

Several girls smiled. A couple giggled nervously. Though he was pleased he'd broken the ice with them, Julie glared at him. Still, she stepped forward to stand shoulder-to-shoulder with him before her little brood.

"Please," Julie said, "can anyone recall anything to help? Cindy?"

"Honest, Julie, it was a total surprise to me when you mentioned onboard *The Manatee* that she'd gone out with him, I mean, out on the Jet Ski. Especially since they had no connection before or anything, not that I knew."

"I think," a quiet voice said, "they were turning toward the right. That's northwest."

Zach noted a pale girl, seated on the end of a long rattan couch, wedged in by four others who seemed to dominate her. At first he wasn't sure she was the one who had spoken, because she was looking at his feet and not his face. She reminded him of a really good informant in Iraq, a young woman whose face and body were obscured by a *chador* and whom no one would have suspected of having saved several lives.

"Bree, you weren't out in the harbor, though, right?" Julie was asking. "You and Jen were on the beach swimming."

"Yes, but I was watching the girls on the Jet Skis. You know, wishing I'd had the nerve. Then—" her voice became almost inaudible "—wishing I'd get to go out with a boy like Randi did. She's had a crush on him—Thad. She told me that a couple days ago."

For a moment, the room went dead silent. Zach heard only the sound of the surf. He wondered if Julie believed the girl. She looked not only upset but angry and she'd shifted away from him for some reason. He might never have had a how-to-read-body-language class in SEAL training, but he'd learned it the hard way on the teams, like so many lessons that had been pounded into him.

Always count your men. Leave no one! The command rattled through his brain from as far back as his early BUD/S training. He had to find Thad and Randi Minton, whom his son was responsible for. And this shy girl, still staring at his feet, had given him intel he had to trust. He'd failed to be accountable for two lives lost at sea. He wasn't here to save Becky, and he'd lost his buddy Garth. But he wouldn't fail again, not with two lives at risk, including his own son's.

"That's a big help," Zach told the girl as he stepped toward her and leaned down to touch her thin shoulder. "If anyone recalls anything else," he raised his voice, straightening, "anything that might help us narrow our search, tell Kaylin, and she'll call Julie on her cell phone. And Kaylin," he said, huddling with her while Julie, still looking shaken, came closer, "keep up on the weather reports. If that storm keeps coming, they'll open shelters inland. Could you get this many girls there?"

"Both Mike and I could drive the vans, though all but two are going home tomorrow," Kaylin said. "They're either flying or being picked up by parents. But if a bad storm comes, what about you and Julie out there?"

"We'll be okay here for a while," Zach said. "As for parents getting in, if there's a mass exodus—either a voluntary or mandatory evacuation—all the roads will be one-way going out from the beaches. Julie, you ready to go?"

"Yes. Girls, I'm depending on you to help Kaylin and to

stick close together if you do go in to the Fish Fest. I'm sorry, but you understand why I need to leave. You've been wonderful. Take care of each other now and, after you leave, *always* take care of yourselves. You're already stronger. You can do it."

Zach hustled her back out to his boat. "I'm just praying that there's been some mechanical malfunction on the Jet Ski," he said, his adrenaline pumping and his mind sprinting ahead. "Or, like I said, Thad ran out of gas. If there's a human element mixed into this somehow, that's a whole new bag."

"Exactly what do you mean by a human element?" she asked as they raced back toward the marina. "Like what? Like how?"

"I don't know yet," he called to her over the sound of the motor. "It's just that I've made a few enemies around here and you never know about someone else causing an accident, that's all."

"That's not all!" she threw back at him. "Like who?"

"Later."

"Not later! Not later about Thad's being expelled from school. Not later about someone who might want to hurt you! Tell me!"

"First, you tell me why you almost went to pieces back there when that girl said Randi had a crush on Thad."

"Because she was wrong. I would have known. Randi's my only child, and I'm close to her. That's what I do—counsel girls. The one who spoke up is one of the most beaten-down young women I've ever worked with, and she's made great strides. So I certainly wasn't going to correct or challenge her in front of the others."

"I guess that's three reasons then. I'll explain some things to you after we talk to Loreen. We're almost there."

* * *

Hearing someone who was very shy but very observant say that her daughter had a secret crush on Thad—a crush she didn't know about, one that reminded her too much of her own past silent longings for Thad's father—shook Julie to her core. That could not be right. Besides, standing before all the girls, she'd felt somehow exposed. It was as if in trying to know and help them, she'd failed to know or help her own daughter.

But for Randi's sake, she thrust all that aside as she hurried up the dock behind Zach. They headed to the Fish Fest, which was going full tilt in the park. This time, the music was an amplified recording of the "Macarena," with some listeners doing the motions. The rides with squealing kids made things worse. One called the Dizzy Dragon whirled by, and then came the blur of another called the Scrambler.

"Keep your eyes peeled for Loreen," Zach told her.

"Let's check around the Seaside Restaurant booth. She was raving about their great mai tais."

He nodded and veered left in the crowd around the Tilt-A-Whirl. The restaurants in this area were all what Julie's friends up north would call "dive chic," and they'd brought much of that tacky ambiance with them here: paper lanterns, what looked like Christmas tree lights edging a sign, a thatched roof. People seemed to rotate by, making her feel dizzy. The smell of fried seafood, coleslaw and hush puppies, baked beans and grits heaped on plates didn't help either. A crowd stood around, cheering for a fish filleting contest as six men bent over their work with sharp knives. People had really turned out for this, but no wonder, since everything in Gladesport was usually bring-or-make-your-own-entertainment.

Julie finally spotted some folks with mai tais, sans the usual umbrella around this rawboned place. Then she saw Loreen.

"There she is!" she said, pointing. "With Clint!"

The moment Loreen saw them coming, her face fell. "Oh, damn, you haven't found them!" she cried.

"We will," Zach said.

Clint nodded, frowning, and took a quick pull of his beer. His plate was heaped with fried frog legs. He smelled faintly of fish, and his skin and clothes glittered strangely in the sun. Julie realized he must have been in the fish cleaning competition Loreen had mentioned, for he was speckled with iridescent scales. It reminded her of the glitter Randi and her friends from the school used to wear in their hair.

"But we're wondering, Loreen," Zach went on, "if you noticed anything that would help our search."

"Well, like I told Julie, I saw them go. She was sitting up straight, so she didn't have to hang on to him, but then she put her hands on his shoulders. She had on a white T-shirt with some red sequined flowers on it and cutoffs, and he wore that old black swimsuit with the purple fish."

Julie bit her lip. Loreen knew what her daughter had been wearing, when she couldn't recall. But then, Loreen wasn't in charge of twelve young women. Loreen was bored out of her mind and had nothing to do all day but watch people and know their business.

"How about the Jet Ski they took out?" Zach asked. "One of the newer ones or not?"

"No, one of the originals. He was good about setting others up with the newer ones, so maybe they could have had engine trouble or something. No, wait—" Loreen cried and smacked her forehead with her free hand. "I don't think he filled that one up with gas. I mean, Grant Towers was in the store yakking my ear off and that always boils my blood, so I can't be sure, but that may be it—low gas."

Julie could have hugged her. "Then they just ran out of gas out there and are on some beach, waiting to be found!" she cried. As Zach nodded at that possibility, she was surprised to see tears in his eyes.

"I'll be glad to go out to help look," Clint said. He'd been sheepishly standing on one leg and then the other while his wife had done all the talking. Julie had overheard him arguing with Zach earlier. Surely, Zach didn't mean that Clint was someone who would want to hurt him, who was an enemy.

"We'd appreciate that," Zach told Clint. "We think they went toward the northwest, so we're going to concentrate on that direction—Cutshin, Halfway, Squatters—in case you want to look closer in. And I'll take extra gas in case it takes a while. Let's go, Julie."

They started away through the crowd. She felt better already.

"While I fill a portable gas tank, jump on my big boat and pull us some sandwiches and drinks out of the little fridge," he told her. "The cabin's not locked and my charter today came in too early to use the stuff."

"Oh, I couldn't eat, but I'll get you some."

"The point is," he called back to her, his voice harsh again, "we may be out a while or the kids may be thirsty or hungry when we find them."

"Right. Okay," she called as he sprinted toward the dock ahead of her.

At the edge of the water, she saw along the shoreline a small crowd and heard voices raised in some sort of altercation. A small group of retired snowbirds—at least they all had silver hair—had surrounded Grant Towers, it looked like. Yes, it was him with a cigarillo. Maybe he'd stepped away from the crowd for a smoke.

"You're turning us out of Winter Park," one old man was shouting, "and we'll never afford another place to live. We been there for years."

"But the land your mobile homes are on is only leased to you," Grant told them, sounding condescending, as if he were lecturing a group of kids. Even though Julie hurried down the dock, their voices carried to her over the water. "You signed an agreement not to own the land, but to lease it, people," he went on. "And now I'm buying that land from the owner, fair and square."

"Yeah," someone else shouted, "for what we hear is millions for new condos."

"Progress is progress," Grant insisted.

Just before she got to Zach and Clint's fishing boats, she noted Grant's shiny white yacht had docked down the first arm of the pier. She was tempted to go back and ask him to take it out to search for the kids, but it would probably be too big to fit in some of the narrow mangrove waterways. Besides, if Thad Brockman was after Grant's daughter, Grant might be angry with Thad or even be one of the enemies Zach had mentioned. She couldn't quite picture Grant being thrilled his girl was hanging out with a Gladesport local. No,

Grant reminded her too much of her own father in that respect, so she left him to his fate with the irate mobile home owners.

"There's nothing you can do." Grant's words still drifted to her over her quick breathing and wash of waves against the dock pilings. "So just take the time to look around and move. If this hurricane hits here, it would be the death of you to be in one of those old trailers anyway."

Julie's stomach knotted tighter at another mention of the hurricane. But everyone at the Fest was carrying on as if there was no danger, and surely, they'd all been through scares like this storm before.

She climbed aboard Zach's big boat. He must have left it in a hurry. A digital camera was just sitting on one of the fishing seats. She took it into the sheltered area of the cabin with her.

Tacked on the wall was a map of Mangrove Bay and the 10,000 Islands. It included water depths at various tide levels, underwater reefs and wrecks and handwritten notes about fishing sites. Wouldn't this be useful, even if Zach knew the area well? At least it would give her a way to follow where they were searching, and she could check off places they'd been.

She untacked it and rolled it up, then stuffed pop, bottled water and four large sandwiches into a plastic cooler she found on the floor. She set the cooler and map on the dock, then jumped off.

Zach was waiting with the motor already going. He took the cooler from her, then nodded when he recognized the map.

"Do you want me to call your friend Ken Leigh on my

cell phone?" she asked as they raced across the harbor. "Maybe he could search in his helicopter while Clint and Jake join us in the search? And Kaylin said Liz Lawson and Nate Tomzak will help too."

"Ken, Clint and Jake head the list of those who don't like me," he admitted. "But since two of them already said they'd help, maybe we're on a roll. Yeah, hand me your cell phone, and I'll call Ken myself to see if he's around. If we don't find the kids soon, maybe he'll take me up."

"Take *us* up," she insisted.

Their boat bounced hard against the waves hurling themselves toward the shore. The wind ripped her hair straight back, and the rhythmic forward thrust and pound, pound vibrated right through her. But Julie's heart was beating even harder as she tried to steady the binoculars before her eyes, searching desperately among the green, leafy puzzle pieces for her daughter.

5

The time is 5:45 p.m., southwest coasters, and it's been a beautiful day, but listen up. An official hurricane watch has just been posted for the western Florida coastline, from Key West clear up to the Panhandle. I repeat, this is a watch, which indicates only that the hurricane might hit here. A warning means it will probably hit here, but we're not to that stage yet. Predictions of hurricane behavior are still imprecise, but Dana, as she heads for Cuba, has just been elevated to a Category Two. That means winds of from 100 to 110 miles per hour, which could cause a possible storm surge of six to eight feet or even more, if it hits at high tide. Although evacuations are only voluntary at this point, boarding up and plans for getting out should be your top priority, especially for those of you on the barrier islands or along the shoreline.

Trying to keep her eyes on the girls, who were scattered here and there in pairs, Kaylin stood in the middle of the Gladesport Fish Fest as the entire thing seemed to deflate around them. Then she heard why. The PA announcement she thought was about another fish-eating contest blared even louder:

"News has just come from the National Hurricane Center in Miami that Hurricane Dana has become a Category Two and may impact our area. Voluntary evacuations are in effect, unless you are on the barrier island or along the shoreline, and then you'd best think in terms of its being mandatory."

The way people reacted, she thought, biting the inside of her lower lip, you would have thought an atom bomb had just been dropped out in the bay. She heard other shouted warnings, passed from person to person like bees buzzing: "Storm surge…hasn't hit here for years…not yet but soon…soon."

People swarmed past, making her feel almost dizzy. Then the crowds evaporated, leaving only the locals. An eerie silence descended as they worked to take things down. She stood for a moment, as if frozen in time and space. She couldn't help it if she was a girl from Michigan who didn't know one thing about hurricanes. Tornadoes maybe, but that meant getting in the northwest corner of your basement, and there were no basements in this entire sea-level area. Wishing for the hundredth time that Julie were here to help make decisions, she scanned the chaos for the girls who hadn't already come running.

"Did you hear that?" Cindy Markland cried as she suddenly materialized with two others in tow. "They're even giving away free food over there!" she added, pointing. "They closed all the rides and are starting to take some down. Oh, man, I wanted to go on Zero Gravity!"

The conch fritters dipped in key lime sauce Kaylin had

just put away suddenly sat like a lead weight in her stomach. Captain Mike had said he could board up the front windows of the lodge before he left with a van load of girls for the airport tomorrow, but he was expecting the roads to be clogged if an evacuation order came. And who knew that gridlock or flight cancellations wouldn't strand them here?

"Kaylin, are we going back to the lodge now?" Jordan De-Muro asked, wringing her hands so hard her fingers turned white. Jordan was one of the girls Kaylin regretted had not made more progress these last two weeks. Every little thing was a crisis that threatened to set her back, though this, Kaylin had to admit, could be a real disaster. "I overheard," the girl said, "they're going to use the local high school for a shelter. Should we go there in case the storm comes early?"

"The storm can't leap over Cuba," Kaylin assured her, then gnawed again at her inner lip. "I think it's almost a hundred miles away. We'll stick to the plan to spend our—your—last night at the resort. Julie will certainly be back this evening after they find Randi. But whatever happens, first thing in the morning, we'll get those of you who are flying out to the airport. If the storm does actually threaten those of us still here, we'll go to a shelter. If you want to take some of the free food or drinks—non-alcoholic drinks—back to the lodge, that's okay, but we'd better head for *The Manatee*. Cindy, please do a count to make sure everyone's here."

As she turned, she saw Nate but Liz was nowhere in sight for once. He seemed calm amidst the human tempest. Leaning against a palm tree, eating something, he was just watching her.

Her stomach flip-flopped and not from fear of the storm this time. She waved and forced a smile, though she'd finally bitten her lip so hard she tasted blood. "Nate!" she called as he hurried over, wolfing down the last of his fried fish sandwich. "I thought you and Liz were going to help look for Randi," she said, as he steered her a little away from the girls.

"You mean, she's not back yet? With this storm threatening?"

"Not that I know of. Zach Brockman took Julie out to search, but they have a good idea where to look now. I'm feeling so guilty! I'm the one who put her on that Jet Ski with him, and they've been searching for hours."

"I'm sorry. Hey, don't beat yourself up, okay? I'll tell Liz, and we'll go out looking."

"Toward the northwest."

"How'd they find that out if they're lost?"

"One of the girls saw them head out of the harbor."

"Listen, Kaylin, I know this is hardly the time, but I was hoping we'd be able to spend some more private time together. But this monster storm—"

"You mean Liz's vengeful goddess of nature, looking for sacrifices?"

"Yeah. It means Liz and I are going to have to batten down all the buildings in the compound, but I want to be sure you and your charges are all right first."

"Liz keeps you pretty busy, even when a storm's not coming."

"You should talk. Julie can be just as demanding."

"She is not! Our work is deeply important to me, as well as her, and it takes a lot of dedication."

"All right, all right. Ditto for my job. Just keep your cell phone on so I can check out how you're doing. And if they don't find those kids, keep me apprised of that, too, because Liz meant it when she said we'd search."

"Thanks for worrying about them and me—for caring."

"More than you know," he said and dropped a quick kiss on her cheek. "I'd do better than that," he murmured, his lips brushing the lobe of her ear, "but your little chicks are all eyes." He lifted a quick hand to their watchful audience and headed at a jog toward the marina.

The girls surrounded her again. "Kaylin, if we can cope with a hurricane coming, I guess we can cope with anything without cutting," Ginger Myers said, rubbing her hands up and down her arms as if to warm them. Despite how hot and humid it was, Kaylin saw that Ginger's skin was all goose-flesh over her web of old scars. All Kaylin needed was for one of these girls to revert to self-injury.

"Let's get back," she said, herding them toward the marina. "Since the Fest is over and this is our last night together, let's build a bonfire on the beach and help Captain Mike board up the windows. Remember, you can do anything you set your mind to. No self-injuring, because you all—*we* all—can cope with anything."

The airplane buzzed over them, dipping its wings, first one, then the other, which read C.A.P. Rescue underneath. It was the Civil Air Patrol, which Zach had called to ask for a search. Julie stood in the boat and waved, until Zach pulled her back down.

"You'll tip the boat!"

"But can that salute mean they've found Randi and Thad?"

"They salute Clint and me like that all the time. They probably just wanted me to know they're out here for us. I told them we wouldn't be in my big boat."

"They're a beautiful sight," she said, feeling both hopeful and deflated as the plane continued southward, flying low, looking, looking. She said a silent prayer they'd find the kids and, with a huge sigh, began to scan the earthbound waterways again.

They'd heard on the little transistor radio Zach had brought that the hurricane might hit their area and that property needed to be protected before evacuation, though that was voluntary so far. They were on the extra tank of gas that he'd brought along. Each turn down twisting paths of water, each narrow beach, every empty ruined house or derelict fishing camp they passed began to look the same to Julie— a blue-green horror house of mirrors. In over four hours, they'd seen absolutely no sign of the lost Jet Ski or their kids.

But at least the Civil Air Patrol search and the three other requests for help they'd made represented progress. Ken Leigh had promised Zach he'd take them up in his helicopter to search tomorrow morning, despite the fact he'd already flown it to Miami to protect it, just as the Civil Air Patrol planes must be evacuated soon. Zach said Ken was flying it back across the Glades tonight. Secondly, they had left a message for the county sheriff, though he and his staff were busy checking out storm centers and policing evacuation routes. And they had phoned the Everglades National Park ranger station to ask them to be on the lookout.

But Julie still feared she was going to cry. The motor droned on as they turned into the next maze of leafy mangrove allies.

"A dead end," Zach said, looking ahead at the thick overgrowth. "I'm pretty sure this used to be open."

He backed them out and went another way. She'd given up trying to trace their path on his big marine map and had stuffed it in her purse to keep it dry. She took another swig of bottled water and said, "Please tell me about Thad."

"About his getting expelled?"

"That, and just what he's like. It must have been so hard for him to lose his mother young."

"It was. Did Randi lose her dad young?"

"He left us—me—for another woman when she was four. He doesn't have much to do with her, a yearly birthday and Christmas gift. He has three other kids, so you can read between the lines on that. She'd love a father, but I've been so busy, I haven't found her one."

He nodded. She felt he understood, though she did note how adept he was at answering her questions with questions. "The thing with the toad at school," he said, then cleared his throat. "After what I'd done with the shark at the resort when I was a kid, I could hardly come down hard on him, for once."

"You're usually a big disciplinarian?"

"Yeah. Tough love in spades—military control. I guess I've been trying to forge us into a team, but not realizing I didn't have a recruit who'd signed up for that. I was so bitter at first about Becky's death. Like all of us who grew up around here, she was a good swimmer…."

His voice trailed off. Julie wondered if he feared his wife might have met with foul play or even committed suicide, but she certainly wasn't going to get into any of that right now. She could see only his stoic profile as he scanned the area while he talked.

"Also, it hit me hard to have to leave the teams—the SEALs—and I came down way too hard on Thad, especially when he turned into a maverick teen. I realized too late, I'd alienated him. I've been trying to build bridges lately."

"The cleaning woman, Rosa, said you used to make him do push-ups. For punishment?"

"Oh, yeah. 'Feet! Drop! Give me twenty! Push 'em out! Suck it up!'" he roared so loud she nearly jumped out of the boat. "I guess," he went on, seemingly oblivious to her, though he kept scanning the area, "Thad ended up educating me more than I did him. Even when I thought I had him under my thumb, he found ways to rebel. He hated my guts at times. No way he'd ever want to follow in my footsteps, he said, becoming a robot, taking orders from others, training to be violent—risking his life."

His voice caught again on that. Hadn't Thad seen the caring man through the tough-guy exterior, Julie wondered, or was this emotion from Zach just the result of Thad's disappearance?

"I told him," Zach went on, "it wasn't like that, being in the service. I told him it *was* a service to others and the country. For a while, I thought, when he gets out of high school—they let him back in," he added, looking at Julie, then away again, "I'd return to the SEALs, but I've made a life with him here in a temporary truce."

"So Thad took a toad to school and let it loose?" she asked after a moment's silence. "That sounds like pure kids' stuff. Are they so super strict at school down here, to expel him for that?"

He pressed his lips together in a grim smile. "This toad was a rare species, a cane toad from South America with poisonous glands which secrete a powerful hallucinogen. They were imported years ago to try to control sugar cane pests. If you lick the stuff, you can get high. South Americans claim it's an aphrodisiac, which Thad and his buds didn't know, but the sheriff charged him with possession of the illegal drug bufotenine."

"The same sheriff you called for help to find Thad?"

He nodded. The thought that the man might consider Thad a screw-up who'd just rebelled again went unsaid between them.

"But where did he get a toad from South America?" she asked, desperate to change the subject, to keep talking.

"He and another kid 'borrowed' it from Liz Lawson's show-and-tell display at the high school because they thought it was 'a neat-looking dude' that wanted out of its cage. Fortunately, Liz didn't press charges for petty theft. I had to get a lawyer, but it was Thad's first offense, so he was only suspended for a semester, and the sheriff made him do community service, picking up litter from boating ramps and picnic areas."

Zach shook his head. "You should have seen me, trying to tutor him and make him keep up with his schoolwork to get back in. I wish you would have been here to work with him then. You know, the catching more with honey than vinegar approach again."

He steered them around another tight turn of mangrove roots, and they both ducked the arch of overhanging branches. She could understand, at least, how Rosa had thought the boy had been expelled for something to do with drugs and sex. Small talk was the local pastime here, and when things got passed on, they were always exaggerated or twisted.

That made her wonder what people were saying about Randi and Thad's disappearance together. Or maybe they were all just too busy protecting their property and getting out of the area right now. Besides, Randi could not have been mooning over a boy she'd barely spoken to. That would be too much like the curse of the mother visited upon the daughter. But had it been mere chance that Kaylin put her on the Jet Ski with Thad—or could her best friend have known something too?

When her cell phone sounded, Julie jumped so hard her head hit a branch. She unsnagged her hat from the leaves and punched on with, "Julia Minton here," just as she had during those years of teaching and counseling.

"It's Nate Tomzak, Julie. I saw Kaylin and the girls at the Fish Fest. You need help with the search? Liz and I have to board up the WorldWise compound and pack our vans, but Liz could come out looking while I pound boards."

"I'm not sure how to tell you to search. The best thing might be to find out where Jake Malvers has been looking and go on from there."

"Jake wouldn't give us the time of day. He might even take a potshot at us. Liz is just waiting for him to try, so she can settle him down with a court order. At the least, he'd accuse us of palm-tree hugging. Liz had better just go look on her own."

"We've pretty much exhausted this northwest sector. We thought they could reach this area on a partial tank of gas from where they were last seen, but no luck. We're doing an air search in the morning."

"Civil Air Patrol? Planes aren't going to be able to stay in this area long."

"I know. The Air Patrol's looking now. I meant Ken Leigh. Zach called him."

"Tell Zach not to sit too close to the chopper door if he goes up with him. Leigh used to be the biggest exporter of shark fins on the east coast—you know, for the Chinese delicacy shark fin soup, not to mention the more altruistic medical uses for shark cartilage that are worth big bucks. The guy's British but lived in Hong Kong for years, before the Chinese took it back from the Brits."

"I didn't know that. I don't know him."

"As Zach's no doubt told you, he's Zach 'The Sharkman' around here because he's championed endangered shark species. He's taken a lot of flak for it—vandalism, threats, the whole nine yards—from his buddies who fish the area. And from, of course, Ken Leigh. You're probably searching through the breeding nurseries right now, and 'tis the season."

She gasped and gripped the cell phone so hard her fingers cramped. "*This* is a shark breeding area?" she asked, as Zach's head snapped around.

"Who is that?" he asked, but she ignored him.

"Absolutely," Nate said, "especially if you're searching sheltered byways off the main bay."

"I see," she said, starting to shake. "Thanks for the information and for anything else you can do."

"Liz Lawson?" Zach asked as she punched off and threw

her phone in her macrame bag. He looked guilty and sounded hesitant.

"Nate Tomzak, though now I know what Leon Malvers meant when he said you were in bed with Liz Lawson—on protecting sharks."

He frowned. "Yeah, we've worked together, but I'm really with the University of Miami on the whole thing, so—"

"Zach, you didn't tell me this is a shark breeding area out here? Is it? *Is it?*" she shouted, with a sweep of her hand that scratched her wrist on a passing branch.

He cut the motor so they nosed into a cluster of mangroves; he reached for her shoulders with both hands. She tried to hit his arms away, but he didn't budge.

"I didn't want you to worry," he said.

"Are you crazy as well as deceitful? I'm already worrying! If the Jet Ski turned over, and they fell in around here—"

"No, it's not like that, and the way you're reacting is exactly why I didn't tell you. For someone who spent time here as a kid, and lived here all this summer, you sure as hell didn't observe much, did you?"

At that, she lost it. Slapping at him, she tried to push him away. He shifted closer to seize her wrists in hard hands. She was amazed at his strength and was furious with him, but she was just as angry at herself. She hadn't known Leon's daughter was Zach's long-lost Becky, she hadn't recalled what Randi wore, she hadn't known that Randi might have had a crush on a boy.... And this man, who was supposed to be helping, had held back all sorts of things from her because he evidently thought she couldn't handle it. He thought she couldn't cope, when she'd cajoled and urged and lectured her girls to learn to handle their hurts and losses....

She went limp and blinked back tears that had threatened for hours. Still holding her wrists, Zach tried to tug her to him, but when the boat rocked, he shoved her over on her seat and shifted to sit beside her, holding her tightly to his side.

"Listen to me, Julie. I've studied these sharks for years. Forget about the *Jaws* stuff. They don't want to be bothered and they don't make a practice of just snarfing up people. When they bite a human being, they have either mistaken them for a fish or someone's invaded their area."

She could barely breathe. "Well, what do you call what we're doing—what Thad did on that Jet Ski? And what about if some kid falls in and is thrashing around?" She couldn't get that picture out of her brain, of Thad taking a turn too fast, spilling Randi off. She wished Zach hadn't mentioned the movie *Jaws*. That first scene with the girl in the water, her legs moving, moving. The camera had looked up at her from the shark's viewpoint beneath and then—

"Don't lie to me," she choked out, "and don't soft-pedal things."

"These are sharks here to mate and nurse. This late in the season, a lot of them are little pups," he told her, his mouth so close to her temple that his breath warmed her ear. "Like dolphins, they steer clear of Jet Skis and motors, not like the big, lumbering manatees that get hit by boats."

Instead of holding herself stiffly away, she sagged against him. "I'm just so scared," she whispered, his shoulder almost muffling her words. "I'm just *so* scared."

"I am too, but we'll find them. Maybe Thad made a raft for them. He could maneuver that, unlike a dead-in-the-water Jet Ski. Maybe he floated them out into the waterway where boats coming in or out from the gulf would see them, but then the tide took them out a ways. I've been agonizing over possibilities, but I'm not worried that any of the sharks could have hurt them. You've got to trust me at least on that."

She was surprised that his admission that he was scared, too, made her feel better. She liked him more for that. She was coming to depend on him—she had to trust him. And perhaps, he had just been trying to protect her, as she was sure his son would protect Randi.

"Okay," she said. "But don't hold back anything else you think I shouldn't know. Anything!"

"We're a team on this. I've been trained to work in teams that leave no one behind when they go out on a rescue."

He moved swiftly back to his seat. Wiping under her eyes with her fingers, she added, "We'll find them. We have to find them before this terrible storm comes, so they'll be all right. I'm sure they'll be all right."

Zach felt defeated and increasingly desperate as darkness fell. The Civil Air Patrol search had spotted no sign of Thad and Randi or an abandoned Jet Ski in the waters of the Everglades National Park, Mangrove Bay, or just off the gulf coast shoreline. They would make another search at first light, but then were going to have to fly their small aircraft inland to protect it.

Zach took Julie back to the resort. After helping Mike board up their ground-floor bay-view windows, he carried her heavy lawn furniture inside, then went to the marina to batten down *The Hooyah!*

He was surprised to see Clint's big boat was not here. Had he gone out looking for the kids, too, and just wasn't back yet, or had he moved her to a safer berth? Zach stowed things inside his boat and triple-tethered it in varying lengths of rope so that, if some broke, the others might hold, even in a storm surge. Still, he knew that the boat he'd poured money, time and love into could be gone in a few minutes if the hurricane hit. Ordinarily, he might have taken Thad and tried to outrun the storm.

At home, Zach found a note from his renters that they'd already fled inland. He saw they'd rolled down the hurricane shutters he'd spent a mint on. He paced his small bungalow, then turned on some lights to check his extra flashlights; power would be one of the first losses in a big storm. It was nearly midnight when he hauled out plywood he'd had stored for who knew how many years and, in lantern light, boarded up the window of the bungalow. He wondered if he should have reared Thad in the bigger house, but he'd wanted to save money for—he'd hoped—the boy's college education. If a storm surge rose over three feet, which it easily could, the lower floors of both buildings would be inundated anyway.

His back ached from helping board up at Osprey Lodge. Working there like a laborer had brought back some bad memories. His shoulder hurt from carting furniture in his rental house up to the second floor, but his heart hurt worse.

Zach made himself a peanut butter and jelly sandwich and forced himself to eat; it tasted like mud. Even eating MREs before a recon or an infil tasted better than this. He opened a beer and stood in the doorway of Thad's room.

On his unmade bed, next to his pillow, was the old, mostly deflated red-and-white beach ball Thad had insisted on keeping because his mother had blown it up for him the day she died.

When he was seven or eight, he had started screaming when Zach tried to take out the valve to blow it up, "Dad, no! Don't! Mom's breath is still in there, and I have to keep it. Grandpa Leon said when she drowned, the water took her breath, so I have to keep that in there!"

Tears stung Zach's eyes. He carried the ball out with his file of important papers, his laptop, and a family photo album, and locked them in the cab of his truck. Even if wind or water took the house, Thad's memento of his mother would have a better chance of survival when he moved the vehicle farther inland.

He returned to his son's room to survey the rest of the messy area. It usually annoyed him for its chaos but now he felt a strange comfort as well as sharp sorrow. His own rack was neatly made and his gear squared away, but he'd quit coming down so hard on his son for disorder like this. He'd preached long enough.

After all, the kid had half Malvers genes in him too. When they were young, Zach—and Clint—had always dreamed of serving their country in the military and getting out of Gladesport. In showing no interest at all in what Zach loved, Thad had hurt him deeply, however much the boy had every right to live his own life.

Zach moved a pile of clothes from the desk chair and sat in it himself. The shelves were lined with CDs and computer games Thad spent his money on—the discretionary one-third of his income Zach didn't make him bank. They'd had arguments about the choices of some of these purchases. Zach hadn't let him buy a couple of video games with too much violence—"But, Dad, you've made your living on violence! You've even killed guys, even if it was to protect others or yourself, haven't you?"

So they'd compromised on a horror series, where the hero was trapped in his apartment and not able to communicate with the outside world. But for his link to Julie Minton in this living nightmare, Zach felt alienated from everyone and everything right now, too.

Here was one with zombies and monsters they'd played together once. Why did Thad revel in this fantasy stuff when the real world awaited him?

Zach pulled out a game he didn't recall vetting. Squinting at it in the dim light, he saw there was another one hidden behind it. And another one behind the next visible one.

"What the hell?" he muttered as he dug out the two hidden ones.

To his utter amazement, the first one was titled, *Full Armor Warrior.* The package said it was based on training for the U.S. Marines and emphasized strategy and graphics. The other one was *Duty and Honor,* described here as a best-selling video game where players step into the boots of a SEAL team in the Middle East.

The rest of the print blurred. Zach sniffed back the tears as he turned the computer on and inserted the SEAL team CD. The screen lit up with maps, strategies, and battle plans of Desert Storm. He startled when a man's deep voice intoned, "You are about to enter a life of hardship and sacrifice. Welcome to the world of the few, the proud, the elite SEAL teams where each warrior must learn to be hard from the inside out."

Zach put his head in his hands and sobbed.

Julie couldn't sleep, not that she'd expected she would. Besides her terror over Randi, she was distraught from having to phone each of the girls' parents to tell them not to worry if they heard a hurricane was targeting this area.

Not to worry—she felt she was lying to each of them, considering the panic she was in, which she mentioned to none of the worried parents. As she assured them that the girls would make their planes and that the airport was supposed to be open at least through noon Sunday, she wished desperately she could get her own daughter back that easily. More than once she'd been tempted to shout into the phone, "You don't even know what worry is! Concerned and afraid? You have no idea what you're talking about!"

As for the girls who had no reservations on the now jam-packed flights heading out of southwest Florida, Julie had assured those parents that their girls would ride out any dangers at an approved storm shelter with at least one of the counselors with them at all times. The parents who were driving down to get their girls were advised not to try to buck the traffic pouring out of the area but to drive to the Jacksonville Airport in northeast Florida so that their daughters could be placed on planes landing there after the storm danger passed and the airlines began to fly again. That left four girls remaining who would have to be safeguarded during the storm, when Julie couldn't even protect her own daughter.

She couldn't bear to go into Randi's room, where she'd thought she might feel more comforted at first. Instead, in the silent lodge, once the girls had gone to bed, she tied a terry-cloth robe around her nightgown and, holding onto the banister rail, went downstairs into the darkness.

The first floor was pitch-black from being boarded up in front. She wished she hadn't run out of money before she bought roll-down hurricane shutters, but for now, the old boards would have to do. Unlike their living area upstairs, this room seemed to close in on her. She hesitated partway down. It was like a wooden coffin, all nailed shut; she felt even more cut off from Randi, whom she was certain was out there in the bay somewhere, waiting to be found. They just hadn't searched the right place yet, that was all.

But at first light, in a helicopter, they would spot them and be spotted in return. Blinking back tears, she pictured Randi and Thad screaming with joy and waving up to them as they hovered overhead.

She hurried the rest of the way down the stairs, not turning on a light despite the fact she didn't want to bump into the big wooden lawn chairs and heavy tables they'd moved inside. She couldn't stand to see how the usually spacious, open room looked so crowded and closed-in. By feel, she went to the second drawer of the breakfast bar at the bottom of the stairs and groped for the flashlight she knew would be there. Following the narrow, wavering beam through the crooked maze of piled furniture, she went into the north wing toward Kaylin's bedroom. She knocked as quietly as she could on the door, then a bit louder.

A light came on inside her friend's room. Looking bleary-eyed, Kaylin opened the door a crack.

"Oh, Julie. I was expecting a crisis with one of the girls. I'm terrified all this will make them lose control. Is everything okay? The hurricane isn't com—"

"I just need to talk to you about something. I'm sorry to wake you, but it can't wait. Mike's taking me over in *The Manatee* before dawn to meet Zach and drive with him to the air strip."

"Oh, sure. Come on in."

Kaylin rubbed her eyes. She wore a wrinkled sleeping shirt, and the sheets on her bed looked churned to waves. Julie perched on the edge of the single upholstered chair and Kaylin sat on her bed, with her back against the headboard. She had her window open, overlooking the bay. Palmetto fronds thrashed fitfully against the screen in the wind, but the fresh air helped clear Julie's head.

"You heard what Bree said about Randi having a crush on Thad Brockman," Julie began, gripping the flashlight. "Did you have any hint of that? And maybe it's why you hustled her aboard his Jet Ski?"

Kaylin sighed, pulled her pillow onto her lap and punched it once, hard. "Yeah, she mentioned it, just that she thought he was really rad or bad or however she put it."

"When?"

"I don't know." Another sigh. "I guess she told me when the first group was here. She'd seen him and chatted with him when she went on errands to the marina when you two were getting this place fixed up."

"She told you six weeks ago? Why didn't you tell me?"

"She wasn't one of the guests, Julie," Kaylin said, her voice suddenly stern. "It wasn't like we were consulting on her. She was your daughter, so I figured if she wanted to tell you, she'd tell. We see and hear enough from these girls to know teens keep secrets from parents, for heaven's sake. I did as a kid, you probably did, too."

"Did she ask you not to tell me? Here I find out she's told you six weeks ago, told Bree a few days ago. Did she say I shouldn't know? I mean, she wasn't actually seeing him."

"You know how desperately she's been missing her friends," Kaylin said in a counseling-type voice that made Julie madder by the minute, as if she were one of the mothers they worked with, one who had subtly harmed her daughter without even knowing it.

"You know she's grieving that she's not going back to school up north," Kaylin went on, looking down at her pillow as if she were reading from a case file. "She's nervous as heck about starting school down here, so maybe she saw Thad as sort of a life preserver for when school starts— you know what I mean. I think they just shared a little small talk, and her imagination—her heart took her the rest of the way."

She looked up at Julie. "And, yes, she asked me not to tell you. I thought it was enough of an escape valve for her that she was unloading all her worries on her friends at home via cell phone and e-mail and that blog site where she has a journal, you know, like an e-diary for teens, whatever its name is—Xanga, I think."

Julie felt she'd been punched in the stomach. In the heart.

No, she didn't know any of that. Randi had told her it would be a real adventure to go to school down here. She knew nothing about a blog diary Kaylin was referring to. Her daughter was missing and maybe she didn't know one damn thing about what she wanted and what she was like.

"You don't think…" Julie said in a near whisper. "Let's say Thad was running away from his father for being too strict, and Randi asked to go with him?"

"You mean, like they staged a disappearance?" Kaylin cried, gaping at her. "No way."

"But was she…could she have been that unhappy or desperate here, and I didn't know?" Julie asked aloud, as tears started to course down her cheeks. "If—if she was unhappy or ran away, without you and Bree, I'd never even begin to know why…." She slumped back in the chair and pulled her knees up and circled them with her arms. Kaylin vaulted off the bed and knelt next to the chair to try to hug her, but Julie didn't budge. What Zach had implied about her today—that she wasn't aware of things outside herself—was all too true. Not only things about this area or other people, but about her own flesh and blood, the person who, she thought, was closest to her in the entire world.

Whether the hurricane came here or not, she already felt blown to bits by the storm inside, the one of fear, regret and grief.

When Julie went back upstairs, she still didn't go to bed. Without turning on the lights in the combination family room and office she and Randi shared, she turned on the desktop computer by feel and watched its screen light an eerie blue, then turn to the swimming fish screensaver. She got online, then did a search for the Xanga site that Kaylin had mentioned.

She was astounded at the size and complexity of the Web site. She'd considered herself a counselor of young women, but had not known about this fad. Here teens, especially young women, evidently poured out their hearts and, considering some of the rules against personal flame attacks, maybe poured out their hormones too. Weren't diaries supposed to be private and precious?

She finally found Randi's—"Randi's Ramblings." More than once, tears blurred Julie's eyes as she read through her daughter's public agonizing, dating over the last three months they'd been in Florida.

…So what good is gorgeous scenery if I can't see my friends anymore?…I'd make a scene, but I do love my mom, 'cause really, she's all I have now that I lost all of you…

If only I had a friend my age here, someone strong to really hold onto, a friend, a guy or girl. I'm telling you, if this school turns out to be hicktown high, I'll be hitchhiking north, ma darlin's…

That scared Julie even more. Surely, Randi didn't mean it, that she'd hitchhike north. Could she have run away? No, it said only if she didn't like the school and she hadn't started there yet, *please, dear Lord, don't let her have run away.*

And yet, if she did, at least she wasn't at the bottom of the Gulf of Mexico or attacked by a shark, or…

Julie shook her head and sniffed hard to get control of herself. After all, here was proof her daughter loved her, though the reason might be that she was all Randi had.

Trembling, she read an earlier entry, a poem called *Someone to Love:*

> I've been left before, been ignored.
> By the first man I ever loved, even if he was my dad.
> Sad if broken memories are the best of him I had.
> Now, looking for a different kind of man,
> One who listens, includes me in his plans,
> Asks me about my dreams, about my day,
> And one who'll just plain stay.

The mouse shook so hard in her hand that the cursor on the screen leaped and jerked before Julie left the site and turned the power off. Her head in her arms on the desk, she burst into such hard sobs she could barely breathe.

6

Good Sunday morning, gulf coasters, though it doesn't look like it's going to be a good day. At 7:45 a.m. our time, as Hurricane Dana bears down on Cuba, I hope many of you are on the roads heading away from the beaches and shorelines, just in case. Even if the mountains in western Cuba slow Dana down a bit, she could still hit there at almost a Category Three. She's moving at 19 miles per hour with sustained winds of 120 with gusts up to 140. Those of you who were considering sitting this one out at home may soon be ordered to leave in a mandatory evacuation. If you have small aircraft, fly them into the middle of the state. Watercraft can be secured on-site or moved north to Naples or Ft. Myers, where you may find more protection than in our flat mangrove keys and barrier islands. And be sure to keep it tuned right here all day.

"You haven't slept," Zach observed as Julie met him at his car to head for the nearby landing strip. He squeezed her shoulder and opened the passenger door of his truck for her.

"And you have?" she countered. She knew she looked

horrible and felt worse, but the dark circles under Zach's eyes and his black beard stubble testified to a terrible time, too. "Were you packing this truck all night? A beach ball?"

She got in, lifting her feet over the things he had piled on the passenger side floor. The narrow back seat was also full of stuff, including the partly deflated ball.

"It's special to Thad," he said only, jamming his key in the ignition and driving them quickly out of his twisting driveway onto Gladesport's main paved, two-lane road. Twice he had to drive on the berm because cars were using both lanes, heading for the highway out.

Julie began to silently berate herself again. She should have gone through Randi's room, picking out some things she'd want saved if the storm hit. But after she'd read Randi's online diary and lost control, she had still checked on the girls and found four of them scared and awake. Comforting other people's daughters took time.

Panicked, as the night stretched on, Julie had tried to make rash deals with God. If Randi turned up safe, she'd take her back to her friends in Michigan. Surely, she could help self-injury-prone girls there. She'd become a stay-at-home mom, if she could just find a livelihood that would allow it. Anything, dear Lord, anything, if Randi could only come home.

Julie just hadn't realized her child was so distraught about leaving old friends and having to make new ones. At least, Randi hadn't been told that she should stay away from the local kids—oh, no, she not only hadn't stayed away but had disappeared with one. Worse, that was exactly Julie's girlhood dream, to ride off into the sunset with Zach years ago. Now, here they were in this nightmare.

Too late Julie realized, as if she were counseling herself, that her seething inner stew of panic, anger and guilt had exhausted her in a way the lack of sleep never could. And she desperately needed to share all that with someone else.

"God help me," she blurted to Zach, "I'm fighting feeling angry with her at times. I'm so screwed-up inside."

"Me, too. Hang on."

"I'm trying."

"Yeah, that way, too, but I mean I'm going to cut through this field to get us out of this traffic."

They bumped over a sawgrass-filled field, then parked near the small single hangar at the airstrip. They heard and saw the helicopter approaching. Black with a bold, white stripe, its doors were off so the pilot seemed to sit in the open air. As it descended, Julie saw stenciled on the side in gold the word *VICTOR* with a smaller *ia* after that, so the entire word read *Victoria*.

"That's his wife's name, right?" she asked, recalling the phone message the woman had left on Zach's answering machine.

"Right. She's English, too, a beautiful woman."

"Really?" she asked, turning toward him.

"One who knows it and uses it," he added, frowning, "and that's not a compliment."

"I see."

"I doubt if you do. Like they used to say, 'Beauty is as beauty does.' She seldom comes slumming in Gladesport. The art galleries and ritzy shops of Marco or Naples—or Miami, where they have another home—that's her usual hunting ground."

Julie didn't mention she knew Zach had taken Victoria Leigh deep-sea fishing or that she'd said she was anxious for another "deep-sea lesson." At least he seemed not to like her, as if that mattered. When Julie made a move to open her door, Zach grabbed her arm and ordered, "Stay put until the rotors stop. The downdraft always kicks up dust and debris."

In a small tornado of noise, the helicopter landed on the air strip near the truck. Julie had never flown in a chopper, but she would have gone up in a cyclone to look for Randi.

"Good, he's got the pontoons on over the skids," Zach said. "If we spot the kids in an open enough area, we can put down."

Julie gripped her hands and pressed them to her quivering lips. This had to work. It just had to.

When the rotor blades stopped, they got out. A short, wiry man stepped down as they went to meet him on the edge of the tarmac, which was completely empty of the usual small planes tethered here.

"Julie Minton, Ken Leigh," Zach said, and she shook a strong hand. Ken removed his baseball cap to reveal thinning auburn hair above a long face and pointed chin. Dark circles hung like half moons under his gray eyes. And this man had a beautiful wife? she thought. But then, he must be very rich. Perhaps Victoria was a trophy wife, but one who refused to just collect dust on a shelf.

"My pleasure, though not under these circumstances," Ken told her. "But if they're out there, we'll spot them straightaway."

"How's Victoria doing with having to leave your new beach house?" Zach asked.

"As we used to say about Queen Victoria, she was not amused," he said with a small shake of his head. "Our hunt lodge on your old property—which she detests for its primitive, rustic nature, though I built her a beautiful bedroom in it—may make it through, but I don't hold out much hope for the beach house if this Dana monster ravages the area. Victoria's closing up the house, then she'll lock up the lodge before she drives to Miami to meet me there. I said I'd pick her up there and fly her over, but she wanted to be sure her new sports car was out of the storm's reach."

He spoke in less of a British accent than his wife had in her phone message to Zach. Though Ken looked like some sort of absent-minded philosophy professor in his ill-matched plaid slacks and pinstriped shirt with the sleeves rolled up, Julie thought he exuded confidence and caring.

"I really appreciate your coming back clear across the state for this when you're trying to secure your properties," Zach told him. "I insist on paying for the gas and your time."

"Nothing you could give me, old chap—except letting up on the shark trade—is necess'ry, but let's not get into that. Onboard, you two. Zach, you'd best sit in front with me. Since I have the doors off, stow anything loose and get those seat belts on."

Julie recalled that Nate had said Ken might want to push Zach out, but that, of course, was just Nate's strange sense of humor. At least she was relieved to see that Zach and Ken seemed to share a mutual if begrudging respect.

She clambered into the narrow backseat. The chopper carried four, but if they did find Randi and Thad, they could certainly squeeze them in. Zach made certain her seat belt was on right while Ken scanned his rows of round dials. He put his feet on pedals and his hands on two sticklike controls. With the rumble of the rotors overhead that grew louder, they were swiftly airborne.

"This is the same kind of chopper often used for law enforcement!" Ken shouted, evidently thinking that would make them feel better about their mission. "Behind Julie, I've stowed life vests, a raft and two pairs of high-powered, anti-vibration binoculars. I'd wager you're used to those from the old days, eh, Zach? Julie, they're in a khaki duffel bag right behind you, so pass one pair up to Zach and use the others yourself, right?"

"Oh, sure. Good!" she cried and squirmed sideways in her seat to dig them out. Above the duffel bag, strapped to the back wall, she saw a strange device, half bow and half rifle, with a big scope attached to it. The bow and rifle handle were in gray camouflage. Did he hunt with a crossbow in his camp in the Glades? Surely, not from this helicopter. With a shudder, she ignored the thing and dug out the binocs.

When she leaned forward to hand Zach's pair to him, she gasped and not just because of the laminated photo of a stunning blond woman she saw mounted above the instrument panel. It looked as if both men were perched on nothing but air. The doors open to rushing, vast, cloudy sky, and the clear bubble in which they rode made it look as if the men were flying on their own.

"You okay?" Zach asked, turning to her and yelling over the blade slap. "You don't get airsick, do you? You look a little green around the gills."

"I'm all right. Since you can see everything out to the right, I'll look out Ken's side."

She threw herself back in her seat and rechecked her seat belt. Everything looked different from the air. The wind blew harder than it did yesterday, and the water moved under them, even cresting to whitecaps. The bay looked deserted; she saw none of the usual fishing boats or pleasure craft. No kite boarders, parasailers or windsurfers, no Jet Skis, kayaks or canoes. Nothing.

The mangrove islands they'd searched yesterday rotated under them as they swept along one after the other, turned, hovered, then moved on. At first Julie couldn't tell how high they were because depth perception seemed strange aloft. But soon she learned to look for dark objects or shadows thrown by the early morning sun. The downwash of the chopper helped too as it pushed waves and spume out from under them in different sized circles, depending on their hover height.

The men talked about currents and tides; she couldn't hear everything they said at times. She kept her gaze riveted on the waterways and islands beneath them.

"Julie, we're going to go over the other side of the bay where we didn't look, though maybe Jake did!" Zach shouted, as the helicopter tilted, then flew toward the south.

It made her nervous that the stick in Ken's right hand, the one between the two front seats, vibrated, shaking even harder than she was. She could tell they were getting more turbulence up here. Was this even safe?

"The helicopter's the only vehicle that has saved more lives than it's taken, love," Ken turned to say directly to her, as if he knew she needed comforting, but his words didn't help. Where were Randi and Thad? It was as if some crazy

Bermuda triangle had snatched them into thin air—the kind they were rushing through so fast she was getting nauseous. No, not exactly sick to her stomach. This was like watching a horror movie, like she was a spectator who knew something dreadful was going to happen to the actors any second. *Disassociation*, that's what they'd called it in psych classes, and it was one key sign of disorientation or shock.

Time seemed to fly, too. "Sorry, but we're gonna have to head back!" Ken told them, and Zach nodded. He reached back to squeeze her knee with one big hand, but neither of them said anything as Ken dipped the chopper back toward the northwest again.

Tears matted Julie's lashes; she blinked them back. She felt as stranded as Randi and Thad must have when they got lost and put in on some key that couldn't be seen from the air. With the evacuation orders and the demands on law enforcement, what could they do now?

"Wait!" Zach shouted, pointing. "Can you circle back around that long, S-shaped key at four o'clock?"

They banked and circled, then hovered. "What?" Julie cried. "Zach, what?"

She pressed her nose to the glass bubble behind the open door first on Ken's side, then switched her seat belt so she could look out on Zach's side. She was appalled when he leaned out, looking straight down with his binoculars, while Ken tipped the chopper to accommodate him. What if Zach tumbled out? If he didn't answer her, she'd unfasten her seat belt and lean out, too!

She saw an S-shaped key, but nothing unusual. The isle had a narrow strip of crooked beach on the gulf side and the remnants of a tumbled hut or small house there, but no sign of life.

"Zach, tell me!" she shouted.

"I see something dark in the water south off Fishbait—that S-shaped key. Naw, it's too big to be a Jet Ski. It's part of that junk old man Crothers dumped there when the Park Service made him leave his old house years ago. It's become an extra reef for the fish, that's all." His voice broke.

He was devastated, too, she thought, and clutching at straws.

"I'm going to take her in," Ken said and glanced back at Julie with a nod.

She watched Fishbait Key blur, shrink, then fade. Ken's words, *I'm going to take her in, I'm going to take her in*, echoed in her mind. If only she could find Randi, take her in her arms, hold her and tell her she'd be a better mother now. She'd tried so hard to be both father and mother. Had she smothered her daughter? Had she drowned her with attention and then turned it all on the other girls, leaving Randi lonely and bereft? And had they left her out there somewhere?

Sitting straight up, her hands still gripping the binoculars pressed to her thighs, Julie cried silently, her shoulders shaking, her eyes seeing only Randi.

Depression and desperation hit Zach hard. Whatever lay out there in that waterway off Fishbait Key, he had to go out for a look and he didn't want Julie to know. And he had a couple of other things to take care of first.

As they drove away from the airstrip, the Civil Air Patrol

called on Zach's cell phone to report they had still not located any sign of the kids and they were going to have to fly the planes out of the endangered area. Even their promise that they'd be back to look again, after the hurricane either passed by or went through, had depressed him.

"If that hurricane does come through here," he told Don Thomas, the C.A.P. volunteer on the line, "it will be far too late."

He almost lost control, as he had last night when he'd found those computer games that had showed Thad's secret interest in the military, maybe even an interest in what Zach had gone through. He regretted he hadn't shared more with his son, opened up to him about his past, especially the failures that haunted him. An invulnerable warrior, a hard-from-the-inside-out SEAL, he was not. And now it might be too late to explain that to Thad. He tried to ignore the fact that Julie was fighting not to cry in front of him again.

The next call was from the sheriff.

"Finally tracked you down, Zach."

"Thanks for calling back, Sheriff. You were pretty hard to track down yourself."

"I'm sure you know why. I've got thousands of lives on the line here, helping move folks out of flood zones. This evac goes mandatory, and it's a whole new kettle of fish. Your boy's gone missing? And with a young woman?"

Although the traffic was now much thinner and heading his direction, Zach pulled over onto the berm so he could concentrate on the conversation. "Yes, he's with Miranda Minton, goes by the nickname Randi, age fourteen. They weren't close or anything like that. At someone else's urging, he took her out for a ride. Randi's the daughter of Julia Minton, who inherited the Osprey Lodge on the edge of the bay. She's here with me if you need to talk to her."

Julie held out her hand for the phone, but he shook his head, concentrating on the sheriff's words because the connection wasn't very clear.

"You understand," Sheriff Ray Radnor was saying, "a teenage boy and girl out on a Jet Ski—the officer who took the call said on a Jet Ski, right?"

"Right. A dark blue Jet Ski from the Gladesport Marina, one with silver trim."

"Have they found it?" Julie cried, but he just lifted a hand to hold her off again.

"Our immediate assumption has to be that there's no foul play involved until it's proved otherwise. You or the mother of the girl suspect any?"

"Not so far. And I know the circumstances of your heading up a search are—"

"Are, unfortunately—even with this bastard storm coming—damned premature. 'Sides, as I recall," the sheriff went on, "Thadeus managed to get himself both attention and trouble to boot this last winter. You sure this couldn't be more of the same, like the kid who cried wolf?"

"I don't care if he robbed a bank, he's still missing!" Zach exploded.

"Okay, calm down. We're all antsy here. Look, Zach, the most I can promise right now is that I'll keep my eyes peeled as I visit the hurricane shelters and patrol the area to guard property from looters. E-mail me photos of the two of them so I can get them printed up and share it with my staff and get them distributed, okay? Height, weight, clothing when last seen, too."

"Thanks. Right away."

"But in this low-lying area," Sheriff Radnor went on, "I'm gonna have to pull my men, too, if the area goes to a mandatory evac. We'll patrol through once to be sure folks are out, and we can look then, but we can't risk other lives if we're in the bull's-eye of a Category Two or Three and its storm surge."

The sheriff went on with assurances that the kids would probably turn up, that he would see their pictures were posted in each shelter, hand it out to local Red Cross and medical volunteers. "Forty percent of kids in that age range who go missing together mean to run off together...." he went on.

Zach just muttered, "We're grateful for anything you can do," and punched end on his phone.

He had to get back to Fishbait. Pulling out on the road, with the traffic now almost nil, he sped toward the marina.

"He hasn't seen them, but he'll look?" Julie asked.

"We'll e-mail him photos and descriptions of them, and he'll get them printed, distributed and posted. His staff will keep an eye out when they patrol the area now and later, if there's a mandatory evacuation."

"I won't go! Without knowing where Randi is, I won't go."

"He thinks they might turn up at a shelter. And if the storm hits here you—we—have to go." He was desperate to get going now, but he had to get rid of Julie first and make sure she didn't do anything rash.

"I guess putting up their pictures and a patrol search could help," she said, but she sounded as enervated as he felt newly energized. "When you take me back to Osprey, I'll give you a photo—or we could scan and send them from my office."

"Do me a favor and pull one of Thad out of that brown album in the back seat. I keep all my fishing photos on CDs to send online to my clients, but the family stuff is in that album."

"Which reminds me," she said as she turned to reach for it, "I've got to put some things in the small resort boat and then in my car. It's parked in the lot where we keep the two resort vans. You know, where my great-uncle used to keep the stable."

"I know. Listen, I'll give you the sheriff's e-mail address and let you send him the pictures," he told her as he pulled in behind the marina and they got out. He hurried her down the dock toward the small boat they'd searched in yesterday. "But before I leave you there, I want to make sure that small motorboat of yours works, since *The Manatee*'s tied down here. Kaylin's going straight to the high school shelter with the girls who couldn't fly out?"

"Right. I'm to join them there, and I will—as soon as I find Randi."

He stopped at his big boat and scooped up his scuba gear he kept stowed aboard in a netted bag. His digital camera was in the cabin, so he secured it in a latched cabinet. He had an answer ready for what he knew she'd ask.

"What's that diving gear for?"

"I just want to take it to the truck with me and didn't want to forget it when I come back. Let's get you out to Osprey and send those photos."

He saw her look down at the close-up of Thad she still held—it was his junior year photo—which she'd selected from the scrapbook.

"He's a very good-looking young man," she said, "but I'd expect him to be. Randi doesn't look as much like me as Thad does you."

Despite the hell they were slogging through, he was touched by her subtle compliment and her honesty about herself. Above all things in a woman, he valued honesty, and he cursed himself for deceiving her, for holding back. He'd promised he wouldn't, that they could be a team, but he had to go back on that. Damn, he wanted to prepare her for what he feared he might find back at Fishbait Key, but he wanted to protect her more.

"Hang on!" he said only and veered away from the dock so fast the small boat's waves rocked *The Hooyah!*

7

It's 2:15 p.m. Sunday, southwest Florida, and it's time for some extra hurricane safety precautions from your chief meteorologist Tim Ralston. But first, let's remember our Cuban neighbors, who are feeling the outer bands of Hurricane Dana right now. Frankly, I'm expecting a mandatory evacuation order here soon for anyone who hasn't left the area or gone to an approved shelter. Meanwhile, listen up for some advice we've been repeating. Fill your bathtubs with water you can use for drinking or bathing. Tie down anything outside that could become a flying missile—anything including lawn furniture, which you can dump in your pool. Women in their final term of pregnancy should head for a hospital, because the huge drop in barometric pressure we're expecting often triggers premature labor. And don't be macho or foolhardy enough to plan a so-called hurricane party with beer and junk food, or you could end up blown away like so much junk.

Julie appreciated Zach's help, though he did seem to be in more of a rush than ever right now. On Osprey, he checked the gas and oil for the small motorboat Mike had set up for her, then hustled her into the lodge.

"Here's the sheriff's e-mail," he said, scribbling on a scrap of paper he pulled from his pocket. "Unfortunately, when Thad had the problem this winter, I memorized it. Go ahead and scan his picture and one of Randi in to him."

"But you need to tell me Thad's height and weight."

Edging toward the door the minute she was inside, he rattled the statistics off to her. It was as if he didn't want to be in this place he'd obviously once resented—but then, he'd seemed okay here when he'd spoken to the girls just yesterday. Surely, he wasn't suddenly panicked about fleeing the hurricane. Julie intended to go by boat, then car to check on Kaylin and the four remaining girls at the high school shelter, but she also planned to come back here, talk to Jake Malvers and search further. Amazingly, she seemed calmer than Zach right now.

"You'll send the info, then head for the shelter, right?" he asked, turning back. "Just phone me if you learn anything."

With the bright light of the sun behind him in the dim doorway, she wasn't sure if he was looking at her or avoiding her intense gaze. Sensing he wasn't telling her something, she stepped closer, staring up at him. She almost asked him if everything was all right, but then, how stupid would that sound right now?

"Go," he said, his voice harsh, as if he were giving a military order. "I've got some things to do back at my place, but if the evacuation becomes mandatory, I'll get to a shelter, too. Julie, we have no other choice."

Before she knew she would move—or he would, too—

they clung together, hard. The man felt like steel and stone, so sturdy in the midst of chaos and catastrophe. Her arms around his lower back pinned him to her; she pressed her cheek so hard to his chest she could hear the quick thud of his heart. He had one arm clamped behind her waist and one snagged in her hair to press her head under his chin. Then, as if they were both shocked, they leaped apart, and he was gone, sprinting toward his boat.

It terrified her that neither of them had said their usual parting mantras, "We'll find them," or "They'll be all right."

She rushed upstairs to the living area and turned on her desktop computer and its peripherals. She took a recent picture of Randi out of its frame—trying not to stare at it or she'd lose control—and scanned it in with Thad's. She typed out Randi and Thad's height, weight, eye color, and e-mailed that too.

As the scanner hummed, she glanced out her side window toward the bay and distant Gladesport. And saw Zach had not headed back to the marina, or even toward his house. Now a small gray dot with a white wake, his boat was speeding back toward the islands where they'd searched all morning.

"You lied to me!" she shouted as if her voice would carry that far. Her insides cartwheeled. Was he returning on his own to search more? Or had he seen something out there— maybe at Fishbait Key, where he'd asked Ken to hover? Perhaps that dark shape in the water was more than old man Crothers's junk, as Zach had called it. And he'd taken his scuba gear with him!

She stood frozen in the window as the desktop whirred,

sending a JPEG of the photos with the e-mail. What should she do? Zach had said they'd be a team, but, her deceitful ex-husband promised that more than once. Dear Lord in heaven, what had Zach seen from the air, and why hadn't she or Ken noticed the same thing?

Julie yearned to follow him, but in the 10,000 Islands she'd get as lost as Randi and Thad. She'd never find Fishbait Key again.

But she heard the echo of her own voice as she'd counseled Bree just last week, urging her not to be paralyzed by indecision or fear. "When you're like that, you harm yourself, because you're afraid to act," she'd told the girl. "Bree, this is a country and a world full of too many choices. We have hundreds of ice cream flavors, forty kinds of coffee beans, way over two hundred cable channels, and thousands of life choices for a woman. I know it can seem scary and paralyze you to the point you turn your frustration and anger inward on yourself. But you must find the courage to make choices, to move forward or outward, even in what is new or uncharted territory...."

The memory faded. "I don't care if a hurricane does come," Julie cried. "I'm going out there, too!"

As if God had approved her choice, she remembered she still had Zach's marine map of the area in her purse. Should she phone Kaylin to tell her where she was going? No, she'd try to talk her out of it, and Kaylin had enough to worry about right now.

Julie grabbed a big bottle of water, her hat and macrame bag off the sofa where she'd thrown them, and tore downstairs. Zach had just checked her small motorboat for fuel, so she was okay there. If he wasn't working *with* her any-more—and it was pretty obvious he resented ever working *for* her family—she'd just do things her way.

Zach's stomach cramped with foreboding and not just from listening to the ominous weather report on the transistor radio he'd left on in the boat. He jammed his feet in flippers, adjusted his face mask, strapped on his tank and checked his air regulator. *Jocking up*, they'd always called it on the teams, though he had no protective wet suit and was just going in wearing his shoes and khaki shorts. This was an easy dive in fairly shallow water with no hostiles around; he'd done more difficult dives a hundred times before, he tried to buck himself up.

Yet as he stared into the shifting water, he cursed the fact he was so reluctant to go down. He wanted answers, but he was afraid of what they might be.

From just sticking his mask in the water and staring through it, he'd seen shapes that were more than a rusted stove down there. He had to recon this entire area if Thad's Jet Ski had sunk. At least, if he found Thad had been speeding and had hit that submerged junk, his fears of foul play could be put to rest. But what terrified him was that, if the Jet Ski were underwater, the kids might be, too. He couldn't bear to admit the possibility.

Besides, they could have been thrown clear. Surely, they couldn't have been pinned or trapped under the heavy machine on this silt and sand bottom—or pulled out to sea with the shifting tides.

He checked to be sure the anchor was secure and far

enough from the submerged debris not to snag or disturb anything. And, as much as he admired sharks, he hoped none of them had their nursing areas too close, despite what he'd told Julie earlier.

Instead of just holding his mask and back-diving, he eased himself over the side of the boat. Because of light refraction, especially since the sun still peeked through the scudding clouds, things looked closer underwater. He could not judge the distance to the metal shapes beneath, and he didn't want to stir up bottom sediment and obscure his vision more.

As he sank beneath the surface, the familiar blue-green water world closed in around him. He loved snorkeling and scuba diving; it was all second nature to him after BUD/S, the basic training he'd had for SEALs. He'd had it pounded into his head that SEALs always kept one foot in the water, that it was not an obstacle but a sanctuary, even the sixty-three degree Pacific Ocean they'd trained in.

And Zach had always loved being in the depths. His father had been a frogman in 'Nam, in the Underwater Demolition Teams called UDT, the forerunners of the SEALs. He'd died there in 1969, when Zach was three, on a mission they'd never learned much about. But Zach had always pictured him becoming a part of the deep blue sea, swimming off into it, like he lived there yet and would protect his son when he swam or dove. Too bad he hadn't protected Becky, Zach thought. Or Zach's SEAL swim buddy Garth, when he'd lost him in the Persian Gulf that night. The SEALs might never leave a comrade behind, dead or alive, but the black night sea had swallowed Garth. Their C.O. had grabbed Zach to keep him from throwing himself from the helo after him, into the propeller-churned wake of the ship they were covertly boarding.

He couldn't bear it if Thad was lost now, too. He just couldn't go on then. He'd choose to die, swept away by the horrors of the hurricane.

Bubbles momentarily blinded him, even from this gentle submersion. Zach wished he had his combat Draeger gear, since it was small and light and didn't produce bubbles. He'd forgotten how much masks could cut peripheral vision too. A manta ray swam close before he saw it above his head and ducked to miss it.

The rusted wreck of an old, wood-burning iron stove and some other random junk metal had made an artificial reef here. Some coral and barnacles had attached themselves among the swaying kelp and pink sea anemones. He saw bonefish and sea trout. Much as Ken's helo had done, Zach hovered over the site. Yes, farther down, nestled against the iron stove—a Jet Ski on its side!

Blinking back tears which could foul his mask, he swam down. Damn it to hell, definitely Thad's! The nose of the machine was caved in and bore reddish scrapes, but surely not blood. Maybe rust marks from a collision with the submerged stove. How fast had that kid been going? He probably wanted to impress Randi or just get a thrill himself. Zach didn't wonder *why* he'd been speeding, but he had to wonder where they were now.

He realized he should have brought a weight belt. With the gulf currents and outgoing tide pulling at him, he had to kick hard and fan his arms just to stay in place. Four small, playful lemon shark pups and a slightly bigger bull shark showed up, gently bumping him as if they wanted him to play tag. However small scientists said sharks' brains were, they were curious creatures.

Ignoring them, Zach went heels over head to try to examine every exposed inch of the Jet Ski. At least he saw no bodies, but with the ebb and flow of several tides since then...

To his amazement, a bonnethead over four feet long appeared from the murk of the rusted reef and stared at him with one flat eye. The size of the shark reminded him of the one he'd let go yesterday when his charter wanted to kill it. From this angle, he couldn't spot that J-shaped scar he'd seen on it, but yes, this one bore a tag, tags like he used!

He jerked slightly in surprise and felt something hot against his left ankle. He looked up, horrified to see a pinkish cloud of blood ooze from his skin. Damn, he'd cut himself on this rusted ruin of the stove. If so, he had to get out now because, even without blood to summon them, the sharks were here.

"They'll find Randi," Cindy assured Kaylin, evidently reading the morose expression on her face.

The crying babies and little kids running around the hurricane shelter wore on Kaylin's nerves, but then, everything did since she'd called Julie and learned they had not found Randi and Thad yet. Here at the new, consolidated high school, the five of them had been allotted cots the Red Cross volunteers had provided—and who knew who'd slept on these last? As much as she hated being in this noisy, packed high school gym, worrying about Randi was making Kaylin feel sick, much sicker than the threat of the storm or smell of the tuna sandwiches they were serving in the cafeteria across the hall where Jordan and Tiffany had gone.

Besides, she had only reached Nate's voice mail when she'd tried to call him, so she was worried about him, too. He'd said he'd call her and would be available, so where was he? She'd tried phoning Liz Lawson to see if she knew where Nate was, but she'd been on voice mail, too.

Kaylin wasn't sure what she would have done without the girls. Tiffany and Jordan gave her no problems, and she was proud of them for pitching in to help the volunteers in the cafeteria. Cindy kept her spirits up, and Bree reminded her how much progress she and Julie had made with some of their charges.

Cindy, Bree and Kaylin had been sitting cross-legged in a little huddle on their cots since Kaylin had returned from the hall where she'd gone to make her cell phone calls. "I mean," Cindy went on, "Randi's with a guy who's really savvy about the area. So what did Julie say when you called her?"

"She was really hard to hear," Kaylin admitted, hitting her fist on her knee. "She said she was in a search boat."

"With Captain Zach again?"

"On her own—just in the bay, she said."

Bree piped up, "She's searching for Randi in *The Manatee*?"

"No, in that little runabout boat. She couldn't talk long, but she said posters about Randi and Thad should be put up in the shelters, so keep your eyes open for that."

"Like they've been abducted?" Cindy cried. "Can they do that Amber Alert thing for them in the middle of a hurricane evacuation?"

"They haven't been abducted, for heaven's sake!" Kaylin snapped. Several Hispanic women looked at her, then away, quickly tending to their children again. Where were their men, Kaylin wondered? Outside, staring up at the clouding sky or still sticking it out at home? One woman was bulbously pregnant, and Kaylin had heard on the radio that this storm could cause premature labor.

Susan Parker, the girls' phys ed teacher at the school who was more or less in charge of keeping order with the kids in the gym, came over. She had her coal-black hair pulled back in a ponytail and looked about as buff as Liz Lawson did, though this woman was much younger.

"Everything okay over here?" she asked Kaylin, tossing a basketball from hand to hand. Susan had organized some games in the back halls since the gym was packed, but she'd just brought the kids back in here.

"Sure. Fine," Kaylin said with a tight smile, though she wanted to scream. Kaylin wished she could switch places— and personalities—with Susan right now. Let her calm and comfort these girls while the so-called counselor did something physical to let off steam, instead of being cooped up like this.

When Susan walked away to talk to others, Cindy tapped Kaylin's shoulder. "Look!" she said, pointing toward the door to the gym under the big red GO GATORS! banner. "Isn't that the woman who runs the marina?"

"You're right, it is Loreen Blackwell," Kaylin said, bouncing up as she saw the suntanned, bleached-blond woman come in, stop and look around. "Stay put a minute, and I'll see if she knows anything new." Actually, in the bitchy mood she was in, Kaylin wasn't feeling too charitable toward the woman who'd told everyone she'd more or less forced Thad Brockman to take Randi for a ride.

"Hi, Ms. Blackwell, it's me, Kaylin McKenzie."

"Oh, right. Any word on the kids?"

"They're still looking."

"My husband went out last night with a search light and a megaphone and again before dawn. And he got another charter fisherman from Marco to help look, the guy he races boats with."

"Oh, good. What kind of boat does he race?"

"The kind Clint and I could never afford. They call them cigarette boats because they used to run contraband in from Cuba years ago. Fast and sleek. White or light-gray to blend in with the horizon," she said, still scanning the crowd in the gym.

"Can I help you find someone?"

"Grant Towers, the king of the luxe Realtors, said he'd meet me here with an offer I couldn't refuse, but he's late, and I'm not waiting. He's slime, not to be trusted, anyway. I've told Julie that, and I tried to tell Victoria Leigh the same when she came into the marina the other day pretending she just ran into him."

Julie had said this woman was a font of local knowledge and gossip. "Maybe he's trying to buy Mrs. Leigh's property, too," she said, hoping to elicit more information. Kaylin didn't know much about Victoria Leigh, other than that her husband had helped Julie and Zach look for the kids in his helicopter. But Grant Towers was a handsome, older guy who'd tried to buy Osprey Island for big bucks, and his daughter was in a soap opera, *Dangerous Women,* that Kaylin used to watch. Some dirt about them could be pretty interesting.

"Julie says the Leighs are pretty well-to-do, so they probably won't sell to Grant Towers or anyone," Kaylin prompted. "And like you said, Grant Towers is rich, too. I wonder if his pull got his oldest daughter an audition for that TV show she's on."

Loreen snorted. "Rich, maybe. We think he's built a house of cards—everything in property and no liquid assets, as Clint puts it. That may be one reason he's so damned desperate to get his hands on our land, so he can keep his little shell game going. But his getting his hands on that looker Leigh is entirely a different matter. Hell, I wasn't born yesterday," she said, wrapping her arms around herself as if she had an upset stomach.

"Look, Carolyn," Loreen plunged on, screwing up her name, though Kaylin didn't correct her, "I just want you and Julie to know Clint and I are trying to help find Randi and Thad. Is Julie coming to join you?" she asked, finally looking directly at her. "If she doesn't now, she will soon, because I think they're going to *make* us leave Gladesport, instead of just *ask* us to. We're too damned vulnerable in this whole area," she added, shaking her head. "I've been through the drill before, even if the worst of it doesn't hit here." As abruptly as she'd appeared, Loreen stalked out into the hall.

"If Julie doesn't find Randi safe and sound soon," Kaylin muttered to herself, "the worst of it already hit here."

Julie ran the old outboard 35-horsepower motor as fast as it would propel the little boat through the mounting waves. They were cresting to good-sized whitecaps now, and she soon learned to steer into them at an angle to avoid being rocked. Still, spray and spume doused and chilled her.

Kaylin had phoned, but Julie hadn't told her she was heading out into the maze of islands. Her call to Liz Lawson to see if she or Nate had searched the area before vacating ended up just being a message she left on her voice mail. Julie wished she'd thought to bring Leon and Jake Malvers's phone number, because she would have called them, too. They might have issues with Zach, but she was certain Jake had gone out searching for his nephew.

She jammed her phone in the pocket of her shirt. She didn't need both hands to steer, for there wasn't another watercraft in sight, but she needed at least one hand free. Digging Zach's folded marine map out of her purse, she tried to stop its flapping and steady it over her knees.

If only she'd known which key was Fishbait the first day they searched. What she remembered from the air was only confusing. No, here it was on the map, that distinctive S shape. It was on the other side of a twisting waterway after the V-shaped key called No Name.

To her amazement, about fifteen diving pelicans suddenly surrounded her. She could see their prey, a school of silvery fish in the blue-gray slide of the waves. The birds rose nearly thirty feet in the air, then, open-beaked, dive-bombed with a splash to come up with fish they tossed back in their gullets and swallowed. Soon, they flapped their huge wings to rise and dive again.

The fish seemed to be keeping pace with her, surround-

ing her. She'd seen such displays before, but the birds and
even the fish, which leaped of their own accord from some
of the waves, seemed crazed. No wonder they called it a
feeding frenzy.

Past what she was certain was No Name Key, she turned
down the mangrove-guarded natural canal that must lead to
Fishbait. Or did it? She turned her motor down to a mere
putt-putt and went almost silently through the marauding
mangroves. The twists and turns of the passage seemed eternally familiar and yet strange. At least the water was calmer
here, and the birds and fish were gone.

She glanced down at the map again, now speckled with
briny spray. When she nervously licked her lips, they tasted
salty.

And then around the next bend, she saw Zach's boat. It
was anchored, but she didn't see him as it scraped in rhythm
with the waves up and down against one of the mangrove
barriers. She cut her motor and just glided.

He must have gone diving, just as she'd thought—had
feared. He must have known something was down there besides the rusted stuff he'd mentioned.

Tears sprang to her eyes, and she almost dry-heaved as her
boat floated quietly closer to his. She felt terrified and terribly alone, even though she heard a radio voice coming from
his boat, that local veteran weatherman they'd all been listening to about the coming storm. Yes, a radio sat on one of
the seats.

Oh—she saw something in the water on the far side of his
boat, something thrashing the surface which looked reddish
with white foam. From the rusted things beneath?

A fin! She saw a smooth gray back with a fin lift, then sink beneath the roiling water.

"Zach," she screamed, "where are you? Zaa-aach!"

8

At 3:30 p.m., Tim Ralston here at your friend in the storm, WSEA-AM radio, Naples. I have been indicating we would probably go to a mandatory evacuation of our area, and that has just been confirmed by the National Hurricane Center in Miami. Predicting how strong a hurricane will grow remains more art than science, but as Dana ravages Cuba and then heads across the Straits of Florida, she will gain strength. Clouds and winds will continue to increase here as the outer bands begin to reach us, and they will be dangerous with lashing rains and powerful winds. If you had planned to ride out the storm at home, you are now required to evacuate to a shelter or head inland. I repeat, the entire southwest coast of Florida is under a mandatory hurricane evacuation order. I'm not a gambling man, but the likelihood is this one's going to be very bad.

To Julie's amazement and relief, Zach sat up from the floor of his boat, obviously shocked to see her. Bare-chested, he'd been hunched over or curled up on his side in the boat. Had he been sleeping?

"Julie! What in the—"

"What are *you* doing? What's all that?" she demanded, pointing at the flurry in the stained water.

Her boat bumped his. She saw his lower leg was bleeding, and he'd tied his T-shirt around it. He still had a swim fin on his right foot, and his scuba gear was dumped in the bottom of the boat.

"I was diving and cut my foot on the rusted metal down there. I saw sharks and got out. A good-sized one is feasting on the smaller ones down there, but at least he didn't come after me."

She held her boat tight to his. The bloodstain seeping through his shirt was as big as his fist, but she was still angry.

"I figured out why you left so fast," she told him. "You lied to me about our working together, about not holding anything back. And about there being no dangerous sharks around here. Did—" she swallowed hard. "Did you find something down there?"

Frowning, he nodded, holding his shirt tightly to his left ankle.

"Zach, talk to me! I'm not some stupid outsider, and I won't faint! Is the Jet Ski down there?"

"Yeah, but no sign of the kids," he said, meeting her eyes at last and speaking in a rush as if to unburden himself or assure her. "I think they hit the submerged rusted stove. The Jet Ski got its nose bashed in, tipped and sank. Now prove to me you're not fragile, Julie, because I'm sure it just threw them off."

"But—just like you, if they got cut on the metal…those sharks…" She wanted to throw herself into the bottom of her boat to scream and cry, but he was right. She had to hold on, to be strong, to never give up unless…unless she had proof Randi was not all right. She bit her lip and managed a nod.

"I'm theorizing," he went on, "they got thrown free, then either tried to hike or swim out or got picked up by some boater who heard about the coming storm and took them along for safety's sake, maybe to Naples, Sarasota, even Tampa or Key West."

She hated to play devil's advocate, yet she had to. "But they would have contacted us already."

"Who knows how long it would take them to get to the bay or the gulf, to even get picked up."

"Zach, this is the age of cell phones."

"Okay, so maybe under this canopy of mangroves, they might not be spotted from the air."

It went unsaid between them that they and others had searched this area already. And that a killer hurricane was coming.

"I suppose," she said, trying to hold on to the remnants of hope, "walking on those weird mangrove roots would be terribly slow. Plus, one or both of them could be hurt. But what if the people who picked them up weren't helpful…"

He looked guilty. It shocked her to realize she was starting to read his moods. "What else?" she demanded, still shaking. "I don't need any more surprises, so just tell me."

"It's a real long shot, but…"

"Tell me, I said." She reached over to grab his wrist so hard he flinched.

"For decades, this area has been a drop for contraband goods."

"Such as?"

"Lately, such as drugs coming in by small plane from the Caribbean or Central America."

"And someone comes out here to pick them up in this mangrove maze? You'd have to be a native to know your way around here so…" Her voice trailed off. "You don't mean," she went on, her voice deadly calm, "that someone could have come along who was picking up drugs and also picked them up? And since they'd seen too much, was afraid to let them call us?"

"I don't mean anything except it's one other wildcard possibility. You don't want anything held back, you've got it."

"And, of course, you'd thought of that from the beginning and kept it to yourself," she goaded. "Because you didn't want weak little me to worry. Or you want to protect locals who are out here picking up the drugs, locals you know!"

"You sound like your bigoted great-uncle or snob of a father! Are you happy to know everything, then? That there are drug runners around here who could endanger our kids, just like they do on the city streets? Yeah, Julie, it's a billions of bucks illegal business, and they don't give a damn who they hurt to protect it!"

She loosed his wrist. "That can't be, it just can't be," she argued. "But… Forgive me for asking this, but are you certain Thad wouldn't have any part in such a thing?"

"Picking up drugs to pass on? You think I wouldn't know at least that he had extra money? And with Randi onboard?"

She'd hated to ask that for more than one reason. It reminded her that she hadn't known Randi's heart or hurts.

And she was furious with Zach again. Still, she had to keep calm. She was going to work on her own, and she needed to know several things from Zach first. Following his lead, she would make him trust her and then do what she had to do.

"I still want to search this key," she told him. "Maybe the others nearby, too. I see this one has dry land. I'm going to get out and check out that tumbled-down hut I saw from the air for any sign of the kids. You saw the submerged Jet Ski from the chopper, didn't you?" she accused, before she steadied her voice again.

"I didn't know if it was just the old rusted junk or not. And I didn't want to drag you out here to check it out."

"Oh, thank you very much. Best to just let me know in a couple of weeks, maybe after the hurricane goes through, if you located my daughter or not."

She was losing the battle to be civil. She wanted to hate this man. But she'd been so distraught when she'd seen his boat and not him and then that roiling water. Yes, she had been afraid for him as well as for their kids.

"Julie, I'm sorry. I'm sorry that Thad's speeding must have caved in the front of the Jet Ski. I'm sorry Randi was with him. But, I swear to you, there is absolutely no sign that they were ever underwater with the ski."

Julie bit her lower lip hard so she wouldn't cry. He'd actually apologized and seemed to read her mind, as she believed she was starting to read his. She could not blame Zach for Randi's being lost, though she had no intention of letting him control the search any more. Whether he knew the area better or not, whether he'd been a SEAL or not, she had to do her own thinking, her own planning and daring.

At this moment, if she could save Randi by jumping into this shark-infested water, she would. Suddenly, more than ever, she understood young women who injured themselves in their frustration and their impotent fury. They had to learn to make decisions and to act on them, and she did, too.

"I have some of that antibacterial hand sanitizer in my purse," she said, digging in it. "Spread this on your cut while I look around the key."

When she handed the small plastic bottle to him, he looked at her, awestruck. Had he thought she would dissolve into tears? She shoved away from his boat to edge hers toward the key. Tying its prow to a mangrove, she stepped out onto the half-submerged, arched roots.

"Did you hear they've made the evacuation mandatory?" Zach asked as he bent over the task of cleansing his cut.

"Just now on your radio," she called to him. "How much time do you think we have before we get blown away?"

"Hours. Not sure how many. Be careful in those thickets. You never know about snakes or other wild creatures."

"Zach," she said, amazed at the strength and determination which suddenly bloomed in her, "I'm just praying that if someone picked our kids up, they weren't wild creatures of some kind."

By pulling on his anchor rope, Zach brought his boat closer to hers. "I need to give this cut a little longer to stop bleeding before I get out to help," he told her. "Keep talking to me, especially if you move out of my sight."

"Sir, yes, sir! Is that an order, sir? Will I have to do push-ups if I double-cross you, the way you did me?"

Without another look at him, she climbed onto the edge

of the key; the mangrove roots looked like talons clawing the water. A few bowed or cracked under her weight, but most held. She saw now how such roots created the keys, for floating things were snagged in them to make soft soil and then land. Liz had told the girls how these mangroves multiplied, dropping their cigar-shaped seeds called propules into the water to drift away and start new plants.

"Now wouldn't it be much easier for *homo sapiens* to breed that way?" Liz had said, her voice as much bitter as humorous. "Not as much fun maybe, but a lot more simple and quicker. Have you ever noticed how Mother Nature has it down right and mankind all wrong?"

As Julie made her way toward the center backbone of the long, thin key, the ground seemed to rise, harden, and become less dense with trees. She spotted the tumbled-down building she had seen from Ken's chopper, the place where old man Crothers had once lived before he'd been turned off his land and had dumped the stove in defiance.

"See anything?" Zach's voice came to her. "I'll be there to help in a couple of minutes."

"I'm not certain we're still a team," she yelled at him, feeling even braver at this distance.

"The hell we aren't. Just be careful in there."

Old man Crothers had once had a decent-sized clearing here, she realized. But the shack was totally tumbled into ruin, so it could not have provided shelter for two kids. She saw no sign of a recent fire, no human footprints on the ground, nothing to give her hope.

Though Zach had said she might see wildlife, Julie saw

nothing and heard not one sound of a bird. Did the animals sense the storm was coming and flee inland, as she should do but wouldn't, at least until the last minute?

Though Zach knew he should just stay put with his leg elevated, he couldn't let Julie recon Fishbait alone. She was right to search it thoroughly, but he was afraid of what she might find. He had to admit, though, she seemed to have a backbone of steel today, and his grudging admiration of her grew.

He wanted to dislike her for the way he'd been treated by her family, by the way they'd made him and his friends feel like dirt. It was as if everyone from Gladesport had been a second-class citizen to her pompous father and great-uncle. But had Zach just assumed Julie went along with them, reveled in their supposed superiority? He was certain that she would be embarrassed if she knew he'd gotten a lecture from her father once about "not being good enough to so much as look at my daughter that way. And from now on, don't even look me in the face. Just keep your mouth shut and do your work around here or you're done, Brockman."

It was then Zach had decided to construct the rubber shark. It was then that he also turned his resentment of the other kids' treatment by Julie's family into a deep-seated hatred that had eaten at him for years.

Trying to protect his cut ankle, he got out of the boat and, gripping mangrove trunks, navigated the seven feet of shoreline before terra firma began.

"I'm on shore, heading toward the Crothers house!" he called to her. "What's your position right now?"

"About two o'clock from you! Maybe twenty yards or so southeast!" she called. Her voice sounded very distant, and very professional. He couldn't fathom having a female partner, but he guessed, in this, he had no choice.

Julie fought her way toward the south, curved end of the S shape of the key and was amazed to find the remains of an old tabby cistern half full of rainwater. Its square mouth was about four feet across. In an island ringed by the salt sea this was how the old man had managed to survive out here. Perhaps Randi and Thad had found this, too, and had a drink. But surely, if the storm surge from the hurricane roared through, it would turn this rainwater brackish.

"Julie?" Zach shouted. "Give me another bearing."

"I'm over here by the cistern east of the hut."

"Wait up."

But she walked on. She wasn't taking orders from Zach Brockman anymore. And with this storm coming, every second counted. She saw the other side of the key through the maze of mangroves and thrashed her way toward it. If she were marooned here, she'd keep close to the fresh water but make a camp on this far side to flag down passing vessels on the gulf.

"Julie?"

"I'm almost to the other side of the key!"

"I'm bleeding bad again. I need to sit down."

"I'll be right back."

She was pleased to see this side of the key was real sand, not just roots in water. But on that thin stretch was beached a mutilated, skinless, limbless torso with huge chunks of flesh torn away.

* * *

Kaylin had not only gotten through to Nate, but he was coming here to see her! With the wind ripping at her hair, she stood outside the high school, waiting for him. Finally, he pulled up in a shiny, new-looking van which had WORLDWISE: Don't let the Everglades become the Neverglades written on its black sides in bright green. Liz, luckily, was not with him.

He killed the motor, jumped out and, with the door to the van still open, hugged her hard.

"I was so worried," she told him. She was surprised how breathy she sounded, as if the rising wind spoke her words. "I couldn't get through to you or Liz."

"We decided we'd both better recharge our cell phones in case the area loses power," he explained, pulling her into the shelter of the open van door. He leaned against it and kept her tight to his body. It cut the rising wind and made her feel the safest she'd been in days. She tried not to cling to him so hard, but she was starting to feel desperate about the storm, about Randi's fate—about all of their fates, even here in an approved shelter built of cement blocks.

"A policeman was just here telling everyone that if the cell phone towers blow down, cell phones won't work anyway," she told him. "He came to post pictures and descriptions of Randi and Thad and check how things were going here. No storm in sight, and I'm going nuts already."

"Liz and I went out in separate boats looking off Goodland and at the edge of the park, but to no avail."

"Thanks for trying. I'll never forgive myself if…if she's lost for good."

"Kaylin," he said, holding her stiff-armed before him, "have you or Julie thought that someone might have taken them?"

"Taken them? No, that can't be."

"There are strangers around here, you know. This area used to attract weirdos of all kinds, outlaws and escaped killers who—"

"Don't say that! That was years ago," she cried, hitting his hands from her shoulders and stepping back.

"Have you checked thoroughly for an abduction note? No one thinks Zach Brockman has much money, but Julie's people must have."

"She inherited that Osprey Key, not bought it!"

"But her family was rich, and everyone knew it. I'm just suggesting you take a hard look at all the angles, that's all. We can't afford to leave any stone unturned."

She was touched that he'd said *we.* "I—of course, you're right. I'd hate to mention it to Julie, but I will."

"And please don't punish the messenger if you don't like the message, sweetheart," he said, pulling her back against him again. "If we did that, we'd have to all go kill that radio weatherman everyone's relying on."

Thank God, Julie thought, the corpse wasn't human, though, at first, it had looked like a body from the hips on up, a human torso minus its limbs. She forced herself to approach it, lean over it. A three-foot shark, but its fins had been sliced off. Had it been alive then? And had the fact that it was bleeding caused other sharks to attack it and take huge chunks out of it like this?

Despite how she was sweating in the heat and humidity, she went icy cold and began to shiver. Her teeth chattered. This could have happened to Zach—maybe to Randi and Thad.

But the fact the fish was definned clicked in her stunned brain. Zach had mentioned that Ken Leigh used to export shark fins for some sort of special soup. Could someone have mutilated this shark for that? She should show Zach, though it sounded as if it would be difficult for him to make it all the way here to see this. But then, what if he pursued this possibility on his own, just as he'd done earlier today? What if Ken or someone he knew had definned this shark and so had been in the area when the kids crashed? But no, Ken had said he'd been across the state, flying the chopper out to Miami.

Hoping she wouldn't be sick from the sight and smell of the mangled mess, she walked around the shark. From the other side, she saw its head was still attached. Part of a big hook and a piece of line protruded from its gaping, razor-teethed mouth. It had been caught, evidently pulled in and definned, then it either pulled or was cut free. But then she saw more proof to link this grotesque sight to Ken Leigh— an arrow in its side. It had broken off when someone evidently tried to pull it out, but it was definitely the pointed end of the shaft of an arrow.

She pictured again that crossbow she'd seen in Ken's chopper. It had a powerful magnifying scope mounted on top of it, and the back part of it had looked like a rifle.

Gritting her teeth, she tugged the arrow from the putrid flesh. She decided then that she was going to question Ken

Leigh herself. He'd be much less threatened if she, instead of Zach, phoned him.

No, better yet, especially since he had flown back to Miami and time was of the essence, she'd visit his hunt camp where he said his wife was closing up, and question her. Or, if she seemed sympathetic, convince her to help. At least, she would know how to reach Ken. If the beautiful Victoria was not at the hunt camp, which wasn't far, Julie would drive to their beach house on Marco Island. The roads were deserted; it wouldn't take her long. Ken had said that his wife was distraught about losing their property. Surely, she could sympathize with another woman distraught about losing her daughter.

And she wasn't telling Zach or taking him with her. Who really knew what his relationship was to the woman he'd taken deep-sea fishing and who had made that double entendre phone call to him? Leon Malvers had sarcastically said Zach had been in bed with Liz Lawson, but perhaps it was true of him and Victoria Leigh. If so, and if Ken had any inkling, maybe he'd want to get back at Zach—even by harming his son, whom he found stranded on an island where he was killing and definning sharks illegally. It seemed like a desperate theory, but she was desperate.

Still trembling, she washed the two-inch broken arrow shaft in the water, then hid it by sticking it in the waistband of her pants under her shirt.

She strode back up the beach and cut across the key toward where she thought the ruins of the shack must be located. Zach sat there on an old door with his left leg propped up. He looked very relieved to see her.

"This door would have made a great raft if they'd been here," he said, shaking his head. "I'll be able to walk okay as soon as I get a couple stitches."

"You're going to the E.R.?"

"No time for that. I'll sterilize and do it myself—I've had basic first aid training. Don't look so surprised. I've got a med kit on my big boat, and I've been cut up worse than this. It's nothing much if I can keep it from bleeding or getting infected. You obviously didn't find anything?"

"Just a dead fish. Here, let me help you keep your weight off that foot back to your boat."

He was so much taller and heavier that she didn't provide that much help. It felt strange to have his arm around her, to have her shoulder fit so well under his armpit. She kept one hand free to grab at mangrove trunks and her other arm around his broad, bare back. His skin was warm, his muscles sinewy and taut.

But suddenly, the roots at the fringe of the key cracked and they almost both went down. Zach grabbed a branch over their heads and kept them from falling. The air was getting cooler now, but the exertion—or his proximity—made her feel hotter than she'd felt all day.

"Our weight together is too much for these roots," she said, needing to say something. The trouble was she wanted to hold him, to have him hold her again. And she hardly needed that when she'd decided to go it on her own.

One root not only creaked and cracked but gave way. Again, he grabbed branches to steady them. The movement swung them both around. Julie found herself staring at a red-sequin flower snagged on the very branch he held.

"Zach, look! It's got to be one of those flowers appliqued on Randi's pirate movie T-shirt!"

She stretched against him to pluck it down. She'd felt strong and determined a moment ago, but she started to tremble again. Cradling the torn fabric flower in her hand, she pressed her cheek against it as he steadied her against his big body.

"Are you sure?"

"Yes, but how could it get there? The tides surely don't rise that high—or could the wind have carried it here?"

"See the broken branches and torn leaves around it— above it?" he said, squinting upward. "If she was thrown through here, and the flower snagged…"

Holding to each other, they both looked down at the web of roots under their feet. Perhaps it wasn't just their combined weight which had weakened them.

"Maybe she fell here, where the roots are broken," he went on, "and that's why they didn't hold our weight as well. The trajectory could be right if they were speeding from over there," he added, pointing.

She saw it horribly in her mind's eye. She and Zach could be walking where their lost kids had been.

"What if," she whispered, "the Jet Ski hit the submerged junk, and she flew off and landed here. What about Thad?"

"I'll get this bleeding stopped and come back out to search the whole area," he vowed. "They can't have gone far without some sort of raft or help. Julie, we're making progress— we're starting to get answers," he added and hugged her hard again.

As they started toward their boats, she almost blurted out

about the definned shark, shot by an arrow. But she needed to follow that lead alone, so Zach would come back more quickly to search here before she joined him. Ken Leigh's hunting camp wasn't far from Gladesport, and she could stop by the hurricane shelter at the high school on her way back out here. At least they had now pinpointed an area.

"I'm going to drive to the high school shelter," she told Zach, glad it was a half truth at least.

"Good. I'll probably end up there, too, when the worst comes. But I'll come right back out here as soon as I stitch up this cut."

"I don't intend to stay at the shelter yet. I'm going back to the lodge to pack up some things and then check to see if Jake Malvers is still willing to search, or if he's looked in the haunts he said Thad might use."

"I can check on the Malverses," he said as she helped him back into his boat, then immediately clambered through his to get to hers. She gently placed the flower in her purse. Dear Lord, what if it was the last thing—the only memento—she ever had of losing Randi?

But she said only, matter-of-factly, "Okay, but good luck. Leon and Jake didn't like you before the storm, so you think anything's changed from when you sent me to talk to them? Oh, by the way," she said, gesturing toward the water near his boat, "those sharks that were attacking each other here—do they ever strip off each other's fins?"

"Not that I've seen," he said, propping his hurt leg up on the seat ahead of him. "It's only mankind that does that, leaving them to bleed to death and often be eaten by other sharks."

"But you said people use the fins for soup? Eating that sounds gross to me," she went on, hoping she sounded nonchalant as she settled herself on the boat seat.

"It's a big tradition in China, Japan and Singapore. The fins contain a flavorless cartilage that gives the soup a gelatinous texture the Asians love. It's a big deal at weddings, birthdays—a prestige food, like our caviar."

"I've heard of shark cartilage in medicines and health food, but did Ken Leigh make a lot of money from strictly fins?"

"Last time I checked," he said, starting to haul in his anchor, "small fins were getting six bucks and big ones up to a hundred dollars a pound. The soup is about two hundred and fifty bucks a bowl and rising as the availability goes down."

"No wonder Ken is upset at your stance on protecting sharks."

"No more than most of the fishermen in the state, including Clint Blackwood. Look, are you going somewhere with all this?"

"Just curious," she lied as she reached for her rope to untie it. As she leaned over, she realized too late she still had her cell phone stuffed in her shirt pocket. She gasped and grabbed for it as it hit the water and sank instantly.

"Oh, no! Damn!" she cried.

"It would be a goner even if we fished it out," Zach said. "I've ruined more than one on the water."

"I'll just borrow Kaylin's. She's in a safe place and…I'm not, yet."

"Tell me her number—slow," he ordered.

"I can write it down for you."

"No, I'll remember it."

She did as he said. Before he could question her more about her plans, she threw her rope in the bottom of her boat and started her motor. She was heading for Ken Leigh's hunting lodge. She only hoped his wife hadn't started across the state to join him in the expensive sports car she wanted to save from the wind and water so badly.

9

It's 5:00 p.m. and our skies are clouding up with outer bands that are forerunners of the hurricane. I have some additional information for you from the Orion aircraft that flies through the storm. Hurricane Dana has been forming a more concentric eyewall, which contains turbulent storms surrounding the eye. NOAA, the National Oceanic and Atmospheric Administration, which flew the plane out of Tampa, warns us that the storm path appears to be through the narrow, warm water channel that separates the Caribbean from the Gulf. If that holds true the next few hours, Dana may just brush us or target us. Either way, as the line goes from that vintage movie, "Fasten your seat belts. We're in for a bumpy ride."

Julie clicked off her car radio and dropped a hand to her waist to be sure her seat belt was fastened before it hit her that the weatherman was just trying to inject a little levity. Her brain had slowed and thinking felt as challenging as trying to balance on crooked mangrove roots.

She'd run straight from the boat to her car and sped along the deserted two-lane road. On her dashboard, the broken arrow she'd pulled from the dead shark seemed to point the way. Next to it, like a beacon, lay Randi's tattered red sequined flower.

She was going crazy, Julie thought, but, after all, she hadn't slept last night and was running on adrenaline. Yet fear was draining her strength and courage. She was dead on her feet, dead…

She nearly swerved off the road before she realized she must have gone to sleep for a minisecond. Thank God, no car was near and no canals lined this road. She broke out into a sweat; her hands gripped the wheel so hard they cramped. Her heart pounded faster as she slowed to reach onto the floor to retrieve the flower and arrow, which had skidded off the dashboard when she'd veered.

In a rush now, despite the fact she needed Kaylin's cell phone, she started past the high school property with its football field and stadium seats, its circular drive and attractive, newly planted royal palms. Each was propped up with three boards, but their fronds were already thrashing in the increasing winds.

Maybe she should take the time to go in for Kaylin's phone now. No, after she was certain she'd caught Victoria Leigh at the hunt camp, she'd stop at the storm shelter.

But as she approached the exit of the curved driveway, she saw Grant Towers get out of a large black car in front of the school. He looked around almost furtively, then, buffeted by the wind, started inside. It seemed ludicrous that a man with Grant's money and clout was staying there during the storm. Of all the newly built properties he'd developed, wasn't one of them safer than this crowded public shelter?

She'd hoped he might have gone out in his yacht earlier to search for the kids. Surely, he'd heard they were missing by now. What if he'd learned something and was looking for her, since he couldn't get her on her cell phone?

She veered into the exit-only driveway and honked as she came up behind him. The minute she began to roll her window down, she heard the sharp ding of the American flag banging against its metal pole as it snapped in the wind. The noise sounded like some sort of horrid alarm clock, clanging, clanging to drag the sleeper from exhaustion and bad dreams.

"Hey, Julie!" he shouted over the din. "I've been wanting to talk to you."

So he had found something out about the kids! She rolled her window all the way down, but to her dismay, he reached in, unlocked the passenger side and got in. The car rocked under his weight as if a big gust had hit them. His hair was soaked, though he didn't seem to be sweating. He looked and smelled as if he'd just taken a shower, though she could still detect cigarillo smoke on him, too.

"I can't stand this wind," he told her, slamming the door, "and it's only going to get worse. Any news about your kids?"

Her hopes fell, but she said, "I'm glad you heard. I thought you might have gone out looking."

"I've had a couple of associates out, guys from Marco," he said, "but they've had to dock and tie up by now. I've been running around like a chicken with my head cut off, making sure my new projects are as secure as possible, and talking to locals. I was going in to meet Loreen, and I'm late, but you're someone else I wanted to talk to."

"Loreen? I don't think she wants to see you on a good day."

"She's a spitfire, all right. But I would think, with what we're all facing, she and you would be ready to listen to reason."

"If this is about property again, Grant, forget it. I've got to go. My daughter and Zach's son are still missing and the only things I'd sell Osprey for right now is their safe return. If you don't know where they are, I'll have to ask you to get out."

"All right, sure. I understand. I'm just grateful my girl Gracie wasn't out with him. I'll tell you, I was about ready to get a restraining order on that Brockman kid."

Aghast, Julie glared at him. "As if you can control your own child," she accused, before she realized she might be talking about herself—about any parent of teens. She plunged on, getting more frustrated and furious by the minute. "You really are here to get Loreen, or me, or anyone else you stumble on who has beachfront land, to sign it over, even right now?" She felt as if her head would explode, and the entire car would disintegrate like one wired with a terrorist bomb.

"Look, the twelve million I've offered you is a lot of dough, and I'm willing to take the risk of loss you could never afford. All of Osprey Island could be blown apart or be under water by tomor—"

"Get out!" she shouted. "You're like one of those sleazy lawyers who chase ambulances, or a vulture just waiting for a disaster you can pick apart. Get out!"

For one moment she was afraid he might hit her, and she

started to unbuckle her seat belt to get out. But, with a vein in the side of his neck throbbing, Grant opened the passenger door and got out. She drove off so fast he barely had time to step clear; the door slammed itself shut.

Julie roared out of the driveway, cursing him. He'd made her lose time. And she'd been close enough to borrow Kaylin's cell phone, but he'd upset her so she'd forgotten about that. She even doubted if he and his so-called associates from Marco had been searching for Randi and Thad.

She tried to calm herself as she drove the last stretch to the area where she knew the Leighs' hunt lodge must be. She'd never seen it, but it was on the site of Zach's old family home, so she knew where to turn off.

On both sides of the road, the woods pressed closer, now thick with craggy slash pine and gnarled cypress. Like the rest of the Everglades, the area surrounding Gladesport was a strange amalgam of prairie and swamp. Elevated areas marked by pines, cabbage palms, and wax myrtles made what were called hammocks, which looked like islands in a sea of blowing sawgrass or reeds in marshy ground.

She recalled that Liz Lawson had told the girls that the precious big cypress had been logged out about a half century ago since they were rot-resistant wood. A lot of private landowners had been bought out by the government to make preserves, or—like Zach's family, evidently—their land had been purchased by independently wealthy interests like Ken Leigh.

She wished Zach's family was still in the area, because they could use more savvy locals to help look for the kids, but they were all scattered now. She'd heard that both of his half siblings had moved away. He'd said his mother had been widowed a second time and had used her buyout money from the Leighs to purchase a trailer in the northern, "cooler" part of the state, from which she spent her small fortune taking cruises with her "significant other." Zach couldn't phone to tell her Thad was missing because she was on a trip to Nova Scotia. He was certain Thad would not have gone north to see her anyway. The boy had never been as close to his grandmother as he'd been to the Malvers men, because Thad hadn't liked Zach's stepdad any more than Zach did.

It was rough and raw beauty the Brockmans had given up here, Julie thought, and the area looked quite unpopulated from here. Liz had said that although four hundred hunting camps once studded this area, only about twenty-five remained.

"Anything we can do to beat back the so-called progress of condos, golf courses and shopping malls is a victory!" she'd insisted. "But men out to kill the animals who were here before they were are not much better."

It was no surprise that people like the Malvers men—and, no doubt, Grant—hated Liz. Julie wondered what the eco-zealot Liz thought of fishermen. Surely, she and Zach would at least be on the same side in the battle to save sharks.

Ahead, on the left, Julie saw the entrance to the camp on a site which, she recalled, had once held the Brockman house and gardens. They'd lived a hardscrabble life, though she hadn't realized that years ago.

She was relieved it hadn't taken long to get here. She could speak with Victoria, then check with Kaylin and be back out to the keys around Fishbait in time to help Zach search for a while before nightfall. Despite the fact that the storm was getting closer, maybe they could even continue looking after dark.

The entry to the Leigh camp looked like a gated ranch from out west. Two slash pines, straight and thick as telephone poles, made the vertical sides of an entrance. A horizontal bar ran across the top, and from that hung a wooden sign, now swaying in the wind, that read TALLY-HO ACRES, K. LEIGH, OWNER. A gate, made to be moved by hand, stood open, so either the Leighs were very trusting or Victoria was still here and had entered in a hurry.

Land Posted and Keep Out signs appeared at regular intervals as Julie drove into the acreage. A rambling lodge appeared through the trees. Rustic but hardly primitive, it seemed to blend with the pines and cypress. It looked totally masculine, but Julie recalled Ken had said he'd built his wife a beautiful bedroom here.

"Thank you, Lord," she said with a sigh of relief when she saw a low-slung, bright yellow sports car parked near what looked like the front door. Victoria was still here. Surely, she would help her either indirectly with information about Ken or directly, by contacting her husband so Julie could question him.

She got out and hurried to the front door, which opened onto an overhanging, elevated porch. Whether the raised area was to keep water or critters out, she wasn't sure. The metal-slatted storm shutters were down on all the windows, making the place look sealed tight.

Yet the heavy wooden front door was open, even if the screen door was closed. Air swept past her down a central hall as if it were a wind tunnel. She saw no doorbell, so she shouted, "Mrs. Leigh? It's Julia Minton from Osprey Lodge on Osprey Island! Could I speak to you for a minute?"

Nothing. She cupped her hands around her mouth. "Mrs. Leigh?"

Ken had said Victoria would be closing up and heading out. Maybe she was inside and couldn't hear with the rising wind, or was tending to the shutters on the other side of the house. Julie could hear a radio or TV voice droning on, so that might be why she couldn't hear. Or the woman might have stepped out the back door. Should she go around or go in?

"Hello! Is anyone here?"

Julie pulled the handle of the screen door. Not locked. She opened it and stuck her head in. "Mrs. Leigh? I'm a friend of your husband's! He mentioned you'd be here!"

A large-screen TV was tuned to the cable weather channel. It displayed graphics and maps of the storm, which looked like a big bull's-eye dragging a scarlet-and-neon-yellow puddle with it, moving closer to the outline of the state. Julie's stomach knotted tighter, but she went farther into the large, high-ceilinged great room.

It should have been dark in here from the closed shutters, but recessed ceiling lights were lit throughout. What if Victoria had hurt herself trying to close things up?

The interior was stunning, with large leather couches and gnarled pine pieces. Ceilings, walls and floors flaunted cypress wood, so the lodge would probably stand sturdy in the storm. The walls were heavily hung with the heads of what must be local game Ken had killed. Antlered stags mostly, looking wide-eyed or startled. A wild boar, so lifelike it could still be slathering and charging, looked down at her from over the brick facade of the raised hearth. Still, she preferred all this to the naked gator skulls and rifles the Malvers men had on their pine and tabby walls.

She gasped as she noted an array of crossbows mounted on the wall behind her, each one in its own glassed and framed case. It was like a minimuseum, with each display labeled. One said, 18th c. Chinese, self-loading, repeating. The next one read, 17 c. Italian for ambushes and vendettas. Another one, Replica, 12th c. Crusader bow, declared by Pope Innocent II in 1139 to be "deathly and hateful to God."

She shuddered and turned away without reading the others. So Ken not only hunted with crossbows, but collected them.

"Mrs. Leigh, are you here?" she called again.

Obviously not, Julie thought, so she must have gone outside. She began to walk the hall, which was lined with woodframed photos of Ken with a crossbow, or maybe with several different ones. In some he was posing in camouflage gear in a covered blind of the same material; in a few others, he was shooting from a platform in a tree.

As she walked swiftly through, she also peeked in the rooms that entered the center hall. They were dark but for the light thrown through their doors from the hall. A spartan man's bedroom, then a very feminine, frilly boudoir that seemed totally out of place. The bed was messed up, as if Victoria couldn't sleep and had tossed and turned. A big bath towel, no, two of them, were dropped by the foot of the bed. She saw two guest rooms, one that had been made into an office, and finally came to a spacious kitchen with huge stainless steel appliances and a large, round wooden table.

On the table lay a gold key ring, loaded with keys, a large

flowered fabric purse, and a pair, no less, of what appeared to be leather driving gloves. Everything looked normal, except that one of four rattan bar stools from the breakfast island lay on its side. And, she noted, a canister holding colored pasta had been tipped and broken, spilling shattered glass and vermicelli out onto the slate counter and into the sink.

Had there been some sort of struggle here? Surely, the wind coming down the hall would not have moved these things like that.

Julie found the back screen door was not only unlocked, but ajar. She went out and scanned the large backyard before the encompassing wall of trees began. This view was more like what she'd expected to find in an Everglades hunting camp, at least beyond the elegant umber tile patio with its carved stone picnic table and matching, built-in barbecue grill.

Past the patio sat a swamp buggy, with its huge balloon tires, which locals used to navigate the marshy Glades, and an airboat on a trailer attached to a truck. She saw several outbuildings, including a thatch-roofed, open-air edifice with posts for support but no walls, what the locals called a *chickee* hut, built in Seminole Indian style.

As Julie got closer, she saw the *chickee* covered a stained, randomly-grooved wooden table. Power saws and knives hung from pegs on the posts. "Ugh," she muttered, realizing this must be where the meat was cut and dressed from the carcasses.

She shuddered again, despite the heat and the warm wind. The tabletop reminded her of the scars some of her counselees would carry for life. Marks like these on Kaylin's arms had first tipped Julie off years ago to the fact that the younger woman might be intentionally harming herself. Yet in contrast to the gruesome table, a chest freezer hummed here merrily.

"Mrs. Leigh!" Julie cried again. She was losing time, she told herself. She'd have to leave. But this had seemed such a logical avenue to pursue. Surely the woman wasn't sitting in her little car behind its tinted windows for some reason— but with the keys and her driving gloves inside the lodge?

Julie turned the corner around the freezer and saw a big kettle with a pile of wood next to it. It looked as if the woodpile had blown over and had bumped the metal bar holding the kettle, for it had fallen too and lay on its side. Farther out, some firewood looked tossed by the wind. Had the wind gusted that hard already? she wondered. Feeling defeated, she turned to hurry back to her car. She'd phone Ken on Kaylin's phone back at the storm shelter. She knew how desperate he'd be when she told him his wife seemed to be missing. Unfortunately for her, Ken would focus on Victoria's disappearance instead of Randi's and Thad's.

Besides, if Ken had been shooting and illegally definning sharks near Fishbait Key, he might be unwilling to admit he'd seen the kids there. Worse, since the shark was definned, Ken must had been there in a boat, not his chopper. And if he'd held back that information from her and Zach while they'd been searching with him, Ken might be dangerous if cornered. Zach had feared the possibility of foul play aimed at harming him. Despite how Ken had helped them search for the kids, could that be a cover for the fact he hated Zach for protecting sharks and might want to hurt him? There might be two reasons Ken Leigh could have taken the kids somewhere—they'd seen him mutilate the shark, and he wanted to get back at Zach or force him to reverse his stand on shark slaughter.

She felt as if she might throw up. Why hadn't she put all these possibilities together before? And would Ken's wife be in on this or not?

But then, protruding from the tumble of kettle, kindling, and larger pieces of wood, Julie saw a limp hand with a gold bangle bracelet. She screamed, pressed both her hands over her mouth and stared, then bent over the exposed arm and to feel for a pulse.

None. The woman was warm but utterly still.

She dropped to her knees, dragging pieces of wood off the body and crying, "Mrs. Leigh! Victoria!"

Faster, faster, Julie heaved pieces away, trying to dig her out, ignoring the splinters and her broken fingernails. She uncovered the woman's head. Pieces of bark were snagged in the long blond hair strewn in a halo on the dark ground. She fumbled for a neck pulse, trying to recall the counting patterns for the new way to do CPR. But the woman was gone...crushed to death? She should try CPR anyway, if she could just get her out from this huge pile, shove off the kettle, and turn her over.

She heard a strange *twang* and felt the wind whistle close by, then a thud.

Julie sucked in a breath and stared agape as an arrow

stuck, shuddering in a large piece of wood she'd just shoved away. Whoever had just fired it certainly wasn't aiming at a woman who was already dead.

10

It's 5:30 p.m., and this is your voice in the storm, Tim Ralston, with you all the way. I know it's been nothing but bad news lately. But since preparation costs about a million dollars per mile of shoreline, we don't exaggerate about the endangered areas. Now for the good side of that. The warnings are given for an area about six times wider than where the storm itself could cause severe destruction. We're going to get hit, but some areas will make it through better than others. The other possible good news of the day is that Dana's trajectory is starting to wobble just a bit, which may keep the height of the surge down. Stay tuned right here for information to ride out the storm, whatever's in store for us.

"Yeah, bud," Zach talked back to the guy on the radio, "but I've got to do more than just ride it out. I've got to find our kids before it hits."

He shook his head at the realization he now considered Randi and Thad as "our kids." And if Julie was part of that *our,* the thought both sobered and scared him, so he forced his attention back to business.

He'd sterilized, stitched and bandaged his cut leg, wrapped a piece of plastic sack around it, then taped down the edges of that in an attempt to keep the saltwater out. He kept it propped up on the seat beside him as he headed back out from Gladesport. As for the jagged cut tearing open again, he couldn't guarantee that it wouldn't any more than the weather guy could promise the brunt of the storm wouldn't hit here.

Zach braced himself from the bounce of the waves as he turned the boat toward the south end of Osprey. He was going to face down Leon and Jake on his way back out to Fishbait Key, maybe even ask for Jake's help to search the area. Leon and Jake had never had a phone—the entire island never had—and even with the advent of cell phones, they'd still refused to get one. Zach didn't like to think it, but if Leon and Jake had only had a way to call for help, Becky might not have drowned. No, that wasn't true. Alcohol and water—lots of both—were a deadly combination.

Zach put in at the same old dock where he and Becky used to sit after dark, making out, then getting in the water naked to escape mosquitoes and cool off—though that actually used to heat both of them up pretty good. Thad had been conceived under that dock one night when Leon and Jake were off catching frogs or gators.

Zach knew he was getting punchy from lack of sleep. Strange to think of Thad being conceived in the shifting water, that same global ocean moved by tides and storms, maybe the same molecules of water his dad and later his best friend had died in. And then for Becky to drown and now Thad to be out there on—please, God, not in—the deep.

Clearly, he saw Garth's face before his eyes, his SEAL dive buddy from the first day of hell week. Despite exhaustion, pain or that damned icy water in training, Garth's grimace always turned to a grin. His dark eyes radiated his love of life.

When the team lost him at sea, they had been forced to break their sacred code of never leaving anyone behind, dead or alive. Black night, those churning propellers where he'd gone into the inky sea, the hostile situation... Without a body or a funeral or memorial, sometimes it seemed Garth wasn't really dead. In his heart and head, Zach still did not want to let Garth be dead!

But Zach was now doubly haunted by the fact he should have shared his best friend's life and loss with Thad. Yeah, Clint aside, Garth had been his best friend ever. Talking about Garth to Thad might have brought them closer, might have let his son understand Zach's black moods when he left the teams. He wished desperately he'd told the boy who hid his video games about duty and honor that he hadn't left the SEALs with duty and honor, but with shame and grief for losing Garth. He didn't want Thad to think he resented coming home to him, when he should have fought on in Garth's name, but with Becky's sudden death he'd had no choice.

Zach sniffed hard and shook his head to stop the flood of memories, but he couldn't hold them back. His father, Garth and Becky, his trio of tragic losses. And now what had seemed like a lot of laughs with Becky years ago only made him sad. If she hadn't been pregnant with Thad, he wouldn't have married her before he went to boot camp. Afterwards, the two of them had changed so much in different ways he doubted if they would have ever made a future together. But, thank God, they had made Thad.

Zach had no more than tied up at the dock and eased his foot off the seat when Jake appeared and Leon wheeled himself outside.

"You ain't found them?" the old man shouted before Zach climbed out of his boat.

"No, but I found their Jet Ski in the water off Fishbait Key."

"Fishbait!" Jake said, facing Zach on the dock as if to block his way in. The waves were hitting the pilings hard enough that the old boards seemed to shudder with each blow. Leon rolled himself close enough to nudge Jake out of his defiant stance.

"Yeah, Fishbait. Thad must have hit that rusted junk old man Crothers dumped in the water, but there was no sign of the kids."

"Damn Crothers's soul to hell," Leon muttered. "The old bastard always was loony."

Zach knew better than to say most locals thought the same of him. "I'm hoping they got thrown clear."

"I'll go back out with you," Jake said. "I been looking since dawn, but not near Fishbait. I just came back to get Pa to a shelter. He won't go."

"Now I got good reason not to," Leon said, pointing a finger at his son. "You and Zach can't spare the time to take me. Get on out and find those kids. Where's Julie Minton?"

"She's checking on her people at a shelter," Zach told him, "but she said she'll come out. So where all did you look?" he asked Jake as the big man bent to untie the ropes holding his twelve-foot fishing boat to the dock.

"In most a the places in the islands or along the shore. Pa took the boy years ago to fill his head with all them old tales 'bout pirate lairs, Calusa shell mounds, and Seminole outposts. Loved that boy, more'n you ever loved anybody, didn't you?" Jake demanded, glaring at his father, his voice almost menacing. "Better'n me 'n' Becky included, so—"

"Jake found nothing," Leon interrupted before Zach could ask, or maybe before Jake could say more.

"I found a For Sale sign on a stretch of beach with that son-of-a-bitch Grant Towers's name on it," Jake said, his voice defiant again. "And a stash of what looked like Clint's illegal lobster traps. And four definned, dead sharks— prob'ly friends a yours."

Zach didn't know whether Jake meant that the men or the sharks were his friends, and he didn't have the time to waste asking or arguing. Right now, protecting sharks was way down on his list.

Besides, he didn't want to rile these two as he had ever since he'd taken Thad to live with him, especially at first when the boy had run back to Osprey more than once to be with his grandfather and uncle because he insisted they let him do anything he wanted.

And he was treading deep water with them because of what he'd really come to ask.

"I'm hoping that someone around Fishbait with a real bad agenda didn't pick the kids up," Zach blurted, looking from one rugged, worried face to the other.

"And not somebody just definning sharks?" Leon asked.

"You askin'," Jake demanded, "if we been running drugs?"

Given how slow on the uptake Jake sometimes seemed, it worried Zach how quickly he came up with that. "I can't leave any stone unturned," Zach explained, staring directly into Jake's eyes as he rose to his full height again. He'd known Jake his whole life and yet he didn't really know the man. Brighter than he seemed, fiercely loyal to his own, he'd never forgiven Zach for reporting for Marine boot camp after he got Becky pregnant, even though he'd married her first. But what Zach couldn't forgive Jake for was the fact that he used to drink too damn much and Becky took it up, too. It had only been her death that had turned Jake stone-cold sober.

"No, we ain't been picking up and passing on for a coupla decades," Leon told him. "Quit when it turned into more than pot and when we found Becky using some of it she snitched on top of the booze."

Zach's mouth dropped open. "She...pot, too? I never knew."

"How the hell could you?" Leon retorted. "Mr. Clean Living, you were off defending the country and saving the world. We never picked us up the hard stuff and passed it on, just marijuana, and she found some, okay? Mother of a child like that should of had her man home with her, not an old coot like me and her hard-drinking brother."

"It's just great you two had both poisons in the house!" Zach exploded. "So maybe she was stoned as well as drunk the night she decided to go for a little swim!"

Jake hit Zach's shoulder with both beefy hands, a quick, hard blow. Zach staggered back a step, then stood his ground again, fists clenched at his sides, ready to lunge.

"Cut it, both a you!" Leon roared. "I'm just telling you we don't know who's running it now, but it's a hell of a lot more than a little pot. It's the big, hard stuff."

Keeping an eye on Jake, Zach asked, "Are you sure you don't know who inherited your job? What about Clint and the guys who've lost so much money when the fishing laws changed?"

"Possible," Leon said, stroking his beard, as Jake turned away and went back to untying his boat. "Or that Britisher who took such a hit when the shark fins got to be taboo. He's got him boats and an airplane to fish plastic wrapped packages out of the drink. Don't know, though, do we Jake? Might as well be you, Zach, making big donations of dough as well as your time to save the damn sharks."

"But it isn't me, Leon. Jake, you still willing to go out and help me look?"

"For Thad, sure—and the Minton girl. She's kind of a loner, goes off by herself when the other girls are busy."

Zach frowned at him, but didn't ask how he knew that or why that seemed to make Jake care about her in some unspoken way. Trying to watch his cut leg, he got back in his boat and untied it.

"Leon," he called to his former father-in-law, "if the hurricane heads for here, Jake will be back in to take you to a shelter, and you *will* go."

"Naw," he said, wheeling his chair backwards up the dock without even looking behind him. "I'll go down with the ship. I ain't leaving of my own accord, not Jake's nor yours neither."

"Thad will be really upset if he hears I let his only grandfather, one he loves a lot, drown in a storm surge or get blown away," Zach called to the old man. He hoped it would be some concession to Becky's father that he wanted him to live—like he'd wanted her to.

"Let's go!" Jake said and started his motor.

Zach nodded and stepped toward the stern to sit by the motor. As Jake went past, he noticed that he had a big net and a rifle covered in clear plastic in the bottom of his boat.

On all fours, Julie scrambled away from Victoria's body, then broke into a run for the freezer. An arrow skidded along the scrub grass as she ran for cover. Panting from fear as much as from exertion, hunched down, she pressed her back to the humming freezer.

It seemed the arrows had come from the sky. And each one had been preceded by the distinct *twang* before it hit.

She recalled the photograph inside the lodge of Ken shooting from a camouflaged blind up a tree. But he was across the state, wasn't he?

Julie's thoughts scattered when the awful sound of the bow spit out another arrow, which bounced off the freezer inches from her head. Could there be more than one bowman, or was the hunter on the move? She had found Victoria dead in an apparently staged scene, with a woodpile and kettle blown over before there had been much wind. Perhaps the woman's killer now knew he had to kill again. A killer who knew how to shoot a crossbow and was adept at hunting with it.

She only prayed that if Victoria had paid the price for being an unfaithful wife, she hadn't been cheating with Zach Brockman.

Keeping as low as she could, Julie ran, zigzagging toward the edge of the clearing. She had to get into the trees, circle around to her car. If she tried to make it into the lodge, he could trap her there. But if she could work her way back toward the front of the lodge, she could crawl to her car and go for help.

Never had she been angrier at herself than when she realized she could have stopped at the high school for Kaylin's cell phone. But, even if she had a phone and called 911, who would come? The police were all out on special assignments. And forget her first thought about phoning Ken Leigh to tell him of his wife's death. Didn't these arrows prove he was her killer? If he'd killed once, he surely would again. Who knew that Victoria wasn't stuck full of arrows under the pile of debris no storm had put there.

Julie made it into the thick foliage as another arrow thumped into a tree trunk. Her feet were instantly wet, but she had no intention of taking off her running shoes, even if they felt filled with cement in this murky bottom she stirred up. No way was she going to chance cutting herself the way Zach had or stepping barefooted on a water snake. One of the girls had asked Liz Lawson about poisonous ones in this area, and she'd mentioned cottonmouths and coral snakes. This was like living a nightmare, where she wanted to run but her feet wouldn't move.

The tea-colored water here was only knee-deep, but it made soft, slopping sounds each time she took a laborious step, stirring up the silt. Fallen limbs she nearly stumbled over impeded her path. She pressed herself behind the widest slash pine she could find and held her breath to listen for pursuit. The loudest sound, one which drowned all others, was her heart, nearly beating out of her chest.

And then another noise. Something—someone—sloshing through the shallows? And then another *twang-thud* as an arrow hit the tree next to her. Was the hunter a bad shot, or just trying to scare her? Or was he or she playing with her, taunting her? It must be difficult to carry and aim a cross-bow in these thickets of trees and brush.

Trying to keep tree trunks behind her, avoiding making too much noise so the hunter could track her, she slogged deeper into the stand of trees. She wanted to look back, but she had to keep going, zigzagging but trying to keep her directions straight so she could get back to her car. She recalled a novel she'd read once, a thriller, where a madman kidnapped people, then turned them loose on his hunting grounds as human game. Dear God, why did she have to think of that now?

She plodded into a clump of cypress trees with their rugged trunks and bumpy growths. The ground cover was thicker here, too. Which way? Which way to go?

She almost screamed as something rose before her in a stretch of shadow—no, just flapping wings. Deep in the thatch, she'd flushed a sandhill crane, which moved just a short distance to another fallen cypress log, scolding her with its mournful "woo, woo, woo."

She wished he'd shut up, or he'd give her position away. But the fact he was here meant all the wildlife hadn't fled the approaching storm. What if a panther or bear were in here, the kind that were mounted inside the lodge? Where had those animals been when they were shot by Ken's arrows?

She froze where she was again, listening for human sounds, for more arrows. The fronds and leaves shuddered in the rising breeze as if the entire swamp were breathing. Huddled against the arthritic-looking limbs of a slash pine, straining to hear, she tried to take deep, quiet breaths.

Nothing now but the trees shaken by the wind. Nothing but her own panting and her thudding pulse, shaken by her flight and her fear.

She dared to peek around the trunk of the sturdy pine. Though the sun had been eaten by the clouds, fitful shadows darted through this Everglades forest. More than once she thought she heard or sensed a person moving, her pursuer, probably Ken Leigh. If she edged her way out of cover, would he be waiting for her in the open?

Continually praying there were no snakes or gators, she dragged her feet through the water, heading for what she was sure was the road into the lodge. Eventually, exhausted, dripping wet from water and sweat, she made it back to dry ground. Her white running shoes looked stained dark brown and oozed muck. If she had to, she could hike out, walk back to the high school, but she'd be totally vulnerable on the road with no one on it but perhaps the hunter, tracking her. And it would take too much time. There was so little time before the storm, so little time to find Randi—to escape death herself.

She wished she hadn't separated from Zach, that she had trusted him and stuck tight. Surely SEALs had skills for self-defense if they were stalked. Until it got dark, she might not be safe even running for her car, but she had to see Kaylin, call the police about Victoria, then get back out to Fishbait and Zach.

When she finally worked her way toward the lodge, close enough to see the clearing, the place looked silent and deserted. She couldn't tell from here if Victoria still lay half buried under the debris, but she had a theory about her death now. Someone was gambling everything on the storm coming through to take the blame for murder.

In thick foliage, Julie parted the palmetto fronds. This was the closest she could get to her car, leaving her exposed the shortest distance. How far did arrows shoot? The rifle and high-powered scope she'd seen mounted on the crossbow in the back of Ken's chopper looked very forceful.

Dear Lord, she prayed, *please let me make it to my car. Please let me get help from Zach and find Randi.*

She steeled herself. If she was shot by an arrow, she would just keep going, get to the car, drive away to the storm shelter. Kaylin would be there, and maybe medical or police help, too.

Amazed she still had her purse over her shoulder, she fumbled in it to take out her keys. She was shaking so hard they jingled.

Holding her door key in her hand, ready to stick in the lock, she rehearsed it all in her mind. Run, keep low, turn key, yank handle, dive in, lock door.

Every fiber of her being ached as if she'd already been shot. Expecting to be a target, holding her purse over her heart for some protection, she ran in squishing shoes and threw herself against the car. The key didn't go in the door lock at first, but then slipped in, turned. She bent so low when she pulled the door open that she almost hit her head on the lower corner of it.

Throwing herself in, gasping for breath, she slammed the door and locked it. Her fears the car might have been disabled dissolved as the motor roared to life. She was so crazed to get away she forgot which gear was forward and jerked backwards until she hit the brake. She pulled away, U-turning on the lawn, squealing the wheels, still expecting a bowman to leap from the trees to rain arrows on the metal skin of the car.

The dirt road out of the hunt camp, then the two-lane road into town blurred by. Safe. She was safe for now, but what about Thad and Randi?

11

Tim Ralston here at 6:15 p.m., tracking this potentially devastating storm. Hurricane Dana, currently a Category Two with sustained winds of 110 mph with gusts to 125, at 28.32 barometric pressure inches and 922 millibars, could hit southwest Florida approximately at dawn tomorrow. I repeat, could hit, if she takes a turn to the east. Her current rate of speed is six miles per hour, but she's still on an erratic course, so we can't yet pinpoint where or when she will make landfall. Some storms are huge, slow and sloppy. Dana's getting smaller, but that means, unfortunately, she's stronger and meaner.

Zach was more panicked than ever. Not only could he and Jake find no sign of Thad and Randi on the keys closest to Fishbait, but Liz Lawson and Nate Tomzak had just arrived in separate boats to say they'd been searching nearby and had seen no signs of them. Still the four separate crafts fanned out, going along at trolling speed, sometimes crisscrossing routes while scouting for signs of human life and shouting for the kids.

Just when Zach thought he couldn't feel worse, he tried to reach Julie on Kaylin's cell phone. He wanted to encourage Julie that he had help, but also to tell her he'd thought of something she could do without having to buck the weather in her small craft to come back out here. Seeing these boats passing back and forth had reminded him of something that might provide a way to identify a boat which had possibly picked up Thad and Randi.

"Oh, hi, Zach," Kaylin said when she answered his call. "Julie? No, I haven't seen her since she left to go up in Ken Leigh's helicopter with you early this morning."

His stomach went into free fall. Ignoring the pain on his cut leg, he sat down hard in his boat, rocking it even more than the mounting waves did. He put his head in his hands. Not only was he worried about what had happened to Julie, but it stunned him how much it mattered. Julie of the arrogant, condescending Whites of Osprey Island, the people who'd made him, his family and friends seem cheap and unworthy of treading the same ground. Damn, but he was coming to care desperately about her, maybe even care *for* her. Even in the blackness of despair, how could needing her have happened so fierce and so fast?

"Zach, are you still there?" Kaylin's voice came from what seemed a great distance. "Did you hear me?"

He pressed the small phone harder to his ear. "She should have been there by now," was all he could manage at first.

"She must have been delayed."

"I can't trace her right now, because she lost her cell phone in the water. It's getting windier and darker, so I've got to keep searching out here. What's it like at the shelter?"

"Growing stress and pressure issues for everyone."

Ordinarily, it would have amused him how much Julie and Kaylin talked in what he was coming to think of as guidance-counselor-speak. Then again, he knew damn well he still thought and dreamed in SEAL lingo.

"Lack of personal space puts a premium on self-control," Kaylin went on. "By the way, Loreen was here for a few minutes, waiting for Grant Towers, but she left and then he showed up."

"They're like oil and water. Was she with her kids or Clint?"

"Alone, it looked like."

"And waiting for Grant?"

"He'd evidently set a meeting up with her, but it's not like it sounds. Which reminds me, Loreen implied Grant and Victoria Leigh had something going on the side. Sorry, I don't mean to get into the soap opera stuff with all that's going on. I'll leave that to Grant's other daughter."

"Grace's New York City sister, Ms. Towers knockout blonde the elder. Thad didn't exactly say so, but I'm starting to wonder if Grant didn't threaten him to stay the hell away from Grace."

He squeezed the bridge of his nose, then rubbed his eyes, sore from lack of sleep and stung by salt spray. Maybe Grant was the first person he should question when he gave up the search out here, for it would have to be called off soon. But even if Grant had threatened Thad, surely a guy with his credentials and demeanor wouldn't stoop to actually hurting him.

Yet, as the old saying went, absolute power corrupted absolutely, and Grant Towers was always throwing his wealth and weight around. Zach couldn't dismiss the idea that some local kid hooking up with an upper crust girl soon heading back to her private school might not be just passed off by her father as a summer fling. Zach knew all about raging hormones in paradise and remembered well how Julie's father had ordered him to keep his eyes off his daughter years ago. Storm coming or not, he had to find and confront Grant.

"Did you talk to Grant?" he asked Kaylin. "Did he say anything about Thad?"

"I didn't talk to him. He came in, looking upset—well, who isn't right now?—then practically ran out. I tried to go after him, but he had his car right in front and roared off."

"Who's that I hear crying?"

"Some Hispanic kid. I feel like crying, too, and I'm supposed to be in charge of our girls here, but I keep worrying about Randi and Thad, blaming myself in a way. Secondary stress."

"Don't overanalyze everything. Julie's beating herself up pretty bad, too—we all are. Gotta go, but I'm going to give you my number. I want you to call me the minute you see or hear from her, all right?"

"Sure, but I've been an idiot again. I forgot to bring my cell phone charger, and it's getting low. I'll see if I can borrow one from someone here who has the same kind. Oh, wait—I see her—Julie. Oh, no, she's—just a sec…"

"Kaylin? What?"

But she suddenly wasn't there. Had she punched off? No, she must just not be holding the phone to her ear, because he could still hear that kid crying. Then the line went dead.

* * *

Julie saw Kaylin coming toward her in the crowded gym, arms outstretched to hug her, until she evidently realized Julie looked like she'd crawled out of the swamps, which she had. Her friend's eyes widened as she took in her sopping, dirty and dishevelled state.

"Is it raining outside already?" Kaylin cried. "Are you all right? You look—"

"Like I've been to hell and back."

Cindy and Bree ran up to her, and many others stared. She probably should have dried off and cleaned up, but she had no time left for anything but finding Randi. Still, she had to contact the sheriff about discovering Victoria Leigh's corpse.

"I'm all right," she tried to assure Kaylin, taking her arm and steering her away from the gawkers, though Cindy and Bree kept up with them. "I had to talk to someone about finding Randi and Thad and ran into a problem. Cindy and Bree," she said, turning to them, "I need to talk to Kaylin alone for a minute. Don't forget to keep buddied up, even in here. Where are Jordan and Tiffany?"

"They've been helping in the kitchen," Cindy explained. "We've been hanging out with Kaylin and helping some of the mothers with their kids. You know, so we won't turn scary feelings inward but keep busy," she recited from one of the mantras from their counseling.

"I'm proud of all of you," Julie said, nodding because she couldn't find the stamina or spirit for a smile. She hoped they accepted being so quickly dismissed, because, despite Cindy's usual *brio*, both of them looked shaky.

"Good," she told Kaylin as she tugged her farther away from the noisy gym, "you have your cell phone."

"Oh, my gosh, I should have told you. Zach just phoned, but I think I just accidentally ended the call. He's really worried about you. He said he's out searching with Jake, Liz and Nate. Isn't that great they're helping?"

"I owe them a lot, especially with this storm coming. But what did Zach say? Any sign of the kids?"

"Oh no, he was going to give me his cell number." Kaylin hit her forehead so hard with the palm of her hand that her head jerked back and a red mark suffused her skin there.

"That's all right. I have it, and we'll call him back in a minute, but I need your phone for another call first."

"I'm sorry I'm such a jerk, when I want to help you find Randi so much. I forgot to bring the battery booster, and it's running down. There's some left, but not much. Julie, I'm so sorry to keep letting you down."

Kaylin's voice shook and she looked ready to burst into tears, which didn't help Julie at all. But she couldn't really comfort her friend now, despite the fact her appearance and actions were starting to remind Julie of the scared, guilt-ridden girl Kaylin had been when she first knew her, when she used to blame herself for all the world's woes.

"Come on," Julie said. "Let's find somewhere quiet in here."

Though Julie and Randi had visited this building to register Randi for fall classes a few weeks ago, Julie wasn't sure which hall led where. She took Kaylin around another corner. They walked past an area labeled BAND AND ORCHESTRA, with a hand-printed sign under it that now read Special Needs.

"Special needs," Julie said. "That's all of us right now."

"The few nurses here are in there," Kaylin explained. "There are about six hundred people in this shelter but I heard fifty-five are special needs people, like the elderly, cardiac patients or people on oxygen. They brought some patients or geriatric types in by school bus a while ago. Julie, I've got to tell you something."

"Okay. Go ahead."

"Nate stopped by to see me and asked if we'd thought about the fact Randi could have been abducted for ransom—if we'd found a note or anything."

Julie almost tripped over her own feet. It had been an early fear, but then she'd dismissed it because Thad was along and Randi's joining him on the Jet Ski had been so impulsive.

"No," she told Kaylin. "No note, and I lost my cell phone only a few hours ago, in case someone tried to call. The sheriff asked Zach if we suspected foul play, and he said no, but since the kids seem to have dropped off the face of the earth, I—I guess I should have looked around better for some sort of note."

"Nate said people know Zach's not rich, but they might think you are."

"I'll mention it to Zach again once we stop searching directly for the kids. But if Nate's out there with Zach, he'll probably suggest it to him, too."

Finally, they'd reached a deserted back hall with some semblance of silence. A sign on the door to the nearest classroom was labeled in big print, NURSING MOTHERS ONLY.

"Who did you go to see about Randi that you got so wet and dirty?" Kaylin asked.

"It's a long story, but one I'm going to try to make short for the sheriff."

"The sheriff?"

Instead of elaborating, she took Kaylin's phone, a replica of her own, and glanced at the tiny bars that registered how much stored power was left. One out of four bars, not much.

"Julie," Kaylin blurted so loudly that she jumped, "I'm so, so sorry I put her on that Jet Ski!"

"I know you are. You think I don't feel guilty too, with the things I've learned? That I didn't know my only child as well as I thought? That I probably let her down by being so obsessed with helping other girls? But we've got to put that aside for now and concentrate on finding her and Thad. Only doing something helps. Calm down, okay, because I'm relying on you."

"But—"

"Sh!" she insisted as she punched in 911. Her hands were sore from firewood splinters and her skin was black from the swamp. Still, however grubby she was, she pressed her shoulder against Kaylin's as if to lend her strength she didn't have.

She heard the call go through, then ringing, ringing.

"Hurricane Emergency Management," came a recorded woman's voice which rattled off a series of options including which shelters were open, how to contact medical volunteers, and finally how to contact the police. Julie punched the last choice and, praying the phone didn't die, listened impatiently to a series of opportunities to leave messages for various agencies until she got to the sheriff's so-called emergency mailbox.

"Sheriff, this is Julia Minton. It's about 6:30 p.m., Sunday. I want to report a death—"

She got only that far before Kaylin collapsed, sliding right down the wall, gasping, eyes wide with both hands pressed over her mouth.

"Not Randi or Thad!" she whispered and knelt beside her, even as she kept talking into the phone. "Sheriff, I went to speak to Victoria Leigh about contacting her husband and found her, evidently recently deceased, under a pile of firewood and an iron kettle behind their hunt lodge." She blurted the rest out in a rush. "It looked as if the wind had tumbled all that onto her, but there's really been no big gusts yet and someone shot arrows at me, which you'll find on the grass near the firewood, near the freezer and stuck in several trees in the Glades to the west of their backyard clearing. Someone chased me for a while, but I circled around through the wet Glades area to my car and got out of there. I'm going back out to Fishbait Key to—"

The phone clicked and a voice interrupted, "This is Sheriff Radnor, live and in person, Ms. Minton. I just happened to be here in my office for a few minutes and monitored your call. Are you certain Victoria Leigh is dead?"

"I felt for a wrist and neck pulse before I got shot at."

"What's your current location? I'm going to send an EMR team to the hunt lodge, but I'll pick you up myself to go back out there with me so I can take a statement while this is all fresh in your mind, have you walk me through your discovery of the body, et cetera. You find your kids yet?"

"No, we haven't. And that's why I can't go anywhere with

you now, Sheriff. We're still looking out near Fishbait Key, and I've got to go back."

"Not with this hurricane coming! And if what you're telling me is true, whether we're talking accidental death or possible homicide, I need you with me. If someone shot arrows at you, I want your statement pronto to get a warrant to pick up Ken Leigh. The spouse always needs a good look-see, and it's no secret the guy hunts with a crossbow."

"My thoughts exactly. He told us he was flying his chopper to his home in Miami, so maybe you'll have to contact the authorities there. I never saw him, but the arrows point to him."

She shook her head at the way she'd worded that. She pictured those dreadful arrows that could have killed her, pointing not at her but at Ken. Kaylin was crying openly now, almost hyperventilating. Julie sat on the floor with her arm around her shaking shoulders.

"You're evidently on a cell phone, Ms. Minton," the sheriff said.

"If I'm breaking up, it's because it's almost out of power. Or maybe the rising wind is shaking the communication tower."

"No, I can tell you're on a cell because the system isn't tracing your call, but you're right. If this storm hits here, we could even lose cell phone communication, so give me your location immediately, and I'll be right there."

"I can't," she insisted. "I'll help later, but I don't have much time left to look for Randi and Thad before it's dark or the storm…"

The phone played the warning notes that indicated little time was left before the battery died. She had to phone Zach, tell him what had happened and that she'd be right out.

"I'm sorry," she told the sheriff, then repeated, "I'll help later, after I find the kids."

"Listen to me, Ms. Minton. I am ordering you to give me your location immediately so th—"

Biting her lower lip hard, Julie punched off and, from memory, hit the numbers Zach had given her for his cell.

"Julie, you wouldn't have been through all this," Kaylin whispered, swiping at her wet cheeks with the palms of her hands, "if I hadn't put Randi on Thad's Jet Ski."

"Kaylin, I forgive you. You did nothing wrong, and I'm sure Randi was thrilled."

"Don't talk about her in the past tense. She's all right, and I've got to help you find her!"

"You've got to stay here and keep the girls calm and safe. Do that for them and me—and Randi," Julie insisted, straining to hear the phone ringing, praying it wouldn't die before she got Zach. If so, she'd have to borrow someone's phone, then get out of here quickly and back to Fishbait before the sheriff came looking for her. For all she knew, he might try to detain or arrest her for refusing to cooperate.

"Julie?" Zach's deep voice came through the phone.

"Zach, yes, I'm all right. I'm ready to head back out. Was there something else besides the fact you've got help out there? Talk fast, because Kaylin's phone doesn't have much power."

She was dying to tell him what had happened, that she might be on the run from the sheriff now, but she heard another trill of music that meant the cell phone was going to shut off.

"I want you to go by *The Hooyah!,* get my digital camera—it's in the cabin's latched cabinet near where the map was on the wall. Develop the film and print out the pics in it. If you don't have the equipment, go break in my house and use my stuff."

"I can print the photos at the lodge. What's on the camera?"

"The wacko charter I took out fishing yesterday shot a lot of pics of boats in the area. I hope I can spot a boat in a photo that I can identify—or one that doesn't belong, which we can trace. We can blow the prints up tonight and search…"

His voice started to fade.

"I'll do it, then bring them out."

"No, don't come back out here! I'll come to the lodge. I can't ask anyone to stay here longer. It's getting too rough, even on the lee side of these keys. We've got to start going at this another way."

He was shouting now, yet he sounded increasingly distant. She heard other voices in the background, also raised. Thank God, Zach had help, but the fact they'd all been searching must mean the kids were not in the area.

"All right!" she said, shouting herself. "See you at the lodge with those pictures. I have a lot to tell you…"

The phone went silent, but she'd been expecting that. It had held on long enough, and that's what they all had to do— hang on long enough to trace their kids. That might mean playing hide-and-seek with the sheriff now.

"Kaylin, can I take this phone? I lost mine in the water, but I'm going back to the lodge and can recharge it there. The girls have cells here, don't they?"

"Sure. Oh, sure. Take it—anything to help. And I just thought of something else. Loreen was here a while ago."

Julie was already up and moving toward the front door. Kaylin scurried to keep up.

"Looking for Grant Towers, I'll bet."

"How did you know? Anyway, she implied that Grant and this woman you found dead—Victoria—were having an affair. I mean, if her husband did kill her, her cheating on him could be a motive, couldn't it?"

"Yes, and it fits her MO. Listen to me—too much cop TV. And, speaking of which, if the sheriff comes here looking for me, you don't know where I am, okay? Don't lie to him—I've been here or you heard my phone call, but you don't know where I am, because that's the truth. I may not be at the lodge for long, and just pray he doesn't come to get me there."

Strangely, Julie felt a bit better for the first time in aeons. She had been hoping Zach wasn't having an affair with Victoria. Maybe Grant was her lover. With that sexy phone call, Victoria might have been trying to hook Zach on her line, too. But all that had to take a backseat to finding the kids.

"We could ask around and borrow a charger for that phone here before you go." Kaylin's voice interrupted her agonizing at the front door.

"No, no time."

She hugged Kaylin, then pushed her away when she clung. There was no time left to comfort her friend. No time.

After Julie left, Kaylin went into a women's restroom and washed her face with cold water. She could have kicked herself for falling apart in front of Julie when her friend was the one who had so much at stake. And Julie was right: she had to stay strong for the girls, to keep their spirits up. How she wished she could talk to Nate right now, but perhaps he was partly helping to look for Randi because he knew Kaylin blamed herself for the girl's loss.

Kaylin leaned on the sink and stared at herself in the mirror, thinking of all the faces of high school girls that peered in here, worried they looked awkward or ugly, worried about an exam, that their families were falling apart, or that some boy didn't like them, or that they weren't worth anything to anyone. That's how Kaylin had felt in high school, and it had helped so to punish herself for that.

She'd thought she was far beyond that now, but lately those feelings had been pulling at her for the first time in years, tugging like that ebb tide she'd swum through with Nate. Even after all the help she'd had from counselors, especially Julie, her studies of aberrant behavior, then helping others, since Randi had been lost, the hopeless, hurting feelings had returned. If Randi was never found, she not only deserved to cut herself but to kill herself.

"No," she said so loud her voice echoed in the large, empty room. "Stop it!"

Too late, she heard the door open and Susan Parker, the phys ed teacher, came in.

"Did I heard you say 'Stop it'?" she asked. "Is anyone in here?" she went on, glancing around. "You sure you're okay?"

"Just trying to buck myself up, that's all," Kaylin said and headed for the door.

"Listen, we're all scared. You're trying to keep your spirits up for your kids, aren't you? Me, too. I've got more than one student here I'm trying to put on a good face for. They think I'm fearless, but I'm from Indiana, where we don't do hurricanes, just twisters—though those used to scare me, too."

"I can believe it. Thanks for sharing," Kaylin said, still moving toward the door. She could have kicked herself for cutting the woman off and sounding so fakey when she was just trying to help, but nothing helped right now.

Smoothing her hair, Kaylin went out to find her charges. She walked by the cafeteria, where many refugees had congregated, some eating, some playing cards or just sitting around talking. In the background, more than one radio droned, tuned to the channel with the local weatherman everyone was listening to as if he were a voice from God.

She scanned the area for Tiffany and Jordan, then spotted them behind the long row of serving tables, set up like a buffet line. Tiffany was pouring drinks, and Jordan was cutting sandwiches in half, then putting them on a tray.

Kaylin went behind the serving line and tapped Jordan on the shoulder. The girl's elfin face lit to see her.

"Kaylin, how's it going? Hey, what's that black, splotchy stuff on your shirt? I mean, it looks gross, like blood or something."

"Julie was here. She's dirty from looking for Randi, and I hugged her."

"Bummer, I mean that Randi's still missing. I'll bet Julie's frantic. You, too."

"Yes, but we all need to keep focused and controlled,

right? You two are doing a great job here. I'm proud of you. Need some help?"

"Okay. You could cut these, and I'll go back to spreading PB and J on bread for the kids. Mac and cheese, PB and J, that's all some of these little ones want."

Grateful to be doing something to help someone again, Kaylin bent over her task. But when the sandwiches were all cut in neat triangular halves, she couldn't stop herself from pocketing the six-inch, serrated knife.

The stiffening wind buffeted Julie as she parked her car behind the marina, then ran around the boarded-up building toward the dock. As she rushed toward Zach's fishing boat, she saw Cliff had taken his somewhere. Maybe he was still out searching for the kids. Halfway down the dock, she realized that Zach's *The Hooyah!,* tethered to the dock like a bucking bronco, would not be easy to board. And it was prematurely dark, with no sunset in sight and clumps of clouds scudding overhead. She needed to turn a radio back on. Had the hurricane taken that turn to the right the weatherman had warned about?

She stared at the rising and falling deck of Zach's boat so she could time her leap onto it. The big craft pulled at the groaning mooring lines with which he'd triple-tied it. Wind whistled through the rigging of several nearby sailboats which were still tethered here, too. Everything seemed to be creaking and straining against the wind and water. She'd have to be very careful jumping on the boat, because she could be easily crushed between the thrust of the heavy hull and the big dock pilings.

She backed up a few steps to take a running leap onto Zach's fishing boat. But before she could jump, something caught her eye and she stumbled to a halt in half-stride.

12

Tim Ralston here at 7:00 p.m. with my eye on the eye of the storm. As for Dana's eye, it's currently eight to ten miles across. Remember, if she targets our coastline, there are two parts to this potentially devastating storm. When the eye goes over, you may even see blue sky, but on the back side of a hurricane, the winds can be worse yet. Unfortunately, Dana is almost a Cat Three and has stopped wavering, though she hasn't made a turn yet. Let's pray that she doesn't.

From the corner of her eye, Julie saw a strange white form fly at her down the dock. She almost screamed before she realized it was a person with loose white clothes flapping in the wind, not flying but running out on the dock toward her. Liz Lawson, alone, buffeted but yet reveling in the elements.

"Liz! You scared me to death! I thought you were out helping Zach."

"I was, but conditions are deteriorating! I just stopped here to see if there's anything I can do to help you before I head back to the compound to tie my boat up with the others. We've got a big old boathouse there that may lend some protection for our ragged little fleet. I'm just hoping the manatees we've been counting, not to mention the dolphins and other wildlife we try to protect, are going to get through this blow—and that we locate your kids."

"How did you know I'd be here?"

"I was close to Zach's boat when he was yelling at you on the phone to get his camera. I had no idea *when* you'd be here, but I thought I might catch you. I didn't have time to check at Osprey Island, if we're going to get these eco-boats back and stowed. The weather guy still says he's not sure, but I can smell that the storm's coming in here."

"You have a sort of sixth sense?" Julie asked as she again eyed the up-down of Zach's boat. She wasn't going to try for the ladder or the railing but leap onto the open back deck.

"Not like the dolphins seem to. I swear they have their own version of ESP to avoid boats that could harm them. Most of us are like the poor, lumbering manatees Nate and I try to protect with our Manatee Guard Protection Program. But I do feel a part of all nature," Liz admitted, thrusting out her arms as if to embrace the wind, "even when she turns terrible and violent, even when she must hurt her own."

Though Julie was almost ready to jump aboard, she turned to look at Liz. Sometimes she sounded so eccentric, but she looked magnificent and mighty with her pale, silvered hair blowing back from her face and her loose clothes flapping— not the Glades ghost, but a goddess with wings.

The vision passed quickly as Liz stooped to grab one of the mooring ropes and pulled back on it with all her weight.

"I can hold it a bit steadier for you," she shouted. "Get ready to jump! Now!"

Julie saw she was right, and, with a two-step run and a leap, landed on the deck feetfirst before she fell to all fours. She thought at first Liz might follow, but she stood, evidently waiting to help her off, with her face turned up to the sky again.

Surprised that Zach had not locked the door to the galley area—though most things weren't under lock and key in Gladesport—Julie went in where she'd retrieved the marine map. In fading light, looked in the latched cabinet he'd described. Yes, the camera was there. She took it, then looked through the drawers in the galley until she found a plastic Ziploc sandwich bag, with which she protected the camera. She wedged that in the top of her bra, held tight by a strap to leave her hands free, then closed the door to run out on the deck. Liz was waiting for her, pacing.

"Want me to take the camera?" Liz asked, extending an arm. "Then I can hold the rope taut again, or try to."

"Thanks, but I've got it handled!" Julie called as she climbed onto the wide rubber tread of stern rail, holding on to the chrome edge of the elevated captain's cockpit to steady herself. Damn, but this getting off was going to be worse than on. Maybe she should give Liz the camera, but she was bending over the main mooring line to try to steady it again.

When the deck rose close to the dock, Julie vaulted off, nearly sprawling, but the camera stayed secured.

"Where'd you put it?" Liz asked, then added, hands on hips, "What happened to your clothes and shoes?"

"Glades water. I fell in. Liz, thanks for everything. I'll see you later."

She pushed past Liz on the dock, for she didn't look inclined to move at first. But to Julie's surprise, the older woman kept up with her.

"If the weather maven says the hurricane's coming here," Liz said, "Nate and I have more injured animals to move from the compound. If not, we may ride it out, but don't think I won't be concerned about Randi! And if you and Zach can't identify the boats he said are on that film, just call me, because maybe I can help. We spend so much time on the water, I could probably ID boats around here, especially ones the enemies of the environment use. That includes Jake Malvern, Clint Blackwell, Grant Towers, even Ken Leigh! He's got a couple of boats, as well as that helicopter, you know."

Yes, Julie thought, Ken Leigh had all the toys, from swamp buggies to expensive boats. But she'd heard Clint Blackwell liked to race both buggies and boats with his friends from the fishing union and they also hated Zach for standing up for sharks.

Though she didn't break stride, Julie turned to look into Liz's face again. They were both out of breath. Julie felt weak and probably looked pale, but Liz looked radiant, flushed with excitement, or maybe just with awe at the way the natural world she loved faced the threat of this storm.

Afraid the sheriff might come looking for her—though no one in his right mind would want to brave a boat trip to Osprey right now—Julie kept her curtains drawn and her office lights off while she worked by the pale blue light from the screen of her monitor. Without changing clothes or washing more than her hands, she copied the images from Zach's camera into a new folder, then was given a prompt, asking what she wanted to name the photos.

ZACH'S, she typed in and waited for the response. The drop-down menu on the view tab offered her the choice GET IMAGES. She hit that, then waited while the photos came up on the screen, picture after picture of boats in the bay where it met the gulf and then boats heading past the keys toward Gladesport. The images even included one of the sheriff's clearly marked patrol boats, which he or one of his deputies took out into the harbor sometimes.

Her eyes were so strained from fatigue, it seemed as if the boats were actually moving through blue water in the sunny pictures. Get images, she thought. Get images, echoed in her exhausted brain.

She remembered one scene from Randi's ninth birthday as if it were a clear picture appearing before her eyes. Randi's dad had said he'd come, for once, and they'd set a place for him. He was late, with no call to say why. Married, with two kids and his wife almost due to deliver again, he was often busy, but he'd promised Randi he'd come today. The child sat stubbornly at the table, even letting her ice cream melt—Cookies 'N' Cream, her favorite—because she insisted on waiting for him. Later that night, he'd phoned to tell his firstborn that his "third child" had been delivered early, so he'd been busy.

"But," Julie recalled he'd told Randi, "I won't forget your birthday again because I'll always remember my new daughter was born that day."

Julie pictured a later memory of Randi arguing that she

should be allowed to wear her flip-flops to school even in the coldest Michigan weather because all her friends did. When Julie had made her leave the house with something warmer than nearly bare feet, she'd found Randi's shoes and socks stuffed in a snowbank. Worse, the flip-flops she'd fought to wear were ones she hadn't touched in Florida, where they would have been comfortable and appropriate. But, no, they sat enshrined on her dresser in her bedroom, as if they were Dorothy's red sequined slippers from the land of Oz, which could take her home again.

Julie realized she was crying and wiped tears from her cheeks with the heels of her hands. The red sequined flower from Randi's shirt—and those ratty flip-flops—she'd treasure such things if she never got her daughter back. And those haunting thoughts and the poem of *Randi's Ramblings* in her diary online for all to read: *Sad if broken memories are the best...I had...* Breaking her heart, those painful lines scrolled through Julie's brain.

She jerked alert again as the images stopped scrolling onto the screen. There were sixteen of them. Praying Zach would be able to make something out of these, she began to print them out, wondering if he would want any particular ones enlarged. Images...images of a boat that might have taken Randi and Thad away.

Over the gentle chugging of the printer, she was certain she heard another sound, a strange one she could not place.

Downstairs? It was dark and desolate in that closed-up tomb. Yet she was sure it had not been an outside sound, not the palm fronds against the windows as they thrashed and rustled, not the wind making even this sturdy old place creak.

She tiptoed to the door of her office, then stepped into the dark hall and closed the door after her, muting the printer. She strained to hear.

Total darkness. And yes, a creak of a board, as someone moved beneath.

She crouched instinctively, holding onto the banisters under the railing to steady herself. Could the sheriff have come out to Osprey, or sent a deputy? Wouldn't he identify himself, even if he was here to bring in what he might consider a hostile witness?

Maybe Zach was here already, but surely he would call to her and not sneak around in the dark of a boarded-up room filled with piles of furniture.

She held her breath. Someone or something moved below with the slightest sound, like the swish of blue jeans legs brushing together. She could not decide whether to call out or click on the downstairs lights. Would that make her too vulnerable or make the intruder panic and harm her? What if it was Ken Leigh with his crossbow and arrows, come to finish the job of silencing her? She had Kaylin's phone in the office, but she'd only started charging it. Why didn't Zach get here?

A stair creaked directly below her. She knew one sometimes did that at the bottom, and another halfway up. Which was that? And why didn't the intruder have a flashlight? Was he coming up? Could it be someone who knew the interior of the lodge well or just someone brave enough to enter by feeling along in the dark?

She nearly screamed with joy when a sharp rap resounded on her side door downstairs. "Julie! It's Zach. Julie? You in here?"

At first his voice sounded distant, but it grew stronger as he spoke. He must have come inside. But she was certain she had not left the side door unlocked, or the back one either.

She exhaled with relief as she heard whoever was coming up the steps go back down, scrambling, maybe taking two at a time. She jumped to her feet and felt for the light switch.

They had him now, whoever he was!

"Zach! Zach, someone's in here!"

She hit the lights, which momentarily blinded her as she ran to the railing and looked down. But she saw only Zach, who rushed in below and looked up, squinting in the sudden brightness. Somewhere, beyond, a door slammed.

"There was someone here!" Julie shouted again as she tore down the staircase, pointing. "Just now—out the back way, I think."

Zach sprinted toward the back door with her right behind him. In the blowing darkness, fronds and other foliage shifted and shook.

"Stay here," he ordered. "I won't go far."

He headed down the dark path, but soon came back, shaking his head. "He only needs to step off in the palmetto thickets, and I'd never see him. Let's get back inside."

They went in, and he bent to examine the door. "Looks like the key lock's been jimmied—maybe just with a screwdriver, so you must not have had the dead bolt on."

"I have no idea. Kaylin helped me close up. With everything going on, for all I know, we might have left the door open. I should have checked, but I was so intent on getting those photos printed."

He closed the door, shot the dead bolt, and pulled her

close. They clung together in the dim hall, her lips pressed to the taut sinew of his throat. The beard stubble on his cheeks scratched her forehead, but she didn't care. His skin had a salty tang, and he smelled of windy sea. She probably smelled of sweat and swamp, but he held her to him with one big, hard hand in the small of her back and one, tipping her chin up so her wide gaze met his intense, narrowed one.

"We'll find them. Let's get going—on land instead of sea this time."

His dark eyes caught reflected light and seemed to glow. Mesmerized, she nodded. For once, but only for a moment, she felt almost safe, almost happy. It was another precious thing that quickly slipped away as they hurried back upstairs.

"The way that guy ran leads toward Malvers's end of the island," she gasped, out of breath from his touch, more than from running through the lodge.

"I know. You think it was Jake for some reason?"

"No, but I think he watches this place sometimes."

"Yeah, something he said made me think so, too."

"All I know is I was terrified what the intruder might do if I turned the light on and caught him."

"You're sure it's a him?"

"No, but the floorboards creaked under the weight of the person, and they seldom do for the girls or Kaylin and me."

He glanced around her office, then ordered, "Stay put while I look around. I'm starting to think someone may have taken the kids."

"Zach, I can't imagine it's connected, but someone's murdered Victoria Leigh."

He looked as if she'd punched him in the stomach. She

rushed on, "I went there to see if she'd help me contact her husband to ask him a few questions because I found a dead, definned shark on the other side of Fishbait—with the stub of an arrow in it."

His expression crashed from astounded to angry, yet his voice was calm and controlled. "And you just forgot to tell me all that before, after you lectured me on leveling with you in this mess?"

"I'm telling you now," she said, gripping the back of her desk chair. "The thing is, when I found her body at the hunt lodge, someone shot arrows at me, so I think Ken Leigh's to blame, at least for that much. I've reported all that to the sheriff, but I refused to go back to the scene with him or be deposed right now or whatever you call it, so I can't wait around here arguing with you. We have to find the kids and I have to keep from being detained by the sheriff!"

Zach finally closed his mouth.

"Besides," she added, hands on her hips, "you omitted telling me a few things about sharks before. And I'm sorry to say, I think we've moved from that kind to the human kind now."

"I agree. I just can't believe that you…never mind," he muttered, heading for the door again, evidently to search the house for other evidence of the intruder. "Someday, I hope and pray," he added, "we'll have time to discuss your hazardous behavior, maybe while we're babysitting our grandchildren. Right now, we have to keep going, looking, thinking about suspects, and you've added Ken Leigh to the list as well as Grant Towers. I'll be right back."

As he went out, Julie wilted into the chair. Our grandchildren? Well, he certainly didn't mean ones they'd have in common. Still, he had treated her like a partner, not like some out-of-control woman, although she felt like that sometimes. But she'd also, of dire necessity, become cold and calculating about whatever they had to do to find their kids.

She'd expected Zach to explode at her, but their lives had been stripped down to raw essentials. It meant no emotions or energy to comfort Kaylin, no time to argue over mutual disagreements or disappointments. Their own safety was only key because they had to figure out who took or harmed the kids they now had in common—and before this hell of a hurricane took a turn for the worse.

After Zach had checked the lodge, while he hunched over her computer screen, enlarging some of the boat photos, Julie took a lightning-fast shower, changed into jeans and a sweatshirt and finally found the strength to go next door into Randi's room. Tonight, Zach had looked in Randi's closet and under her bed, but Julie hadn't been here since she'd read Randi's online diary.

But since Kaylin had asked if Randi could have been abducted, this place needed a closer look.

Images, she thought. Get images of Randi and hold them close. Try to know her now in a way perhaps you never did.

"Hey, there's even one here of the sheriff's patrol boat in the harbor," Zach called from the other room, his deep voice startling her in this realm of adolescent femininity. "You might know he was out there and evidently saw nothing unusual. Julie, you okay in there?"

"More or less. I'm just looking around Randi's room."

"I really lost it, doing the same thing in Thad's."

She felt strangely close to Zach, because he seemed to be so open with her. He'd accepted what she'd done at the hunt lodge and gone on. They shared so much, including an electric-jolt attraction that had nothing to do with their common tragedy. Former SEAL or not, macho boat captain or not, he'd reached out to her and trusted her, and she could not help but respond. She needed him, not just to find Randi but to find herself.

Julie stroked the old, brown plastic flip-flops on Randi's dresser and whispered as if her daughter could hear, "I should have come in here more, but I was trying to give you some space—and I was too damn busy with the others. I'm so sorry, sweetheart."

Her eyes skimmed the cluttered desk with the stacked CDs next to a lava lamp, and the dusty plastic box with her retainer she never wore anymore. As if this were the overflow catch-all place, an eyelash curler and several hairbrushes lay next to a stack of *InStyle* and *Teen People* magazines, last year's issues with their Michigan address.

But for a few shells Randi had picked up on the beach, there was so little of her new life here, so much of the old. A clump of key chains with silly plastic add-ons, photos of friends, a trophy from her eighth-grade lacrosse team Detroit-area championship.

Draped over her mirror, above countless tubes of lip gloss and nail polish, above the bulletin board with stickers and cut-out comics, were the long-deflated silver balloons from the farewell party Randi's friends had given her.

Fighting tears, Julie sank onto the edge of the unmade bed and stared at the array of e-mails, printed out and cropped to fit the bulletin board. She stood and started to read them. Most were from Randi's friends at home, but one was a brief, terse, "Good luck in Florida," from her father, dated earlier this year. A typed message on a big piece of paper Randi had not cut down to fit in the jumble of things was tacked over some of them, right in the center of the board. It had large, bold print and the paper didn't look faded from the sun.

Julie skimmed it. And screamed for Zach.

Zach's first instinct was to rip the ransom note to shreds, but he didn't. He stood, bent close to it beside Julie, and read it several times:

IF YOU WISH TO HAVE YOUR LOST PROPERTY RETURNED, TWO FOR THE PRICE OF ONE, THE CHARGE IS 10 MILLION DOLLARS. THIS IS A PRIVATE SALE. YOU WILL BE CONTACTED LATER ABOUT DELIVERY. MERCHANDISE NOT PAID FOR IS NONRETURNABLE.

"How long could this have been here?" Zach asked. His stomach churned with rage. He flexed his fists, tempted to put them through the wall.

"I don't know," Julie admitted, seizing fistfuls of her hair with her elbows up and out. He was amazed she didn't dissolve in tears, but she went on, "The intruder you scared off could have put it here, for all I know. I just assumed he was only downstairs, but he could have been up here before I heard him. But ten million dollars? Why, that's almost as much as Grant Towers said he'd pay me for..." she got out before she stopped and just stared at him.

"Hold that thought," he said. "Come hell or high water—literally—I'm going to see Grant Towers."

"*We're* going to see Grant Towers. I can tell him I've changed my mind about selling Osprey at the last minute."

"Okay, that may work. You know, one of the boats I was looking at in those pictures could have been his—not the yacht but the cigarette boat he tools around in sometimes."

He didn't tell her that Clint's racing buddy had a boat just like that one. But Clint couldn't have anything to do with hurting Thad, could he? Clint had a son of his own.

"Wouldn't this ransom note too obviously point to Grant?" Julie asked. "If Grant is behind everything, his asking for an amount just under what he offered for Osprey is too blatant and risky. You know," she went on, frowning, wrapping her arms around herself, "I told him the only thing I'd sell the island for was getting my daughter back. Two for the price of one...means Thad's with Randi."

"I may have a duplicate note at home, but a kidnapper would probably know I'd never be able to raise the money, even if the banks weren't all closed. You're right, though," he added as he reread the note yet again. "It too obviously points to Grant, even though we could surmise that he wants Thad out of his daughter's life."

"But she's gone back to college and Thad's still here."

"Right. As for suspecting Ken Leigh, no way he needs money either. But it's cleverly worded, not something Jake would write."

"Jake? He can't be in the mix. But what was that you mentioned about his watching the girls or Randi?"

"He said something about Randi going off alone sometimes while the other girls were busy. I guess, since he's living on the island and goes all over in his boats, that's not a very ominous observation. But he did blurt out to his father that Leon always loved Thad more than he did his own son, so he might have harbored a deep-seated jealousy toward Thad all these years. And what if Thad found out that Jake was still running drugs?"

Julie pressed both palms over her eyes. Her hair stood out in tufts where she'd grabbed it, still damp from her shower. He wanted to hold her again, but he didn't. They had to get going.

"Jake still being into drugs is a big 'if,'" she argued. "But *if* it's true, maybe Jake thought Thad would tell him or the authorities. And if Leon doesn't know, he's about even with what I knew about my daughter. Zach, everyone knew more about Randi's heartaches and needs than I did!"

He grabbed her wrist with one big hand. "I regret mistakes I've made with Thad, too. But despite all the possibilities, I still say we start with Grant Towers."

"All right, if we keep Ken Leigh in mind, not only for Victoria's murder but the kids' abduction," Julie argued, putting her free hand on his arm. "The definned shark, the arrows, and the motive of your ruining his shark fin trade could mean he thought he'd get to you through Thad. And something else."

"What?"

"When I went to your place yesterday morning to see if I could find Randi, I was walking past a window and heard a call come in from Victoria for you. It sounded as if she was really offering herself for more than another deep-sea fishing lesson. Now, I'm not judging that," she said as he pulled away, "but you don't think Ken could believe that she wasn't only cheating on him with Grant but you, too?"

"Let's just say, she tried," he admitted. "She is—was—a good-looking woman and very willing, but that's not the game I play. I'll find my own willing woman," he said, looking directly down into her sea blue eyes.

"I believe you," she said and took a step back, too. "So that means we're going to go for Grant first, and hope the sheriff brings in Ken Leigh. If so, maybe you can get the police to question Ken about his whereabouts when the kids disappeared," she added, pulling a tissue from the box on Randi's dresser. He thought she'd wipe her eyes, but she used it to take down the ransom note without touching it directly.

The woman impressed the hell out of him in more ways than one. She was thinking ahead and acting calmly and coolly, despite her obvious panic, just as he'd been trained to do from BUD/S training hell week and on. He heard again his favorite instructor's voice, finally not screaming at him and his buddies after they'd survived that grueling time: "Things get tough in life, but you've learned to suck it up. This mental and physical agony will be your benchmark for pain, panic, exhaustion, danger."

He'd believed that then. But this nightmare he and Julie were slogging through shrank SEAL hell week down to nothing.

"One more thing about Grant," Julie said. "I'm not defending him, not for the pushy, callous way he's been pressuring me to sell Osprey, but you said one of the boats in the photos might be Grant's cigarette boat. I could testify to the fact that he was in the marina store about the time Randi and

Thad went missing. So doesn't that clear him?" she asked as they hurried back to her office.

"It does sound like the perfect alibi if the mother of one of the victims can vouch for the suspect's whereabouts when the crime was committed, but the time frame may not be that clear-cut." He picked up the stack of photos he'd strewn on the desk to shuffle through them, then looked up at her as she placed the ransom note in a manila envelope.

"Let's go ask where he was before and after the time the kids went out on that Jet Ski," he said. "Hurricane threat or not, we've got to start rattling cages around here, and he's the place to start."

13

Tim Ralston here at 8:30 p.m. Sunday, southwest Florida. This time of year the sun sets at 9:00 p.m., so it would usually be dark in about half an hour, but the outer bands of clouds are making it seem later. We'll get our first rain soon. I'm continually scanning the First Alert Dual Doppler Radar, which shows the storm in real time. I regret to say Dana's veering slightly to the right—not a hard turn yet, so I can't predict landfall time or place. Remember, landfall is technically when the eye of the storm hits land, but we'll see a lot of wind and rain before that. For properties close to the water, the real devastation could be in the storm surge which will be pushed ahead of the eye. Normally, we'd have sunrise at 7:00 tomorrow, but whatever happens, don't plan on much daylight.

As the double darkness of the approaching night and storm raced toward them across the gulf, Julie drove herself and Zach toward Marco Island to confront Grant Towers. Occasional gusts of wind hit the vehicle like a shove from an invisible, giant hand. They'd taken her car, because they didn't want Grant to spot Zach's truck. Since Grant had almost turned violent the last time she'd talked to him, Zach planned to be her covert backup if Grant seemed to know more about the kids' disappearance than he was saying.

Her stomach churning with foreboding, Julie left Kaylin's cell phone recharging in the cigarette lighter but turned off the car radio. No reason to risk running down her car battery, since she had the headlights on and would soon need the windshield wipers. Besides, they wanted silence. Zach dialed Grant's number for her on his cell, then leaned close, holding the phone to her ear and listening intently while she tried to explain why she'd decided to sell Osprey.

"I know it sounds like a sudden change of heart, Grant, but I might need to hire a private detective to find Randi and Thad as soon as the hurricane passes and that could cost big bucks—not to mention the storm damage possibilities. I'd like to seal the deal for Osprey right now, if you can meet me before the storm really hits."

"Sure, that's great, but we'd better meet on the mainland. I've got my boats tied up, and it's getting too rough for me to come to Osprey."

"I'm heading toward Marco right now. Where are you?"

"Checking my last piece of property before I hole up somewhere. I'm at the partly constructed Beach Bay Luxury Condos off Winterberry. Know where I mean? I'm ready to close up the sales office, but I'll be here. Julie, I'm glad you've seen reason and I'm glad the money will help to find Randi. And, like I said, you can build a new state-of-the-art counseling center somewhere safer."

As she ended the call and Zach punched off, she told

him, "He's glad I've seen reason and knows I'll build some-place safer, the big phoney. He thinks he's a brilliant manip-ulator."

"And I think your meeting him on his turf will give him a false sense of security, but I'll be your unseen bodyguard. If he gives you any trouble, it's two against one. But you'll have to get him to step outside so I can keep an eye on you."

"It's going to be pitch-black soon," she said, "so it shouldn't be too hard for you to sneak up on us, like you did that first time I talked to Leon and Jake and that was in broad daylight. I was surprised Grant didn't ask where you were just now, but he saw me alone last time, so he must think we're working independently to find the kids. And since he says he's been checking his properties, I wonder why he was meeting Loreen at the high school earlier. If he thought she or Clint would sell the marina land to him, he's really crazy."

Zach went back to putting new batteries in her flashlight and his. They were trying to plan ahead, for when even nor-mal storms hit this time of year, the area often lost power.

"That new high school storm shelter is close to where you found Victoria," he said. "Grant might have gone to see her at the hunt lodge, since she thought Ken was across the state."

"Then Grant had an argument with her which got out of hand? But the arrows—"

"Yeah, I know, lead to Ken, but I'm not saying she was dead when he left. Maybe Grant met Victoria at the lodge, and Ken saw him leave. I don't know. I told Kaylin not to overanalyze everything, but that's exactly what I'm doing—what we have to do."

He turned on one flashlight to be sure it worked, then started on the other.

"Did Grant sound surprised," he asked, "that you'd changed your mind so fast after telling him off at the high school?"

"If so, he didn't let on. His lust for money and building may make him not only ruthless but nearsighted. As for telling Kaylin not to overanalyze, forget it. That's what she and I do for a living."

With the bright beams on under an increasingly ominous sky, they sped past the Everglades National Park entrance and turned into Everglades City, with its broad streets pompously laid out to resemble those of Paris. Once built to be the capital of the area, the Collier County seat had gone to Naples, and few but tourists and sportsmen passing through had visited here for years. There was not even a traffic light in the place, so they went quickly past the Captain's Table Restaurant where she, Kaylin and Randi had eaten once. Even in normal times, Everglades City looked eerily deserted, like a frontier town when a gang of bank robbers was expected.

As they left the city behind, the headlights of another vehicle came at them. Both cars dimmed their brights, but they could tell a red truck barreled toward them on the two-lane road, the first vehicle they'd seen.

"That looks like Clint's truck," Zach told Julie, leaning forward, his chest and shoulders straining against his seat belt. "He might not spot me in your car, but I'd like to talk to him. Blink your headlights, and I'll hit the horn."

As the vehicles neared, Julie also rolled down her window and waved. The driver hit the brakes as he passed, then backed up. It was Clint, with two kids in the dim car.

"Zach, look!" she cried. "He has a boy and a girl with him! Maybe he found—" she got out before she could say no more.

Her wild hopes were short-lived. Both sets of headlights indirectly illuminated a girl in the back seat who was taller than Randi, with reddish hair frizzed like a Brillo pad. The boy, sitting beside Clint, had his hair buzzed so short he looked bald.

"Hey, any news about your kids?" Clint yelled. With the increasing blasts of the wind, he shouted to be heard.

"We're still looking!" Zach said, leaning over Julie to yell out her window.

"After I searched, I took my fishing boat to Ft. Myers to tie her up in the river. Kids went in my truck to meet me with a buddy I just dropped off, but we're gonna join Loreen to ride it out here."

"Not at your house!"

"Prob'ly the high school shelter. But I got my racing boat and swamp buggy still here, so where should I go looking for your kids, once I get my family stashed?"

"We think someone in a boat must have picked them up from near Fishbait Key," Zach told him. His shoulder pressed hard against Julie's. He was leaning so close over her that the glowing dashboard etched his profile and the sea scent he always emanated made her nostrils flare. His increasingly distinct beard shadow seemed to make a mask on the lower half of his face.

"You know anyone else," Zach went on, "except you and

me on our charters who was out in the bay near Fishbait when they went missing? One of your fishing union buddies, maybe? I've got a photo that shows a boat like your charter close to a cigarette boat in the bay."

"Oh, yeah, I spotted this friend of mine I mentioned, and we tied up for a few minutes, that's all. The fishermen I had onboard didn't mind seeing a great boat heading for Key West for some weekend races. I can try to call my buddy if you want—see if he saw anything fishy, you know what I mean, but he didn't say so, did he, kids?"

If his children said anything or so much as moved a muscle, Julie didn't see or hear it. In the awkward lull, she asked, "Key West is holding boat races on a weekend a huge storm is coming?"

Clint gave an exaggerated shrug. "Prob'ly cancelled by now. Listen, got to get these two safe to their moth—" he got out, before having the decency to look embarrassed he'd put it that way.

"Call me, Zach," he said. "I don't care if Armageddon's coming, I'll go out looking for Thad and the girl again if you give me the say-so."

Without waiting for Zach's reply, Clint hit the gas and tore away.

"What do you think?" she asked as she sped up in the opposite direction. "I'm surprised he didn't ask us where we were going."

"All he wanted to do was get away from us. I guess he could be that nervous over the storm, but he seems like he's running from something. I'm hoping it's only the fact he hasn't really searched that hard for the kids, and he's ashamed."

"Zach, I don't recall a photo of two boats linked up."

"Call it a fishing expedition," he muttered. "I lied to him. But more than once I've seen his Ft. Myers racing and fishing friends tie up to him momentarily. And I've wondered where the fishing union was getting all their money for lawsuits to fight the shark bans in Tallahassee and even D.C."

"Then you do think he might be guilty, that he might even have written us that ransom note, then just pretended he's been out of town?"

"Not exactly. I've been fighting admitting it, but I think he could be running drugs. But no, I can't believe he'd ever do anything to directly harm anyone. Clint's known me all my life and Thad, too."

"But if he's in with drug runners, maybe they're making him do desperate things—or they did it themselves and are just forcing him to keep his mouth shut with threats of exposure or harm to his kids, too, using ours as examples."

"Julie, despite our differences lately, Clint and I have been friends for years, and his boy and Thad have played together…"

His voice trailed off, and Julie heard him sniff hard. She wanted to look at him, to comfort him, but she kept her eyes ahead and both hands on the wheel, because the rain suddenly started, slanting across the road from the direction of the gulf. She turned on her windshield wipers, and they talked louder over the slash-slash, slash-slash.

"But don't you think," she asked, "we'd better keep him as number three on our list, after Grant and Ken? Or maybe number four, after Jake?"

"Clint's acted pretty squirrelly, but he can be that way.

And Jake…I don't think so. Let's just focus on Grant. The thing is, with this rain starting, you're going to look ridiculous if you insist on speaking to Grant in the open. I think we're going to have to take him on together."

"Good," she said, gripping the wheel tighter and squinting at the rain-blurred road ahead. "Good."

Kaylin figured the sheriff was looking for Julie the moment she saw him enter the high school gym. The sudden thudding of rain on the roof made her think of a drum roll to announce his arrival. The Red Cross volunteer he was with pointed to Kaylin, and he headed her way, despite how people he passed tried to stop him to ask questions.

The man was tall and quite thin with a long, somber face, probably in his early forties. Kaylin gripped her hands together so hard her fingers went numb. She almost felt as if she would be—should be—arrested for something. As he came closer, she wondered if he'd be able to spot the knife she had hidden in her pants pocket. No, of course not. Besides, she hadn't done anything wrong, that is, nothing illegal. Oh, yes, she'd done something wrong to hurt Julie and Randi, and she did deserve to be punished for that.

Her initial impression of the man was that he was all gray, as if he'd brought the storm in from outside. He had unsnapped his thin plastic raincoat, but his uniform was the same pale color. Beads of water clung to him and darkened his pants legs beneath where his raincoat reached. His hair was graying at the temples and even his visored hat was covered with a gray, plastic protector. Only his heavy black belt stood out, weighed down with a walkie-talkie, a holstered pistol and several other items she couldn't identify.

"Ms. McKenzie, I'm Sheriff Ray Radnor, looking for your friend and coworker, Julia Minton," he said, touching the brim of his hat. His eyes swept the room, then focused on her again. "She here somewhere?"

Kaylin tried to keep her voice steady. Julie had clearly told her what she could say to help.

"She was, but she's been gone for, oh," she said, looking at her watch, "over two hours."

"And went where?"

"To pick up some things at the lodge. I'm here with the four girls we still have with us. That's all I know—really."

"What's her cell phone number?"

"She lost her phone in the water."

He frowned at that, as if he didn't believe her. "You know why I need to talk to her?" he asked, as Cindy walked up. The sheriff took one look at the girl, then motioned her to step away.

"I assume because she happened to find Mrs. Leigh's body. Sheriff, I just feel terrible for Julie, to stumble on that when her daughter's missing. It's her only child, and you can understand why she's desperate to keep looking for her. I'd give anything to help her—"

"Bet you would," he said, his voice accusing. "You see her, you just tell her that her story doesn't hold water."

"What do you mean?"

"She told me someone shot arrows at her, but there were none around the scene, my deputy says. Not a one. She still with Zach Brockman?"

"I don't know. The last I knew he was out searching the islands for his son and Randi. But as for the arrows, I know Julie wouldn't lie about that—or anything."

"Yeah, well," he said, evidently not listening to her, "I have Zach's cell phone number, so maybe I'll get some straight answers out of him."

With that, he strode away. Everyone watched him, then looked at her. Cindy and Bree came back, then Jordan and Tiffany, to stand in a protective little circle around her, asking if he came to say anything about finding Randi.

Kaylin felt as if she were in the middle of a big, bloody bull's-eye of guilt with everyone knowing she was somehow to blame.

As she spoke calming words to the girls, she put her hand in her pocket and pressed the point of the knife right through the lining until it pricked the skin of her thigh, hard and sharp.

Just as they drove over the bridge onto Marco Island, Zach's cell phone sounded, and they both jumped. His heart started hammering, even harder than it had been.

"I hope Grant isn't cancelling through you because he can't reach me," Julie said as he pulled his phone from its case on his jeans and answered it. "Or else Clint realizes he sounded like a jerk."

Zach pressed his ear to the small phone.

"Zach here."

"And where would that be? Sheriff Radnor here, Zach, looking for Julia Minton. You know where I can find her?"

"I'm sorry, what did you say?" Zach asked, thinking fast

that they dare not bring the sheriff up to speed on what they were doing, and what they suspected of Grant Towers. Not only could they be dead wrong, but even if the sheriff agreed to help them, since they had a ransom note, they didn't need to wait for him or have him crashing in on Grant before they could confront him. Grant would lawyer up and they wouldn't get anywhere. They'd be out of even more time with this storm bearing down. Someone smart enough to mastermind a kidnapping wasn't going to leave fingerprints or DNA on the ransom note to ID himself, so it's possible the sheriff would think they had nothing to point to Grant.

"I can't hear you," Zach said, putting a hand up toward Julie like a traffic cop so she wouldn't blurt something out. "Maybe it's the wind—you're breaking up. Who is this?" he asked again before he punched end, then turned his phone off.

"Sheriff Radnor," he told her, "looking for you and trying to find out where I am. If he figures out what I just did—what we're doing—it'll be both of us he's after."

"At least the officers he would normally contact to look for us aren't on the streets. No one is. Here, is this the turn?"

"That's it, that big skeleton of a building up there."

"Look at the size of that thing. It's huge," she said, craning her neck as she slowly drove closer and it emerged from the gray slant of rain and scudding, low clouds.

"But not as big as the guy's ego."

Julie estimated the high-rise condo was almost twenty stories, and it was not completed yet. Much of the masonry skin was on the steel skeleton already, so it could probably weather a hurricane well. Only the top three floors looked open to the elements. A tall, wooden construction wall surrounded the site, but a tower crane stood close to the building.

The monstrous edifice dwarfed an attractive, lighted sales office where a wooden billboard displayed an artist's color rendition of what the place would look like when it was finished, towering over the beach and water. The painting of Beach Bay Luxury Condominiums rattled against wind gusts.

Ordinarily, Julie would have pulled her umbrella from under the seat, but what was the point? She had no makeup or decent hairstyle to protect, and the umbrella would probably turn inside-out. Like Zach, she got out without protection, then closed and locked her car.

As they ran for the office, she made the mistake of looking up. With the fast-moving clouds overhead, the entire colossal high-rise seemed to lean toward them, ready to topple and crush them.

She gave an involuntary shriek and jumped back.

"What?" Zach said and pulled her to his side then under the small overhang of the sales office.

"Nothing," she admitted with a shiver. "It just seemed for a sec the building was moving."

Grant opened the door before they could knock. "Hey, I didn't know you were both coming. Come on in before you drown in this mess. Any news about the kids? The police in on it yet?"

"They will be soon," Zach said, surprising Julie. She wished they'd planned out better what each of them would say. Was Zach going to tell Grant they had a ransom note?

"I've got to level with you about something," Grant said

as he indicated they should follow him into his office. With a glance at each other, they entered a large room with side windows and doors front and back.

The combination office and display area sported pine-paneled walls. An ecru Berber carpet covered the floor. With vertical blinds drawn back, the two opposite picture windows looked like black mirrors, reflecting their every move. Around the room hung drawings of the future interiors of the condo project. The far end of the room held a sitting area with black leather couches and a small, oval conference table. Grant had a carton on his spacious desk he had evidently been throwing papers into, and Julie saw it held a laptop too. She'd like to get her hands on that, but she glanced back up at Grant and listened in expectation to what he would say.

"I actually thought Thad might have gone to see my daughter, Grace, in Connecticut—she left just after Thad went missing. But then, why would he take Randi with him, I told myself. Grace lives with her mother there—we've been divorced for years—while our other daughter's in New York City."

"Yes," Julie said, amazed at how self-centered this man was. Even with her and Zach's kids missing, the world still revolved around his family, his property. It angered her beyond belief. Whether or not Zach had intended to try to set this guy up, she just couldn't hold back.

"Everyone knows your oldest girl is in *Dangerous Women*, but frankly, Grant," she told him, "that's what I'm becoming, too. Do you know what we're going to have to tell Sheriff Radnor and probably the FBI? That you've offered me twelve million dollars to sell you Osprey and, when I refused, my daughter was abducted for ten million, according to a ransom note we recently received. Now, what a coincidence!"

"What?" he demanded. "A ransom note? Then she and Thad were abducted? But you don't think that I had anything to do wi— You're right, it's a coincidence. I'd never stoop to that. I'm one hell of a lot smarter than th—"

To Julie's astonishment, Zach lost it, too. Calm, controlled Zach Brockman exploded past her at Grant, slamming him back into the wall behind his desk so hard the pictures jumped and shuddered.

"We were going to play a game with you, like you've been playing with us," Zach said, his voice low and menacing, "but we don't have the time, Towers. A big storm's coming that could erase evidence of the crime. Actually, two crimes, counting Victoria Leigh's murder."

Grant's face seemed suddenly wiped of all expression before it registered shock. Julie came closer. Zach had the man pinned against the wall in some sort of hold, with one elbow pressed across his throat.

"Victoria's—dead?" he gasped.

"We know it's a loss to you," Julie put in. "If you think your affair with her was a secret in gossipy Gladesport, you're wrong."

"Dead wrong," Zach muttered. "*Dead* wrong."

The man's eyes filled with tears, but he blinked them back. "But I just saw her today—earlier," he whispered. His voice quivered. "I didn't know—didn't do it. What happened?"

"You tell us what happened to our kids," Zach demanded.

"I swear to God, I don't know!"

"You came by boat to and from the marina about the time they disappeared!" Zach roared.

"So what? I didn't even see your kids. There were lots of boats out, even outsiders around for the Fish Fest."

"And Victoria? You'll be one of the first the cops will look at. For all I know, they're on their way here right now, so maybe we should all just wait for them."

"She was alive when I left her at their hunting place. If anyone hurt her, ask her husband."

Julie said, "We won't have to ask him what the motive was, will we? But let's get back to our kids, and the ransom note the FBI will no doubt link to you."

"You're both crazy! I'm calling a lawyer, so get your hands off me, Brockman!"

Zach released him so quickly, Grant almost fell. But he propped himself back against the wall and cowered there.

"Just tell us anything you know about the kids, and we're out of here," Zach said, stepping back only a few feet. "Otherwise, I'll tie you up and deliver you to Sheriff Radnor myself, hurricane or not."

"I said, I swear I don't know anything. Sure, I want Osprey Island, but I'm not going to hurt anyone to get it. Yeah, I told Thad to keep away from Grace, but she defied me as much as he did. Hell, they're kids. I knew she was going back to school, so I accepted their summer thing, even though I didn't think—"

His voice trailed off. He eyed Zach warily.

"Didn't think my boy was good enough to even look at her, let alone touch her," Zach finished for him, his voice tinged not with anger now but bitterness. He glanced at Julie. She couldn't quite read the look in his narrowed eyes.

"Let's go see the sheriff," he told her. "We have a lot to tell him, and we can't stay here, so—"

A sharp *bang* blasted the air; a side window shattered, spraying glass into the room. Julie screamed, and both men ducked. Zach grabbed her and shoved her flat on the floor, facedown on the far side of the big desk, while Grant dove for the floor behind it.

Zach pressed her down, his body covering hers, but he kept his weight off by both elbows. They breathed raggedly, in unison. Despite what had happened—what *had* happened?—she felt strangely safe.

"Did someone shoot at us?" she asked, her voice muffled against the carpet.

Zach lifted his head to peer over the top of the desk. "That side window broke," he said. "Look. It's boarded up!"

"No, it isn't," Grant said, scrambling away from them, but keeping low. He peered carefully at the window, too. "The promo sign must have blown tight to the window. The highrise glass will take up to 153 mph winds, but not these. Now get out of here, both of you. Go ahead and call the sheriff, because I'm calling my attorney. I'll see you in court, once this storm blows through. Now get out of here!"

Julie could see Zach hesitate. He'd threatened to take Grant to the sheriff, but they were both digging deeper holes for themselves with law enforcement, even though the approaching storm made the sheriff pretty powerless right now.

"Let's go," Zach told her and took her arm to hustle her out of the office. But he turned back at the door and shouted,

"You change your mind and recall something I should know, my cell is 774-3474, Towers!"

Outside, he took her keys and put her in the passenger seat of her car. As he closed her door and walked around to drive, she saw the large sign the wind had evidently loosened which had broken and sealed the window. The painted side was toward them, and one of the outside floodlights, even through the slant of rain, illuminated the words, *Relaxation in Luxury Living*.

She couldn't stop the tears as Zach got in, and drove them away.

14

Hang in there, southwest Florida. At 9:45, this is Tim Ralston, here with you through the night and through the storm. Try to get some sleep, despite the increasing wind and rain, because it looks like Dana might come calling and we'll all need our strength during and after. She is still veering slightly in our direction, but I hold out some hope, since only a sharp right will bring the brunt of everything directly into our listening area. Keep it tuned right here.

"I suppose we'd better at least go ride out the night at the high school shelter," Julie told Zach as she swiped at her tears in the dark before he could see them. The partners of SEALs, she was certain, didn't cry.

"The weather guy said a while ago that the worst can't hit until around dawn. I'm going to take you to the high school, then join you later."

"And go where? I want to stay with you!"

"That's music to my ears, sweetheart, but it's not a good idea. You know what I was thinking back there, when that bastard almost admitted Thad was too low-class for his girl?"

"If you mean you were thinking of us, we weren't ever close to dating back then."

"It scares me how good you're getting at reading my mind." He turned up the windshield wipers one more notch and leaned farther forward, as if that would help him see the road better. "Your father said that to me once, that I was beneath you, that I'd better not so much as put my eyes on you, let alone my hands."

"I can believe that. Even though you only had eyes for Becky then, he'd think the worst of you and want to keep me isolated."

"Who says I only had eyes for her? Maybe he read me right."

Strange, how that thrilled her, even in the midst of this crisis. They had no time for themselves, not until they found their kids.

"I know you detested him," she said, blowing her nose and dabbing at her eyes. "I've got to admit, I did sometimes, too."

"You're kidding. I can never grasp how someone couldn't love their father. I lost mine young, and I would have given *anything* to have him as I grew up. I would have adored him, even if he'd come back from Vietnam a drinker, or the loud-mouth my stepdad turned out to be."

She put her hand on his shoulder, then took it back to wrap her arms around herself in a sudden chill. "When we were home, up north," she told him, "my father's study had a light outside it in the hall, right above the door, as if it were a dark-room. As long I can remember, the rule was when the light was on, I had to stay away, not open the door or knock on it, and I had to stay out of the hall, too, so I wouldn't make noise.

Not that I was allowed to 'bother' him other times either. Of course, Mother would go in and out of that inner sanctum. I'd hear them talking or laughing in there. When he turned the light out, maybe then he had some time for me."

Zach reached over to squeeze her knee, then quickly put both hands back on the steering wheel. The howling wind no longer slanted rain across the road but seemed to throw it at them in giant fistfuls.

He pulled off in front of a deserted restaurant in Everglades City, the Oyster House, right across from the entrance to the National Park. Their headlights lit up the sign in front of the rustic place. It advertised Stone Crab Claws In Season and the wooden tower behind it offered Great Sunsets Over The 10,000 Islands And Photos From This Highest Point In the Glades.

Those rain-blurred words were obliterated by the shadow of Zach's big shoulder as he unsnapped his seat belt and reached for her. She turned sideways within her belt and they held tight over the gearshift console between them. But, somehow, less and less stood between them all the time, with new lessons and new losses binding them.

"And your mother? She didn't tell him he was nuts to do that?" he asked.

"For all I know, she put him up to it. They were terribly in love, and I was just in the way of the greatest marriage of all time. I was like…like," she stammered, glancing at the restaurant sign, "an irritating piece of sand in their oyster, one that never produced a pearl. I don't mean to sound bitter, because I've worked hard to put it behind me, but I'm so mad at the entire world right now—except you."

"We'll find Randi and Thad," he whispered. "The SEALs

leave no one behind, living, or—or not. I swear to you, Julie, we will find them." She started to nod, but, as if to sanction that vow, his mouth descended in the dark.

She opened her lips to his, slanting her head sideways, trying to take from his warmth and his strength, and give him her trust and something like love. His big hand grasped her hip through her wet jeans to partly lift her toward him, pressing her hipbone and thighs against the console. Rain rattled against the car and, for the first time, lightning struck and thunder rumbled to mute the vibration of the engine.

They shifted slightly apart. "It's getting worse," she whispered, out of breath, "the storm."

"But we're getting better," he muttered and set her back to shift the gears to drive again. When she steadied herself from that sudden assault on her senses, she asked, "What are we going to do next? Grant may have been telling the truth, but—"

"I don't know how or how soon, but we've got to ask Clint where his racing boat buddy is holed up for the hurricane. And then, I hate to say it, but we're going to have to get help from Sheriff Radnor so he can question Clint, at least start with the drug running possibility and maybe go from there."

"But if the storm hits here, the sheriff will be too busy, and now with Victoria's death—"

"We've also got circumstantial evidence to link Grant Towers to both of the crimes Sheriff Radnor has on his hands, our missing kids and the dead and probably murdered Mrs. Ken Leigh. We're going to have to use and trust Radnor, until something else turns up, and then—"

His cell phone sounded. "I've got to keep my hands on

the wheel," he said. "Take it out and answer it. If it's the sheriff, tell him we'll meet him at the high school shelter."

Julie wanted to argue they had to keep working on their own, but she knew he was right. They'd run into a dead end. Ken was out of reach right now, Grant was stonewalling anything he knew, and Clint would obviously evade questions. She'd like a chance to question Jake, but he might turn up at the shelter with Leon anyway.

"Zach Brockman's cell phone," she answered, expecting to hear Sheriff Radnor, but hoping Kaylin was calling.

"Julie, it's Grant. You've got to come back. You're the only ones nearby who can get here fast."

"Who?" Zach whispered.

"Grant," she said.

"You called us crazy," she said, "but do you think we're *that* crazy? I suppose you've set some trap for us to—"

"No, I swear to God, that isn't it. I didn't even have time to call my lawyer. Someone's outside with a megaphone—a man—saying I'm going to die for my sins. You two aren't still here, are you?"

"That's not us. We're clear through Everglades City."

"What?" Zach demanded. He slowed down, then pulled off the road again.

"Grant swears that someone's threatening to kill him," she said as Zach grabbed the phone.

"Towers, what?"

Zach frowned as he listened. "That's so lame and bogus, I actually believe you. A man's voice? British accent? You think it's Ken?"

Grant must have shouted into the phone, because despite

the rain, Julie distinctly heard every word he said: "I don't know who it is, but listen!"

Zach listened, then handed the phone to her. The voice was muted, but she heard it: "You are going to die for your sins, old chap."

"Old chap?" Julie said to Zach. "I don't care if the voice sounds British, would Ken say that to a man who's been sleeping with his wife?"

"Ken has a sarcastic streak—a mean sense of humor you didn't see," he said and U-turned so fast Julie bounced against the door. She had to grip the phone hard not to drop it.

"I'm going out the back door," Grant was saying, "and up into the condo building. I've tried to call the police but just got a recording. Julie, tell Zach to come back. It might be your man out there—Ken. You're my last hope."

"We're coming, but since he's out in the storm, can't you hunker down there? It will take us ten minutes or more."

"No. He broke the other window. I don't have a gun here, and I'm scared he's coming in. And with what happened to Victoria…"

"Grant, if it's Ken, watch your back. When I found her body—"

"You did?"

"—someone shot arrows at me."

"Why didn't you tell me? You knew damn well when you were here I didn't kill her, and I swear on my life I didn't so much as see your kids."

"But—"

"Just listen, please! I'm going into the high-rise until you get here. I'll take the buck hoist up and keep it on the top floors where he can't get to me without one hell of a climb. I know my way around there and he doesn't, luckily, because I'm a sitting duck for him here. When I see you below, I'll send the buck hoist down for you."

"What's a buck hoist?" she asked, but the phone had gone dead.

Kaylin settled the four girls in their little area in the gym, playing the card game Fish with some Hispanic kids who spoke almost no English, and set out for the back hall with the restroom she'd been in before. Mostly, women were using the ones closer to the front of the building. If she just hid out for a few minutes in one of the stalls and cut herself a little— maybe on her thigh, where it wouldn't show—it would ease the tension and the shame that were making her heart pound.

But as she walked out of the gym, she heard a familiar voice, raised not in its usual determination, but in anger.

"Why can't I keep them there?" Liz Lawson's voice boomed from the main office where those in charge of the shelter were staying to man the phones and the PA system. A Red Cross worker had just come out of the office, and the door was slowly closing. Through the glass walls, Kaylin could see her in a neon yellow slicker with sopping wet hair, hands on hips, facing down a balding, short man who looked distracted and distressed.

"I can see why you can't keep pets or wildlife in here," Liz went on, "but surely you don't mean I can't put some endangered animals in that concrete bunker used for storage under the football stadium seats, so they can survive this storm!"

When the door swung closed, muting Liz's voice, Kaylin went in the office. She hoped Nate was here, too. The balding man whom Kaylin had seen giving others orders stood with his arms folded over his chest, facing Liz across the tall counter that stretched halfway across the front office. He'd backed up against a desk, looking as if he feared Liz might vault the counter to get to him. Around him, Red Cross volunteers looked up from desks; teachers' mailboxes lined the far wall.

"We don't have authorization to use that area, Ms. Lawson," the man replied. His Adam's apple bobbed when he spoke or swallowed. "And I don't doubt there are things stored in it already."

"Things," Liz repeated, her voice contemptuous. "So you would value things over living creatures. I'd advise, since this may soon well be a life-and-death situation, that you have the courage to make an independent, life-saving decision. Isn't that what your assignment here really entails?"

"But animals, compared to people—"

"These are ill or injured animals my WorldWise ecology protection program has tended and saved. I have four injured birds, an osprey, a Muscovy duck, an immature bald eagle—our national bird, sir, a protected bird for which there are stiff fines and jail time for harming. And a wood stork, and they are definitely endangered. Oh, Kaylin," Liz said, evidently noticing her in the middle of her tirade, "tell this man about the work we do."

"These are extraordinary times," Kaylin said, looking at

him and leaning against the tall counter beside Liz, keeping her voice both controlled and compassionate. "What would be the problem with endangered Florida animals being taken to a safe outer location? I imagine you'd be cheered as a hero once this is all over and media coverage begins."

"Well," the man drawled, "is it only birds, and do you intend to stay with them, Ms. Lawson? We can't have people in an unapproved shelter. I've been sent here to be responsible for people, not for animals," he repeated.

"Then," Liz declared, smacking the palm of her hand on the counter, "*I* will stay in here, and *they* will stay out there, all in their appropriate cages. We have otters and snakes too, as well as a Florida panther still back at our compound, another indigenous animal, totally endangered and—"

"All right!" the man cried, raising both hands as if he were being robbed at gunpoint. "I think I know where those keys are kept, but once you unlock the storage area and secure your critters, you'll need to bring the key back!" Shaking his head, he disappeared into another room.

"Critters," Liz said and sniffed, rolling her eyes. "They were all here before that little man or any of us, and they'd take protective steps on their own if they weren't hurt." She leaned closer to Kaylin and lowered her voice. "Short men have a Napoleon complex, you know. A little power goes straight to their heads to make up for their small stature. I suppose I should have buttered him up like you did, but that's what you psych majors are good at, not tackling or assaulting stupidity head on, which is my preference."

Sometimes, Kaylin thought, Liz Lawson seemed as

strange and exotic as her animals. "Is Nate waiting in the van with the caged birds?" Kaylin asked.

Liz shook her head. "He's still at the compound, trying to batten down the hatches, secure equipment, boats. Kaylin, could you and perhaps your girls help me get the animals safely placed? It's raining cats and dogs."

Liz smiled at that, and Kaylin found herself smiling back.

"Nate will be along soon," Liz promised as she took the key from the annoyed man and hustled Kaylin out of the office.

"I can't take the girls outside," Kaylin told her, "but I'll go out to help you, since Nate isn't here."

"Good," Liz said, giving Kaylin's shoulders a swift hug, "because I want to ask if there have been any new developments finding Randi and Thad since Nate and I helped Zach search. We'd probably upset your charges talking about all that. Can you meet me out in back by the stadium? And be careful, because it's wet and windy already, and the worst hasn't even hit yet."

"Hit *yet?* Did you hear the hurricane is really going to hit here?" Kaylin cried, tugging Liz back as she started away. "People have their radios on in the gym, and neither the news reports or the weatherman said that."

"But we have to be prepared for the worst, don't we?"

Kaylin stuck her hands in her pants pocket and gripped the handle of the knife again. "Yes. Yes, we do."

As distraught as Kaylin was, she realized that Liz had just unwittingly done for her what her and Julie's efforts had hopefully done for their girls this summer. Thanks to Liz, Kaylin now had a project and a purpose, so she wouldn't turn her despair inward.

* * *

Julie's heart nearly beat out of her chest in the twelve minutes it took Zach to drive them back to the Beach Bay Luxury Condos. He parked about half a block away, in case, despite the fact they had both heard the metallic, amplified voice threatening Grant, this was some sort of trap for them.

"Julie, I want you to stay here."

"No way. I'm with you all the way. I've already been shot at, even if it was with arrows, and I'm not sitting here while you might be facing down our two top suspects or find some trace of our children."

He expelled a rush of air through flared nostrils, then nodded. Holding hands, each with a flashlight stuck in the band of their jeans and covered by their shirts, they sloshed through ankle-deep puddles toward the office where they had spoken with Grant less than an hour ago.

Peering from behind the trunk of a thrashing royal palm, they saw the office's front door stood open. Lights shone from inside. There was no one outside and no cars parked anywhere around. Was Grant hunkered down in there or had he fled, going up into the building in something called the buck hoist?

Julie had told Zach that Grant must mean the crane, which was evidently used to hoist materials. Zach had argued they didn't lift people up that way, so Grant must have meant some sort of elevator. Grant had indicated he'd be safe up there, but he'd also said someone could climb to get him. They'd gone back and forth about what to do, but mostly, on their ride back, she and Zach had discussed whether they could be heading into a trap.

"What if he did take the kids and now figures he has to get rid of us, too?" Julie had blurted before she'd realized it sounded as if she thought the kids could be dead.

"But what if he took them and has them stashed on that property?" Zach had countered. "No doubt, he let the workmen leave the high-rise and made it off limits to everyone at least a day or two ago, because of the storm. A partially completed, supposedly empty building would offer a lot of possible places to stash someone until a ransom could be paid."

"And if Grant panicked we're on to him, he could fake that voice to make it sound as if Ken is after him and to blame for Victoria's death, too. They could have some sort of loudspeaker around a work site. Grant might want to either harm us or get rid of the evidence…the kids…"

She could not believe she was saying such things. *Dear God,* she prayed, *please let Randi and Thad be there and let us find them safe and sound.*

Zach jolted her back to the present as he pressed his mouth close to her ear. "At least the rain's letting up a bit. Maybe it's a good sign the hurricane will pass us by. Damn, I wish I had a gun. Let's find the closest entry into the work site and then go not in that one, but the farthest one from the sales office. If Grant or anyone is hoping to stop us or drop something on us, we'll try to fool them."

To fool them. The words revolved in her head. Were they being fools to attempt this? And to rescue the man they were convinced only an hour ago might have abducted their own flesh and blood?

Flesh and blood…the images that phrase evoked terrified her. Randi hated to see blood. As a child, she almost passed out when she so much as cut her finger. She had to lie down and look away when a nurse drew blood or gave her a shot, even if a cotton ball and bandage immediately covered the tiny drop of blood.

"Aren't we going to check the sales office first?" she asked as Zach pulled her away from it.

"No way. It could be like a kill house in there—close quarter fighting, I mean. We're going around and then up."

Gripping Zach's hand even tighter, she sprinted with him through puddles and mud toward the tall, solid wooden fence surrounding the huge structure.

15

Tim Ralston here, at 10:15 p.m., still tracking the storm for you. Don't be fooled by the wind and rain letting up sporadically. We're experiencing the outer bands of deadly Dana. The storm could go up and down in power, but she will continue to strengthen. Listen up, southwest Florida. Hurricane Dana has veered to the right, and that puts her on a trajectory toward our area. Although the brunt of her might is still due around dawn, she's heading for us. I repeat, the hurricane is still about eight hours out, but she is heading for us.

"Actually," Liz told Kaylin as they carried cages into the large concrete-block storage room under the stadium seats, "I may just get Nate, and we can camp out here with my babies."

The gust-driven rain had picked up again, but it calmed quickly at times; if you were leaning into it, you almost fell over. Suddenly Liz cried, "No!" when Kaylin tried to turn the eagle's cage around to get a better grip on it.

Kaylin jumped so she almost dropped the cage.

"*Never* turn a bird of prey away from the wind. They must

always be facing into it," Liz lectured her. "Believe me, even though Liberty is caged, you do *not* want an up-close and personal display of where the saying comes from not to ruffle feathers. He's healing from a broken wing, but he'd probably beat us both black and blue, not to mention his talons. Nothing wrong with those, right, Liberty boy?" she cooed to the bird.

"Sorry," Kaylin said, correcting the way she held the cage. "So," she went on, eager to change the subject, "Nate's coming soon with the bigger animals, like the panther?"

"When he can close up at the compound. I insisted all our interns head inland or back to the university a couple of days ago, so the two of us have to handle things ourselves. I didn't tell little Napoleon inside there," she said with a dip of her head toward the school, "but I'll need at least four strong people to lift the panther's cage in here. Despite its broken foot, we were able to walk him into a cage at the compound, but this weather might make him bolt. Animals know more than we do about what's coming. That's partly how I knew the vengeful goddess they're calling Dana would target our area—the animals told me."

Kaylin shuddered and not from the chill of wind and rain. "I can help lift its cage in here," she offered, "but I can't bring the girls out to help. I won't risk getting them hurt."

Each toting a cage, they went back into the dank-smelling space where Liz had clicked on a bare lightbulb in the ceiling. They'd already shoved straw-stuffed bull's-eye archery targets, a box of arrows, a stack of track hurdles, and two soccer nets off to the side to get more space. They'd checked out a small adjacent room, but it was only about six feet by four and housed the control board for the stadium lights, so, in case any of the fuses popped or blew, they'd decided not to put animals near it.

"It must be really hard on you," Liz said as they went out to the van, "to stay here with those girls when you're dying to be looking for Randi."

"I'm trying to be strong," Kaylin said, "but I'm frantic. I'm the one who put her on that Jet Ski with Thad." She couldn't stop the gush of tears.

"Don't blame yourself," Liz insisted, putting an arm around Kaylin's shoulders and squeezing once before she let go. "You couldn't see the future and you did nothing wrong. You've got to get hold of yourself to protect your girls and help me with these animals who need our help, too. Come on."

"This place does seem sturdy," Kaylin said, sniffling, as they went back into the storage room with mesh cages of small snakes. "How did you ever think to bring the animals here?"

"I just assumed since the school was evidently built well, there must be an outbuilding or two of the same stuff. When I drove up, I saw this and knew I'd better get permission and a key for it."

"The school walls seem safe but that flat metal roof over the gym must be holding water, even if they have drains. And it kind of creaks when the wind gusts."

"Nothing like good concrete or cinder block," Liz said, patting the wall much as she'd been reaching into the cages to pat her animals. "How I wish I had some sort of haven like this for the manatees we've been trying to protect with our new Manatee Guard Protection Program. The most we've been able to do with them is coax them into large holding tanks out in the islands if they're injured or nursing their young."

Kaylin was so impressed with Liz, for reasons that went far beyond her protection of endangered wildlife. No whining, no excuses from her, just boldness and action. She was nurturing, yet a proponent of tough love and high standards. Kaylin wished she could be more like that, not only with others but herself.

"Here," Liz said, after she locked the door, "keep this key in case I somehow miss Nate on the road, and he gets here to put more animals inside. I'll let him know to find you for it, though I bet he'd come looking for you anyway," she said with a soft punch on Kaylin's shoulder.

"Will do," Kaylin promised, trying to sound more upbeat. "And anything else I can do to help, let me know."

"Just don't give that key back to Napoleon until this storm is over and we can retrieve the animals. He's in way over his head, trying to run things. I say he has a Napoleon complex exacerbated by the Peter Principle—you know, people being promoted to their level of incompetency. How's that for psyching him out? Besides, he won't miss the key."

It half annoyed and half amused Kaylin how Liz held grudges, but she was always impressed by the breadth of the woman's knowledge in areas of study not her own. "You're not driving back clear to Goodland, are you?" Kaylin asked her.

"No choice. Get in, and I'll drop you at the front door of the school now that there's room for you in here."

They were both so soaked and windblown they looked like drowned rats, Kaylin thought. And the van smelled of animals, but she was grateful for the sheltered ride back. As Liz fumbled to get the key in the ignition, Kaylin noted the wind was on the rise again, sweeping the rain sideways. Forks of lightning stabbed at the horizon, and the thunder rumbled its pain.

"Can you call Nate while I'm here, to see how he is?" Kaylin asked, but her voice was drowned out when the radio popped on full blast just in time to hear the familiar weatherman's voice.

"…listen up, southwest Florida. Hurricane Dana has taken an even sharper turn to the right, and that puts her on a trajectory toward our area…"

"I knew it!" Liz cried, hitting the steering wheel with both fists.

"But Julie and Zach are still out there somewhere," Kaylin wailed, "maybe Randi and Thad, too."

"Where are they now, Julie and Zach?"

"They didn't want me to know in case the sheriff questioned me. After Julie found Mrs. Leigh's body—"

"What?" Liz cried, twisting toward her and shouting over the radio before she muted it. "Ken Leigh's wife? You mean she's dead? What happened?"

"They're not sure. Julie found her under a pile of wood and a big kettle at their hunt camp. And someone shot arrows at Julie, and chased her."

"But she's safe?" Liz demanded. When Kaylin nodded, she plunged on, "Ken Leigh must have killed his wife and shot arrows at Julie when she stumbled on the scene. I mean, if someone chased her with arrows—she does know he hunts with crossbows?"

"I guess so. The police went out there. It's in their hands now."

"A man who can massacre sharks for their fins, throwing them back into the water alive so their own kind can feed on them, it wouldn't be a big step for someone like that to kill his own wife. But why? Frankly, it makes me fear for my own life. He's out of control, and he hates me with a passion for working so hard to get that shark fin and fishing ban— with Zach Brockman's help."

She shifted the clutch, driving the van slowly toward the school as its lights swam at them through the swirl of wind and rain.

As soon as Zach located the entry into the work site closest to the sales office, he pulled Julie away from it and led her around the circumference of the plywood wall, hoping for a second entrance. There had to be one, because the front entry was too narrow to take large equipment or even the dump trucks that must come in and out here. Someone had to cart out the debris from the Dumpsters at the bottom of the tall trash chutes he could see.

But when he found the entry he wanted, just beyond an empty guardhouse, it was chained and padlocked.

"Think you can squeeze through here under the chain, if I hold the door open?" he asked Julie.

She nodded. If she was crying again, it didn't show because her face was slick with rain. Even so, she looked bold as well as primitively beautiful, especially when distant lightning etched her fine features, so alive with fear but determination, too. For a split second, their gazes snagged and held. Like that crackle of lightning, something raw and elemental leaped between them.

"When I get through, I'll hold it for you," she told him.

"That's my girl—partner," he amended and lifted a quick hand to cup her chin and cheek. "Once we're inside, no talking at first unless absolutely necessary until we're sure no one's waiting there. We'll try hand signals, okay?"

When she nodded, he tugged at the edge of the big plywood door which was evidently opened by hand when trucks or other equipment went in or out. The padlocked chain was just long enough to give them a space to squeeze through, though Julie's full breasts stopped her for a second. In a wet T-shirt contest, he'd vote for her, he thought, then thrust those feelings away for now. If they only had time someday, time together after they found their kids...

She held the crude gate ajar for him, and he shoved and scraped himself through. He kept telling himself that this would be nothing next to the SEAL O-courses he'd banged himself up on years ago. Even now he heard his BUD/S instructor's voice shriek in the wind:

"Get the hell through that obstacle course or your pain will be legendary, Brock—man!"

"Hooyah, Instructor Stenton!"

"Suck it up! You want to earn that bird? Don't let your crewmates pull your weight!"

"Hooyah!" the wind howled.

Was he starting to hallucinate already? This was only his second night without sleep, when he'd been up three nights straight during the grueling exhaustion of hell week before he'd started hearing and seeing things. But this sort of emotional and mental hell was worse…worse…

They slogged into the work site's sopping sand and pressed their backs against the wooden wall. Though nailed to support posts, its sections strained and rattled in the wind. Heavy plastic sheeting flapped in the wind over piles of materials tied down.

Covering his eyes from the rain as if he were staring up into the sun, Zach noted that the condo had fifteen floors so far and was going higher. Lightning flashes revealed that windows were in the first eleven, but the ones above lay open to the elements. And Grant had gone up there for refuge?

Julie tapped him on the arm and mouthed "buck hoist," pointing upward to the crude-looking elevator which was mounted to the side of the building. He wasn't sure, but from here the metal box which took workers up and down looked suspended between the top two floors, with access to neither. Julie shrugged her shoulders, evidently asking him if that was the buck hoist or if they should shout for it as Grant had instructed.

He shook his head, put his mouth to her ear and hissed, "Inside stairs."

Since Grant had mentioned his harasser could climb, Zach was assuming staircases lay within, even if it was too early for interior elevators. Grant had said he'd send the buck hoist down for them, but no way he was trusting that. He supposed such a thing could be made to drop on them, or with them in it. He was unwilling to even trust that the floors it had stopped near were where they'd find Grant, but they would skip the lower levels and start high.

Or, what if Ken Leigh was behind all this and lay in wait for them with a gun or other tricks up his sleeve? Since he'd possibly staged his wife's death and not killed her with arrows, Zach was pretty sure he wouldn't want the evidence of those sticking in any of his victims, except maybe that dead, definned shark Julie had seen. As for Clint being behind any of this, he couldn't believe it. Surely, he couldn't have taken his kids to Loreen and then come back here this quickly, though there were two routes he could have come by.

"Let's go!" he whispered. They ran for the building and pressed against its sturdy white stone wall. Here, at least, the wind and rain seemed lighter.

Once they went inside through what Zach judged was a side entrance, he heard Julie fumble with her flashlight and put out a hand to stay her. Getting right in her face, shaking his head, he pointed to both of his eyes to indicate they should let their eyes adjust to the darkness. It had been gunmetal gray outside, but this was pitch-black, at least at first.

When shapes—support beams, room dividers—emerged in the vast space of the mostly open first floor, Zach pushed Julie to a squatting position behind what must be a long counter in the condo lobby. He held up his finger to indicate "wait here a sec." She nodded.

He easily located the stairs, which were evidently the only thing lit inside this monster edifice. Signs indicated that concrete stairs went up above this lobby level. Gripping the cold metal banister, he strained to listen and heard nothing but rain and wind. Wishing he didn't have Julie with him, he went back to get her and they started up.

His admiration for her grew. She kept up with him and

seemed to sense their need for silence in the echoing cement chamber of the tall stairwell.

When, out of breath, they reached the twelfth floor—he noted the next one was labeled 14, no doubt to avoid unlucky 13—they stopped. The door from the staircase to the building stood open. He motioned for Julie to flatten out against the wall, then ducked inside. This level was one vast area with no room dividers. Its lack of windows made it wet and windy.

Zach shot his big flashlight beam quickly around, shifting his position in case someone had a gun and would pinpoint his light. Empty, deserted. He'd hoped desperately they would find the kids tied up here someplace—and whoever had taken them. He missed the security of his old Sig pistol or, even better, an M-4 rifle. He was dying to shout for Thad and Randi, but they could be gagged or unconscious. He kept quiet, wishing he had a SEAL team or buddy with him instead of a woman he was worried about protecting.

This was taking too much time, but he feared just going to the top floor and somehow getting trapped up there. Besides, Grant or whoever had been after him could escape in that buck hoist or even climb down the ladder attached to the tower crane if he didn't move fast. He had to go up all the way into the higher areas.

But he had another thought. Was this a ploy to lure them into the building, to steal or wreck their car and strand them here with the storm worsening? He wished they hadn't parked so far away, so he could look out at the car, but he'd never get to it in time if it were tampered with or hot-wired and driven off.

Suddenly, he didn't know what he was doing here. He was

getting punchy, too desperate to think straight, but he had to.
Had to…

They huddled along the wall, next to a window opening.
The metal trash chute, about as wide as a barrel, was just past
the window.

His mouth pressed to her ear, his arm went around her to
stop her trembling. He'd seen that before, involuntary shud-
ders from nerves. "Unfortunately, I'm betting," he told her,
"that either Grant or whoever was chasing him is on one of
the top floors. I want you to stay here while I go up to either
surprise him or flush him out and down. If you hear anyone
go down either on the stairs or in that buck hoist, don't let
him see you but wait for me here. Got that?"

"I want to stay with you."

"Stay here where you can see the stairs and that suspended elevator go by outside. I can move faster without you
or worrying about you. I'll pick you up on the way down,
but if I don't, go down the stairs to—"

"I can keep up with you."

"Just do what I say, Julie!"

She glared at him, but nodded. He hugged her hard, and,
keeping low, ran immediately for the stairs, holding a two-
foot piece of board in his right hand as if he were a caveman
instead of a former, highly-trained naval commando.

When Zach disappeared up the dark stairs, Julie almost dry-
heaved from fear. She wanted to flee this colossal stone-and-
steel skeleton, but perhaps it was a safe place to be in the coming
storm—except for the top floors, where Zach was headed. But
was it safe from Grant or whoever had threatened him?

Keeping her flashlight off, hoping she could use it for a weapon if she had to, she sat back on her heels on the concrete floor until her knees hurt and her haunches ached. And then she heard a grating sound—or something sliding. Louder, nearer. With a whoosh of air, discernible even in the wind, something came close, then passed and the sound faded.

Her pulse pounded. What had that been?

The big trash chute the workers used to dump debris was just a few feet behind her. Could something have slid down that or had she heard the wind drag something across the floor in here?

Keeping low the way Zach always did, she crept closer to the trash chute. It dipped past like a giant metal snake, almost touching the building, its wide, dark mouth open to this floor, and no doubt, others. She shone her light into the maw of the chute. Nothing to be seen inside but a dangling rope the workers must use to lower items they didn't want to go down in a free fall. Wet streaks and speckles of something glinted inside the chute. Who knew what they'd dropped down it?

Shuffling carefully to the edge of the building, Julie looked down into the large Dumpster the chute emptied into below. She'd seen at least one other Dumpster; maybe there was one on each side. She didn't bother to shine her feeble light down that far. For the first time, the height got to her. On this twelfth floor, she must be at least a hundred and thirty feet in the air.

Buffeted by the wind slapping around and from the chute, she returned to the spot from which she could see the staircase and the wide opening to a nearby balcony. Thrust out into the black, windy night, it was only a concrete slab floor with crude two-by-four railings the workers must have put up for their own safety. It was near the spot where the buck hoist would pass.

To calm herself, Julie tried visualization, something she used with her clients sometimes. She tried to imagine how lovely the views would be from these lofty balconies, once the place was finished. The azure Gulf of Mexico; the wide strip of sand beneath edged by ribbons of white surf; glitzy Marco Island at its feet; and the 10,000 Islands in the distance as the sun set each night.

"Picture your favorite place," she'd tell the girls. "Isn't it lovely there? Take yourself there for a minute. Doesn't it feel so safe?"

The image shattered, and not only because she dared not close her eyes. She was here, looking for Randi and Thad, without Zach, and scared to death. All she could visualize was darkness and danger and three faces she imagined floating in it, just out of her reach. Randi and Thad, of course, but Zach now, too.

Zach realized he should not have brought Julie back here. They had to follow leads about the kids when they could, but it kept eating at him that Grant would not have been stupid enough to write a ransom note demanding a sum so close to what he'd offered Julie for Osprey Island. Nor, he thought, would Grant risk so much to kidnap the kids.

"Keep your head in the game." He heard the repeated order instructors had shouted at him when he was struggling with training exercises. He'd told himself that on the

pitch-black night they did hydrographic recon of a beach in Oman during Desert Storm. Garth had said that on the stormy night he'd been lost: "Keep your head in the game."

Zach shook his head to clear it. On the fourteenth floor, he decided to go for broke and run clear up to the last open-sided floor, then work his way down. And the moment he reached fifteen—bingo!

He spotted someone across the wide concrete space near the edge of the building, dressed in a shiny, dark-colored slicker with a hood pulled up. Zach didn't even need his flashlight, because a jag of lightning illuminated a man's form and reflected off the dark vinyl from pointed hood to knee-length hem.

Zach's first instinct was to shout Grant's name, but instead, staying in a half crouch, he started for the target. It took him a minute to realize that the man was moving away from him; the flashing sky outlined his shrinking silhouette. It looked as if he intended to hurl himself out a balcony door opening into oblivion.

Suicide? Or was the guy going for the buck hoist?

"Grant? Grant!" Zach shouted, shining his flashlight beam toward the figure. The man's slicker was dark green.

Thunder partly muffled his words, but he was certain the man looked back. Then he kept going. Zach saw that the buck hoist, which had been between two floors, now hung here, blotting out part of the balcony. The guy either intended to jump or take the buck hoist down. Either way, Zach had to stop him.

He sprinted toward the guy but slipped in water and went to his knees, then his open hands, dropping his two-by-four board with a clatter on the concrete. No, he wasn't in water, but something pink. Paint?

In the next flash of lightning, he saw he'd skidded into a puddle of not only rainwater, but blood. Yes, still sticky. Was it warm? He scented deep in his gut that acrid, coppery smell that evoked his worst nightmares of missions long past.

He jumped up, wiping his hands on his jeans, and ran more carefully toward the boxy elevator as the man leaped a few feet from the balcony into its open end. Zach saw now that the buck hoist was a metal enclosure with wire mesh walls. No light came on inside as Zach heard something grind—a lever or shift?

"Grant!" he shouted, but he knew now it wasn't Grant. The peaked hood and dark slicker obscured the height and girth of the man, who kept turned away from him. It could be Ken Leigh, who was stocky and short, but he couldn't tell, not from this angle above, not through the cage as it began its descent.

Standing on the balcony floor in the strong rush of open air, Zach had just an instant to decide. He had to get to that guy, who might be a link not only to Grant's fate but the kids. He'd never catch him by running down inside the building. The top of the buck hoist looked like a solid sheet of metal, impossible to see through from here.

Zach wedged his flashlight against the small of his back in the waistband of his jeans. He stepped over the temporary, low wooden railing to the edge of the windy balcony precipice and jumped for the roof of the moving metal box below.

16

Tim Ralston back with you, at 12:30 a.m. Monday morning. I've just had a couple of hours of shut-eye, the last I'll be seeing for a while, because I'll be riding out Hurricane Dana with you all the way. Now, if you have not evacuated to an approved shelter for some reason, it's almost too late to change your mind, so I want to repeat some advice for getting through this thing. Get to a confined space, if at all possible, one in the center of your house, a place with no windows in case of flying glass or other airborne debris. A bathroom or a closet is usually small, so even if the roof blows off, the walls might offer some protection. Get away from those outside walls. One-story block or masonry buildings stand the best chance of surviving a hurricane intact.

Zach hit the metal top of the buck hoist on all fours, hard. Hoping he hadn't broken his kneecaps, which stung like hell, he immediately flattened out and pulled himself to the edge of the outside of the elevator to try to catch a glimpse of the man inside. But it was obvious that, despite the howl of wind, the guy had heard him. Not only did he not look up, but he began to jerk the controls so that the hoist went up, then down, then up.

He was trying to fling him off, Zach realized, and gripped the edge of the hoist even harder, curling his fingers into the top of the wide metal mesh that made up the cage. His flashlight came out of his jeans where he'd stuck it and rolled over the side to drop away. Something under him was hurting his hip, something sticking into him.

He shifted enough to realize it might be a handle. A handle to lift a hatch into the hoist. Yes, they'd probably have that safety feature in case the hoist malfunctioned and the workers had to escape.

Still trying to stay on, fighting the push of the wind and the hoist's bucking motion, Zach lifted the hatch.

Heavy—very heavy. He grunted and put more into it, praying his efforts wouldn't topple him off if the guy jerked the cage again. He had to kneel to get enough heft to lift it.

The hatch opened slightly. He banged it up and over, where it gave a dull thud rather than the clang he was expecting. As the cage slammed to a stop, Zach gripped the hatch itself to keep from flying off, clawing at the mesh as his torso rolled and his legs dangled over the edge of blackness.

Julie thought she heard the sound again—the rushing sound from the chute—but it must be coming from somewhere else. With the thunder and the thudding of her own heart, she wasn't certain what it was.

And then the square form of the buck hoist dropped into

view. Before she could move toward it, she heard Zach's distant, distressed voice, but from where she couldn't tell. He must be in the hoist.

She shone her flashlight toward it. Dull red metal. It jerked to a stop.

"Zach?" she screamed.

"Julie, look out!"

For what, she wondered, gripping her flashlight so hard her hand and wrist went numb. But then, as the buck hoist swayed to a stop level with this floor, a black form exploded from it at her.

For one instant, she thought it was Zach, running from someone and she turned to run with him. But the person had a pointed head—a hood. She gasped, turned, and tried to train her flashlight beam at the man, at his face.

She screamed when she saw beneath the hood. At first, all she could think of was the Phantom of the Opera, with a black hat partially obscuring his white mask. But no, this man had a black baseball cap pulled down under his slicker, and under that, a white mask tied across his nose and mouth. Only the slits of his eyes showed, and they were in deep shadow. And he wore black gloves. Gloves, here?

Julie raised her flashlight to hit him, to stop him. She landed a blow, but it skidded away on the floor. He tackled her, taking her down onto her back to the concrete. Her head hit, stunning her.

Pain. Dizzy. Zach screaming her name. Where was he?

Holding her back to his side, the phantom hauled her to her feet and began to drag her. She saw stars, bright blurs of pulsating color.

"Leave the woman alone! Put her down! Put her down now!" came Zach's fierce, loud command.

She didn't want Zach to leave her. She wanted him to hold her, comfort her, want and love her. To need her. She needed help. Her head hurt like Zach's leg must have hurt when he cut it, swimming with his sharks. But now her heart hurt, hurt because she'd lost Randi, because Zach had lost Thad.

The man ignored Zach, but picked her up instead, cradling her the way she used to hold Randi. She would like to just go to sleep, so tired. Was Zach putting her in bed, taking her to bed?

And then her head cleared, and she realized where she was. The man who had leaped off the elevator from the black storm of night was trying to put her down the snake's mouth, into its body so she would fall far, far below.

Despite the pain, she shook her head. She was in the unfinished condo, looking down into a dark trash chute that dropped twelve floors, almost straight down!

She grabbed the chute opening with both hands and screamed. The sharp edges cut her palms. Her shrill voice echoed in the sheet-metal depths. The man let her go, shoving her aside now. Julie sprawled on the wet concrete floor.

But she got right up. The man might take the buck hoist again, and she had to stop him, to help Zach, but where was he? And where had the man disappeared to, as if there were a drop hole in the stage of the opera house?

Zach! She saw him, his hips and legs, hanging off the roof of the buck hoist, trying to swing his body into it, reaching with his feet toward the door the man had come through.

"Zach! Don't drop! Wait, I can help!"

"Just stay back! Where is he?"

Though her head spun, when she glanced around and still didn't see the man, she staggered toward the open balcony door. Zach must have been on the roof of the buck hoist, riding it down. She gaped at him as he swung himself inside the metal cage and dropped. He backed up a bit, took a short running start, and leaped over a four-foot space to the balcony where she stood.

"I'm too late!" he cried. "Too late to ID him or help you."

"He tried to drop me down the chute, then just let me go."

They clung together hard inside the building, pressed to the wall between the balcony door and the trash chute.

"Maybe you scared him when you shouted. But who was it?" she asked as Zach set her back. She pressed her hands hard to her head to stop it from spinning, but her palms stung and her left temple was slick with warm blood. Still, that wasn't going to stop her. "Could he have thrown himself down the chute?" she asked, wiping her temple with the sleeve of her soaked sweatshirt, then blotting her palms with the wristbands. "There's a rope inside he could have used."

"A rope in the chute?" he asked and ran toward it. "Where's your flashlight? I dropped mine."

She retrieved hers from the floor and shone its beam inside the chute again. At least, she was not crazy. The rope she'd assumed was for the workers to lower things still dangled there, shifting in the wind. Zach reached it and moved it easily.

"No tension," he said, taking the flashlight and staring down into the chute as she leaned over to do the same, trying to ignore how her head spun again. "Maybe he either fell or killed himself by leaping down the chute."

As they looked over the side of the building, they knew Zach was wrong, that everything had gone wrong here. Twelve stories below, thanks to the fitful lightning, they glimpsed a man climb out of the large Dumpster. He disappeared from view, as if he'd run back into the building, but he was probably only using it for protection from the rain or from their surveillance.

Zach swore under his breath, then returned to the chute. "There are blood drops and streaks in here, too," he said, shining her light back into the chute. "Maybe he's hurt."

Julie felt like a failure, a feeble fool. Had the kids' kidnapper had his arms around her—tried to kill her—and she had nothing to show for it but a hurt head and cut hands?

"He wore a black baseball cap and a white handkerchief over most of his face. I only saw his eyes, hard, cold, narrowed," she said, trying to recall details. "Did you find Grant upstairs, waiting for us like he said?"

He shook his head. "For all I know, *that* could have been Grant. His eyes are more than I saw. He must have heard me hit the roof of the hoist, but he evidently wasn't sure I was there until my flashlight rolled away and I opened the hatch. I almost had him, and he knew it," he said, banging his fist on the chute so it echoed, "so he decided to bail out. I've been trained not to panic, but that's exactly what I did when I realized he was stopping at the floor you were on."

"But you didn't panic when you leaped on that thing or almost fell off," she told him. She leaned against him, shoulder to shoulder, to reassure him and just to rest in the security of his presence. "I think he was running too fast to be Ken Leigh," she said, "but who knows how fast anyone can move when they have to. And the way he came at me and grabbed me…still, I didn't really get his height or weight."

"That's hard to judge when your head's being bashed into concrete," Zach said and touched her forehead gently, shining the light there so she closed her eyes at the sudden brightness.

"Ow! Don't!"

"Your pupils are dilating normally, but you're still bleeding into your hairline. We'll have to take care of that."

"I don't want to go down in that buck hoist!" she insisted, not telling him about her cut palms. "I saw it rocking and jerking."

"I was rocking it as much as the wind, once I saw he was going to get out here." He saw her expression. "All right, I suppose the thing could be booby-trapped to drop us. Let's just go down the stairs and check the bottom of the chute to see if the bastard left a clue to his identity in there. But first I want to call Grant's cell phone number. Can you remember it from earlier tonight when you called him?"

She wondered if he thought she might have a concussion and was testing her memory. But he dug his cell phone out of his jeans pocket, only to see its slim lines were smashed even flatter. He swore again and jammed it back in his pocket.

"I've got Kaylin's recharging in the car," she told him as they started down innumerable flights of stairs, peering carefully over each to be certain no one was lying in wait.

Her head still pounded and drying blood stuck her hair together. Her palms stung, but they seemed to have stopped bleeding if she didn't flex them. The storm was worse, louder, brighter, rougher. But despite everything, there was no other man on the planet she'd rather go Dumpster diving with than Zach Brockman.

Thanks to the way Liz had lifted her spirits, Kaylin had found the strength to talk to her four charges about things they liked most in life, an indirect counseling session, really.

"You mean we should sing, 'These are a few of my favorite things,' from *The Sound of Music*?" Cindy had asked.

"I'd prefer it to the drumming and rattling of that roof," Bree had added, and soon they'd all come up with a lot of bright, neat things.

But best of all, the session had perked her up even more, Kaylin realized. The knife was still in her pocket but she'd return it to the kitchen when she could do so without drawing attention to the fact she'd taken it. Right now, she carried it as a sort of badge of courage, a sign she could have it near and not want to use it again—she hoped.

She was surprised to see Loreen Blackwell and her two kids come into the gym with their sleeping bags, because no one new had come to the shelter in a long time. And, although many of the Hispanic men she'd wondered about in the beginning had been late in arriving, it didn't look as though Clint was with his family, despite how bad the storm was getting.

Kaylin gave the Blackwells a little time to get settled, then made her way over to talk to Loreen again. Her kids were playing poker on their sleeping bags and arguing about who was cheating. This time, Kaylin assumed, Loreen wasn't looking for Grant Towers. If nothing else, she was good for updates on local events. Kaylin prayed that could include good news about Randi.

"Hi, Carolyn," Loreen greeted her.

"It's Kaylin, Mrs. Blackwell."

"Oh, sorry. My head's not on straight, that's all."

"We're all uptight. Do you think the marina will be okay?"

"No, or our house, either, if this thing's as bad as predicted. But it's the risk you take if you want to live and work where we do. We belong to the land and water, just as much as it belongs to us, and, frankly, we'd rather see a storm get it than some greedy developer."

Kaylin just nodded, amazed she was still on her anti-Grant crusade. "Did you hear that Victoria Leigh was found dead at their hunt lodge?" Kaylin asked.

"Just heard it," the woman said, making Kaylin realize she'd probably never be able to tell Loreen something she didn't already know about people around here. "Sheriff Radnor stopped me on the road bringing the kids here and gave me what-for for being out so close to when the 'cane's s'posed to hit. He's really going to ream out Clint if he finds him."

"He's all right, though? You know where he is?"

Loreen gave a snort. "I've known Clint Blackwell all my life, but I almost never know where he is. Just remember that when you get hitched someday. Even when *The Happy Hooker*'s in sight—that's his charter fisher—I don't think that man's really there, know what I mean?"

"Not exactly."

"He's always thinking about racing or fishing or being

with his buddies. He went to be sure his boat and Zach's is battened down before he comes here, then said he might go out to Osprey and talk to Jake Malvers and try to get him and the old man—Leon—to come in here before it's too late, couple of old fools that they are. If they insist on staying out there, I told Clint, there's only so much you can do, like you can drag a horse to water but can't make it drink—damn, what a thing to say right now," she said, rolling her eyes toward the flat metal roof overhead, thudding with rain. Shaking her head, as if their conversation were ended, Loreen went out of the gym and turned toward the cafeteria.

Kaylin hoped for Loreen's sake that Clint would show up soon. And for her own sake, that Nate would. But not as much as she prayed that Randi and Thad would turn up, wet and scared, no doubt, but finally found.

It took only one moment's glance in the Dumpster for Zach to realize they could scratch Grant Towers's name off the list of possibles for the man who had assaulted Julie— and maybe taken the kids, too. Bloody and beaten, if it wasn't the fall that did all that, Grant lay in the big, otherwise empty trash bin as if it were a vast coffin, one with a foot of rainwater in it already and a rivulet from the chute spouting into it too.

Zach muttered, and Julie gasped.

"Now the sheriff will want to lock us both up," Zach said. "I'm not going to lie to him about roughing Grant up a while ago—or why."

"Grant must have been telling the truth on the phone. And he has—had—plenty of enemies," she said, recalling the argument she'd heard between him and the senior citizens on the dock yesterday. "That man, who tried to kill both of us, has literally trashed Grant Towers. His body sliding down the chute—I think that's what I heard right after you went up the stairs to find him."

They stared at each other in the reflection of the flashlight for a moment. "Don't look at me like that," Zach said. "I didn't even see him up there, dead or alive."

"I didn't mean that."

"If not, it's because you're not the sheriff."

"I think all this points to Ken Leigh."

"Our concern right now is whether Grant's murder and Victoria's death tie in to the abduction of our kids."

"Assuming this was not a suicide," she said. "I don't believe that for one minute, especially not after my attacker tried to dump me down here, too."

"Maybe our mystery man figures that, if a storm surge comes in here, it will wash a lot of evidence away."

"But Grant's protected by this heavy Dumpster."

"Julie, what's coming can move or tip a dump truck or a Dumpster, believe me. At the rate this rain's falling, especially if there's a big storm surge, he might even wash out of it."

"Then it could seem the storm killed Grant, just as it killed Victoria."

"And that's why we've got to go to the evacuation shelter. But then we're sitting ducks for Radnor. He'll put an end to our search for the kids, especially when he hears about this."

"Can we keep this a secret for a while?"

"Despite the fact Grant wasn't our favorite person, it's too risky."

"Who would have a rope long enough to stretch down the entire length of this building?"

"Yeah," he said, craning his neck to look up at the dangling end of it, which stopped just about four feet above the big Dumpster. "Actually, it looks like a rope off of old drag nets. Some fishermen might still have them from before fishing with them became illegal, too."

"Clint, you mean?"

"Or Ken could have had access to one like that. I don't think Sheriff Radnor will be getting fingerprints off it, although I'm sure he'll try."

"But the man wore gloves."

"You didn't mention that. Maybe he wore them in case he needed to slide down the rope. But can you picture someone dragging that much coil clear up those stairs with him? Maybe the rope belonged to the construction site, and he just saw it and used it."

"And found construction gloves, too? And didn't plan all that ahead?"

"You're right," Zach said. "Your head may have been slammed, but I'm the one doing fuzzy thinking."

"We're both zombies."

"Don't say it that way. Zombies are the walking dead, but we're still alive and kicking and we're still going to find our kids. The thing is, it may have to be after the storm. I just wish there was someplace safe we could put up nearby besides the high school, where Radnor could locate us. Yeah, we need him, but I don't want him taking over, forcing us to do things his way. It could really slow us down—or stop us."

"I know this sounds crazy, but could we ride the storm out

at the lodge? Osprey's a barrier island, but the lodge has withstood hurricanes before."

"Number one," he said, taking her arm, to lead her toward their car, "we'd have to get out there."

"And number two," she added, "Kaylin will be frantic if we don't join her."

Zach was relieved to see their car was still there, though a palm frond had plastered itself over the windshield and other sopping foliage clung to it. But he was not relieved to see the sheriff's official vehicle sitting right behind it. Ray Radnor sat inside. He rolled his window down and, as if they could miss him, hit his light bar and nearly blinded them with pulsating red, blue, and white beams.

"You're both under arrest or protective custody—whichever way you want it," he bellowed over some sort of loudspeaker system and opened his door to get out.

17

This is WSEA-AM's chief meteorologist Tim Ralston at 2:00 a.m., hoping most of you are getting some rest. Our First Alert Dual Doppler Radar indicates that Hurricane Dana is on track to impact our listening area in approximately six hours. She is currently a mid-Category Three, but unfortunately, since she has more warm gulf water to cover, I'm afraid that may go up. Although the Saffir/Simpson Hurricane Scale can register storms up to a Category Five, do not think this will be an average-impact storm. I predict Dana will hit us as a high Category Three, which means extensive damage to windows, roofs and doors. Mobile homes can be completely destroyed, and, with the storm surge, flooding can occur up to six miles inland, with complete inundation of our barrier islands. We've been monitoring police emergency calls, and one death has already been reported. Near Gladesport, in the south end of our listening area, a 37-year-old woman was evidently crushed under wind-gust debris, including firewood and an iron kettle. Batten down the hatches, southwest Florida, and keep it tuned right here through the storm.

* * *

Locked in the back of Sheriff Radnor's cruiser as if she were some sort of criminal, Julie worked to clean and bandage her bruised temple and cut palms with supplies from his first aid kit. They followed Zach, who was driving her car, inland. The sheriff had ordered them to ride to the high school shelter in his cruiser but he was letting Zach park her car in a safer place, not so near the shore.

The sheriff had explained that his radio operator had monitored a panicky call from Grant that he was being threatened at his sales office on Marco, though after that initial information, his phone had gone dead. Since the sheriff's cruiser was the closest, he had taken the call.

Julie and Zach had shown him Grant's body and explained what had happened, including their earlier argument with him. Whether the sheriff believed their story or not, Julie wasn't sure. He had peppered them with questions, then said he would put them both under arrest if either of them tried to evade custody before the storm passed and he could take them into headquarters for a formal statement.

Perhaps, Julie thought, now blinking back tears that blurred her vision as the rain blurred the windows, their search for their children was over until after the hurricane.

She and the sheriff had to speak loudly. Rain drummed on the cruiser, the windshield wipers thumped, and the police radio crackled, even when he wasn't using it.

"It sounds like the radio station has made its own conclusions about Victoria Leigh's death," Julie shouted, as he clicked off the latest WSEA-AM weather forecast. "I'll bet that's exactly what the murderer wants everyone to think. And if Grant's body was battered in the storm surge, his death could be declared an accident in the storm, just like Victoria's."

"That radio info about Mrs. Leigh's possible accident is what my office put out so far. The last thing I need is people freaking out about a murderer loose in all this."

"Especially a multiple murderer, if these two deaths can be linked. Zach and I are just praying none of this ties to our kids' disappearances, but we're afraid it does. What do you think?" she asked, wincing as she daubed antibiotic ointment on her cuts.

"I think I've got the safety of hundreds, maybe thousands, on my hands until this storm passes, Ms. Minton. And then I'll have some time to look into all that."

All that? She wanted to scream at him. Despite the other lives he had to worry about, he called the abduction of two kids *all that*? They'd told him they had a ransom note, one she'd bagged and left at the lodge so it wouldn't get wet or lost. She bit her lip hard not to shriek at him, not to beat against the mesh divider and throw a raving fit.

Sheriff Radnor stayed hunched over his steering wheel, trying to keep Zach's taillights in view and control the cruiser. "You see, Ms. Minton, just like with this storm, things are getting darker and thicker."

"Meaning what?"

"Meaning any moron would find it real funny that one woman keeps turning up bodies—two in two days—and reports she's been shot at by arrows at Ken Leigh's hunt camp, when my people can't find a one of them around."

"I would never have made that up. If Ken Leigh shot

them at me, he could obviously have picked them up after I fled. Sheriff, Zach and I are desperate to find our kids and follow leads to anyone who could know anything! They're the only ones we want to find—and not…not like I found Victoria and we found Grant," she stammered. "When you see the ransom note I found in Randi's room, you'll understand why we suspected Grant."

"And must have been—pardon the word choice—dead wrong about him."

"Maybe. But if Victoria and Grant did have an affair, the obvious disgruntled party is Ken Leigh, and since neither you nor the Miami police have found him yet—"

"The obvious link so far, like I said, is you! But we'll look at hard evidence…" his voice trailed off.

It panicked her that he was being so stubborn, so accusing. Her stomach knotted even tighter. It was hard to tell where they were, but Julie saw Zach had turned into a gas station. The sheriff pulled up behind and kept the cruiser motor going.

"The ransom note *is* hard evidence." She picked up their argument. "We were careful not to leave our prints on it. And the fact Zach admitted he roughed Grant up—we would hide that from you if there were anything…well, anything to hide."

"*We?* Sounds like you two are suddenly quite the team. Look, Ms. Minton," he said, swivelling around to face her through the wire mesh screen, "I sure understand you're scared about your kids, especially with this big blow coming. But I can't ignore that someone killed Grant Towers while you two were on the scene. His bruises don't look like he could've gotten them from jumping or falling down that chute. Yeah, I heard you both about some masked mystery man. But let's face it, ma'am, Zach Brockman's a trained, covert killer—all of those special ops guys are."

Julie gasped as he went on, "I take it you really don't know Brockman all that well. The SEALs have a macho-hero rep, and it's who they think they really are. They're trained for speed, stealth and ambush. For the SEALs, missions in the dark, even underwater, or in a lot of rain—why, it's their bread and butter. And with his boy missing…well, enough said. We're all getting goofy, between no sleep and waiting for this monster to hit," he said, turning back in his seat.

No, Julie told herself. Even though Zach had lost his temper earlier with Grant, even though he had some time upstairs with Grant when she wasn't there, it was her attacker who killed him. True, she hadn't known Zach well or that long, but she did know him, the inner man—didn't she? Zach would have questioned Grant, not executed him. It was obvious her attacker was the one using the chute. How dare the sheriff even consider Zach! So what if he had been trained to serve his country? Was the sheriff crazy? Had the entire, rational world she'd once known gone crazy?

She tried to steady her shaking hands and her voice. "Sheriff, all I know is that I couldn't possibly rest until I find Randi, and Zach feels the same way about Thad. You can't hold that against us."

"I don't. I completely understand why you searched the keys and panicked when you found their Jet Ski. I've got posters up around, and I'm trying to help. I'll check out that ransom note. I sympathize, but my hands are pretty much tied right now with the storm and these probable murders."

She was going to argue that this was the age of cell phones, but hers was in the gulf and Zach's was smashed, so maybe the kids couldn't call them. Still, Randi knew Kaylin's cell phone number—unless that accident had knocked Randi out. She and Zach had to phone hospitals all up and down the gulf coast, she realized. But no, someone would have contacted the sheriff by now if two unconscious or amnesiac kids turned up. Or two bodies.

"It's not that I don't feel your pain," the sheriff said while they waited for Zach, as if he was now trying to soft-pedal other things he'd said.

"Do you have children?"

"No kids, no wife. Married to the job. Now listen to me. You two get some sleep back at the shelter before the worst of this hits. But don't think you're off the hook of being interrogated about the murders. And speaking of evidence, I managed to get a forensic guy to the Leigh hunt lodge, but my deputy and the volunteer EMR team's gonna be lucky to even recover Grant Towers's body in this wind and rain, let alone find clues in the Dumpster or on those open top floors of that monster high-rise."

So, Julie thought, even the sheriff didn't like Grant's huge buildings popping up all over. How long had the sheriff been in the construction area? Before he'd heard Grant call for help? He had a loudspeaker function in this cruiser, maybe like Grant's attacker had used.

She pressed both hands to her mouth as the wild possibility hit her. Zach's photos of boats she'd printed included one of the sheriff's shore patrol boat. Sometimes his deputies took it out, but she'd seen him in it from time to time. What if he'd come across the kids and Thad or Randi had been mouthy or tried to outrun him? He probably already thought Thad was a troublemaker. If he'd chased them, and they'd had that accident by Fishbait and were hurt, maybe he didn't want to be blamed. And someone like Grant or even Victoria discovered that and were trying to blackmail the sheriff, so he had to get rid of them....

No. No, that was as impossible as Zach being guilty of killing Grant. She was grasping at straws in the wind. If the sheriff would have seen anything amiss, he would have told them, and it could have been a deputy out in the boat that day. There was little chance the sheriff could be guilty of any of this, but she might run her improbable theory by Zach when they were alone.

She gasped when Zach's taillights went out, until she realized he had simply parked her car and turned them off. He'd put the car under the shelter of the car wash attached to the gas station. His big form emerged from the rain as the sheriff unlocked the back door. Soaking wet, he got into the back seat beside Julie and slammed the door. She heard the locks go down; they were the sheriff's prisoners and he had, at the least, a revolver and a rifle up there. It scared her even more that her mind was darting to the worst scenarios, things she would never ordinarily think.

From under his shirt, Zach produced Kaylin's newly charged cell phone, and lifted a hand to his lips. She nodded and put it in her wet purse, surprised to see it sitting next to her on the car seat after all they'd been through.

No one talked much on the rest of the ride toward the high school. Rain slashed at the cruiser, and wind smacked it like unseen slaps. The sheriff concentrated on keeping the vehicle on the road. Zach held her hand, and evidently felt the bandages on her palms. She hadn't told him about her cuts, but he only lifted her left hand to examine it, then turned her inner wrist up and kissed her soft skin there. That tiny act sent shivers up her arm and a pulsating heat even into the pit of her stomach.

He reached out to tenderly touch the bigger bandage on her temple. They were both cut now, she thought—his leg and her palms. But unlike the poor cutters she had counseled in what now seemed another life, they were cut not because they blamed themselves. Not like Kaylin, who had been so unstable once, and the other girls, turning their anger and agony inward...

For one moment, she thought she slept and dreamed that Zach was touching her, holding her, but no, it was all really happening. She supposed she and Zach could have whispered, but they sat quiet, tensed up, tight together, wet and cold but sharing body heat as the sheriff drove. The sheriff sometimes talked to the deputy and the EMR squad he had sent to recover Grant Towers's body. He told them to go slow, to watch for standing water on the road.

It seemed an eternity before they pulled up to the front of the school where Julie had argued with Grant about nine hours ago. How time had seemed to both expand and collapse in their frenzied search for their kids, their kids who should be coming to this very place later this month, ready to start school.

Her head jerked onto Zach's shoulder before she sat bolt upright. Had she nodded off? She was so bone-weary that waking and sleeping were starting to merge. The sheriff was outside, opening their back door. Julie scooted over and got out into the blast of wind and water, then Zach.

"Brockman," the sheriff said, "you so much as disappear to the john without permission from the deputy I've got assigned here for the duration of the storm, and I'm putting you under house—school—arrest. You got that—you got me? The lady's already used up her last chance to stay put. We get through this hurricane horror, I swear I'll help find your kids."

If Zach answered, she didn't hear it.

"As if," Julie told Zach as they sprinted for the boarded-up front doors of the school, "this hurricane horror won't erase any possible clues about what happened to Randi and Thad."

"I'm just praying," Zach said as he opened the door for her, "it won't erase absolutely everything."

Kaylin was thrilled to see Julie and Zach, until she took in everything they were saying: no kids, and Grant Towers dead. When Zach stepped away to talk to the deputy assigned here, she huddled with Julie in the front hall. She'd instantly awakened from a deep sleep when Julie had bent over her cot in the crowded gym to touch her shoulder.

"Grant Towers is dead, too?" Kaylin had asked as she'd followed Julie away from her four sleeping girls into the front hall. "I mean, in addition to Victoria? And no sign of the kids? Here, Julie, take my sweater. You're cold and wet, and they've got the AC on in here."

"We're going to take hot showers and get something else to wear out of the Red Cross bin the sheriff mentioned," Julie said as she turned to face her. "No, don't hug me, because I'll just get you soaked. Are you doing okay?"

"How I am doesn't matter, especially since I see…are you cut?"

"Yes, my palms," she said, holding up both bandaged hands, "but my head's just bruised. It doesn't matter."

"It does to me, but I understand. Nothing matters but getting Randi and Thad back."

"The girls seem to be okay—sleeping, at least."

"Exhausted. We've been keeping busy. I helped Liz Lawson put some animals out in the storage room under the stadium seats. She said Nate was coming with more, but he isn't here yet. I have the key to the place. Here, let me find you something to wear, and I'll come with you to the girls' locker room. I used the shower earlier, so I can show you where it is, then maybe you can get some sleep and food before the worst hits. I'm so glad you're here safe…."

Kaylin wished she hadn't put it that way, since Randi still wasn't safe, but she darted into the main office and dug through the big box of clothing items someone had already donated. She came up with a pair of cropped navy pants and a red T-shirt with an American Eagle emblem on it and the faded words United We Stand. The shirt reminded her of the eagle Liz had called Liberty, out in his cage in the storage room.

As Kaylin went back out into the hall, she saw Zach was still talking to the deputy, and Julie to the sheriff, who had appeared from somewhere. "I'm going to take a shower, change clothes, and use the bathroom, *if* that's all right," Julie was telling the sheriff. Kaylin was surprised at her sarcastic tone.

"You two just check in every coupla hours with Deputy Barnes here and let him know where you are," Sheriff Radnor said before, to Kaylin's amazement, he went back out into the storm.

Kaylin was grateful to see the locker room was now deserted but for the phys ed teacher Susan Parker, who was stretched out on a pile of towels right on the concrete floor in the middle of the long, central row of lockers. The woman sat straight up and stared at them, so she must have been awake.

"Is it here already?" she asked.

"Sorry if we startled you," Kaylin told her. "My friend's just arrived, and she needs a hot shower, that's all."

"Oh, Kaylin. Don't mind me, and have a towel," she said, tossing one to Julie. "I just have to get away from everyone sometimes, and this bank of lockers under a low ceiling seemed safer than that big, open gym. Hey, I heard Liz Lawson stowed some of her animals out in the sports equipment storage room."

"I helped her put them there and more may be on the way. She figured there had to be someplace safe for her endangered animals around here and spotted the room under the stadium seats."

"No," Susan said, getting to her feet, "she knew about it from when she was here to teach my classes—the week after she lectured to all the biology classes about saving the manatees and all that. She helped me carry the archery targets out of there and set them up."

Kaylin could tell Julie needed to get into the shower; she was shaking and her teeth were chattering either from the AC or shot nerves. But why would Liz bother to say she just happened to find the storage room if she already knew it was there?

"Why would Liz Lawson be teaching phys ed classes?" Kaylin asked as Julie started toward the showers. "Was it something about swimming with dolphins or what?"

"Oh, nothing like that," Susan said, shaking her head so hard her ponytail bobbed. "Way back when, as she put it, she was a state champion archer in college—Florida State, I think. The days she was here lecturing in biology classes, I started talking to her in the teachers' lounge, and she mentioned it. She gave all five of my classes a demo and tips on archery—and, of course, talked to them about never using bows and arrows to shoot animals, which then segued into a long lecture about environmental ethics or something like that, which went way over most of the kids' heads."

Kaylin saw Julie spin around and stride back toward them, listening intently with her head cocked.

"She didn't shoot a crossbow, did she?" Julie asked.

"No, a recurve Olympic bow. I thought I was a good shot, but she's *really* good."

Kaylin put in, "I saw those targets out in the storage area. But she didn't say a thing about—"

Julie dropped the towel on a bench and started digging in her purse. She pulled out a wet, red sequined flower Kaylin immediately recognized, then a broken arrow, which she thrust at Susan.

"Do you know if this piece of arrow is anything like what

you use—like what Liz uses?" Julie asked as Susan took it from her.

"Where'd you find this?" Susan asked, scrutinizing it.

"Actually, stuck in a dead shark. Is it a crossbow arrow?"

"No. See this tungsten point? Ms. Lawson said it gives better performance in the wind, better than a steel tip. And even though this shaft is broken, you can see it is slightly barrelled, you know, narrower toward the tip. It's what Olympic archers use, what Ms. Lawson uses, way more expensive than what we can afford for supplies here."

"So, to the best of your knowledge, this is not from a crossbow?"

"No, their bolts are steel or cow's horn with a square base. The ones I've seen have what they call leather wings wound around it to make it rotate in flight, not fly straight like these should."

Kaylin saw Julie was shaking even harder now, but her voice came steady and crystal-clear.

"I know this may sound like a crazy question," she said as Kaylin just stared from one woman to the other, "but do you know what sound a crossbow makes when it shoots, compared to a regular bow and arrow?"

"Actually, I do," Susan said, handing the arrow back to her. "I shot a crossbow once on a hunting trip, but don't tell eco-maniac Ms. Lawson or she'd cook my goose for sure. It was noisier than a rifle with a silencer," she said with a little laugh. "These regular bows go twang-thud, but a crossbow goes thud-twang when it releases its bolt. You want me to explain why?"

Julie wasn't about to answer her, because she was running out of the locker room full tilt.

* * *

It couldn't be, it couldn't be, Julie kept thinking as she tore down the hall toward where she'd left Zach. Liz Lawson couldn't be behind any of this and yet, Liz hated Grant Towers. She had no beef with Victoria Leigh, but she no doubt hated Ken. Could she simply have gotten his wife by mistake—or could she be devious enough to make it look as if he'd killed his wife?

Yet Liz had an alibi for the time surrounding Grant's death, because she'd evidently been here with Kaylin, stashing her animals. But Liz also had Nate. How much was he under her thumb?

Still, did it matter that Liz had told Kaylin she just happened to find a safe place for the animals when she knew it was there all the time? Maybe Liz didn't have time to go into all the details about teaching an archery class and then lecturing students about environmental ethics.

Zach was nowhere in sight. With Kaylin still on her heels, asking questions, she headed for the boys' locker room.

That area looked deserted, too. "Julie, what? What?" Kaylin cried when she caught up with her at the locker room door. "Liz hated Grant but she'd be shooting at Ken Leigh, not his wife. And you said you found a shark shot with that arrow. She'd *never* do that!"

"She might, if it meant Ken Leigh would get blamed. You know, sacrifice one animal to save masses of them. And she has help."

"Nate? You don't mean Nate Tomzak could have anything to do with this? He's back at their compound, trying to close everything up—that's probably where they both are, or on the way back here to put more animals in. Look, here's the key!" she cried, producing a silver one. "Nate would never be party to anything like that."

"I'm desperate, Kaylin. Go on back to keep an eye on the girls, please."

"I want you to use my cot. You've got to get some sleep. You've lost sleep and blood—"

"And now I'm losing my mind, right? Please, Kaylin, just take care of the girls and leave me alone for now."

She could tell she'd hurt her friend again, but she couldn't help it. Kaylin stiffly handed her the dry clothes. Taking them, Julie opened the door to the boys' locker room and shouted, "Zach, it's Julie! Are you in there? Zach?"

She heard nothing, so she went in, closing the door in Kaylin's face. "Zach? Zach Brockman, are you in here?"

This room was a mirror image of the girls' area. She heard a shower hissing in the distance, and strode through the deserted locker bay. Sticking her head around the double corner of the area labeled SHOWERS, she saw a steamy, large room with shower heads and stall dividers without doors. Only one shower was on, though she couldn't see who it was behind one of the dividers.

"Zach, are you here?" she screamed, and her voice echoed. She was prepared to explain to him why she was here, but she was not prepared for the fact he would vault out into the open, naked.

"What?" he shouted, starting toward her. So much bronze skin and dark chest hair and more.

"I found something out!" she cried, spinning away even as she heard him flap a towel open.

"Liz Lawson shoots arrows," Julie said to the wall, her voice still echoing. "She was a college archery champion, and she lied to Kaylin about not knowing where to store her animals. I know it's not much, but she hated Grant almost as much as Loreen and Clint do."

"Is Liz here with the animals somewhere?" he asked as he turned her to him, his hands hard on her shoulders. He'd tied a towel around his flat waist, but his skin and hair gleamed with water. He felt so warm and looked so clean, she longed to throw herself into his bare arms.

"She put them in the storage room under the football stadium, but Nate may be coming with more. Kaylin has the key to the storage area out back."

"And maybe that information you uncovered gives us a new key to go through a new door, too!"

"You mean we should sneak out to wait with the animals?"

"Get in there and take a hot, fast shower while I get dressed and watch the door," he said, his voice crisp and hard, as if he were giving military orders. "Then we're going to borrow Kaylin's car—"

"It's a little Volkswagen. It will never stay on those roads right now."

"Then we'll use Loreen's truck, if she's here. Or steal one—the deputy's car if we have to. I thought we'd hit a dead end, but we're going to head for the WorldWise compound. Liz and Nate have some explaining to do. If they catch us breaking in, I'll just say I wanted them to look at the photos of boats in the harbor we have. Liz volunteered to look at them and help me identify their owners or operators."

"I don't think I told you, but she was waiting for me on the marina dock when I went to get your camera off *The Hooyah!* She even wanted me to let her hold it while I got off. That's one more thing that *might* point to her. She could have overheard what you told me was on that camera, because you were yelling into the phone, remember? But, Zach, we have to report to the deputy here, and Sheriff Radnor said—"

"Let them lock us up, if they can find us. I figure we've only got about five hours until the hurricane really hits, and I say we don't spend it sleeping."

"I agree. And I don't need the shower."

"Do it, but make it quick."

"You don't intend to leave without me? I won't let you, Zach."

"I swear, we're in this together," he said, squeezing both her shoulders, then propelling her back toward the showers. "To the end."

18

*T*im Ralston still here with you, awaiting the worst of the storm. The time is 3:00 a.m., and I want to share some hurricane trivia that really isn't trivial at all. You can expect the rain to start to taste salty soon, as the winds scoop water out of the gulf—though I hope no one is outside to notice that. The big barometric drop in pressure could possibly cause premature labor in late-term pregnant women, and it may also make your teeth hurt, cause pain in your ears, or give you trouble swallowing. Unfortunately, those things are the least of our worries. Stay prepared and ready, those of you who are riding the storm out in the shelters. It's highly likely we will lose electrical power and that land phone lines and cellular phone communication will be spotty at best.

Julie could have stayed in the rush of hot water forever, but she took the shortest shower of her life and jumped into the clothes Kaylin had given her. Her underwear was still wet, but she'd be sopped the moment they went outside again anyway. Shoving her feet back into her muddy shoes, she joined Zach, who was dressed in dry jeans and a sweatshirt that was too small for him.

"We're going to have to sneak out of here," she told him, lowering her voice as he led the way back out into the hall. They tiptoed past rows of men in sleeping bags she hadn't seen earlier, but she hadn't come this way before.

"National Guard troops," he whispered and kept going. "Do you know where to find Loreen in that crowded gym?" he asked when they returned to the front hall and, blessedly, didn't see Deputy Barnes anywhere.

"No, but I'm sure Kaylin does, and I know where she is."

"Go try to get Loreen's car keys. Go!"

Feeling as if she were on a stealth mission, Julie wound her way through sleeping families toward Kaylin, who sat cross-legged on her cot as if she'd been assigned to guard the entire, crowded room. When Julie motioned to her, Kaylin got up and stepped over people to head straight for her in the middle of the dimly lit gym.

"Nate can't be involved," she whispered to Julie, picking up their discussion as if they hadn't been apart. "Liz may be an eccentric fanatic, but Nate would have nothing to do with anything like that, an abduction or murder. He cares for me and knows I partly blame myself for Randi's disappearance. I know Nate's the one who suggested you should look for a ransom note, and there it was, but that's all circumstantial. He was just trying to help."

Julie didn't tell her about the mystery man who had nearly killed her and who had killed Grant. She had no time to discuss this, though she understood why her friend defended

Nate. Julie had been incensed when Sheriff Radnor had cast doubt on Zach's actions.

"It's probably nothing," Julie whispered, "but we have to follow any lead."

"But Liz and Nate helped you search."

"We just have to talk to them."

"Julie, everyone you talk to ends up—"

"Stop it! Can you just tell me where Loreen Blackwell is in here? She did come here, didn't she?"

"At the far end," she said, pointing. "She's with her two kids under that basketball backboard."

"Got it."

"Why Loreen?"

"I have to ask her something."

No use, Julie thought, getting Kaylin even more upset by telling her they were going back out in the storm. And she could not confide anything that Kaylin might have to divulge to the sheriff. Instead, Julie reached out and hugged her hard.

"We've been friends for years," she whispered as Kaylin returned the hug, but stiffly, almost warily. "I need your strength and courage now, but from a distance, okay? Please take care of the girls and of yourself."

"I still think you're partly blaming me for—"

"No, I'm not. I said I'm not. I'll see you later."

She set Kaylin back and turned away, walking through the maze of bodies toward the other end of the gym. Several adults raised their heads to look at her. No one but kids seemed to be sleeping this night, and Julie prayed that Randi and Thad were resting well and safely somewhere. Dare she hope that somewhere was the WorldWise compound? What if the kids had hurt a manatee, and Liz had seen it and decided to teach them and their parents a lesson? But that would be beyond fanatical; it would be psychotic.

As Julie stood over the sleeping forms scattered under the basket, it was only Loreen's bright blonde hair which identified her. Like the phys ed teacher, the minute Julie approached, Loreen sat bolt upright.

"Julie?" Loreen whispered. "That you? I thought it might be Clint."

Julie knelt by her sleeping bag. "He's not here? We saw him a little before nine this evening with your kids."

"He brought them to me at the house, and sent us here, but he insisted he had to go to Osprey to try to bring Jake and Leon in."

"To Osprey? Now?"

"It was hours ago, and Clint being out on rough waters is the least of my worries. He said he'd get out there, at least, 'cause the island would brunt some of the wind, then he'd make a run for it back in with the wind. I told him those old coots are too stubborn, 'but they're native Crackers, just like us,' he said. I argued their safety is on their heads, but he wanted to do it for Zach—and himself. He said—I'm just gonna tell you—that he thought, if Jake found Thad, they might keep him there for a while, 'cause they never forgave Zach for taking him back.'"

Her words came in a rush and Julie had to lean close to hear. She saw that Loreen had been crying. The dull light through the gym doors reflected tear tracks on her weathered bronze cheeks.

"And," Loreen went on with a sniff, "Clint said he had to find Thad so Zach wouldn't suspect him."

"Of what?"

"Not of kidnapping! Of running drugs, I guess." Her son stirred and rolled over, flopping his arm onto his mother's sleeping bag. Loreen lowered her voice again. "Clint's buddies done that from time to time, but not him, though he's been running a few illegal traps lines for Florida lobsters and sharks. Look, I shouldn't be spilling my guts like this when you've got your kids missing—are they still?"

Julie was deeply moved by the woman's honesty and her need. She wished she had time to stay to talk, to help her, but she said only, "Yes, they're still missing, but we have a lead. Zach wants to know if he can borrow your truck."

"Talk about Clint on the water! You're not going out in this again!" she said, reaching to grip Julie's wrist. "Listen to that rain on the roof. The whole building's creaking, and this is s'posed to be a safe shelter!"

"Please, Loreen, we need your truck. And letting us take it could get you in trouble, because the sheriff told us if we try to leave, he'll lock us up. Just tell him I stole the key from you—if you'll trust Zach and me."

Julie almost burst into tears when the woman immediately fumbled in the dark for something and came up with a rain slicker. She dug in the pockets of it and produced a ring of keys. She pried one off and pressed it into Julie's hand.

"The same red truck you prob'ly saw Clint in earlier," she told Julie. "In the south lot, close to the building. It's got a NASA Challenger Disaster Memorial license plate. And here, take this, too, my raincoat. Clint has one just like it, and I know he'd give his to Zach if he was here."

"I can't thank you enough. I—I guess you should know that someone killed Grant Towers tonight at his newest high-rise on Marco."

"Killed him? Hell, I wanted the man dead and gone more'n once, but some other leech on the land will just take his place. He really was killed?"

"Yes."

"Can't say I'm sorry, and Clint will prob'ly drink a toast, but I'm sorry for his two girls." She looked at her kids, sprawled next to her in their sleeping bags, breathing heavily.

Again, Julie's eyes filled with tears, but she blinked them back. "I've got to go. We owe you."

"You just find your two!" Loreen whispered, her voice fierce. Watching where she stepped, Julie headed for the door, holding the key and raincoat to her. Only when she was out into the stronger light in the hall did she see the slicker was dark green—and Loreen had said Clint had one just like it.

Zach fought to keep the truck on the road. In their head-light beams, the rain came down in silver sheets like cleavers, slashing at them. Sometimes gusts of wind shook them, moving them slightly sideways on the road so that he had to steer left as well as straight ahead. Water had risen so high in the canals along one stretch between Gladesport and Goodland, where the WorldWise compound stood, that they went through waves as if they were in a boat at sea. When he tested the brakes, the truck hydroplaned, skidding a circle and a half until he regained control.

Thank God, despite the fact they had their seat belts on, Julie had braced herself against the dashboard and door. She'd searched Clint's glove compartment and under the seats as Zach had asked, looking for what he didn't know. She'd found a small tool kit, candy bar wrappers, a flashlight to replace Zach's, a reel of monofilament fishing line on the back floor of the truck—and a piece of rope similar to what was hung in the condo chute.

The windshield wipers barely cleared their vision before the glass was coated with rippling gray rain again.

"It's like driving underwater," he muttered as he slowly U-turned the truck, and they started off again.

"Sheriff Radnor said SEALs do everything underwater."

"Did he? I'll show you some day. But it's grain-of-salt time when he says anything about SEALs, Julie. Ray Radnor DOR'd."

"He what?"

"Ray was in SEAL training years ago," he explained, "way before he went into law enforcement, and he 'dropped on request' because he couldn't get through drownproofing. He's a local kid, too, though he wasn't one of our buddies and never worked at the lodge. Even as a kid, for some reason, he always panicked in the water. The rest of us swam like fish. He was okay in a boat but not in the gulf—or a BUD/S training pool, so he would have been disaster on the teams. I never could figure why he had to try for it."

"Drownproofing sounds like what we're going through now," she said as they drove through water up to the hubcaps again.

"Yeah. Actually, it's learning to swim with your feet bound and your hands tied behind your back."

"I sure can't blame him for dropping out of that!"

"I'm not blaming him, never did, though he probably doesn't believe that. One in five don't make it in the SEALs and get reassigned to the fleet. It's not for everyone—that's the point, but he's still bitter about it, so I wasn't thrilled when he got to pass judgment on Thad's screwing around at school."

"Oh. You mean it's not only grain-of-salt time for Sheriff Radnor, but sour grapes?"

"Not to mention he always liked Becky, too. But no way I'm going into all that. You psych majors might want to, but us Florida Crackers-turned-jar-heads-turned-SEALs avoid that Freud stuff."

"That isn't Freud stuff. It's mass media mavens, good old Dr. Phil common sense about how all of us never really escape our childhoods. In other words, nothing is ever really in the past."

"I got you, doc, even though we don't have a couch here I could lie on. But I've got other things to worry about."

"I know. You did hear me when I told you Loreen claims that Clint has a rain slicker identical to this one, didn't you?"

"I heard everything you said about Clint—and Leon and Jake. I don't think they would keep Thad and me apart. Whatever they think of me, they would never hurt Thad."

"But maybe they'd just keep Thad there to nurse him. When I walked up to their door that first day, Leon was supposedly taking a nap, but what if he was tending Thad or Randi, too? Zach, Jake wouldn't hurt Randi, would he? I mean, I know he watches the girls sometimes, but I've always trusted him."

"And rightly so. The guy's a loner, eccentric, but he's no pervert or worse. He was over-protective of Becky, and he lost her, so now maybe he just worries about the girls. I know that sounds lame, but that's how I see it. He may be a little weird, but not the way you mean."

"And he'd be even more protective toward Thad."

"Yeah, but he showed real anger at his dad about his loving Thad more. Still, I don't think he'd hurt either of the kids."

"Well, I don't think Liz would either. She loves talking to kids, educating them and—"

A large plastic garbage can came vaulting across the road just as they were about to take the low bridge to Goodland. Rather than risk braking again, Zach just hit it and it flew off somewhere. Julie gasped but said nothing else.

He wondered how long she could hold up. The tension and terror were eating at his self-control. All the training he'd had, the real-fire practices he'd had—all of it meant nothing if he couldn't *make it happen*, as they used to say. He had to find Thad and Randi. Soon. Now!

"What's our plan, going into the compound?" Julie asked after the silence had stretched too long between them.

She was still on task, so why was he letting himself get down? She sounded like his buds on the old teams, ready to go in.

"What's that you said before?" she went on, gripping his shoulder hard as if to give him strength. "Plan the dive, then dive the plan?"

"You ever been inside the WorldWise compound, team-mate?"

"Sir, no, sir."

"Then I'm the commanding officer, and I'm going to de-scribe it just once for you before we go in unannounced. This time it's not a head-on assault, like we did with Grant or you tried to do with Victoria. Games aside, sweetheart, this is war."

Although the two towns almost shared the same piece of land, Goodland was light years away from Marco, Julie thought. Marco had a glossy cachet about it, so much so that the denizens of Goodland referred to it as "Mark-Up Is-land." Goodland had a *Happy Days* 1950s feel about it, which was exactly what its residents and retirees wanted. The local joke was that Goodland was a drinking village with a fishing problem—and don't try to change anything about us, thank you very much.

Old Spanish documents showed its recorded history reached back to a visit by Ponce de Leon, who named it Goodland for its fresh water, which was rumored to keep those who drank it ever young. Yet, even in the wind and rain, Goodland felt like backwoods Old Florida. With its almost ramshackle exterior, Liz Lawson's WorldWise compound was probably the most technologically advanced place around the tiny town.

"It's interesting that Liz never invited your girls to visit here," Zach said as they neared the compound, looking for a place to park where falling trees or limbs wouldn't block or wreck the truck.

Julie had started to gather up the flashlights and Kaylin's cell phone, which she stuck in the pocket of her slicker. Zach too had borrowed a rain slicker, which he'd turned inside out so the black plastic lining showed instead of the exterior red.

"Too many kids to transport, I guess," she said. "Liz always came to lecture us on-site, or walked us on little nearby field trips toward Leon and Jake's. What's your point?"

"I described the inside to you, but not the buildings. I came here two years ago to a meeting about shark protection, which she held in an outdoor *chickee* hut. It was a beautiful day and no one thought anything about not being invited in at the time, especially when her four college interns working on her manatee count project served an entire meal to us al fresco."

"She didn't even display the animal clinic she's so proud of, or the monitors that show the view of some keys from what she calls her 'Manatee Cams'?"

"No, though the place isn't exactly off limits. Those Florida State interns had the run of the place—until lately when she evacuated them. And then there's Nate."

"Right, Nate. Kaylin's fallen for him, so for her sake, I hope he's not involved. But that man who attacked me at Grant's was in good shape—strong, maybe young."

"Let's go," he said, jerking the truck to a stop. "And until we have to abandon it, we stick to the plan."

The plan, such as it was, Julie thought, was a covert search, whether Liz and Nate were on the grounds or not. They had noted first that no vehicles were in the unlocked garage, which sat outside the compound, but discerning if someone could be inside still might be harder than they had envisioned.

The compound was right on the water; they could hear the pounding of the surf even over the shriek of the wind. It was surrounded by a stockade fence which at first reminded Julie of the one around the high-rise condo. But slight spaces showed between the boards here, and it was wanly lit inside from a single, short pole lamp. When they walked quickly along the fence, even in the driving rain, they could catch broken glimpses of buildings within. It was like looking at one of those old-time, flickering movies, she thought.

"As far as I can see, it looks deserted in there," she whispered to Zach as he spread the door in the fence as far its chain would allow. Just like at the condo site, the entry was chained and padlocked, but this time without any room to squeeze through.

"I don't want to have to go in through that old boathouse on the water," he said, frowning and looking up at the top of the fence. "Left foot on chain, then up and over with your right leg. You go first so I can boost you."

Her stomach cartwheeled, but she nodded. She grabbed the fence as high as she could reach and fitted her foot in the chain. Zach put his hands on her waist, then her bottom to get her up. She swung her free leg over, grabbed the top of the fence and half scraped, half-dropped her way inside the compound. She barely had time to stand back before Zach was up and over.

"Outer, working our way in," he whispered and started toward the first building in a crouch she tried to emulate.

Then *bam!* Bright lights came on, blinding them. Julie

froze and threw up her hands to shade her eyes, but Zach tackled her, taking her to the ground. She thought he'd hit on top of her, but he rolled under, then over again, somehow keeping his weight off her.

Jammed in the hibiscus bushes, Julie expected the worst. Magenta and yellow spots danced before her eyes. She could feel Zach's heart beating hard but he breathed low and regular, while, trying to keep quiet, she gasped for air.

"Just motion detector lights, I think," he said in her ear. "They may flash on everywhere we go, but since we haven't roused anyone, maybe they're not here."

"They shouldn't be here. These clapboard buildings and that shaky stockade fence won't make it through this storm. But they could be looking out a window, watching us."

"Remember our cover story about bringing the photos here for them to see. We knocked on the gate but we figured in the wind no one could hear us so we just came in. Since we haven't been yelled at or shot, let's go."

In the bright lights that threw their shadows, she followed him along the back fence toward a long, narrow wooden building. The three main structures in the compound had their windows boarded up; several smaller ones, and the open thatch-roofed *chickee* hut, were on their own in the brutal wind and waves.

Only when Zach produced a wedge, wrench and screwdriver from his jeans pockets did Julie realized he'd come prepared to break and enter. She didn't so much as flinch, but she felt like a fool. Had she thought this man, who had come to mean so much to her, could simply will locked doors to open, *abracadabra*?

"I visited the janitor's room at the school while you were talking to Loreen," he whispered. "Watch my back, 'cause here we go."

Julie figured the sounds of wind and rain and a shutter banging somewhere would cover any sounds Zach made, though they were assuming that Liz and Nate had evacuated the place. Yet if they weren't at the high school shelter, where else would be safe to go, Julie wondered, as Zach jimmied the door and stepped inside the dark building.

She followed so close behind she bumped into him, a wet but warm wall of firmly muscled back and buttocks. He closed the door, then flicked on Clint's flashlight. Four pine bunk beds and desks filled the room, so this was probably where the interns stayed. Huge combination bulletin boards and chalkboards covered both ends of the room. Clicking on her light, Julie went to examine the things on one, hoping she'd find something with the same print or paper as the ransom note from Randi's bulletin board.

This display was all about mangrove trees and how important they were to the local environment. They were like giant sponges catching and storing excess water. *Mangrove peat absorbs water during periods of heavy precipitation and storm surge, and even buffers wave action during hurricanes or tsunamis.*

"Anything?" Zach asked, as he walked the other end of the room, shining his light under bunks.

"Ecology stuff. It all looks legit."

"Next building. Let's go."

"Wait, let me check on the other wall." She looked this bulletin board over even faster. "This is all about their Manatee Guard Protection Program," she said, noting a newspaper article she recalled from *The Naples Daily News*. "They have remote cameras focused on manatee sites on three keys—Pine, Crayton, and Buttonwood. You can access the cameras online from the WorldWise site. Do you know where those keys are? You don't think they'd go out there in this storm, do you?"

"I'm starting to think we can't put anything past her. And yeah, I've been on or to all those keys at one time or another."

"Liz told our girls that she and her crew count and nurse injured manatees on-site, but the cameras watch the place when they can't be there in person."

"Let's go, Julie. We've got to search the rest of the compound for signs of the kids."

For signs of the kids. His words echoed in her head. Didn't he share her hope that the kids themselves might be here? Then again, Liz was a very smart woman. She'd never have any sign of abducted kids on her property, surely not. Julie's desperate hopes crashed again, as they had so many times these last endless days.

The next building was evidently the animal clinic. Julie saw skulls of various animals on the shelves, as well as formaldehyde jars of floating bats, seahorses, an embryonic shark. She tried not to show Zach how much those upset her.

Spaces where the cages had been, perhaps the ones Liz and, supposedly, Nate took to the football stadium shelter were missing. They had all sat on newspapers, which were yellowed except for the spots the cages had been. Some were still in place but stood empty.

In various-sized aquariums, fish glided back and forth with wide eyes, as if staring in fear of what was to come. In the largest tank, her flashlight beam caught an eel, baring its fangs at her through the glass.

She gasped and jumped back. When Zach saw what it was, he just went on looking in cabinets and closets. Nothing seemed of help here; they carefully relocked the door behind them when they went out.

Ignoring more motion lights that popped on, they entered the third of the large buildings on the compound, obviously Liz's living quarters. The furniture was strictly utilitarian, but the walls held prints of Audubon reproductions of local birds and large, heavy-framed color photos of dolphin and manatee. Electrical cords hung from the photos, so Julie assumed they were usually lit from within.

They went into the long, narrow kitchen together. "I've seen bigger galleys on subs," Zach whispered, shining his light around. It reflected in aluminum pots and pans hanging on the walls.

Playing her flashlight beam before her, Julie went first down the short hall, past a bathroom where she boldly ripped the shower curtain open, only to stare into an empty—and dirty—tub. Sand marked with random footprints coated the bottom of it. At the end of the hall was a single bedroom, a surprisingly large one, considering the rest of Liz's bailiwick, but then Julie saw it was an office, too. A bank of four dark computer screens lined a long desk made from planks and bricks. At least, Julie thought, Liz wasn't lavishing WorldWise donations on her own creature comforts.

Zach came in right behind her; his light darted around as

she went to the mirrored, double-doored closet and slid one door, then the other open. She skimmed her light along the floor, then parted some of the clothes to look behind them. It took her a moment to realize that men's clothes as well as women's hung here.

"Zach, I think this is Nate's bedroom, too!"

19

Though I know it still feels like the dead of night at 4:45 a.m., I'm betting the increasing wind and rain is waking you up, if it hasn't been keeping you up. Tim Ralston here at WSEA-AM, going through it all with you. Just a word about the water, both the rain and possible storm surge. We're soon going to have torrential downpours, between six to twelve inches per hour. The height of the storm surge will depend on several factors, including winds, pressure, shoreline configuration, bottom topography and the size of the eye. Obviously our regular tide will also play a big part. I'm expecting a surge of ten to twelve feet, but that may change. Everything can change, except that we are right in the middle of the target of this potentially catastrophic storm.

When Julie realized that Liz and Nate must be lovers, she thought she was going to be sick to her stomach. Poor Kaylin. But even more importantly, it meant that Nate could indeed be working not only for, but with, Liz.

But sleeping with a man who must be twenty years

younger hardly proved Liz capable of worse things, nor was it a crime. Nor was lying to Kaylin about not knowing the storage area was under the football stadium. So what if Nate suggested they look for a ransom note, when they should have thought of that themselves? And Liz's reveling in the power of the coming storm hardly meant she would use it to cover up homicides.

"Yeah, Nate sleeps here," Zach said as he rummaged around in a bedside table drawer. "On this side of the bed. Here's a deodorant stick for men and a couple of gas receipts with his name on them. Come on—we've got other places to check, including one more important one."

"Where?"

"Their boathouse on the water."

They locked up, looked quickly in the three small storage sheds on the property, then Zach showed her the entrance to the long, low boat shed. At least they didn't have to climb the fence to get to it.

"I came by water that time and entered through here," he said, almost shouting in the noise of surf, wind, and the groaning of the old clapboard boathouse. But they both froze at its padlocked door. They could hear a banging inside as if something—someone—wanted to get out.

"Can that be a person?" Julie asked.

"Too rhythmic. I think it's just boats banging. But it would follow a pattern if this is a murder scene that will get wiped out by the storm."

Anger at Zach flooded her, but then, she, too, had begun to think of the possibility that the kids could be…could be lost. Although she was running on adrenaline again, clear reasoning was like slogging through the swamp near Ken Leigh's hunt lodge.

"Don't talk or think that way," she insisted. "We're going to find Randi and Thad, and they're going to be all right."

"Stand back. I'm going to break this door in."

It was harder than it looked, but he managed, not only kicking at it, but throwing his shoulder into it four times before it burst open. The moment it was freed, it banged out toward them with a gush of air and a blast of salt water. Julie swallowed some and started coughing; it stung her eyes. They clung together, holding on to the door frame, trying to see inside.

"One or more of the outer doors for the boats must have blown in already," he yelled. "Brace yourself against me and then against the inside wall."

They fought their way inside, edging along the only wall which was anchored to solid ground. The roof was still intact, but the boats pulled at the posts so hard Julie feared they'd yank them loose and knock the entire ramshackle place down before the hurricane did. Even with two of the three double doors still closed, waves were crashing in so high they broke over the narrow board walkways between the boats, and the roof rattled with the downpour.

They steadied themselves and trained their pitifully small beams of light on the boats. The two vintage WorldWise *Don't Let the Everglades Become the Neverglades* boats were here, yanking against their tethers. But between them a third craft, graceful and long, sleek and white, rode the waves.

"I didn't know they had that," Zach shouted. "I've got to

get on it." He took off his slicker and handed it to her, along with the key to the truck.

"Maybe the boat belongs to a friend or donor."

"There's a boat like that in the photos, one I couldn't place. And it's the kind that usually runs drugs."

"But they'd never do that."

"Just stay put. I'll make this fast."

He took a running leap onto the craft and, with his flashlight retrieved from his back jeans pocket, disappeared into the cabin. Julie was tempted to jump aboard the two old boats, but she'd wait for Zach. What was taking him so long?

"No trace of kids or drugs," he bellowed when he reappeared. "But there's a big net inside edged with rope like in that Dumpster chute at the condo. It may mean nothing—or everything. It's a lot like a net I saw in Jake's boat."

She could not fathom a connection between Jake Malvers and Liz or Nate and just shook her head. It still hurt, and she hoped she didn't have a concussion. Her thoughts thrashed, just like these boats, but wandering, not tied to anything to hold them down. She felt so exhausted, so defeated at every turn. Surely, Liz Lawson was no more running drugs than Loreen Blackwell, unless they were the kind Liz needed to drug her sick manatees when people ran over them in a boat…then she watched the manatees on cameras to protect them…like she and Zach should have protected Thad and Randi…

She snapped alert, staring at the sleek watercraft again. Where did the money for this expensive boat come from? Just ardent WorldWise donors, or had Liz somehow taken earning a fast buck into her own hands, money to support her beloved animals, not herself? It kept haunting Julie how Liz had referred to this storm as an avenging goddess. Avenging anyone who harmed the environment? Even kids on a Jet Ski, out in the keys where her protected creatures, the manatees, sharks and dolphins, lived?

Waiting for Zach as he briefly checked the other two boats, Julie pressed against the boathouse wall, thinking, thinking. She and Zach might have found nothing on the compound so far, but if Liz and/or Nate had been out on the water in that fast cigarette boat about the time Randi and Thad disappeared, surely they must have been doing something innocent, such as going to check on their manatee cams. No, they couldn't have even been in this boat because Kaylin had said they'd showed up on Osprey in one of these others. But even if she and Zach were wrong—again—they had to follow any lead.

When Zach jumped off the last boat, she grabbed his arm and shouted in his face, "Do you think those laptops in their bedroom are their manatee cams? What if they're trained on something besides manatees? Like where a drug drop is to be picked up? Maybe the kids made it to one of those keys, stumbled on the drugs, and Liz and Nate had to lock them up somewhere, like in a manatee holding tank. They couldn't decide what to do with them, but when the storm approached, they decided it could solve their problem, just the way it would cover up eliminating Grant and Ken Leigh."

"You mean, they were clever enough not to kill Ken directly like they—Nate—did Grant, but to set him up for his wife's murder? Or if Grant's death was proved a homicide, Ken could be blamed for that, too, because of the affair?"

"It makes as much sense as anything else we've tried to pin down."

He frowned. "But the keys with those manatee cams," he said, "are not close to Fishbait, where the kids had the accident. Still, you could be onto something. I don't know if the laptops inside are those cams or if they're even working, but we can go back in and check. Like I said, I know where all three of those keys are, but if we have to go back out into this mess looking, the cams might help us narrow it down."

Leaving the boathouse door banging on its hinges, they reentered Liz's house. In the combination bedroom and office, Julie saw the surge protector for the laptops was unplugged. They knew better than to plug in such stuff in a bad electric storm like this, but nothing was going to stop them now.

Julie plugged the system in, and Zach turned each laptop and monitor on. Two of the screens lit royal blue, the other two gray.

"How are we going to get them to bring up the cameras?" Julie asked as she knelt before the two left monitors while Zach bent over the other laptops.

But a blessing was bestowed on them at last: all four screens displayed a start-up menu that included Manatee Guard PP. When they double-clicked the icons, the next screens showed a moving image of a raging storm, with sideswept rain and thrashing palms barely discernible in the darkness. They turned up the volume, but there was no audio, just a dark, visual horror. The cameras shuddered and the lenses looked like windshields with no wipers in a maelstrom from hell—and the inner bands of the hurricane were supposedly still a couple of hours away.

"Live time?" she cried.

"I think so. But we're not going to be able to see a damn thing—except, look! Lower left corner—it's labeled which cam is which key. See, I've got Pine and Crayton, and you've got…what?"

"Buttonwood and Cistern. But Cistern wasn't mentioned in the newspaper article, and I don't think it's one she mentioned to the girls when she visited the lodge either."

"Maybe they've added a new site and cam? Let me see if I can make anything out on that screen."

"If it's named Cistern Key, it must have a cistern on it, maybe like that one I saw on Fishbait."

"Several of the bigger keys where people used to live have those. Yes, as I recall from years ago, it had one that was pretty intact."

"Could they keep injured manatees in a cistern to nurse them?"

"No way—too narrow and deep. The manatee tanks are large metal vats, long and low, like a huge coffin. To get the big beasts in and out, they use some kind of portable hoist."

"Couldn't prisoners be kept in a cistern or a manatee holding tank? How deep are those?"

"The cisterns can be ten to fifteen feet deep and fill fast with rainwater."

"I remember the one on Fishbait was half-full—and that was before this deluge."

"The manatee tanks are not half so deep but bigger, longer, easier to get out of—unless someone's tied up."

"But someone could not climb out of a cistern, unless it filled with enough water to swim out."

"It would take a lot of treading of water first. I don't think escape would work unless the prisoner was some sort of rapeller or mountain climber."

"And not," she said, swallowing hard, "if someone was tied or injured."

When Zach bent so close to the screen labeled Cistern Key that his nose was almost touching it, she cried, "What is it? Do you see something?"

"I think I can make out a square hole, darker, smaller than the rest. It could be the top of the cistern and not a manatee tank. It's starting to make sense—crazy sense."

"But if the kids are in there... The torrential rain's one thing, but a storm surge— Zach, we can't wait until daylight to see better. It may stay this dark, or the cameras may blow away. We've got to go out there. Can we? Is there any way? How far out is it?"

"Under normal conditions not far, but a ways south. If I could get far enough down the beach and fight through the surf, I might be able to scuba to it, but getting back in to shore with them if they're there—especially if they are hurt— might be impossible."

"What about in your boat?"

"Bucking the wind and waves? I don't know, but I mean to try."

"*We* mean to. When Loreen said Clint went out to Osprey, she said he was trusting that the island would brunt some of the wind on his way out, then he'd make a run for it back in with the wind. If we use Osprey for protection, then get on the lee side of Cistern Key, can't we try the same?"

"I can't risk you, too. You'll drop me off and go back to

the high school, tell the sheriff everything we know so he can mount a rescue operation the minute the storm's through, in case I don't make it. It would be too late for him to try to stop me, but you could insist he send help after this is over."

"You're not going without me!"

"All right, all right," he said, lifting both hands. She was relieved she had so easily convinced him, but then, he'd promised they were a team. "At least we can leave a note in Clint's truck," he went on, "telling the sheriff to come here, to check these monitors when it gets light, whenever that may be, to prove th—"

A nearby boom knocked the video off the row of screens.

"They may reboot," Zach said, but the screens stayed black.

"Fried, despite the surge protector?" Julie asked, but he didn't answer. Instead, he pulled her out of the room and the house. He closed the door but didn't relock it. As they ran across the yard of the compound, none of the motion detectors turned on lights. Julie wondered if the entire area had lost power already.

"Goodland often blows its electrical transformers before other places," Zach yelled to her as he boosted her and she climbed over the fence. The power might be gone, she thought, but not our strength. They were going to risk their lives on conjecture, on desperate desire and in the very teeth of this hurricane. Surge protector…they needed protection against the storm surge. They had to find their kids, even if they died trying. Yes, she could think that now, could face now, that they might die trying, but at least they would be together.

Holding on to each other like drunks in the wind and rain, they staggered toward the truck.

* * *

Kaylin left her cot and paced back and forth in the long front hall of the school. The plywood over the windows and the row of six doors rattled as the storm snarled around the building. Where was Nate? Why hadn't he come to deliver the other animals? She'd tease him about being a modern-day Noah with his ark, saving animals endangered by a flood. She put her hand into her pants pocket and felt for the key to the storage area, then checked her other pocket for the knife. Like the key, it was warm from the heat of her body.

She turned into the last set of locker bays, the ones farthest from the gym. The carpeted aisles between the lockers were empty and dimly lit. Putting her back against a locker, she sank to sit on the floor.

And then the lights went out, leaving her in utter blackness.

She sat there a moment, eyes wide, seeing nothing. It was as if she peered into her deepest fears, her blackest self.

She told herself that she had to act. The girls would be terrified. She must get back to them. But then, lights blinked back on, at least some of them, a bit dimmer. She'd heard that the school had a generator system in case the electricity went out. It was dim in the gym and the girls were sleeping anyway, so she sat here, staring at the bright blue lockers across from her.

She recalled her pale-gray high school locker, how bare she'd kept it inside when others had rock stars in color, bright posters, or friends' pics plastered all over the interiors of theirs. But she'd preferred her locker pale, plain and empty—that was how she felt years ago.

She took out the kitchen knife and ran her finger carefully down its serrated edge. When she'd cut herself back then, she'd used sharper ones, so it wouldn't hurt so much and the cuts would keep clean. It was just the idea of seeing her blood she needed, bleeding out those awful feelings of hating her parents, or at least hating how the two of them hated each other and ignored her. Yes, she and Julie were sisters in that at least. But Julie seemed so strong about her parents, when poor Kaylin McKenzie was still just pretending. She needed Nate but where was he?

She took a tissue out of her pocket and wiped the knife blade with it. Julie claimed she didn't blame her for what had happened to Randi, but she was just being kind, just trying to keep her from slipping back to those days when things swirled around her so dark and she had no control, except control over the way she could cut herself to release the pain...

She pressed the knife blade high on the inside of her arm. She could hide the cuts there, press this tissue between her breast and arm until the bleeding stopped. She had done that years ago, so she could always say she slipped and cut herself shaving her armpits—just slipped, just bled a little bit...

She tried to steady the knife, but she was shaking, trembling like this entire building.

A light shone in her face; she screamed and dropped the knife.

"Kaylin McKenzie?" a male voice said. "Didn't mean to scare you."

"Y-yes?" she stammered, moving her leg to cover the knife on the carpet.

"Deputy Barnes here," he said, shifting his flashlight off her. She saw he was blond with a crew cut. It was hard to make out his features from this angle. "I been looking high and low for Zach Brockman and your friend, Julia Minton. They in one of these dark locker bays, too? They were s'posed to report to me by now, and they didn't."

"They were exhausted. Maybe they fell asleep somewhere."

"Like I said, I've been looking, and you better, too, because I got sheriff's orders to lock them in a windowless classroom for the duration of this if they don't cooperate."

"I don't know anything, honestly."

"What you doing back in here?"

"I wanted to be alone for a few minutes."

"Better get on back with the others."

"Yes, I will. I just can't stand how that gym roof creaks. Would it be okay for me to take my four girls out to another area of the building with lower ceilings, like a few families have done?"

"Just don't be riling others over it," he ordered as she got to her feet, hiding the knife under her foot. Then, when he stalked away, she slipped it back into her pocket.

"We'll have to buy Clint and Loreen a new truck if we leave it here with the storm surge coming," Julie told Zach as they parked the car behind the marina. She had not been able to stop chattering all the way back, though he seldom answered her and looked deep in thought. "But I can sell a few parcels of Osprey to get the money for that and for repairs. I'll probably want to take Randi back to Michigan, where she was happier. I didn't know she was so unhappy."

Julie realized she was starting to sound like Kaylin, making herself the target of the blame game. She should have eaten something at the high school. When was the last time she ate?

"We'll have to eat something for strength!" she shouted to Zach as they got out of the truck. "Do you still have stuff onboard *The Hooyah!*?"

He nodded and held on to her as they started down the dock. "Here, you keep the truck key," he said, suddenly turning to her and pressing it into her palm.

She quickly put it where she'd secured Zach's camera last night, nestled in her bra. Holding each other, they bent into the wind, going from mooring post to post on the marina dock, making their way toward Zach's bucking boat. When they talked, rushing wind filled their mouths, shuddering their cheeks.

"I'll give it all she has to try to get into the lee of Osprey," he said when they reached the boat. "You just stay as safe as you can, promise me."

"Yes, but can't I be up steering with you? It may take both of us to hold the wheel."

"Julie, just hold onto this post. I'm going to get onboard, loose the main lines and be sure she'll start. Then you'll toss off the last two lines and get on at the last minute. Got it?"

"Got it!"

He surprised her with a quick, hard kiss, probably for good luck, then patted her bottom the way football players did. Despite her terror, that touched her deeply. They were a team. They were going to do this together.

Though she'd noticed Zach's cut ankle had made him limp lately, he took a running jump and made it onboard. Timing his motions to when the mooring lines went momentarily slack, he began heaving off ropes, which, though heavy and similar to what Grant's killer escaped on, blew almost straight out in the wind.

Julie held to the post, her eyes watering from the sting of salty wind, trying to watch Zach's every move. He climbed the ladder to his pitching wheelhouse where he was mostly sheltered from the wind and rain. As jagged lightning split the sky, she saw him click his flashlight on. She heard the rumble of the boat's engine, even over the roar of surf and echoing thunder.

He turned and windmilled his arm at her, and she tried to make it to the two lines holding the boat. She almost reeled off the dock, so she got on all fours to crawl. She heaved off the last ropes. But as she did, she realized he couldn't come down from the wheelhouse to help her onboard without having *The Hooyah!* take out the dock.

She gasped and began to sob as she realized what he intended.

He meant to leave her on shore with the truck, to get back to shelter, while he tried to make it to Cistern on his own.

20

Tim Ralston with the hurricane report for 7:00 a.m., south-west Florida. The outer bands of Dana have arrived. We've already lost electrical power in our southernmost listening area, evidently from a small tornado Dana spawned, so we're hoping here at the station in Naples that our broadcast tower is going to stand. Southwest Florida is a mix of water and land, so keep these sayings in mind through the storm and even after: "Run from water, hide from the wind," and, "If you're not going to drown, hunker down." If you want hard statistics, I want to warn you that ninety percent of people who die in a hurricane drown, so do anything you can to keep high and dry.

Zach wished he hadn't read the book *The Perfect Storm*, because the good guys die in it. This was the most insane thing he'd ever done, and yet it made desperate sense. He was a trained SEAL; this was his most important mission. The evidence was piecemeal and circumstantial, but the kids could be on Cistern Key, and, if there was any chance of getting to them in time, it was worth risking everything.

Everything except Julie's life. He'd tricked her, betrayed her, and she'd probably hate him for it, at least unless he found and rescued—please, God, don't let this be a recovery mission—Randi and Thad.

He looked back toward the dock once, but flying spume and spray obscured his vision. Once he was away, she'd have no choice but to run for the truck and head for the high school. He snapped on the small light mounted on the console in front of the helm and scanned his instruments. The GPS system would do him no good for this, so he'd rely on his depth finder and compass. But in the compass's glass dome, the black disk with its white numbers floating in clear liquid rocked and rolled, making him even dizzier than the boat's pitch and yaw. He might just have to find Cistern with nothing but dead reckoning.

Cistern Key was half-moon-shaped, larger than most of the 10,000 Islands. In May through August, snook fishing and manatee watching was good there in the warm, shallow water of its small, slightly protected bay. More than once, he'd seen sharks chase schools of mullet just offshore, too. Some long-gone pioneer family had once called it home and no doubt fished in their own little bay—and built their own cistern.

He flipped his single-side-band radio to his usual VHF channel, but they were streaming the local WSEA weather reports on it. He shouted a bitter laugh when the guy warned everyone to "run from water and hide from wind." Shaking his head, he snapped the radio off. It was coming in all crackly anyway, and he could barely hear it with the shrieking of the wind and smash of waves.

Hoping he'd be able to tack like a sailboat to at least make minimal headway through the brutal waves, he'd gone about fifteen yards out from the marina dock in a zigzag pattern when a large blast of water hit him sideways with a whomp. The bow lurched and turned, the boat listed. He felt *The Hooyah!* struggle to find her heading toward Osprey, where he hoped to find some shelter to get farther south, but he'd already gone off course.

Damn, the wind and water were driving him back into the dock. He spun the wheel and pushed the throttle up to full. At least there seemed to be slight lulls between the biggest gusts. He had to use one of those breaks, try to tack again so the storm would push him between Osprey and the shore.

Please God, let Julie be in that truck and headed for safety, he prayed, bracing his rear against his captain's chair and spreading his legs stiffly to take the back-and-forth dipping of the elevated wheelhouse. He turned on the pump to discharge overboard water from the bilge, because the fighting deck and cabin would soon be awash.

He was getting too near the marina dock. If he took it out and crashed shoreward, his propellers would go, too, and he'd be shipwrecked right where he started.

Julie knew she should run for the truck, but she clung to the mooring post and watched Zach fight to keep the boat away from the dock. Salt water stung her eyes, but her tears did, too. All her security and pride in thinking they were a team, but he'd set her up. Granted, he meant to keep her safe, but she needed to be with him. She needed to be out there, looking for Randi, no matter what the cost.

She hunkered down, gripping the post as she saw *The Hooyah!* rock and push back. Was it too hard-going already, or did he realize she was still here, that he needed her?

But what if the boat wrecked the dock and she was thrown into the water? They'd never get to Cistern Key hiking south along the shore, not with the river that bisected the beach, not with the trees that would no doubt go down in this blow. It was Zach and that boat, running in the lee of Osprey to reach Cistern, or nothing—nothing left at all to love and live for.

The swing of *The Hooyah!*'s stern slammed the dock once and scraped it hard. Creaking, groaning, it shuddered under her. Despite the screaming wind and whitecaps breaking through the slats of the dock, she heard Zach trying to rev the engine. He was going out—he was still going to try.

Again, the back end banged the dock before he made some progress to start to pull away one foot, then two. "Go, Zach!" she whispered, though she wanted to scream her support. "Go. Go!"

Then she knew she had to go, too. She'd made it on to the boat's tilting deck that time she'd retrieved his camera, when Liz was so helpful. *I feel a part of all nature,* Liz had said, *even when she turns violent, even when she must hurt her own.*

Julie half crawled, half scrambled to the next mooring post. From this angle, the wind would help her leap onto the back of the boat—or else crush her between it and the dock to drown.

No, she was going to make it. She had to do this.

Before Zach could take *The Hooyah!* farther out, she

stood, ran two steps and leaped. The wind lifted her, but she slammed against the stern, half in and half out, her hands grasping the rail. Dangling from the hips down, she clung as the boat bucked. The sea seemed to pull at her heels.

Anger flooded her; adrenaline poured through her. She pulled herself up, scraping one thigh and then her belly over the stern rail, and fell onto the tilting floor of the deck.

Stunned, she rolled with the pitch of the boat and clung to the bolted-down base of one of the fighting chairs, curled around it in a fetal position, bracing herself in case the boat hit the deck again. Each time *The Hooyah!* tilted, onboard water sloshed back and forth over her and more foam doused her. But she was aboard, and the boat was intact. If Clint's *The Happy Hooker* had been in its usual berth, both boats would be tinder by now.

Had Zach seen her? Heard her? And if he knew she was onboard, would he try to take her back in? She'd just stay put until she was certain he was in whatever shelter Osprey would provide while he plowed these monster waves south toward Cistern.

As she pictured her beloved Osprey Lodge facing this on-slaught, she thought of all the sunny, simply breezy days there years ago. Her parents, playing bridge in the shade with their friends, had just hoisted their 5:00 p.m. cocktail flag and were awaiting their drinks. She saw herself sitting with her tutor on the porch, sneaking looks at Zach on his elevated lifeguard chair on the beige beach, his lanky body bronzing in the sun. Could he guard her life now, from that elevated chair in the wheelhouse, and save the kids, if they could be found?

* * *

Kaylin startled when the school PA system came on with the high voice of the man Liz had called Napoleon. The PA had not been used before, and it either woke everyone or just panicked them more.

"We have been advised by the weather service that the leading edge of the hurricane may contain tornado-strength winds. This is somewhat unusual, but should such a perilous and potentially injurious condition occur, we will use the fire alarm to warn you," he went on, giving directions about putting sleeping bags over heads and being accountable for each child.

Kaylin shook her head. A lot of the people here spoke English poorly and the guy was talking so fast and way over their heads about "perilous and potentially injurious conditions." They'd be better off if he piped that straight-talking weatherman in here.

Bree just rolled her eyes. All four girls were awake, listening intently. Kaylin felt ashamed she'd almost cut herself, when one thing she'd vowed to do was keep them from slipping back into such destructive behavior, such perilous and potential injurious conditions, as Napoleon was saying again.

"…with possible destructive winds, even more than we expected," he droned on. "As you can see, we are on generator lighting, because rotating winds have taken down transformers…."

Transformers… Kaylin wished she could be transformed into someone strong and sure of herself, someone who wasn't obsessed with why Nate had not come. She had to talk to him, be certain he had nothing to do with Randi's abduction, that he hadn't gotten close to Kaylin just to lay plans for leaving a ransom note and for knowing when the girls would be out on the water. Jake Malvern used to give her the creeps when she saw him go by in his boat or on the island path, just kind of watching. Now the thought of Nate using her really creeped her out—but then, everything did right now.

"Let's get an early breakfast, because it's going to be a long, crowded day," Cindy piped up, rubbing sleep from her eyes. "I mean, we've got to keep our strength up. I know, I know—'How can that stocky girl think of food at a time like this?'" she mocked herself, probably, Kaylin surmised, in the tone her mother often used. "Well, why not? Some people can't eat a thing when they're a nervous wreck, but not me."

"I think we ought to stay together from now on," Kaylin said. "If Cindy wants to eat, we'll go with her, even if the idea of it could personally make me puke."

Tiffany grinned, and Jordan's pale face seemed not so gray, even in these generator lights. People were sitting up and looking around, chattering in English or Spanish. Why did life have to be like this? Kaylin wondered, as the five of them wended their way out of the gym. Always waiting for something to happen, never quite controlling events instead.

She sniffed back tears and said a little prayer for Julie and Zach, hopefully safe in some shelter together, waiting out the storm until they could start their search again.

Somehow—he wasn't sure how—Zach had wrestled waves and wind to get *The Hooyah!* onto the lee side of long, thin Osprey Island.

But the boat still pitched and yawed. He braced himself against his captain's chair because he couldn't stay in it. At least the engine hadn't quit. Now, he was fighting to keep the boat out of the shallows and sandbars where his inboard motor propellers would choke and quit on him.

It was still as dark as night, though the sun would be up by now. Layers of black and gray clouds shifted and swirled overhead as if to mirror the turbulent gulf below. He felt he was a ship in a bottle being shaken, shaken.

Trying to judge and read the most violent surf he'd ever seen took him back to SUBOBS, surf observation training. "Hit the surf!" used to mean running across the beach and getting wet. Two-mile ocean swims, brutal water lifesaving practice on breakers crashing into boulders—somehow, all that paled next to this. Hell, the waves had not even been this bad on the nightmare mission where he lost Garth.

Keeping the black, low form of Osprey in view, Zach wondered how Leon and Jake were doing, riding out the storm there, if they had been defiant enough to stay. He hoped Jake at least had the brains to take Leon to the lodge with its sturdier tabby construction, because their clapboard place would surely be a goner. Julie had thought that Leon might have Thad there, taking care of him the way the two of them should have taken care of Becky better. No, losing her—her slide into booze and even drugs—was something Zach could have stopped if he'd come home sooner. Now, he only wanted to save Thad where he'd failed Becky, save Thad and Julie's Randi and have a chance to care for Julie in a way she might never allow, now that he'd deserted her after all their talk about being a team.

Bracing himself even harder as he ran *The Hooyah!* out from the shelter of Osprey, he felt not only the blast of the storm coming in, but the way its winds rotated.

Surely, they wouldn't take him out to sea so he'd over-shoot his trajectory past two other islands and then to Cistern. But the storm turned him ninety degrees, back toward Osprey.

He wrestled to bring her around again, fighting the storm and his own boat.

Julie crawled into the cabin of *The Hooyah!* and got a bottle of water from the small fridge she recalled seeing in the galley. Everything in here was rattling or shuddering, despite how shipshape Zach kept the interior of the cabin.

Water, water everywhere, but she was desperately thirsty. Good, there were six bottles in here, because Randi and Thad would need some when they got to them. She guzzled one bottle, took one for Zach, then pulled out the other four for their kids. They had to find them and soon. When did a storm surge come, anyway, that is, if rainwater and rising surf hadn't already inundated a cistern or a manatee holding tank?

She left the fridge door open for its meager light, but the rocking of the boat slammed it shut, so she had only her flashlight beam. She rummaged through a drawer of Zach's things and came up with exactly what she wanted—a backpack, which she stuffed with water bottles and put on. Under the long, leather-padded bench at the table, she found life preservers and took four. Struggling out of the backpack, she put a vest preserver on, then strapped the backpack over that. She tied two other bulky vests to hers for Thad and Randi and left Zach's out with his bottle of water. She'd show him how valuable she was in this rescue mission.

She felt weighed down as she went to the door of the stern and tried to judge where they were. Was that the next key after Osprey, or had there been one she'd missed? It should be daylight, but no hint of dawn peeked through this suffocating cover of racing clouds and pouring rain. Should she try to bail out some of this sloshing water?

Thank God, she didn't get seasick, but she felt soul sick. What if this was a wild goose chase? What if the kids were never there, or it was too late—too late to save even themselves in this storm?

Leaving the cafeteria and heading back for the gym, Kaylin heard what sounded like a freight train roaring nearby. An unearthly shriek followed, then a huge metallic banging and ripping. Then only human screams.

She grabbed Cindy's hand and put her arm around Jordan, the first girl she could reach. Standing in the hall, they were sucked hard toward the door to the gym. A woman's scream shredded the air nearby. No, the scream was her own.

The five of them slammed into the wall by the trophy case as its glass shattered, spewing out onto the carpet and at them. The sucking ceased, but the shrieks and screams got louder.

Then the fire alarm sounded with its deafening, robotic beep—beep—beep!

Still holding Cindy's hand—the girl had gone pasty white

and was vomiting—Kaylin peeked around the corner into the gym.

The entire vast roof was missing. Standing roof water and slanting rain poured in hard and fierce on stunned and scrambling people. The closest basketball backboard had shattered. Then, even the generator lights went out and the fire alarm died.

It wasn't easy, geared up like she was, but Julie had to face Zach, to let him know she was here, that she wasn't quitting and he wasn't alone in this. Dragging three life jackets, looking like a hunchback, the bottle of water for Zach stuck in the waistband of her jeans next to her flashlight, she laboriously climbed the ladder to the wheelhouse.

Zach looked like a man possessed, braced but thrown from side to side as he tried to steer. There was no door on the back of his wheelhouse, but he was protected on three sides. Still, the wind was deafening. She didn't want to startle him. Should she shout or turn her flashlight on him to tip him off?

With still two more rungs to climb, she screamed, "Zach!"

He didn't turn.

"Zach, I'm here!"

And then, when she was again trying to decide whether to surprise him or wait longer, he simply turned to look at her, as if he'd sensed her presence. He noticeably jerked but didn't let go of the wheel. He said something, but—perhaps, fortunately—she couldn't tell what.

She didn't care. He might be macho-SEAL, as the sheriff had called him, but she had an equal stake in this mission, too.

She climbed the rest of the way up. He reached out to drag

her to him and shoved her in the corner of the wheelhouse with one hand before returning it to the wheel. He was still muttering, maybe cursing.

"I have some water for you!" she yelled as she tried to hold herself in the corner. "And a life jacket you've got to put on. And water and jackets for the kids."

He shook his head in disbelief once, went straight-armed on the steering wheel as if he'd wrest it from its base before he yanked himself back over it.

"Okay!" he shouted, his voice calm and controlled. "I'll take some water."

Amazed they were just going on as if he'd wanted her here and they'd never been apart, she realized he couldn't spare a hand to take the plastic bottle. She unscrewed it for him and asked, "Should I take the wheel?"

"No way! Tip it to my mouth!"

He drank greedily, spilling some down his beard-stubbled chin when the boat tilted again. He nodded, and she twisted around to shove that bottle in her backpack, too.

"Can you swim?" he asked.

"Of course, I can swim!"

"I mean really swim. I'm going to try to put in to the little harbor, but we might have to abandon the boat."

"But how will we get back to shore before the storm surge then?"

"How about we build a raft like the Swiss Family Robinson?"

"But we'd never have time…"

He shouted a harsh laugh. "And now I've got you to take care of, too—if the kids are there."

She flushed hot, but she should have expected he would not be pleased or pleasant. Oh, she hadn't meant pleasant, but she was losing her focus again, losing the strength she thought she'd found. She was wet and cold and clammy and scared to death, but she wasn't giving up. She wasn't going to let Zach search for her beloved daughter without her, come hell or high water, and they sure had plenty of both.

21

Tim Ralston, your voice in the storm, here at 7:30 a.m. We're really getting into the thick of it now, southwest Florida. We've had reports of several tornadoes, with one in the vicinity of the Gladesport High School storm shelter. Let me clarify the difference between tornadoes and hurricanes, which are also called tropical cyclones.

The two have little in common. Tornadoes are smaller scale, a single storm occurring over land with a lifetime of minutes. Tropical cyclones can contain dozens of storms and are oceanic phenomena with a lifetime of days.

And one more clarification—the storm surge of hurricanes will not occur in the middle of the eye. Storm surge is caused by the winds pushing the ocean ahead of the eye on the right side of its track. The bigger the eye, the worse the surge. So far, Dana has been strong and compact, but the closer you are to the shore, the higher the surge will be.

Kaylin could not believe her eyes. The roof of the gym had been peeled back like the top of a can. Chaos reigned in the dark of storm and night. She'd left her flashlight under her cot, but no way was she going back into the disaster of the gym for it.

"I'm cut—cut!" Tiffany screamed. "Bleeding!"

"That glass case," Jordan said, looking stunned. "Me, too—two places on my arms."

"Bree? Cindy?" Kaylin said, her voice shrill above the other voices.

To Kaylin's amazement, Bree clicked on a flashlight she hadn't seen and shone it first on her friends, then calmly pulled a piece of glass out of Jordan's arm. "I think we're all cut from that trophy case breaking," Bree said.

Kaylin appeared to be the only one not cut, but she didn't say so. "We'll get into a restroom and wash those cuts. Let's get the glass out, then use paper towels to bandage you. We can't go back into the gym."

Napoleon and Deputy Barnes rushed past to stand in the door, where Napoleon spoke through a megaphone. "Keep calm and come out into this hall. Be sure everyone comes out into this hall. Do not panic. We are going to wait in the halls until the eye of the storm, then transport everyone farther inland in school buses."

Were they nuts? Kaylin thought, as she pulled the shaking Cindy to her and urged the girls down the hall toward the closest restroom. Take all these people out in this, in lumbering school buses with their glass windows? She'd heard it was almost impossible to predict how long the eye would take to pass and then the winds on the back side could be even worse. She wasn't going out in those with girls entrusted to her care, no matter what. Liz had been right; Napoleon was in over his head in all this.

"Shouldn't we just wait in the hall so we can line up for the buses?" Cindy asked as wind and rain swept around the corner toward them from the gym.

"No—I have another, a better place."

She knew now where she'd take the girls. They would have to be outside but only for a short distance. They surely wouldn't be doing a head count to know they were gone. Yes, they had Bree's flashlight, the girls had their cell phones, and she had the key to their safety, right here.

When it came time to steer directly toward the small harbor on Cistern's south shore, Julie was thrilled that Zach motioned for her help to turn and hold the helm to starboard.

"We're going to have to run her aground in the sandy bottom of the little bay," he explained, his voice as calm as ever. "Then we'll get in the rest of the way—not far, I hope—on our own. All those life vests will keep you up, and don't worry about me. I'm used to surf swims. There are no rocks on the flats there, just eel grass."

"Eel grass? Like that eel we saw at the compound? Is that where they live?"

"You're sounding like a novice again, and I need a tough teammate."

"Right. All right. Eels or sharks, I'm ready. But will we be able to use the boat to get back into shore before it gets worse or the storm surge hits? However big it is, it will surely cover all these barrier islands."

"I'm hoping the increasing tide and then the surge will lift *The Hooyah!* free once we're back on it and drive us into shore. If not, we'll find debris or tree trunks to make a raft, because we can't stay long on the island. I'm taking fishing line in with us to make a raft if we need to."

"We can do it!" she said, just before a length of low-lying land appeared before her eyes, black in the mix of grays. "Is that Cistern?"

"It had better be, because we're going in!"

He pushed the throttle forward, then cut the motor. The boat headed in a ways, then tilted so hard Zach was thrown into her and they were both pinned in the corner of the wheelhouse. But at least the violent rocking motion was muted now.

"We're aground," he gritted out. "I was hoping for a better angle, but this might keep her here until we're ready to go. Come on. And leave your flashlight. Mine's waterproof."

With all the stuff she'd strapped on herself, she would not have made it down the steps to the stern deck without Zach. She felt as fat as Santa with a stuffed pack. Zach took his life vest from her and strapped it on. He threaded fishing line around his waist, through his belt loops. Four times around, he wrapped a long rope and tied it tight. She had a hundred questions, but she kept quiet, her hands gripped together, waiting for him.

"We'll try to stay together," he said, "but I'll see you on shore."

Waves washed in as they slid to the lower side of the boat. Julie knew how much Zach must love *The Hooyah!*, but he'd spent it so easily for the chance of finding his son. Yes, she'd give anything, too—anything…

She was shocked as, without another word, Zach took her arm in an iron grip and lifted her up, then pushed her over the edge of the boat into the roiling water. She gasped in a breath before she hit, but her head didn't go under, buoyed up by the three life vests and the backpack.

At least the water was warm. Despite the bandages on her hands, the salt water instantly stung her cuts.

She started to swim, but got turned around somehow. Which way was in?

An undertow, a sucking, sweeping backwash took her somewhere. In? Out? Farther from the shore? If she never made it in, she'd be no help to him, lost in this black belly of the storm.

Then Zach appeared, swimming with one arm and dragging her with the other. Up, down, slammed with spray, ripped inward, then shoved out. She swallowed salt water and spit it out, trying to suck in a breath before another breaker hit her. She kicked hard, trying to help him, and felt one of her shoes, then both sucked away. But she was with Zach. She always wanted to be with Zach.

"Feet!" he shouted.

She didn't know what he meant at first, but he must be walking now, still dragging her. She fought to find her feet, only to be blasted away, out of his reach. Huge whitecaps crested over her and banged her, belly down, on a sandy, water-swept shore.

Tasting gritty sand and salt water, Julie hacked and spit as she tried to get to her knees. A large turtle was cast ashore here too, clawing its webbed feet in the sand, trying to escape the next breaker.

Zach lifted her. Her legs were wobbly, but she staggered out of the foaming, pounding surf with him. If a beach had been here, it was being devoured by the surf now.

They sloshed past the first line of mangroves and into a stand of palms, bending and flailing their fronds. As Zach produced his flashlight from somewhere and turned it on, one tree nearby broke with a resounding crack that sounded like gunfire.

Zach threw himself at her, and they went down. She was sure he said, "Incoming!" as the weight of soaked, rustling fronds settled hard around and atop them. At least the trunk had missed them.

"You okay?" he asked, leaning into her and breathing hard. His thigh rode hard and high between her legs; the backpack was skewed to the side.

"Y-yes."

"I'm going to crawl out backwards and pull you. The manatee cam's a little ways from here. Stick tight to my six—to me."

He'd gone into combat mode, Julie thought, as he did exactly what he said he would do, dragging her out behind him. This time she kept her mouth and eyes shut to avoid sand. Once they were both on their feet, he started immediately off into the dark, and she hurried to keep up, hobbling in her bare feet, following the erratic beam of his flashlight he used to shove and slash foliage aside as if it were a machete.

"We're going to get soaked out there!" Tiffany cried as Kaylin and the four girls stood at a back door of the school. Behind them, echoing through the halls, they could hear the rumble of voices.

"Soaked and blown away," Jordan muttered.

Kaylin had cleaned and bound their cuts with toilet paper

and paper towels; thank God, it wasn't worse. Strangely, they seemed more upset by getting wet than by their blood. Though she was trying to hide it, Kaylin was certain she was more shook than they were, but she fought to stay steady and strong.

"I'm making a decision," Kaylin told them, "that I think is best for all of us. We'll have to spend a few hours with some animals in cages, but the storeroom is sturdier than this building—with no windows. And we're not going to split up, so I'm not taking a vote on this."

She was pleased that she sounded so assured. Despite the terrible decision she'd made that might have cost Randi her life, she was certain this was the best thing to do now.

"We don't have far to go," she told the girls. "We'll go along the chain link fence until we're nearly there. No one lets loose of the other two in line and Bree comes last. I have Bree's flashlight, but I'm going to keep it dry so we have a light inside if the electricity's off in there, too. Now let's go."

"All for one and one for all," Bree said, though her voice broke. "Just call us the five musketeers."

As scared as she was to lead the girls outside into the screeching wind and pelting rain, Kaylin was bolstered by how brave Bree had become. The shy loner had blossomed into a courageous young woman. She and Julie could be so proud of that.

The moment they were out the door, the wind smacked them. They bent double, at first unable to move, despite how the building blocked the worst of the wind. Then, keeping low, turning sideways, they made for the fence. Once they reached it, the wind plastered them there as if they were being barbecued on a grill, but they managed to inch their way along.

They were all instantly drenched, but then so was everyone who'd been in the gym when the wind had peeled the roof away. Just lifted it off like the top of someone's skull, Kaylin thought, and then rain had poured down like blood—

Oh, no, oh, dear Lord in heaven, help me, she thought. These terrible visions of violence—they had to stop. She hadn't used the knife, she didn't want to. Three of the girls had been cut by flying glass, but she hadn't been touched, she hadn't shed her blood, even if she deserved to.

Two of the girls intentionally dropped and rolled toward the shelter of the concrete stadium steps, but they made it around to the door. Kaylin expected it to be more sheltered here, but the wind whipped around the corner with vicious strength.

Bree huddled over her, holding the flashlight while Kaylin worked the key in the lock. Liz had done this before. It worked hard, then turned.

She hadn't realized how difficult this would be. It took three of them to keep the door from banging inward. It was blacker than black in here. Kaylin shook so hard that when she took the flashlight from Bree and turned it on, its beam zigzagged back and forth across the cages before she realized they were not alone.

Sopping leaves and fronds whipped Julie's face and arms and clawed at the life vests and backpack as she plunged after Zach into the black heart of Cistern Key. Twice she tripped but scrambled back up; they were almost running, and she could feel the land getting slightly higher.

"If we don't spot the cistern right away, look for the foundation of an old homestead here somewhere. And don't fall in the manatee tank. It's got to be here, too, closer to this side of the key."

Julie spotted the long, metal tank off to the right and ran to it. "Nothing in here!" she shouted.

"The cistern's here somewhere!"

Julie turned to her left and ran right into it, its hard tabby stone outcropping knee-high. She slipped on a coconut—they were all over the ground here—banged her knee and almost tumbled in headfirst. Zach saw the cistern, too, and ran to lean over it and shine a light down into its dank, dark depths. The beam bounced off the roiled water in the cistern as rain pelted down.

Julie squinted, still unsure.

Could it be? After all this struggle? Or were those floating coconuts instead of heads? No, two bodies, but alive or dead?

"Randi!" she screamed, her voice echoing weirdly in the well and in her head and heart. "Randi?"

22

Tim Ralston here in the storm at 8:30 a.m., in case your clocks have quit in the power outages which have been reported. With the help of First Alert Dual Doppler Radar, I'm estimating the storm surge preceding the eye of the storm is very close to our shoreline, although the surge is something our state-of-the-art radar does not pick up. Again, I warn you not to be deceived by the calm and beautiful character of the eye when it appears. I repeat, the worst of the storm can come after the eye, when you are least expecting it.

"Nate!" Kaylin cried and hugged him hard as he stepped out from the dark corner of the crowded room. "I'm so glad it's you—that you're all right. How did you get in here without the key?"

"Are you all okay?" he asked in turn, crushing her to him, then setting her back and looking at the four startled girls. "I was going to look for you at the school, but when I arrived, I saw the roof had been ripped off, so I headed straight for here."

"It happened about a half hour ago," Kaylin told him, still

out of breath. "Evidently, some sort of tornado went through. It sounded like a freight train."

"Oh, yeah—I think I heard that. Sounds seem really muted in here."

"The shelter officials are waiting for the eye of the storm to evacuate everyone into buses and go somewhere else," Kaylin plunged on, so relieved and excited to see him. "But the girls have already been cut from flying glass, and I thought this would be safer."

"I agree with you, unless our door gets ripped off, which I thought was happening when you came in. We may have to get inside that little electrical room, because all kinds of things could go airborne and hurt someone in here if the door goes."

"But how did you get in here?" Kaylin repeated, leaning gratefully against his strength. He was amazingly dry compared to the rest of them; she saw he'd draped his dark green slicker over part of the eagle's cage. "Liz said she'd leave me the key," she said, "and I still have it."

"When I saw the roof was gone, I was so panicked to get out of the wind, I actually jimmied the lock," he explained, giving her another hug with his arm around her waist. "That is, when I pounded and you didn't open the door for me. I've been worried sick about you. Liz's voice broke up bad on her cell when she called me, but I thought she said you'd be waiting for me here. I was really upset when you weren't and now, apparently," he rushed on, "cell phones are not working at all for some reason. Or maybe it's just the fact we're as good as encased by a concrete bunker in here, which is exactly what we need."

"Oh, rats," Cindy said and sniffed hard. "I was gonna call my mom again to let her know I'm okay. I'll try anyway, just to see," she said and turned on her phone.

Its small blue screen glowed in the dim light as she punched the numbers in. Nate stepped closer to her to look over her shoulder.

"Aw, you're right," she wailed. "It says 'call cannot be connected.' It could be her phone's off, like she's recharging it or something, but I doubt it. Not with all this going on."

"See?" Nate said and came back to put his arm around Kaylin again, holding her to him. She shifted slightly away. She'd just been reminded of something which had been bothering her last night, when she couldn't sleep despite her exhaustion.

She hadn't been able to reach Nate or Liz by cell phone for a while yesterday. When Nate had stopped by the high school, she had asked him why. He'd said it was because they'd both decided to recharge their phones in case the area lost power. That had sounded logical, but her numerous calls to them had actually gone through. Their phones had rung, and the voice-mail option was available. Could it be they just weren't answering, for some reason? That would have been about the time someone sneaked into Ken Leigh's hunt camp and killed his wife.

And then, of course, Nate had ingeniously suggested the possibility of a ransom note just before Julie found one, which ended up making Grant Towers look guilty. Kaylin had been so thrilled to see Nate here safe, but she had to keep reminding herself that Julie and Zach didn't trust him or Liz right now. Even if he was safe, she suddenly didn't feel that way.

"Would you listen to that howling out there?" Nate said and went to the door to put his ear against the crack in it. "I'm going to shoot the bolt on this, but if it gets much worse outside, we'll put the young ladies in the back room for safety's sake and you and I will guard the frontier, Kaylin."

"No, I promised them we'd all stick together," she insisted, stepping back among the girls.

"But that was before you had me to take care of you—all of you," he said with a nervous laugh. He didn't meet her eyes as he leaned against the door and crossed his arms over his chest.

Suddenly a strange, almost primal fear of this man clawed at Kaylin. Her hair prickled on the nape of her neck. An icy shudder slid down her spine, raising gooseflesh that was not from being soaked or the dank chill in here.

"So where are Julie and Zach Brockman in this mess?" he asked.

"That reminds me," she said, her voice trembling, "I was going to ask you if Liz is okay and where she is."

"Safe, I'm sure, just like all of us."

She forced a stiff smile and a nod. His eyes narrowed as he seemed to assess her anew, and not quite the way he used to, with sexual heat. He seemed different now, calculating and cold.

"Mom! Mom? Is it really you? I've been dreaming, drifting… Is it you?"

"Yes, yes, we're here. Is that Thad? Is he okay?"

"He's been a goner since the Jet Ski threw us. I mean, he's breathing, but he's like, still unconscious."

Julie and Zach gripped each other's hands so tightly Julie winced. She could have danced in delirious joy, but reality smacked her hard. If they didn't move fast, they could all drown.

"Randi, I'm Thad's dad," he said, leaning over the well. Despite the shriek of wind, his deep voice echoed, the words crisp and controlled, though he was shaking as hard as Julie. "We have to get you both out of there and off this island. This is a really bad storm with high water coming, so I'm going to lower a rope. If you can tie it around and under Thad's shoulders, we'll haul him up, then you."

"Thank God you're here, 'cause this water's rising really fast. I'm on a pile of coconuts to keep our heads up, but they keep slipping. I've been drinking rainwater, but we're going to go under, and I'm so stiff and sore. I think we've been here two days."

"It took us almost three to find you," Zach said.

"Thank you, Mr. Brockman," she cried as both Zach and Julie untied and unwrapped the rope from his waist. Julie kept working but she shook her head and cried harder. Her little girl, her baby, after being kidnapped, was being polite in the middle of a deadly hurricane.

"Call me Zach, okay, Randi? I really owe you for helping Thad, for not letting him go under. Who put you here? Keep talking, Randi, okay?"

"I wish I knew, because I'd stick them down here! Two guys in a boat, one steering and one who grabbed us. He threw a big net over us and dragged me underwater. Thad was already out cold. When I saw I was bleeding from my nose and was cut up, I think I fainted. I'm still pretty weak."

"She always faints when she sees blood," Julie told Zach, then called down to Randi. "I'll toss you a bottle of water."

"I couldn't grab it. Just get us out and keep talking, okay?"

"Can you describe the man you did see?" Julie asked.

"He wore a baseball cap and a handkerchief—like some bank robber in a Western. I didn't recognize the boat. If Thad did, he didn't say when we were trying to outrun them. But we saw floating drugs, wrapped up, and maybe the boat came to get them."

"Drugs," Julie said to Zach. "Then it might not be Liz and Nate. It could be almost anyone."

Randi called up to them, "I don't think I can let go of Thad to tie a rope around him. I've got him propped up against me just right, or he'll go under, and it's getting deeper. I'm better now that you're here but still kinda dizzy."

"Julie, I can't go down because you'd never haul me back up," Zach said, not yelling down the cistern this time.

"I'll go down."

She peeled off the backpack and all her life jackets, as Zach made a large noose and tied knots. "Put yourself in this to keep your hand cuts from opening again," he said as they heard another coconut palm go down nearby, evidently taking several others with it. This time, neither of them so much as flinched.

"It's okay. Nothing matters but getting them up and out of here."

In the cistern, Julie wished she hadn't lost her shoes because the rubber soles on these old tabby bricks would have helped. Rather than trying to walk her way down, she just hung still, bumping and sliding her way down, with a bottle of water clutched in her hand.

"Mom—oh, Mom!" Randi cried as she got near her level. The girl pressed her shoulder hard against Julie's hips and burst out crying. "I thought I would die, never see you again."

"Randi, don't push on me now, or I can't get lower. My darling girl, I'm so sorry, too. Randi, get back, sweetheart!"

Julie's feet hit water, and she went down about four feet. The cistern bottom was murky, slimy. She nearly twisted an ankle on a coconut that slipped aside from Randi's pile of them, then popped to the surface to nearly hit Julie in the face as Zach trained his light on them. It wouldn't have taken much more rain for these kids to drown, and the storm surge…

Julie held the water bottle to Randi's lips, and she drank greedily. She tried to get some down Thad, but it just spilled back out.

"Julie! Let's go!" Zach shouted.

She stuffed the bottle in her pants and put the loop in the rope around the unconscious Thad. Her fingers kept slipping. Both of her palms hurt, her bandages were soaked, and the ropes, too.

"Thad's breathing for sure," she shouted up to Zach as she worked while Randi still held him up, "but he feels cold."

"I'm cold, too," Randi said. "So cold, I'm numb, even in this hot, humid weather."

"I'll boost him," Julie cried. "Lift him! Now!"

She'd thought Randi could help heft him, too, but once Thad's dead weight started up, Julie realized Randi was nearly frozen into the position in which she'd held him. Despite the musical howl of wind over the top of the cistern, as if some giant blew across a bottle top, Julie could hear Zach grunting to get Thad up. Near the top, the boy's inert body scraped on the side and hung there as if caught, before Zach somehow both kept the rope taut and reached over the edge for him.

Julie cradled Randi to her, kissing her cheek, her forehead, rocking her like a baby. If the storm surge came even now, at least they would be together.

"Oh, Mom, I love you, oh, Mom." Randi kept up an almost incoherent chatter. "I was so scared. I can't wait to get back on dry ground—am I going to be grounded for this?"

"For life, baby," Julie managed and cried harder herself.

"I don't care. I don't care, just don't leave me...."

"Julie!" Zach bellowed as the rope flopped down again, hitting her on the head. "Randi next!"

"Come on, honey. We have to hurry. The storm's going to get even worse."

"Did they try to get money for us?" Randi asked.

"Not now. Later, when we get home," she promised, slipping the same big loop under her daughter's armpits.

"All right—go!" she shouted to Zach. His flashlight beam left to leave Julie alone in darkness as she hoisted Randi and he hauled her upward, faster, easier than he had Thad.

The rope flopped down again; the light illuminated her in this hole that had held Randi, so scared, so alone. It sounded as if her daughter had agonized about things, too, the way she had.

Julie looped the noose under her armpits and dared to shout, "Hooyah!"

She bumped and turned on her way up until her head cleared the top of the cistern and she put her arms out to grab hold. "These trees keep coming down," Zach gritted out as he hauled Julie over the lip. "But at least they were thick here to keep the rainfall in that cistern low. Randi," he said, as Julie scrambled to put a life vest on her, while Zach had already put one on Thad, "can you walk?"

"I think so—I'm just hurting, but at least I'm not bleeding now."

"I'm going to carry Thad, and we're heading back for the boat. Julie, take my flashlight and hold onto Randi and lead the way. If you hear another tree go, everyone hits the ground."

Julie took Randi's wrist, ignoring the pain in both hands. She held to her daughter as tightly as she had years ago, heading into a crowded football game in Ann Arbor or at the state fair when she was little. She used Zach's flashlight to hack through, the way she'd seen him do, ignoring everything but getting back to the boat. This storm be damned, she felt wonderful now. She had Randi back alive, and they were going to be closer, better, always. And surely, Thad would recover, too.

Randi stumbled behind her, sometimes lurching along, but there was no time to help that. She could hear Zach's heavy breathing behind, hear the swish and smack of sopping foliage as he carried his son away from the place where he could have died in her daughter's arms.

After an eternity, staggering against the blast of wind and thickening downpours, sometimes going from tree to writhing tree for support, Julie led them to the edge of Cistern Key where she thought they'd left the boat.

"Isn't this the place?" she cried. "Where is it?"

"It must have blown away already."

A moaning sound escaped from deep in her throat, an involuntary keening. She put her arms hard around Randi, and they swayed in the wind together, leaning back against a trembling tree trunk with surf rampaging at their feet.

"Let's move!" Zach ordered, his voice harsh. "That storm surge is overdue. Julie, find some pieces of trunks you can lift, while Randi stays with Thad. It's Swiss Family Robinson time."

Julie nodded and pushed her daughter down to sit just off what must have once been the beach. Zach put Thad next to the girl, with his head in her lap, and handed Randi two bottles of water.

"Mom, doesn't he mean Robinson Crusoe?" Julie heard Randi ask and couldn't help smiling through her tears and the stinging rain.

How long, Kaylin thought, she had wanted to get Nate alone, but now that he'd proposed exactly that, she felt frenzied. She had to protect these girls. She had to stay with them. No way was she going to agree they should be shoved into some small electrical room, as Nate had called it.

Nate tried to pull her away to speak with her alone, but she shook him off. "I think the door to the outside is sturdy enough to hold," she insisted. "I don't want the girls in that other little room. They might get claustrophobic in there. I know I would."

"Even animals know when they are better off in cages," he told her and swept his hand toward the eagle.

Still, she didn't budge. From across the room, she nodded to the girls to encourage them and wished they weren't trying to give her some space with Nate. They were clumped in the corner near the door to the electrical room as if they were willing to be herded in there.

"Okay then," Nate said, almost whispering now so she had to read his lips at first, "let's leave them here and go out into my van. It's in a sheltered area. Kaylin, I really need to talk to you alone—please. I think I know who took Randi and the Brockman boy, but I need to bounce it off you before I take steps. You said you were partly blaming yourself for Randi's loss. Getting the people responsible will make Julie forgive you."

He did care and was trying to help! "Then tell me here," she whispered back. "No way we should go back outside— not for hours."

"You've changed. What's with you?"

She wanted to trust and love Nate, and she desperately wanted him to love her back. It had been years since she'd cared deeply for someone, and she didn't want to lose him, too.

"The storm, on top of our losing Randi, is getting to me," she said.

He smiled as if she'd said something funny. *He* was the one who had changed, she thought, and not for the better. But her protest died in her throat. Pulling her to him, not too tight, so that it probably looked the way he'd hugged her in front of the girls before, he put his hand in his pants pocket and, using her to block their view, showed her a gray metal gun.

She gasped, her mouth open, her eyes wide. He dropped it quickly back in place, but kept his hand on it.

"Kaylin," he said, his voice quiet and icy-cold, "tell your little chicks to step into the electrical room for a minute. I'm dead serious about nailing Clint Blackwood for taking those kids—he and his poaching, fishing and drug-running buddies—and you've got to help me."

Clint Blackwood!

Scared, confused, Kaylin turned to her girls, who were still trying to look away as if to give her some privacy with her guy. She said to them, "I think it might be safer for you in that little room, just for a few minutes until we can test the door to the outside to make sure it doesn't blow in to harm these animals or us. And we can't be standing here if the door really blows."

Could Nate have proof that Clint and his fishermen friends were to blame? Had Julie and Zach considered that? If only she could help find who took them. As Nate said, it might make up for her sending Randi out there. But Nate's gun scared her to death, and she had her own reason for wanting the girls out of this immediate enclosed area.

If she couldn't grab that gun and hold it on Nate until the girls could come back out and tie him up, she was going to surprise him with the knife in her pocket and do what she had to. And she couldn't afford to have former cutters, who were already cut once today, see that—or be hurt or killed by ricocheting bullets.

23

Tim Ralston here at 9:30 a.m., with you in the belly of the beast. What we're experiencing now is not the eye, but what is called the moat of the hurricane. That is a relatively light rain region between the first rain bands and the eyewall, so the storm surge is imminent. Not only will the surge inundate our barrier islands, the smaller keys and our shoreline, but expect to see rising water far back into the Glades. Remember, this will displace sea and land animals, including our gator friends, by driving them quite a ways inland onto what was formerly dry ground. Keep it tuned right here and don't venture out for a peek, even in the moat or in the more benign-appearing eyewall. In this case, what looks like relief could ravage you.

"The rain's let up a little," Julie told Zach as she and Randi held pieces of palm tree trunks while he quickly lashed them together with fishing line and the rope they'd used to rescue the kids. "Maybe the storm is not hitting this area directly," she added, trying to sound hopeful.

"We can't wait around to find out. I wish we had a radio, but then I wish we had a lot of things."

"Like *The Hooyah!*"

"If she's gone, it's a small price to pay. I'm hoping we'll find her beached somewhere after this is all over."

That did sound hopeful. The raft looked finished to Julie, and she guessed it was when Zach lifted Thad onto it and tied him down with the last of the rope. She realized that the other loops of fishing line in each of the corners were for handholds.

"Julie here, Randi here," he said, pointing. "Hang on to Thad and your loop of line which will tether you to the raft. If you get swept away, let your life preserver hold your head up, and the storm should take you into shore."

"Where are we compared to Gladesport?" Randi asked, as she threw the last empty water bottle away.

"South," Zach said, "but the storm's heading to the northwest, so it may take us close to home. But it may also change the shoreline as we know it. The three of us will have to get the raft on solid ground somewhere and try to find shelter before the back side of this thing hits. That old lodge of yours may be our best bet, if we can find it. Let's go. Help me get the raft out into the water."

Julie gasped. "I thought we had to wait here for the storm surge to lift and take us in."

"Not in a raft," he said, shoving it into the next breaker that foamed around them. "We'll need to be in the water so it will lift us, not bash us. Go!"

"We'll find the lodge, Mom!" Randi cried. "We're heading home!"

Tears blinded Julie's vision, but she managed to keep her feet. Although Randi had been so unhappy at the lodge, could this horrible abduction have changed her mind about what was home?

The three of them pushed the raft out. Randi went to her knees in the sweep of gray water, but Zach boosted her onto the raft next to Thad so that only he and Julie had their feet down.

"Time our push just after the next breaker!" he shouted. "It took *The Hooyah!*, it should take this."

But the blast of water spun them and thrust them back, both clinging to the raft. Again, again they tried until they were ripped out, afloat. To Julie's surprise, Zach pushed her up with the kids and stayed in the water with only his upper torso on the raft. The makeshift thing was about six feet square, but there was room for him. Julie motioned for him to come up and held out her hand. He took it, squeezed it and let it go, shaking his head. He had his arms through the fishing line handholds, so Julie concentrated on holding Thad steady and on praying silently and fervently.

She didn't think they were making progress toward shore but she glimpsed Cistern Key shrinking through the rain and mist. The wind seemed a perpetual roar in her ears, the flying foam and smash of waves normal now. But the tilt and slide of the massive black water seemed to tip them so much harder than it had *The Hooyah!*

They soon settled into the dip and sway until a wall of water washed over them. It swept them up, up, tipping and ripping at the raft. Randi screamed. It became a roller-coaster ride down, down with Julie hanging onto the kids and her stomach falling away as they smashed into a maelstrom of white water—and then Zach was gone.

* * *

Kaylin gripped the knife in her pocket. Of course, it would be no match for a gun, but she was clinging to the hope Nate had it on him just to protect the eco-compound from looting after this was over, or because he really intended to try to question or even capture Clint Blackwell.

But she knew better. And she feared she knew why. Nate and Liz always wanted more financial support for their causes. And they held huge grudges against those who got in the way of their mission in life. So could ransom money—or the drug money he'd mentioned in the same breath with Clint—be something they could justify? But even if she could imagine their wanting to hurt Grant Towers, Victoria and Ken Leigh, or Clint, why would they ever harm Julie and Zach's kids?

"You're scaring me with that gun," she told him. "Are you hoping to question or even get the drop on Clint with that?"

"Get the drop?" he said, his voice mocking. "That's a good one. More like waste the bastard for what he's done to those kids—and to Julie and you, not to mention to Zach Brockman."

"Yes, Zach has helped Liz in the fight to protect sharks," Kaylin said, choosing her words carefully. Anything to keep him talking, to find out whether she could trust him or not. She wanted to, she needed to, but she had to let go of all that and be strong.

"But Clint Blackwell is Zach's friend, isn't he?" she asked. "Why would he want to hurt Zach or his son?"

"Clint is Zach's competition. Not only a rival for charter fishing clients—ones Clint lets kill and keep sharks—but they became enemies over that shark legislation we fought so hard for. No, it's Clint, and I can prove it. When someone steps over the line like that, they deserve what they get."

That reminded her so much of some things Liz had said, that nature would avenge itself on those who abused it. But she'd never realized until now that Nate shared that zeal that edged into fanaticism. She'd seen Nate as exciting before, but now she saw him as dangerous to her and the girls. This storm, this crisis, had ruffled Nate's feathers to make him strike out, just as this eagle almost had yesterday.

"Tell me about Clint," she said. If he pulled the gun on her, she'd have to be close to him to use the knife. Very close, so close he didn't see her pull it out. "I'll be grateful to you if you can prove he took the kids and find out where we can get them back."

"Exactly," he said. "That's one thing this is for."

He drew the gun slowly, held it loosely. Though her gut instinct was to duck and run, she stepped closer.

"I'll bet you'll need something like that to make him talk—to tell the truth," she said.

"Which reminds me, I need to know where Zach and Julie are, so I can tell them my theory and deliver Clint to them as soon as this storm is over. Do you know where they went? And don't tell me they're with the poor saps waiting for school buses," he said, gesturing toward the door.

She moved closer to it. She'd never run out into the storm or leave the girls behind with this man, but she had a plan, if she could only open that door.

"The sheriff told Julie and Zach to stay put," she said, "but they kept defying him to find the kids, so last time he left the shelter, he took them with him. I only hope he hasn't actually put them under lock and key."

She shook her head and tried to look worried as she took another step closer to Nate and to the outside door. He suddenly stepped between it and her, reached out and pulled her against him, full length. One arm snaked around her waist, the other held the gun straight up, jiggling its muzzle back and forth, more or less pointed at her chin. Her fingers tightened around the knife in her pocket.

"You're lying," he said, "and I'd hate to think why. I met the sheriff on the road on my way in here, and he had no one in his cruiser."

"So, he came back for them after. He—"

"Where are they?" he said, still keeping his voice low and glancing past her, evidently to be sure the girls were staying put in that little room. "Storm or no storm, I need to talk to Julie and Zach about Clint before he hurts them," he said, his voice and look so menacing that Julie knew for certain he intended to hurt her. But the girls could later testify who she'd been with—unless he planned to eliminate them, too. If Nate and Liz were the ones using the storm to cover their crimes, what would five more lives be, especially if they'd already hurt Randi and Thad? And she'd be at fault for taking these girls away from the others in the shelter, just like she was at fault for losing Randi.

That thought made her desperate. And absolutely furious.

"Let me go and put that gun away," she said, a new edge in her voice. "Julie and Zach never tell me where they're going, so I don't have to lie to the sheriff when he asks. You'll have to check with Loreen Blackwell about Clint and Julie. The last time I saw Julie she was talking to her."

"So maybe they're on to Clint, too! What else do you know about who they suspect or why? Did they think it could be Grant Towers? I swear, Kaylin, you *will* tell me what you know."

He pressed the gun to her cheek in the same moment she pulled the knife. "All right, I'll tell you," she said, but she yanked back, took a wild swipe at his ribs, slicing him in the side just above his waist.

He shoved her and staggered away from the door. The gun banged once, blasting a bullet into the ceiling. Just behind her, the eagle went wild in its cage, flapping huge wings against the wire bars. Kaylin prayed the girls would not come running out. Perhaps that little room was almost soundproof, or the roar of the storm was too loud.

She took another swipe with her kitchen knife at the astounded man who held his ribs with one hand and leveled the shaking gun toward her with the other. This time she got him high on his right forearm. The gun went flying, but so did the knife.

Looking stunned, he stared at blood on his hand.

Then, somehow, Nate got to the gun again. The bullet pinged past her as she half crawled, half rolled toward the eagle's cage and reached up to yank it open. Nate staggered toward her. She scrambled for the outside door, certain he would shoot her, kill her. Her head and body grew hot, waiting for a bullet.

The door must have been damaged when Nate broke in, because it blasted open at her as soon as she shoved the dead bolt.

Fanning its huge wings, the eagle flew free. The bird rose into the blast of air, pumping upward, its talons spread. She wasn't sure if Nate shot again, but he went down to his knees, holding his side as the huge bird tried for the door, then got swept back, clawing Nate and beating him with its wings.

Kaylin scrambled for his gun, but the wind blew her hard against Nate. It swirled, shoving cages, tipping some as she fought free of the wounded man, kicked him away. She managed to pull a soccer net down over him, then a second one, then a third. The metal frames banged against the concrete floor as the three heavy nets held him captive. Even as the winds scoured the room, the big bird settled itself on top of an archery target in the corner behind the door and glared down at them.

Kaylin was both giddy with relief and horrified at what she had learned—and done. She'd never manage to get the door closed again, so she'd have to try to get into the small room with the girls, leaving Nate out here under all that, and hope he didn't get away. Clint Blackwell was just a smoke screen, wasn't he? It must have been Nate and Liz who had taken Randi and Thad.

The gun in her hand, covering her head to protect it from flying debris, Kaylin crawled toward her girls.

The moment Zach was swept away, then sucked down, he knew he'd underestimated the entire storm, especially its surge. A trained combat swimmer, at the utter mercy of the water he'd always loved.

He tried to find and fight for the surface, to get a breath.

He had a life vest on, so he should pop up, but he was being swallowed, lower, down.

Go low to stay under longer, he heard his BUD/S instructor's words. *More pressure in the lungs, the farther the oxygen goes.*

He'd learned to relax in water, go with the flow, use it, to not panic. He'd learned to count his kicks to know how far he'd gone in the depths so he could come up just where he needed to set the demolitions off. Two-mile ocean swims, pool harassment drills…he had conquered it all. But now, he was helpless.

They had to secure a beachhead, so where was the Zodiac? Hadn't the C-130 dropped the Zodiac yet? They had to mount the outboard motor from the drop. He'd made the free-fall parachute drop, but where was the CRC? He needed that combat raiding craft. The roaring in his ears—was that the C-130 or the motor? Maybe Garth had already mounted and started it.

No, Garth was dead. He could accept that now, because he, too, stared death in the face, held by the water's strong embrace. He and Garth had come to love the water, the power of it. Yes, Garth was dead and he could let him go, not blame himself for his friend's death anymore, for Garth was at peace, too….

But Garth would want him to live. To fight to live…

Where was up? The bubbles all around him were swirling, not pointing his way up. Was he tangled in his parachute lines? He had no breath. He was exhausted, hadn't slept in days, going through hell week…

Then he remembered. He wasn't looking for the plane or

the Zodiac, but for a raft. Where was the raft and Julie and the kids, all alone now on the fierce sea? Even if they were lost, he was the one who would die.

Black ops, black water, black death. The sacred sea had taken his father from him years ago, taken Becky, taken Garth. He'd swum with sharks, and they'd never hurt him. Was that big, black body swimming close to him the shark he'd tagged the day this all began, the shark that nodded its thanks for being released and not killed…just released, released…

Or was that his father, gesturing to him, come…come deeper with me. Garth, saying it's okay his swim buddy couldn't save him. And was Becky there, her hair streaming out behind her? In her recklessness, she'd chosen her own death, and it wasn't his fault.

He wanted Julie now, to save Julie, love her and those kids…

He broke the surface with a whoosh. Riding a wave, surfing? Maybe he was swimming underwater, like that day off Osprey with the fake shark he'd made to show those snobs that the local kids who worked there weren't nothing, weren't only to be seen and not heard—not even seen…

He sucked in huge gasps of air before the next wave washed over him. Choking on sea water, spitting it, he still breathed deep.

Reality returned. Treading water, trying to keep his head up, he scanned the waves for the raft. But again, churning water sucked him down, up, down, around. Even when the next huge swell lifted him and he could look around, he saw nothing.

Nothing but the storm, tearing at the sea.

* * *

Julie clung to Randi and Thad on the raft as waves washed over them, then hurled them onward and around.

"Do you see him?" Randi screamed.

"No, but he's a strong swimmer! I—I think we're riding the storm surge that took him. We have to be going in the same direction!"

But everything seemed circular now, without direction. The wind, the patterns of white wash atop the waves. The way the raft rotated, with no rudder and no course or control. This pounding, sweeping dizziness in her head from exhaustion and hunger and from her need for Zach. She had Randi back and Thad was alive and had to have medical help, but she needed Zach.

And she needed to help Zach.

Fastening her feet and legs as best she could in the ropes on the raft, she raised her head and shoulders to try to spot him. But if she did, he'd never hear her scream his name in this shrieking nightmare. She'd never get the raft to him. Zach would want her to keep Thad safe, to get him into shore.

And so, sobbing, mourning, she and Randi held to the unconscious boy, who looked so much like his father, through each peak and valley of the sea until she dreamed that the waves went still and the sun came out.

24

Tim Ralston here at 11:00 a.m. The eye is beginning to pass over us now, but as I have repeated before, do not go outside. That is, except for those at the Gladesport High School shelter, where a tornado ripped part of the roof off and folks are going to be relocated farther inland. Remember, the winds are always worse at the back side of the eye, only this time they go clockwise instead of counterclockwise. In the eye itself, the winds will drop, but the waves will continue to be pushed along. The passage of the eye can take from ten minutes to several hours, but I estimate with Dana's relative compactness, we are looking at a little under an hour. As for the storm surge, we have flooding inland along the coast and are waiting for reports on that. Water is coming up into the estuaries. Keep safe out there.

At first Julie thought she was dreaming. Though the ocean still roared and breakers smashed behind them, the raft rested in some sort of lagoon. But there was no place like that anywhere she knew around Gladesport. She had no idea where they were or how much time they had.

Straddling Thad, she stood on the remnants of the battered raft and shaded her eyes from the sun. Had they died and been cast into paradise? But it would never be that without Zach.

"Mom," Randi cried, "a bunch of leaves are poking between the pieces of the raft."

Julie looked down and gasped, even as her right foot went through between two pieces of palm trunk and she almost pitched into the water. They seemed to have been snagged in the top of some mangrove trees. Where were they? And where was Zach? She couldn't bear to lose him after all he'd done for them—and how deeply, beyond anything they'd been through, she cared for him.

On her knees, as the raft continued to shift in two-foot waves that seemed like nothing now, Julie kept scanning the lagoon. She nearly jumped off the raft when Thad moaned and moved.

"No, he does that sometimes," Randi said. "He still doesn't wake up. He even yawns."

"Hold him still. Zach must have been washed in here, too—he had a life jacket on. And he's a good swimmer."

Her voice broke. She fought to keep from crying. The kids had to be her first priority. Zach would demand that.

"Mom, what are we going to do?"

"We'll have to paddle farther inland before the back side of the hurricane hits."

"The back side? You mean it's not over? Paddle with what?"

"Our hands. No, it's not over."

Julie knelt next to Thad to make sure he was still breathing, then lay on her stomach and started to dip her arm into the water, but that only swung them in a circle. Tears blinded her and dripped off her chin, salt water into salt. Randi shifted to the other side of the disintegrating raft, sprawled out and paddled, too. They soon hit a stride and moved off the tops of the mangroves. What key or island was beneath this storm surge, this flood, Julie wondered. Could it even be Osprey?

The silence of the eye was almost deafening, and the air seemed to have a strange smell. But the raft was breaking up under then, pulling apart to strain the fishing line Zach had wrapped around the palm tree logs. Her back muscles and arms were killing her, her newly opened cuts on her hands stung in the salt water, but none of that mattered. Zach had given them the gift of life—and, even if she'd lost him forever, whether he had meant to or not, he had also given her the gift of love.

Caught up in the storm surge, Zach couldn't tell where he was until he saw a large piece of the roof from Leon and Jake's house. Clinging to the ragged hole where the chimney must have been and braced against a bent stovepipe, Leon was the only one in sight. Now, how did a paraplegic get up there, evidently on his own, Zach marveled as he started to swim toward the roof.

His bulky life vest slowed him down, but it had probably saved his life and he might need it again. No, he'd put Leon in it to fight the other side of the storm when it came through.

About a third of the Malverses's roof had snagged against the bare branches of a row of gumbo-limbo trees that had somehow held in the wind and water. If those trees were where Zach was thinking, the roof hadn't gone far before it had caught. What was left of it was rocking and bumping against the trees. And solemn, stoic Leon, covered by a long length of clear plastic, was wailing so loud Zach could hear him from here.

The old man didn't see him until Zach heaved himself onto the edge of the roof, rocking it even more.

"Leon! Where's Jake?"

Leon gasped and looked up, shading his eyes in the sun. "Zach? My boy's gone, swept away, getting me up here. I didn't see him again. Went the way of Becky and your boy."

"No," Zach shouted, backing up the roof in a crab walk. "Julie and I found the kids on Cistern Key. Thad seems to be comatose, but he's alive. They're on a makeshift raft out there somewhere—got to be near," he said, shading his eyes, too.

"Who done it to them?" Leon demanded with a loud sniff. Every time he moved, the heavy plastic crinkled. "Jake stayed out too long, still looking for them. When he come back for me, it was almost too late. He got me up here, but then—" He sniffed hard again.

"We think Liz Lawson and her lackey Nate took them."

"Damn 'em. The Glades ghost? Now I got somethin' to live for, to get gator garrotes 'round the necks of those two."

His hand on Leon's shoulder to steady himself, Zach stood carefully, straddling the peak of the roof. It was the first time he realized he was barefooted. He guessed he could get higher than the roof if he climbed into one of these bare-branched trees, leaf-stripped by the winds.

"And Clint was here right 'fore it hit," Leon told him. "Wanted me to leave, wanted to know all 'bout where you were and if you knew who'd taken the kids yet—and who was running drugs. I pulled a gun on the damn fool to make him head back for the mainland, 'cause he's got family. But then, when I lost Jake, trying to make me leave here, too…"

"You were thinking of just jumping in and ending it, weren't you, Dad?" Zach asked him, still scanning the horizon.

"What if I was? And you ain't called me Dad since you come back from playing hero."

"Don't you do it, because I'll need your help at the hospital with Thad and then at home."

"But you said they're lost."

"Nope," Zach said and screeched a triumphant cry. "I see the raft, and I've got to get there fast, because Julie and her girl will never get to shelter fast enough before the eye passes."

Zach unbuckled his life vest and tossed it to Leon. "Put that on. The only place around here all of us might pull through the back end of this storm is at the lodge, so we'll come by to get you. Jake may turn up yet, determined and stubborn as he is." Zach gripped Leon's shoulder hard. "Be here when I get back with them."

"That an order?" Leon yelled after him but Zach skidded down the slant of roof and then jumped, feetfirst, into the water.

Without his vest, he set a good pace toward the raft, which he reckoned was a half mile out in a sort of lake the storm surge must have made. Kick, pull, pull, kick, pull, breathe.

A lot of debris cluttered the water, limbs, entire trees, an occasional dead fish or bird, but not many. With their strange sixth sense, animals often fled bad storms before they hit. They probably sensed the drop in barometric pressure and left the area. But if he got his hands on Liz and Nate, he wouldn't stop to discuss that with them.

He was a good fifty yards away when he realized that Julie and Randi were not only moving away from him, but there was no raft.

The raft had fragmented under them. At first Julie had tried to string pieces of the trunks back together with the broken fishing line and the short piece of rope which remained, but that was useless. So they had kept the largest piece of log and draped Thad over it at his armpits. On one side of him, Randi held his wrists while Julie held onto the log and tried to kick to steer them inland.

"I'm kicking, too, Mom," Randi called to her. "I'm so tired, but I'm trying. How long will this calm last?"

"I don't know. The sky still looks okay. The thing is, I've been in the Glades recently, and I don't want us to have to go clear in there."

"Gators and snakes? Liz Lawson will be ticked if they got hurt in this horrible storm."

Their chatter had helped Julie, because it had seemed so normal. It was wonderful to have Randi back. She wanted to tell her their suspicions about Liz and Nate, about all that had happened, but her strength was fading and breath was precious.

"Maybe," she said only, "the gators and snakes all went inland to shelters, like people with any sense."

"Yeah, but what about sharks? Mom—a fin! I'm not kidding—I did see a fin! There's a shark in the water, oh, a shark, a shark!"

Julie froze, hanging still. Every inch of her underwater felt icy cold, then hot. She saw that horrid scene from *Jaws* again, the woman in the water, but Zach had said he'd swum with sharks. Surely, Randi was wrong, and it was something else.

But she, too, saw the fin and the sleek gray body gliding by beneath it. Circling. It was a shark, and it was circling.

She stayed quiet, her hurt hands gripping only the top of the log in case she was bleeding, looking at Thad, so oblivious to everything. She couldn't see Randi. Fighting to keep from just screaming, she said, "Zach said they come to vibrations. Don't move or talk."

Julie couldn't tell if there was one shark or more. This one made ripples in its circuit of them, rocking them. It came so close she felt the water from it bump her, move her—or had the shark itself done that?

Curious, Zach had said. They were curious.

She shuddered and her body went from flushed to freezing. She wanted to scream out her instinctive fear, just as she had these last days about losing Randi. What if she lost her now—this way?

Zach. She needed Zach. Somehow facing an entire hurricane seemed like a swim in a pond next to facing this. To come so far and then this.

Zach stopped and treaded water once to shout at Julie and Randi to stop paddling inland, but they had kept going, so he did, too. They were evidently afloat on a piece of the raft; at least he was moving a lot faster than they were. He was amazed at how quickly he was catching up.

And then he saw why. They'd stopped dead in the water. And at least one shark was circling them.

Using the fastest Australian crawl stroke he knew, he swam closer, then treaded water with his legs to cup his hands to his mouth.

"Stay still and be quiet! It may be hurt or disoriented. I'm going to draw it over here!"

"Oh, Zach!" Julie screamed. "Thank God, but—"

"I said shut up!"

"I thought you meant just stay still in the water."

"Julie, shut up!"

"I don't want you to get hurt either. Zach, I need you!"

Whatever happened to him now, he'd be happy, he thought. Thad had survived, Julie had Randi—if they could get to shelter before the rear end of this storm hit. But why couldn't that woman follow orders?

He began to thrash in the water. He'd seen that draw them before, because they thought it was a wounded fish and scented blood whether it was there or not. If the shark didn't leave them alone, he might have to open the wound on his leg again, to use his own blood for chum. That would be the end of him, but he was praying the shark's presence was an aberration—that his movements wouldn't summon a whole school of them.

The shark came straight for him. He saw it and stayed still. They had a blind spot right in front of their noses, so he could try to hit him hard there. He'd never done it, but he'd heard you could spook them like that. But if he saw an open maw and rows of razor-sharp teeth, it would be too late for that or anything.

It rushed toward him so fast, it created a wake that rocked him back. But it slid past him, a hammerhead, one with a yellow tag. On the next pass it made—he tried to ignore Julie and Randi's shrieks as they foolishly paddled closer to him— he saw the familiar J-shaped scar it bore. Yes, the shark he had freed the day this nightmare began—it had to be.

To his utter amazement and awe, the fish circled him once, then cleared the water in a corkscrew leap over him, dove in and disappeared.

"Where is it?" Julie cried.

"Great team partner, you are," he choked out and ducked his head once in the water to hide that he was crying with relief. "I tell you to shut up and—"

"Is it gone?" she demanded. "Randi and I aren't kicking any more until we know it's gone."

"I see you kicked your way clear over here after I told you not to. Besides, it was a friend of mine, just checking you out."

He stroked to them to kiss Julie, then got behind the log to point it toward Osprey and kick as hard as he could. "Kick, ladies," he said. "And that's an order I'm asking you, pretty please, to consider obeying."

"To where?" Julie asked, and he saw she was crying, too, but there was no time to comfort her.

"To pick up Leon on the way to the lodge. That lake with the tree tops sticking up ahead—that's Osprey."

* * *

In just under an hour, Julie figured, their sweet blue sky was gone and their world turned gray again, then blindingly black. It was bizarre to have the winds sweeping in the other direction, to have that glimpse of paradise devoured by the return of the shrieking storm.

They picked up Leon, clinging to a stovepipe on a ruined roof. As they swam toward the lodge, not knowing if it would be intact or visible, they found the winds had scoured the backbone of the key dry.

"Maybe the storm surge is receding," Julie said, overjoyed to feel somewhat solid earth under her feet again. "I think this ridge is right along the path that linked the lodge to Leon's." But she still felt she was rocking on the waves. She wove as she stood; they all did.

"I'm going to carry Thad again!" Zach yelled. "Can you two pull Leon on this piece of plastic he's been using for a raincoat?"

"Go on without me!" the old man said, gesturing them away. "I'll never make it without Jake, 'n' you all can go faster without me."

"I told you, Thad needs you!" Zach shouted as the horrid whine of wind picked up.

"I need you, too!" Julie told him. "Whatever's left of the lodge—when Randi and I visit here from Michigan—I want someone who knows the past of this place to tell tales to the girls I'm counseling."

"Visit here?" Randi cried. "I can see our doing more re-decorating together to fix the place up again, but I've been thinking a lot down that well. I don't want to go back to Michigan, honest. I mean, I was homesick, but I just want to start school and make a few new friends that aren't gone in two weeks like your girls, that's all."

"*You're* my girl," Julie told her, "first and always."

When they tried to walk, they staggered, not as much from the wind as their dizziness from being pitched about on the water. No one said anything else as they plodded through the lashing storm toward where the lodge should be. Julie kept telling herself it had withstood other storms, though maybe none so bad as this. But even if it was gone—like her daughter had been for three terrible days—she still would not want to leave Osprey.

To their dismay, it seemed the water was on the rise again; some of the surge which had covered most of Osprey was back. It broke in waves over their path, so Julie and Randi lifted Leon between them and wobbled on behind Zach.

"Lightning coming closer!" Zach shouted. "Knee-deep in water's not a good…" he got out, but the resulting rumble of thunder and the downpour drowned his words.

Most of the pines and some of the palms were gone and Julie couldn't tell how far they'd come, how close they might be. Like Leon's house, the lodge could be gone. If they were washed away, too, would these life vests save them? And could Zach, since he'd given his vest to Leon, make it into shore? What used to be the shoreline could be miles inland now.

She heard a bang-banging from the dark. It reminded her of the WorldWise compound where the ships had hit against the boat-house. And then, when the next stab of lightning lit the slanting deluge, she saw the silhouette of the old lodge, a skeleton in the storm, beckoning to take them in.

25

Tim Ralston with you all the way, southwest Florida. As you know, the eye has passed, and we are in the back eyewall winds, possibly the worst of the storm. We've had gusts up to 125 mph, but our anemometer, which measures wind force and speed, has just blown away here at the station. I'm hoping our tower holds up. I know we can stay strong through the rest of the wind and water—wait, it's going. The tower is shaking and shud—

Zach realized they didn't have to look for a way into the lodge. Either the winds or the storm surge had ruined the screened porch and the front double doors. Some of the plywood from the windows now gaped like lifeless eyes. And the banging—he was shocked to see the old lodge ferry trapped in the embrace of what was left of the front porch.

"I can't believe Captain Mike would come back and bring *The Manatee* out here in this!" Julie shouted to him.

"He's left the key in it for decades. My guess is Clint came out in it, but he should have gone back in by now."

Fear twisted in his gut. Clint could have indeed been running drugs, then been forced to grab Thad and Randi when they saw him and his cronies after picking up those Randi had mentioned. If only Thad were conscious, he could describe or identify the boat. But maybe it was a blessing he'd been knocked out, because if he'd confronted drug runners, he might have been eliminated on the spot.

But whoever had taken the kids had hesitated to harm them outright. Because the kidnapper had a son himself or was a friend of the boy's father? Or was it Liz and Nate, who knew how hard Zach had worked to save sharks? Maybe Ken Leigh had pulled all this off and had some alibis to avoid a double murder charge.

Half staggering, half treading water, they made a human chain and were swept into the lodge. Distant lightning strikes occasionally lit things in here through the missing doors and windows. Unidentified things, some large, floated around inside. The aisles between the furniture and boxes kept shifting, like in those mazelike video games Thad loved. Zach prayed they didn't get swept right through the place and out the back door into the bay, because the winds and water were worse.

"Head for the staircase!" he shouted. "With that lightning, get out of the water!" He put Thad into a rescue hold to pull him through the clumps of debris. Thank God, the water only covered the first few stairs. He could even put his feet down. Between the erratic lightning strikes he went by feel, depositing Thad partway up, then going back to help Julie and Randi with Leon.

Julie was holding to a floating rattan sofa which would never fit through the back door of the lodge, even if it was blown out. He grabbed Randi first, gave her a push toward the broad staircase, then went back for Julie while Leon held to the sofa.

"I'm so exhausted," she said in his ear. "Can we sit the rest of the storm out here?"

"If I'm invited upstairs again."

"My bedroom's large and at the back," she told him as he pulled her toward the stairs. "That will do."

"Reminds me of my place or yours, sweetheart. Hold that thought."

Julie wanted to laugh and hug Zach as he delivered her to her own staircase, but she ached all over. Still, she found the strength, with Randi, to help Leon climb the stairs, one at a time, backwards, in a sitting position.

"I'll be right back to help," Zach said. Bending over to lift and carry Thad again, he went ahead.

They got the old man all the way to the top of the stairs, but no Zach. Standing at the top of the staircase in almost the same place where she'd heard the intruder just yesterday, she shouted, "Zach?"

"I hope Thad hasn't taken a turn for the worse," Randi said. Her beautiful daughter looked as exhausted and bedraggled as she felt.

"Let's get Leon in there and see what's happened," Julie said and lifted the old man's right arm over her shoulder. "Randi, is there a flashlight somewhere in the stuff in your room?"

"Amid the mess, you mean? I think so, if only I can remem—"

Zach vaulted at them from the dark of the hall—no, not Zach. A form in white, lit by lightning.

Randi screamed, and Julie echoed it.

Liz. Liz, with a gun which glinted in her own flashlight beam!

The tiny black bore of the muzzle looked as big as a cannon. Time seemed to slow, then stop. Julie no longer heard the wind, only her own ragged breathing.

She tried to duck, but Liz shoved hard at Leon. He fell, somersaulting backwards down the stairs and into the water below. Julie went off balance, but grabbed the railing. Randi fell to her knees, clinging to the banister on the other side of the stairs.

"Zach! It's Liz!" Julie screamed, but Liz only shouted a laugh.

"Oh, it's Liz, all right," she cried. She jerked a large flashlight beam and the black pistol from one of them to the other. "But Commando Zach has joined his son in la-la-land and didn't know what hit him, either. I regret that, but not the other risks or losses."

"You—you didn't shoot him?" Julie demanded, squinting into the light. The woman also had a length of rope thrown over her left shoulder.

"I gave him a good, old-fashioned knock on the head with this," she said, still moving the flashlight from one of them to the other. "I never figured you'd find your kids or make it back through the hurricane. Well, in the end you won't. I had to be sure you weren't holed up here—and that you'd found the ransom note. Julie, if I could just have rid the area of the others, I would have, but you've upset things, so you and

Randi will have to be victims of her righteous retribution, too."

"Of the storm's? Of yours, you mean."

"Surely you can understand."

"Understand that you've been running drugs, too? Have you? Poisoning thousands of people, besides murdering Victoria and Grant and trying to set up Ken Leigh for a life in prison? I'm going down to help Leon now."

"You move, and I'll have to *really* get rid of Randi this time."

"But why did you take our kids in the first place?"

"It was their own fault for being in our way at a drug drop. For all I knew, they'd ID us or call for help on a cell phone. They had to be stopped quickly, because I'd already planned the fates of our enemies—in complicity with the storm, of course. Anyway, they should have been punished for running that horrid Jet Ski through an area where we've often counted manatees, not to mention the fish nursing grounds there. Perhaps they've learned their lesson, but none of you seem to be able to listen to reason."

"Reason? You can say that with what you've done?"

"Just listen! Wildlife, both flora and fauna, are on the way to a boutique existence in the Glades, in the country, in this world, if someone doesn't step forward to salvage things! The global environmental movement has stagnated and must be completely transformed. That takes big money and a new, no-holds-barred approach, or we're doomed."

Doomed. To save plants and animals, this woman doomed people and justified it all, from drugs to kidnapping to murder. I need to keep her talking, Julie thought, so she doesn't shoot Randi first. I can get to her, take a bullet, stop her.

"I guess I see what you mean," Julie said, amazed her voice sounded so calm when she was shaking with fury and fear. She slowly raised one hand to shield her eyes from the light, so Liz lowered it slightly. "You always were good at explaining anything about wildlife."

"Saving wildlife is best for people, too. This kind of war is the only way to solve the ecological problems which ultimately endanger and threaten humans. Zach would understand a righteous war. Randi, my regrets," she went on, turning slightly toward the girl, "but I must fight back like this, or in my next visit to speak to schools or other groups, I'd have to tell them that we regret we screwed up our world—and that simply is not an option."

"Let us go," Randi said, "and we won't tell."

Frowning, Liz shook her head. The upward reflection of her flashlight beam caught her features and made her look like a fright mask with her hair wild about her head.

"Where's Nate?" Julie asked, hoping to get Liz's attention back to her instead of Randi.

"Checking on some things for me."

"Then he was the man in the mask!" Randi cried, just as Julie was about to say the same thing. Suddenly, Julie knew how Zach felt when she kept insisting on helping him, on staying with him despite the dangers. If only Randi weren't here, and if she'd shut up. She had to deflect Liz's anger from her daughter, draw it to herself.

"You and Nate not only abducted the kids but killed Victoria Leigh," she accused. "You staged an accident for her, then tried to scare me off when I stumbled on the scene—with arrows you hoped would implicate her husband. But you got cold feet and retrieved the arrows before the police came. Then you had Nate kill Grant."

"The animals and their natural habitat can't fight back for themselves anymore," Liz said, shouting to be heard over the roar of the wind. "Someone has to be bold enough to do it for them!"

"I realize Nate was your lover," Julie plunged on, "probably a worshipper, not at the altar of your storm goddess, but of you."

"At least, Nate is someone who understands, who sees the truth of things. We're so desperate to save the planet and its innocents, that the ends *must* justify the means. And those means include tying up your daughter right now with netting rope I've brought. Then all of us—Zach and Thad, too—are going for one last ride on that little ferry of yours I brought out here. One by one, you'll be quickly knocked out and rolled into the bay. Drowned, battered—you'll get ashore, all right, but none will live to tell that you simply risked too much and drowned."

Julie just gaped at her.

"But the storm's worse out there than before!" Randi protested. "You might not make it in, either!"

"What a clever girl. You, see, I'll borrow all your life vests. Even if that rickety little ferry breaks up or goes down, I'll make it in. But if I'm lost, too, *no price* is too great to rid this once pristine area of those who insult and abuse it. As for the rest of you, I'm sorry, but you were—what is it that they say? Collateral damage."

"When this story comes out," Julie made the last argument she could think of, "you'll set back all the good people who champion the environment—sane ones."

"Enough! I just wanted you to understand, and you don't. No one does. Now tie Randi up, and then I'll do the same for you. Now!" she shouted as she raised the gun stiff-armed at Julie.

Maybe, Julie thought, as Liz threw her the length of rope, she could bend over Randi, then rear up under Liz to knock the arm which held the gun. Liz always seemed in good physical shape, but if only…

Julie startled when Leon yelled from below, "Julie, the sheriff's here! He made it out!"

Liz jerked just slightly, turned her head. She must have known it couldn't be true, and yet it surprised her, too.

Julie lunged, throwing herself at Liz, concentrating on hitting her arm, on getting that gun. They hit the hallway floor and rolled against the wall.

Julie managed to get on top of Liz, but she was sinewy and strong and threw her off. But Randi was there, pummeling her, trying to take the gun.

"Randi, get back!"

The gun cracked close to Julie's ear. Randi screamed. "Mom, my arm! Blood!"

Julie knew Randi would faint. It was up to her. Zach and Thad hurt, Randi hurt, Leon—Leon crawling by his arms, dragging himself up the stairs, not here yet.

Power Julie didn't know she had poured into her. She seized Liz by the hair and hit her head hard into the floor, once, twice. She held one of Liz's flailing arms down and then—then, Randi stood with both feet on Liz's other wrist, even as drops of blood speckled everyone.

Julie grabbed the rope and fiercely wrapped it around Liz until there was no more of it. Leon dragged himself higher, closer by gripping the banister rails until he rolled across the landing to lean an elbow hard in Liz's midsection.

"Remind me not to pay you the rent late, Julie," he muttered and spit at Liz. "Best tend to your girl, then see to Zach and Thad. You and me got us a lot of walking wounded here, now don't we?"

Leon pulled the end of the rope taut around Liz's throat, looking for all the world as if he'd just hog-tied a gator. Finally, the bruised woman looked afraid.

"See, Mom," Randi piped up, "I didn't faint at the blood, even my own, because you needed me."

And then she fainted.

Zach regained consciousness in Julie's arms. She was bathing the bump on the back of his head gently, but he flinched the moment he opened his eyes. It hurt to even turn them, but he did.

"Thad?" he whispered. "Okay? Still out?"

"Yes, in a coma I think," she said, gesturing to the side, "but we'll have help for him soon. After all he's been through, he has to be all right."

"He's been through?" Zach echoed and turned to look for his son. Thad was still on Julie's bed, where he'd put him before the entire world went black. Had a piece of flying debris hit him? He saw now he was on the daybed in Julie's bedroom, his head in her lap.

"Wha' happen'?" he asked, but his words sounded mushy.

"Liz Lawson hit you from behind with a flashlight, then held a gun on me and Randi. She shot Randi, but she's okay, just a nick on her arm, though it did bleed. I would never have been able to wrestle the gun away from Liz and tie her up if Leon hadn't shouted after she knocked him down the stairs. Got all that, partner?"

"Hooyah," he whispered, a pitiful rendition of that battle cry, and his eyes filled with tears.

"The winds have gone down, and I think we may have made it," Julie added. "I'm just hoping Kaylin and the girls are all right, because I have a feeling Liz sent Nate to see what she knew about our suspicions. For once, Liz is not talking. Oh, Zach, thank God we came through!" she blurted, unable to keep up the pretense of being in control anymore. And yet she had been and she was. This lodge she'd loved for years had lasted through the storm—she and Zach had lasted through it, too.

"We make a great team—all of us," he said.

"I agree. Don't I have to ask you questions to be sure you don't have a concussion? Maybe you'll need to get to the hospital like Thad," she said, shifting her thighs under the weight of his head. "Do you want to sit up?"

He put one arm around her hips and settled his head closer against her. "I think I'd better stay put right here so you can protect me and spoil me at least until my head stops spinning. Then all of us—Leon, too—will get Thad some help."

"Swiss Family Robinson?" she whispered.

"South Florida family Brockman-Minton."

And then she knew he had no concussion, though they might both be out of their minds.

"Mom, Mom, it's really calming down outside!" Randi cried, coming in from the hall. "And Liz was cussing out Leon about poaching, so he stuck his shoe in her mouth. But I can't get anything on the local radio to find out if the storm's gone or the hospital and police station are open. Or restaurants. I'm starving, and Thad will be, too, when we get him some help."

"Welcome home, Randi!" Julie said, gripping Zach's hand. "Welcome home."

26

Tim Ralston here, proud to announce that we've had another beautiful day in southwest Florida, this Wednesday, February 18. Today marks the sixth-month anniversary of Hurricane Dana. We've had a high of 78 with a gentle sea breeze—in other words, great boating weather. Despite piles of debris and the battering our area took last summer, we've all pulled together to begin to rebuild. After all, the real purpose of the barrier islands and keys, which took the worst of it, is to protect the mainland, and to move and change shape if nature so dictates.

My worst memory of the storm is when our radio tower went down and I lost the ability to make it all the way through with you, and my best moment was when I heard the evacuees from Gladesport High School had been safely relocated to another shelter. We hope you'll be part of WSEA's best-worst storm moments contest and e-mail or snail-mail your memories to us.

"You gonna send something in to that contest?" Randi asked as Julie turned the radio off and began to set the large metal picnic table under the umbrella on the lanai of the lodge.

"Hey, how was school? I didn't hear you come in. About that contest, no, I don't think so."

"Come on, Mom. There were lots of good moments mixed in with the bad. I mean, if I can say that, you can, too," she said, flinging her backpack into a new rattan porch chair.

"Great moments, fabulous moments!" Julie said, hugging her and waving to Thad as he went off down the hall toward the wing where he, Zach, Leon and Captain Mike, who helped care for Leon, lived. Since *The Manatee* was still being rebuilt, Thad and Randi rode a Jet Ski in to shore each day to catch the school bus. Both Zach and Julie had been against that at first, but maybe it was like climbing back up on a horse that threw you. Besides, life went on. The fish and birds were back and what was left of the leafless landscape showed signs of greening up again.

"Without that storm, Zach and I might not have spoken, and certainly wouldn't be engaged," Julie admitted, glancing at the ring on her left hand. She'd insisted she didn't want a diamond, that he should spend the money on refurbishing *The Hooyah!* which had been found beached nearly at the spot the marina used to stand, as if the boat had brought itself home. But he'd been adamant, and both Randi and Thad had talked her into the ring, too.

Because the lodge had stood, while the marina and Zach's bungalow were devastated, Julie had taken everyone in, but that meant she had extra help rebuilding the first floor, too. She'd even invited Clint and Loreen to stay at the lodge for a while, but they'd been living with Loreen's parents, though they were coming out for dinner tonight.

Strangely, the devastation to the area had not kept tourists and fishermen away, but had brought them out in droves. To make extra money, Clint had even begun hurricane tours in *The Happy Hooker*, taking Leon along to tell tales of times past and regale everyone with how he was rescued from a floating roof. But he always demanded a moment of silence for those who had died in the storm—especially his hero son, Jake—though Julie had heard he always talked about his hero son-in-law and grandson, too.

"You're acting kinda strange, Mom," Randi said, taking the flatware from her and continuing to set places.

"Zach's overdue, that's all."

"You think with what he's been through—and all that special forces training stuff—he won't be here? Don't sweat it, Mom."

Julie heard *The Hooyah!* before she saw it. Most of the docks in the area were gone, so anyone with a boat just tossed out an anchor lately and rode a dinghy in. That is, unless the boatman was a former SEAL.

She watched Zach dive in and swim ashore, then hurried down to the beach to meet him. The sand was strewn, not with refuse and debris, but driftwood, seaweed and shells, just like the old days.

Holding up her tie-dyed skirt, she waded out knee-deep into the gentle surf and hugged Zach hard, even though he was dripping wet.

"Kids get home okay?" he asked, swinging her up into his arms and striding out of the water.

"On time and still handling the big brother-little sister stuff well. But once Mike gets *The Manatee* fixed, I think they should take that in to catch the bus."

"Once baseball season starts, Thad will be coming home later than Randi anyway. Clint and Loreen here yet?"

"No. You've got time to change, if you don't want to sit down to dinner soaked like that. Besides, you and Clint are supposed to grill."

"Oh, right," he said and stopped on the sand to kiss her hard. She tightened her arms around him. "Julie, I've been thinking about possible honeymoon spots."

"Not a cruise, I think."

He laughed.

"Zach, I told you, the ring was enough, and we should put the money into rebuilding things."

"We are rebuilding things—our lives. But I'm going to sell my land to our renters, since Thad and I have a free ride here now."

He grinned at her, and she punched his arm. "I'm the one getting the free ride now," she told him, swinging her bare legs. "Besides, we might have to spend part of our honeymoon testifying in Tampa, since they've moved the venue for Liz and Nate's murder trials. Zach, not to change the subject, but did you see the shark today?"

"Not today. You think I'm nuts, don't you?" he asked as he put her down and they walked up the beach toward the lodge, arm-in-arm.

"I just don't want you to turn into a wacked-out Captain Ahab, looking for a yellow-tagged shark every time you go fishing. It just can't have been the same one."

"I've tagged a lot of sharks, but this one's distinctive," he argued, shaking his head, then turning back to scan the sea.

She stood beside him, looking out, remembering the peril and the power they had faced out there together to find their kids. But the spell was broken when they heard Clint's voice behind them.

"Hey, lovebirds! Some of us been working hard today!" Clint bellowed and windmilled his arm. "I just got a call that the builders for the new marina gonna start tomorrow."

"I can't wait to get Kaylin back next year and start counseling cutters again," Julie told Zach as they walked toward the lodge. Clint and Thad were wheeling out the grill and Leon rolled his wheelchair to the edge of the stone lanai. "And for everything we've planned to do together. You know, this is almost like the old days at the lodge with guests, only a million times better."

Loreen had something under her arm, which Julie thought looked like a loaf of bread, until she extended it to her.

"I was thinking this might be a special wedding present, but it will do for a hostess gift," she said.

It was the antique life preserver Julie had always admired at the marina, one she'd tried to buy from Loreen more than once.

"I know you got you a bunch of these up on your wall inside," Loreen rushed on, "but I think you always favored this one. Someone found it up a tree inland a ways, and knew where it was s'posed to be, but I think now it's s'posed to be with you."

Tears flooded Julie's eyes as she looked down at the gift in Loreen's brown hands. The stenciled word *Gladesport* was barely visible, but it could still be read. *TRUST ME*, it said on the lower half, words that had come through the storm still looking crisp and clean.

"The others on the wall are for the girls who will visit here," Julie choked out, "but this one will be for my new family. I hope it means that all our hurricanes are over."

She blinked in the brightness of the sun, and tears speckled her cheeks. Clint and Zach were arguing about fishing spots; Randi was telling Thad that her new friend Marla thought he was really cute, and he was insisting he'd never date an underclassman. Leon was just gazing out into the blue bay.

And Julie had never been happier.

Author's Note

Just as I never base my characters strictly on real people in my contemporary fiction, neither did I base Hurricane Dana on an actual storm. Dana is a conglomeration of hurricanes I studied. Weatherman Tim Ralston is also fictional, as is his radio station.

Although people often ask where I get ideas for my books, I think the basis for *Hurricane* is obvious. We live part-time in southwest Florida and were there when Hurricane Ivan, the third of four terrible storms to hit Florida that season, approached, while we were examining what Hurricane Charley had already done to the area. Ivan went on to impact the Panhandle of Florida and other southeast states farther north, but I interviewed many people who had gone through Charley, Frances, and Jeanne. Both awesome and awful, hurricanes fascinate everyone; even those devastated or sick of them at the time had a story to tell.

I would like to thank the following people for help with researching background for this book. Any mistakes are those of the author.

—John Hawkins, Vice President and Senior Partner, for

WCI Developers, and Gary L. Muston, Superintendent, Kraft Construction Company, Inc. for a great tour of a condo high-rise under construction.

—Rachel Conner and her friends for advice on fourteen-year-olds.

—The many Floridians who told me their individual survival stories.

During Hurricane Charley, a school shelter did lose its roof, necessitating that 1,400 people be relocated by school buses.

About the shark situation: in mid-November 2004, the United States proposed international measures to reduce the slaughter of sharks and to study threatened shark populations throughout the world, including a ban on shark finning. However, many nations have no intention of taking such measures, and not only Asian countries, where shark fin soup is still a delicacy. As late as March 27, 2003, the European Parliament voted to allow shark finning. Sixty-six percent of sharks caught by European Union vessels can be finned. (According to the United Nations, more than 100 million sharks and related species—skates and rays—are killed each year.)

As I was writing this book in the winter of 2005, famed *Jaws* author Peter Benchley visited southwest Florida and said in his lecture that "...he made errors in writing about the great White Shark. 'Now we know they don't attack humans or boats,' he said. 'They don't react out of instinct, they are capable of learning.'" [*Naples Daily News,* Jan. 20, 2005]

As ever, thanks to Don for the many trips to the Everglades, Marco Island, Goodland, Everglades City and parts south.

I have been on many boat trips out into the 10,000 Islands, some sponsored by the Everglades National Park. Although Liz Lawson and Nate Tomzak in this book went overboard in more ways than one, the Everglades are always endangered and, without continual watch, could indeed become the "Neverglades."

Karen Harper
Naples, FL
April 2005

The Fyre Mirror

❧ AN ELIZABETH I MYSTERY ❧

KAREN HARPER

In the latest installment of Karen Harper's acclaimed mystery series,
Elizabethan England comes alive as its young queen struggles to
stop a serial killer who uses fire as a weapon...

Smitten with spring fever, Elizabeth Tudor escapes London for fantastical Nonsuch Palace in the sweet Surrey countryside. There she hopes to relax and pose for the official royal portrait for which she is holding a competition. But one of her artists is burned to death, and portraits of the queen are going up in flames. When she hears that her rival, the dangerous Mary, Queen of Scots, has been peering in mirrors and announcing, "I see the next queen of England!" Elizabeth summons her Privy Plot Council. Time is running out, because the enemy who stalks the queen means to destroy not only her portraits and artists, but her very life.

"Tudor England's answer to V. I. Warshawski."   —*Publishers Weekly*

"Harper's facility with historical figures is extraordinary." —*Los Angeles Times*

ISBN: 0-312- 99622-5

AVAILABLE FROM ST. MARTIN'S / MINOTAUR PAPERBACKS

MKHSTMARTIN05

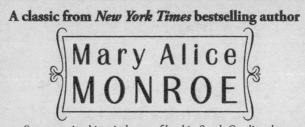

It was an affair…to regret

Laura Caldwell

Rachel Blakely's charmed life is significantly tarnished after her husband Nick's infidelity, but she wants to give her marriage a second chance. Then a business trip to Rome leads to a night of passion with a stranger. Rachel returns home, determined to put the past behind her, and at first, life seems golden again. Nick is more loving than ever and, following his promotion, the couple is welcomed into Chicago's high society, where beautiful people live beautiful lives. But there's a dark side… one that sends Rachel's life spiraling into a nightmare.

It's clear everyone is guilty of something. But whose secrets will lead to murder?

THE ROME
AFFAIR

Available the first week of June 2006 wherever paperbacks are sold!

www.MIRABooks.com

MLC2309

A field of lavender…full of promise

JEANETTE BAKER

International-relations attorney Whitney Benedict hasn't
completely given up on marriage, but she does have a
checklist of qualities for the man of her dreams: affluence,
intelligence, good looks and, absolutely no prior baggage.
So when she travels to California to make an offer on
behalf of the Austrian government for Gabriel Mendoza's
famous Lipizzan horses, no one is more surprised than
Whitney at the effect Gabe, his children, his stepchildren,
his ex-wife, his mother and the rest of his zany family
have on her heart. And she soon realizes that a checklist
isn't always the final measure for happiness.

The Lavender Field

"Baker's sweet romance will appeal to young
and old alike."—*Booklist* on *A Delicate Finish*

MIRABooks.com

We've got the lowdown on your favorite author!

KAREN HARPER

32043 DARK ROAD HOME	___ $4.99 U.S.	___ $5.99 CAN.
32115 DOWN TO THE BONE	___ $4.99 U.S.	___ $5.99 CAN.
32116 THE BABY FARM	___ $4.99 U.S.	___ $5.99 CAN.
32179 DARK ANGEL	___ $7.50 U.S.	___ $8.99 CAN.

(limited quantities available)

TOTAL AMOUNT	$ _____
POSTAGE & HANDLING	$ _____
($1.00 for 1 book, 50¢ for each additional)	
APPLICABLE TAXES*	$ _____
TOTAL PAYABLE	$ _____

(check or money order—please do not send cash)

To order, complete this form and send it, along with a check or money order for the total above, payable to MIRA Books, to: **In the U.S.:** 3010 Walden Avenue, P.O. Box 9077, Buffalo, NY 14269-9077; **In Canada:** P.O. Box 636, Fort Erie, Ontario, L2A 5X3.

Name: _____

Address: _____ City: _____

State/Prov.: _____ Zip/Postal Code: _____

Account Number (if applicable): _____

075 CSAS

*New York residents remit applicable sales taxes.
*Canadian residents remit applicable GST and provincial taxes.

MIRA®

www.MIRABooks.com

MKH0606BL